A SIN OFFERING

A Detective Robert Lui Story #2

GLENN BURWELL

Somewhat Grumpy Press Inc

Published by arrangement with Somewhat Grumpy Press Inc. Halifax, Nova Scotia, Canada. www.SomewhatGrumpyPress.com
The Somewhat Grumpy Press name and Pallas' cat logo are registered trademarks.

ISBN 978-1-7387998-2-4 (paperback)
ISBN 978-1-7387998-3-1 (eBook)

First Printing, August 2023

A SIN OFFERING

Blessed is he whose transgression is forgiven,
whose sin is covered.
Psalm 32

CONTENTS

Three people were in the cold room. One was bound and shackled to a chair, which was bolted to the concrete floor in the room's centre. Blood, vomit and sweat formed an atoll surrounding the chair. The other two were standing, one hanging back, just out of the cone of light over top of the chair. Gurmit tensed his arms. Sweat trickled into his eyes, his eyebrows doing nothing to stop it. The man standing over him was at least three hundred pounds and stank of fried food and body odour. Greasy, long, corn-rolled plaits hung down either side of a large, fat face, the hair style seemingly out of place on a man of South Asian descent. The eyes were pinpoints of darkness above a wide squashed nose. Manny grinned as he grabbed one of Gurmits' fingers and bent it backwards until it snapped. Gurmit would have screamed if he could have, but black duct tape had been wrapped around his head, keeping his mouth tightly shut. Gurmit had long ago given up the name of the other undercover policeman working within the Gupil gang. The large man was amusing himself. Gurmit noticed a gun's grip sticking out of the fat man's pants. A much smaller man with black eyes, an electric blue turban, and a carefully trimmed black goatee above an extra long neck, hovered in the background, watching.

'Mr. Goatee' or the Guru, as he liked to call himself, wasn't sure whether their victim had given up everything he knew, but his guess was that he had. The duct tape underlined that they weren't interested in anything further Gurmit might want to say. Either way, he had become useless, except for one more act, more in the form of a message. The man with the turban was after some property of his that had gone missing. Gurmit had volunteered the information as to where he thought it was and who had it. Volunteered was one way of putting it. The Guru had been sloppy in finding out the details. The officer strapped to the chair now knew who was running things. Prior to this encounter, Gurmit had not seen the Guru. In the process of fixing this mistake by getting rid of Gurmit, the problem was about to be compounded. The concentration on Gurmit's fingers was per a request by the Guru's new-found business partner, Edward. He didn't know exactly why this particular fetish was being asked for, but Manny seemed to be enjoying himself. He looked the fat man in the eyes and nodded. He had assumed it was only a single cop who had infiltrated his gang, so the revelation of a second embedded informer by Gurmit was very troubling.

"Come on, let's go for a ride, do some swimming." Manny said.

As he unshackled Gurmit and raised him up, the fat man snapped one more finger for good measure. Gurmit's legs buckled, which didn't make the fat man happy, so he snapped the remaining two fingers that had escaped his attention. Gurmit had none left pointing in the correct direction, and he was missing his two smallest fingers. Gurmit fainted. When he came to, he was in a confined black space. It seemed like he was moving, so he guessed he was in the trunk of a car. The pain was blinding. Even if he could make a play for the man's gun at the end of this trip, with all his broken and missing fingers, he doubted if he could even hold the weapon, let alone shoot it. All his police training was as nothing in this moment as he contemplated the final transgression yet to come.

* * *

The still and humid air deadened noises. Robert Lui drove his undercover police car carefully along the dyke road next to a slough in south Richmond. A call had come in early that morning about something in the water next to the Fraser River. Robert wouldn't normally be attending to such matters, but he was on his way to the local RCMP detachment in the area and called in to say he would take a look. He shook his head. There were lots of things in the water these days, mostly the detritus and leftovers escaping local sawmills farther up the river, stray logs from booms, and rarely anything of interest. He wondered who would have called. A couple of houseboats and stilt homes in the slough seemed to be inhabited. By whom, he didn't know. He hadn't heard of any houseboat communities in Richmond.

He supposed that a jogger or cyclist could have made the call, but it was early in the day, the sun only now trying to make its presence known. This portion of the river was part of the massive delta that emptied into the Salish Sea and Pacific Ocean beyond. As a result, the river current was disrupted by tides twice daily, the difference in water level felt by the residences and commercial interests along the riverbanks.

* * *

A foghorn echoed across the water four times, the river traffic trying its best to avoid one another. March days along the Fraser River brought mist and chilled bones. The Fraser, one of the mightiest rivers in Canada, started in the Rocky Mountains hundreds of miles to the northeast. It was many things to many people, but by the time it reached the Lower Mainland of Greater Vancouver and the sea beyond, it served as a highway for river-borne commerce. Most of the businesses on its shores didn't care about the natural history of the waters and surrounding land. For thousands of years the delta lands were visited and inhabited by aboriginal groups interested in the lush berries and the bountiful fishing. The European settlers in the 20th Century made sure all the berries were rounded up onto farms. A hundred years of pollution crushed the once-excellent salmon and ooligan fishing. Some of the finest agricultural soil in the world served only as support for ever-expanding suburbs. For many people, food came from a supermarket, not a farm, and they gave little thought to the land where they lived other than its price, which was getting steeper all the time.

One type of item that came up the river was drug

shipments from far away countries, usually piggybacking or hidden with something more mundane like cars or other goods aboard cargo ships. Vancouver, like any other port city, became a gateway for drug entry to a country. It also happened to be the first major stop for ships from Asia, so Vancouver probably got more than its fair share of product. This spawned many bad things, but employment on both sides of the game was not one of them. There seemed to be never-ending opportunities for lazy young men on the gang side. On the opposite side, ambitious young people could make careers chasing the lazy ones.

Robert slowed his cruiser as he pulled onto the road next to the silted waterway. A few house boats of a dilapidated nature sat at un-horizontal angles. Drinking coffee in any of these homes would be a challenge, mugs sliding off the table, the result of a low tide settling the houseboats onto the slough bottom. He wondered how one could possibly live like that, even-keeled half the time and the other half, at some cockeyed angle. It happened twice a day, every day. Perhaps cockeyed people enjoyed it. The remainder of the homes sat on stilts or piles next to the dyke, making a forlorn attempt at being horizontal. Humidity dampened the weathered grey wood of long abandoned fishing boats and houses. The place looked like a wreck, on the verge of being abandoned.

No one seemed to be around. Maybe ghosts lived aboard the houses, not real humans. Evidence of habitation abounded. Cords of firewood lined the river side of the road next to narrow entry points to the homes and boats. Electrical connections had been made to the overhead lines running along the north side of the dyke road in long ellipses, so someone must be allowing these squatters some slack. The ragged remnants of an elementary school long past educating anyone could be seen leaning into the water on the southern arm of land which provided protection from the force of the Fraser River. The beaten remains of a wooden footbridge tried to maintain a connection between the sides of the slough. The north side of the road framed farmer's fields displaying varying types of crops or attempts at crops. The fields contained mainly water and rotting pumpkins left over from the previous fall.

Robert stopped his car on the road, slowly opened the door and got out. It was silvery grey every way you looked, the mist likely to take a few hours before it burned away, if it felt like leaving at all. Sometimes fog decided to mask south Richmond all day. The pavement was dark and wet, everything else slick and dripping with moisture. The air tasted thick and heavy. He had parked at the western or open end of the slough, and started walking east, keeping an eye on the water. The tide seemed to be ebbing, the houseboats going to be resting on the mud bottom soon. A third of the way along the road he spotted something dark hanging from a pier on the far shore, partially in the water. It didn't take Robert long to figure out that it was a body, seemingly tied to the pier. He stood for a while looking at it and at the adjacent homes. Something about the form looked familiar, but he wasn't sure. Nothing stirred. There were better places to be going for a swim, Robert thought. Two gulls flew low over the water, but even they were silent, the fog swallowing them quickly. The mouth looked black, maybe the result of being taped up, it was hard to tell as the mist moved past. Robert wondered if another message was being sent. There was a drug war going on and the police didn't seem to be coming out ahead to date.

* * *

Robert was a mixed-race officer; father Cantonese, mother Anglo-Canadian. Being tall, his thinness only accentuated his height. He moved with the ease that came from being in the best shape of his life. To anyone falling under his gaze, the eyes seemed dark and penetrating, gifts from both of his parents. Slightly prominent cheekbones and short black hair surrounded the eyes and gave him a certain movie idol look that many women found attractive. Men were less attracted to him, particularly those of his colleagues who resented someone partially Asian rising above a certain level in the force. As far as they were concerned, Chinese officers were on the force to deal with Chinese crooks, nothing more. And it certainly didn't matter that the head of the force had Chinese heritage. To them, it was only a display for the Vancouver public; window dressing, nothing more. Robert always had his antennae tuned for the looks and the comments that told him of his place.

* * *

The body looked like it was staying put, so Robert knew the crime scene people would have something less than eight hours to do their work and retrieve the remains before the river rose again. He pulled the cell from his jacket's inside breast pocket, made the call to the local RCMP detachment, and waited for the action to start. It appeared that the locals were going to be in for some disruption to their sedate aquatic existence. The eerie sound of a siren eventually wavered across the fields, the local RCMP post being close by. Robert watched to see when someone would open their door to find out the cause of the commotion. He was both disappointed and impressed by the apparent lack of interest. Looked like the residents would need to be rousted by the uniforms that were drawing ever closer to the dyke road. It wasn't Robert's jurisdiction, but he decided to hang around and watch the action after he had briefed the officer in charge of the recovery.

Some locals got ejected from their cozy hideaways, eyes shifting around as they submitted to constable's questions. Robert eventually got bored, and even though it was early in the day, decided to head back to the centre of Richmond to eat. This locale had become a new Chinatown for the Vancouver area in an unfortunate way, as it had evolved in a manner that discouraged walking. However, some of the best Chinese cuisine in the world could be had in any of the strip malls populating these roads. All one needed was a car, and a bit of knowledge about where to park it, lest it be damaged by new drivers. He decided on a restaurant at one of the smaller malls on No. 3 Road where noodles were also a specialty. He pulled into the lot and looked for the remotest parking stall. He remembered something from a few weeks earlier about a jeep the size of a small country rolling aimlessly through the same lot, ignoring the aisles, driving over medians, the driver obviously having better things to do than to pay attention to his driving. Before he got out, he reached down and adjusted his hidden holster. He had started carrying a Beretta as a second gun after re-joining the anti-gang Taskforce and its nest chaffed his ankle. Robert was still in the re-adjustment phase for many things.

Robert went inside the restaurant, took a seat, and was looking over the menu over when his cell rang.

"It's Gurmit in the slough, and he wasn't treated very well." The officer said.

Robert knew what this meant. "Is Troy there? I need to talk with him right away. I'm coming back to you, right now." He got up and nodded to the girl at the door as he left the restaurant, thinking about how miserable the gang's life was going to become because of this violence.

He put this thought to the side and considered the problem the Taskforce obviously had. Only a couple of people knew what Gurmit had been up to. Someone was leaking information, so in addition to the revenge that Robert might organize, he was also going to have to go on a mole hunt. What the Gupil gang had done, if it was indeed them, seemed to be blatantly stupid. Killing a Delta Police officer, no matter what he was doing, seemed a big step beyond the usual. Robert wondered if something larger was going on. He got back into his car and returned south along No. 3 Road, trying to avoid the usual mess of bad driving this stretch of street was famous for. The

SIG Sauer in his shoulder holster was also bothering him. He hadn't been armed at all when he was a detective at the Vancouver Police Department, so the hardware was annoying. He also knew it was necessary. He thought it would be good to arrange another session with his trainer, Siegfried. The morning's events signified trouble ahead.

Robert drove back to the river and parked his car along the side of the narrow road, inches from a deep ditch. Several more cars and a van had pulled up. There were officers everywhere. As he got out of his car he spotted Troy Geelham, who was the local RCMP lead on the Taskforce. He walked over to his car. Troy's face was grim.

"They messed him up Robert. Likely the Guru is behind this; this is how he would arrange things." Troy then added, "He was tied to the piling and must have drowned when the tide came in, assuming he was still alive. Shitty way to go. None of the residents are admitting to seeing anything so far. He was tortured, that much is clear. Missing a couple of fingers, and the rest are broken."

"Have you been able to contact Farhad?" Robert asked.

"He's been told not to go to his next meeting. He's safe, so far. He is going to need to disappear for a while. The Gupil guys, if it's them, will be looking for him."

"No need to let too many people know where he goes." Robert stared at Troy. Troy nodded. "We have an internal problem that I'm going to need to solve." Robert added, so Troy was clear about the issue at hand. Robert was certain the problem didn't originate with the RCMP, as they were not privy to the details of the undercover operation. "Who is going to let Gurmit's family know?"

"Someone from Delta will do that. Thank God he didn't have his own family." Even though Delta was a small community, it had its own police force, which both Gurmit and Farhad were part of. Various other nearby municipalities used the RCMP for their policing. There was no particular reason why some cities used the RCMP and others didn't, but it didn't help communications between the forces any.

"The press is going to have a good time speculating about what is happening. I'm going to head back downtown. I have some thinking to do." Robert shook his head and gave a half-hearted salute to Troy, then added. "Someone will need to be a restraining force on the other Delta officers. They're going to want blood, and fast." With that, he returned to his car. The mist was lifting and, as his hunger had disappeared, he headed north, through Richmond and back over another arm of the Fraser to Vancouver, where the Taskforce was headquartered.

Gurmit's body had been cut loose and the coroner had given it the once over before seeing it quietly into an ambulance for its final journey. No one was smiling. The locals were being treated with less than kid gloves; the officers wanting answers and coming up short.

* * *

Robert parked his car in the underground garage of the Cambie Street police offices and slowly made his way up to the third floor where the Taskforce was centred. He waved at Gladys as he passed by the reception area. She smiled but didn't say anything. It seemed she was giving him the cold shoulder ever since the revelation that

Camille Laurent had moved in with him. They started living together after Robert returned to the anti-gang Taskforce. Camille was a detective for the Vancouver Police Department and had worked in the same office as Robert. They were on a case together the previous year that had provided the impetus for their relationship. Robert realized that some professional distance would be needed if they both continued with the VPD, hence his shift to the Taskforce.

He checked Thomas Harrow's office for signs of life, Thomas being the head of the Taskforce. He would have to be told about the morning's events. Finding his office empty, Robert decided to head out for some coffee. While walking slowly up Cambie Street, he dialled Siegfried's number, taking care not to walk into a power pole or another pedestrian while looking down.

"Siggy, it's Robert."

"Hey Robert."

"I think we need to ratchet up our sessions. I sense trouble brewing. I'll tell you about it when we meet next."

"How about tomorrow, say ten?"

"Good, see you then." That confirmed, Robert turned and entered Cafe Paulo waving to Gilberto as he walked up to the bar. Carmelita was behind the espresso machine today, Gilberto seemingly busy with his laptop. "Double long *per favour*." Robert asked Carmelita. She smiled as she served up the cup. He went over to his usual table by the window to try to make sense of what was happening. The Taskforce had succeeded in intercepting an unusually large quantity of fentanyl recently, likely originating in

China. In doing so they had also arrested one of the Gupil gang members, who was now in remand, awaiting trial. If this murder was a response to that, then a line had been crossed. Robert wondered if someone else was pulling the Gupil gang's strings; promising things or threatening them in order to make them to do things they wouldn't normally do. He sipped at his coffee, unable to make any headway. One thing he knew, this wasn't going to turn out well for the gang. He got on his cell to try again for Thomas before leaving the cafe.

"Thomas, this is Robert. We need to talk. We have a problem." Robert was gambling here as he left the message. The problem with a mole hunt was knowing who you could trust. He felt Thomas was a good guy. If you couldn't trust your boss.... He left that thought for the moment. Robert finished up and waved at Carmelita as he left. Compartmentalize and lay traps, that was how you did it. Someone would be needed as bait. Maybe Farhad might be up for it, that is, as long as he didn't see what the gang had done to Gurmit.

* * *

When Robert got back to the floor, he went to Thomas's office, peeked his head in, and asked him to go for a walk. Robert looked up at the pewter sky as they walked out the doors of the building, turning north, following the path he usually took when he wanted to get away from the noise of the precinct offices to do some thinking. The mist cloaking south Richmond was also evident up ahead in

False Creek as they walked toward the seawall path. Rain might or might not follow, the sky impossible to read.

"The RCMP just pulled Gurmit's body out of the Fraser River, Thomas. He had been tortured, then tied to a piling to drown to death. It wasn't good. You should call the Delta Chief Constable to rein them in before someone does something crazy. They'll be after retribution if I know them. I also think we have an internal problem. And from what I know about moles, how big of a problem may depend on who is behind this."

Thomas stopped walking, turning to look at Robert. "So, you don't think Gurmit screwed up somehow and exposed himself?"

Robert stopped as well. "It's possible of course, but unlikely. Gurmit was damn good at what he did, and he had been inside the gang for some time." The pair started walking again east towards Olympic Village, a legacy from the 2010 Winter Games. They stopped talking whenever someone drew near, whether on bikes, roller blades, or merely walking as they were. Paranoia was starting its insidious penetration into Robert's professional life again, much like the first time he had been on the Taskforce.

His children had been targeted with threats during his first time with the force; leading to Robert's decision to leave and rejoin the VPD as a detective for a year. Some of his fellow Taskforce members thought him cowardly for this defection and let him know their opinions. Assholes, he thought to himself. They didn't have children and had none of the cares that girls and boys brought to a parent.

"We'll need a list of people who knew what Gurmit and

Farhad were up to, both here, and in Delta." Robert added. "Then we'll lay a trap."

"It will be a short list. Me, you, and Gladys." Thomas said. "Do you think the Gupils are behind this? Seems a little daring for them from what we know about the Guru."

"As far as I know, they've never worked with another gang, or for another gang, so it's a mystery. We should talk to Farhad, see if he has any clues. He was contacted to stop him attending his next meeting. He is going to need to go to a quiet place." They both stopped, looking north at the water, while running through the complexities of what lay ahead. The condo towers beyond were peeking through rifts in the mist, visible for a couple of minutes, then vanishing in the grey silk. The fog stuck to the water, seemingly afraid to creep over the adjacent land.

"I'm meeting Siggy tomorrow. I need to get ready, or readier, to be blunt."

"Good. You look pretty fit already. Let's head back, I'm getting cold."

Siegfried Damler was a trainer specializing in small arms and unarmed combat. He came from the special commando forces of the Canadian Army, and never talked about what he had done while overseas. Robert knew that he needed to be as prepared as possible for any problem that might rear its ugly head. He met with Siggy semi-regularly, but stepping up the sessions wouldn't hurt. Robert had no interest in meeting the same fate as Gurmit. Robert didn't know much more about Siegfried. He didn't know who else he worked for, or how he got through life after the army. Nor, it seemed, did anyone else know much about Siegfried Damler.

* * *

After the two had returned to the station, Robert's hunger returned, so he headed up to Broadway to fill up at his favourite noodle restaurant. After a satisfying round of eating noodles and dumplings with the occasional vegetable, he returned to his office. His first move was to call Troy at the RCMP to find out where Farhad was holed up. Robert guessed he'd be somewhere in Delta, a sister community of Richmond on the south side of the Fraser River. Siggy's shooting range and hideout was in west Delta, near a small town called Ladner, so he hoped to get both things accomplished tomorrow.

"Hi Troy, I'd like to meet with Farhad and get him out of Delta. Where are you keeping him?" Robert asked.

"Hey Robert. He's in a house in Ladner. And I agree, he shouldn't spend much time there. We told him some of the details about Gurmit, so if you guys can arrange a place for him in Vancouver, that'd be better."

"I'll visit him tomorrow and bring him back. Let him know. I don't want my head blown off when I knock on the door, okay?"

"Thanks Robert. A word of warning, the Delta Police are an unhappy bunch right now. I'm worried things may get out of control. They know enough about the Gupil members that someone might try something. I hope not, but things happen, you know?"

"Yes Troy, I do know. I'll try to drop by there tomorrow

to further calm the waters if I can." Robert hung up and stared out the window as he baked up a strategy to lure out the mole in their midst. After about an hour of this, he wasn't making much headway, so he called Camille on his cell.

"Hey beautiful, where are you?"

"You can't say that at work, that's sexual harassment."

"I can't? Does that mean you're going to punish me?"

"Yes," she said softly. "Later tonight."

"Excellent. It's a date. Grilled salmon good with you tonight?"

"I'm so lucky. A can of Spam and crackers used to be my main course before we met."

"Spam is under-rated. I'll get some items after I'm done here. Meet at 5:30 at the car? I'll tell you about my day. Things may be getting busy soon." After cutting the call, Robert called home to tell Robin what to expect for dinner, and to check on him and his sister. He was trying to remember if Robin had a hockey practise or not. Robin told him that it was the next day. That settled, he headed out to the local grocery store to get a couple of sides of steelhead, the fish that was half salmon and half trout. An appropriate dinner he thought for two kids that were half and half themselves, or at least something approximating that equation.

* * *

Camille moving in had been a blessing for Robert. With the passing of Robert's wife from cancer a couple of years earlier, Robert had struggled to keep his family's life on track. His life as an investigator made his hours impossible to predict. He guessed that his two teenage children were fine with this as it gave them the illusion of more freedom. What it didn't give them was much guidance, or protection. Robert was particularly concerned with the latter issue after the two kids had received some gang pressure a few months earlier. Added to that was a vague threat made to his family during his first stint with the Taskforce, the result being a constant nagging worry about the safety of his children.

Camille and Robert were attracted to each other, but Robert was worried about how the children would react; whether Camille even liked children, and second, if she did, would his kids accept Camille. This all went more or less okay at the start. It was probably going better than Robert had a right to expect, at least to date. Camille warmed to the children almost immediately, but the feelings were not reciprocated, at least from Sophie. It was a lot to expect of his children, Robert realized. Having a second adult in the home, once Camille moved in, was great in Robert's eyes. However, the children felt it was an intrusion upon their life with their father and their departed mother. Even though Susan was gone, she was still a part of the children's lives. They thought about her every day, and Sophie especially missed her mother. It would take time for Sophie to confide in Camille, but Robert was hopeful.

$$\sim \ 2 \ \sim$$

Later that same evening, Michael and Dal, undercover officers with the Delta Police Force, were driving up Scott Road to a recently opened East Indian restaurant that promised great things. Scott Road was the dividing line between Delta and the City of Surrey, where gang violence was carving its own niche. The two had heard about Gurmit and the state that he had been found in. To say they were antsy would have been a huge understatement. They did not know who exactly had done the nasty things to Gurmit, but they did know several members of the Gupil gang by sight. They had nodded when told by their superior officer to not retaliate. In their minds, the nodding indicated that they had heard what the officer said, nothing more. The two men were about to spend a late night following some gang members as they did their drug rounds and wanted sustenance before the long road ahead. As far as the two knew, the gang members they were to follow belonged to a different gang from the one suspected of killing Gurmit. Dal was driving their undercover car. This was one of the drawbacks to some of their work, driving bad North American products around, all in the effort to blend in. In Dal's mind, they were standing out, precisely because their car was crap. That aside, he was looking forward to dinner. The new restaurant had been highly recommended.

* * *

Dal parked their car in the farthest reaches of the lot behind the restaurant. The two officers sauntered in, all the while looking the place over, checking out every diner and the wait staff. As they were led to their table, Michael caught Dal's eye and slightly nodded at the window seats. Dal glanced over, ever so briefly, then looked back at Michael, a small glimmer in his eye. Seated by the window was a thug they knew as Jonny, a Gupil member. His partner was a young raven-haired girl in a printed flax yellow dress. Jonny was dressed in black jeans, ultramarine shirt, with a black sports jacket. Some gold jewellery in the form of a necklace and wrist bangles completed the look that said, 'I'm somebody'. They resembled a South Asian Ikea couple, impossible to ignore. Outside, the light was fading, spring about to make its appearance, but the days were still on the short side.

The two cops sat down and after the hostess left, pondered both the menu and their next move. "If we can't separate them, it'll be too bad about the girl." Michael said.

"That's what comes from hanging around scum. It is a shame that it won't be a learning moment for her. Let's order, I'm hungry." Dal seemed to be all business. Almost as an afterthought, Dal smiled, then said, "Nice that he wore black, red will look good against it." When the server finally came to their table, they ordered chicken samosas, a chickpea masala, and a lamb vindaloo dish, along with a couple of beers.

"You don't have your silencer, do you?" Dal asked.

"It's in the car."

"That's okay, probably a little risky doing anything in here anyway."

Michael was troubled that Dal would even think of this. How crazy was this guy? "Let's see how things go, we can always tail them." At that moment the first of their dishes arrived, the men lost their focus and attacked the samosas. A couple of minutes later, the girlfriend got up and walked off to the ladies room. Dal was watching and it gave him an idea.

"If dickhead Jonny goes to the men's room, I'll follow and take him out the back way. You pay the bill and join me outside. That way, the girl gets left out, okay?"

Michael nodded and kept eating. The other dishes arrived, and the two men made short work of them. The bistro was as advertised. Too bad they probably wouldn't be able to return after what was going to happen. They had pretty much given up on the washroom scenario and were paying their bill when Jonny made his move to the men's room. Michael left cash on top of the bill and ambled out the front door, while Dal followed Jonny.

A minute later, as Michael waited by the car at the rear of the lot, tape in hand, around from the back came Jonny followed closely by Dal, his gun firmly in Jonny's back.

Jonny smiled. "Do you know who I am, dickheads?"

Michael grinned in return. "Jonny, correct?"

Jonny briefly wondered how other gang members would know his name. "You guys are so screwed."

"Really? Think you've got it backwards, but that's what we'd expect from a dimwit." With that he laid a piece of duct tape across Jonny's mouth. They then turned Jonny against the car, zip-tied his wrists together, and opened the trunk lid. Darkness had fallen. Their car was in the dimmest region of the lot to avoid any surveillance cameras. Before pushing him in, Michael relieved Jonny of a gun and two knives. Twenty seconds later they had the car started and were exiting the restaurant parking onto Scott Road, heading south. After a few blocks, Dal turned west and headed over to a huge conservation area known as Burns Bog, the largest remaining peat bog on the west coast of America. The bog was large, and it was also devoid of people, a perfect place for a conversation about the niceties of gang warfare.

* * *

Dal turned off the road and travelled west on a gravelled path little wider than the car, probably used by the city maintenance people to access the bog. He pulled over and stopped, killing the engine. Silence reigned. Michael screwed the silencer onto his pistol and they both got out of the car, walking around to the trunk. Dal opened the lid and pulled Jonny out and stood him upright. Michael immediately shot him through his right foot, so he wouldn't get any ideas about leaving the party. Jonny's eyes were as wide as they could get. Muffled noises came from behind the tape on his mouth. Snot dripped from his nose.

"Time for a short discussion Jonny, and I'm sorry to say it's going to be a little one sided. Word is that your gang murdered one our brethren yesterday. Yes?"

Jonny shook his head, rather violently.

"Not what we heard, Jonny." Dal took aim at Jonny's right kneecap and let loose a round. Jonny collapsed, his head shaking from side to side, moans coming from behind the tape. "You can't go around torturing and killing police officers without expecting some *quid pro quo*. Don't know whether you understand Latin or not, but maybe you understand this," Dal then shot out the other kneecap. Jonny seemed to be losing control at this point. Michael pointed to the other foot.

Dal nodded, "Michael points out my love of symmetry, which, to be perfectly honest, I didn't know I had, so I'm going to have to shoot you in your other foot, just so you are all matched up. A hole in one shoe kind of makes the pair useless anyway, do you agree Jonny?" Jonny was shaking his head wildly at this point, but it was hard to tell if he was agreeing or disagreeing. Dal put a hole through Jonny's one remaining good foot. Michael started looking for the shell casings.

Dal stood there, thinking, "I'm getting bored with this, so here's what we're going to do. I was going to kill you, but I've changed my mind. You'll notice that we left your cellphone with you. If you have the wherewithal to get it out, you might survive, we don't really care. Bye Jonny, maybe we'll be seeing you again. And don't bother getting up, we're not big on formalities." With that piece of advice dispensed with, the two policemen got back into their crap car, turned around with some difficulty and drove slowly back up the track.

Dal looked at Michael with a small grin. "I don't know about you, but I'm still hungry. Think we dare go back to that place? The food was awfully good, and I don't think we got a fair sampling of the menu the first time, thanks to Jonny."

Michael looked back at Dal. This guy was nuts, but he had a good point. After this got out, they would probably never be able to eat there again. "Ok, why not. Agreed, that food was excellent. Let's go back. I wouldn't mind trying the fish pakora, and maybe we need the chicken tikka masala." Their minds were already locked onto food, the bloody mayhem they had just caused Jonny fading quickly.

About the same moment, back at the restaurant, the girl in the yellow dress was getting angry. Where was Jonny? He had been gone almost fifteen minutes. She reluctantly decided to go to the men's room and call for him. After yelling his name a couple of times at the men's room door, a young man came out.

"Is there anyone else in there? She asked.

"Sorry, just me, will I do?" The young man tried some humour on the girl.

"Fuck off." She turned and went back to her table, confused by events she didn't understand. As the waitress came up to the table with the cheque, she decided to call a girlfriend. So much for hotshot gang members, they couldn't even pay for dinner, or drive you home. She was seething. After she reluctantly paid for dinner, she waited another fifteen minutes before her friend drove up. As she left the restaurant and was about to get into her friend's car, she noticed that Jonny's car was still sitting where it had been all evening. Weird, was the only thought she could come up with as they left.

* * *

That same evening, the media finally twigged to what had happened in south Richmond, and the news was starting to buzz about the fact that a policeman had been killed —in apparent gangland fashion. The media liaison people from the police had very little to say to the press about anything to do with the case, other than the obvious, that the murder was targeted. Radio, television, and the local papers were trying to make a story of it. After Jonny was discovered the next morning, they wouldn't have to try very hard, but the hows and whys would remain elusive for the reporters.

~ 3 ~

The next morning, Robert drove into work, dropping Camille at the station on Cambie Street before heading south to Delta. On the way, just before going through the tunnel under the Fraser River, he pulled off at Steveston Highway to stop at RCMP headquarters in Richmond. The detachment was very close to the highway exit, placed there so squad cars would have an easier time going any which way they wanted. He walked into a lobby that would have made a prison proud. Whoever had picked out the finishes and colours definitely must have done time in a maximum security institution somewhere.

He was led into Troy's office. "I don't want to whine, but this place is dour. Spend a lot of time outside the office?"

Troy smiled. "We don't get a lot of say in where we work, so yeah, I try to get out when I can. And it's not like there is any place to walk, so it's cars all the time. Going to see Farhad?"

"Yes, I'm getting him out of Delta to a different place. I would think the Gupils are actively looking for him." Robert added, "I haven't quite figured out how this mole hunt is going to go, but I think I have to assume there may be more than one. The triads like to do things in pairs."

"You think a triad is behind this?"

"Perhaps. This killing is way over the line, so maybe someone else is pulling the Guru's chain here."

"Want some coffee, Robert?"

"Thanks, but no, I have a meeting with Siggy shortly. Have to stay light on my feet when he starts working me over. I should get moving—talk soon." Robert would have never accepted the offer of office coffee, as he had long ago stopped drinking what he considered to be lethal brew. He was too polite to explain the reasoning behind it to Troy.

* * *

The Hong Kong triads were clever, or at least imagined they were. From long history in many countries, the loosely connected members knew enough to keep a low profile within the communities they infiltrated. They purposely let the flashier gangs steal all the limelight. They had businesses to run. Sometimes, when it was to their advantage, the triads would align with a local gang to use them. If there were issues to deal with, they dealt with them quietly and forcefully. Money was the only important thing to them. There were a couple of Hong Kong triads with branches operating in the Lower Mainland, the Wide Bay Boys being one of them.

One thing the triads didn't want was to wake up the police forces to their presence. Of course, the police knew about triads and that they were operating in the Lower

Mainland. However, with all the other gang activity in the headlines, sometimes the triad issue moved to the back of the line. Certainly, the lack of news coverage about the Chinese gang presence helped the triads. Another part of their business involved knowing what their opponents were doing, sometimes before they knew themselves. The triads made it a priority to gather intelligence, and using moles planted within society's organizations was their preferred method to achieve this.

In Hong Kong, the head of the Wide Bay Boys was Jacky Chow. He had been discussing local issues with his lieutenant, Cedric. Cedric had been searching for some ideas to help deal with their ongoing Kowloon problem, an officer with the Hong Kong Police Force by the name of Winston Chang. Winston continued to be an impediment to the smooth functioning of the triad by arresting their members, sending some to trial, and even killing one in a kidnapping gone wrong. No one else on the force got under Jacky's skin like Winston and he wanted something done about it.

* * *

Earlier that same morning, a Delta municipal works truck slowly made its way into Burns Bog along one of the eastern service roads. They hadn't gone very far when they spotted Jonny laying by the side of the track.

"Jesus, what's that?" The passenger said.

"Looks like a body. This isn't good. Let's go see." The driver replied. He was both repelled and interested. They stopped, got out, and walked up to where Jonny lay. They could see the obvious signs of some gunplay, and the tape across the mouth. The driver knelt down to touch the body, knowing full well that this was some kind of gang thing, and that just maybe, they should turn around and get the hell out of there. Jonny jerked a bit. The two workers jumped.

"Holy, he's alive. Call 911." After making the call they cut the ties around the guy's wrists and took the tape off his mouth slowly. They didn't know what else to do. It had taken a few moments to explain to the woman on the other end of the phone where exactly they were. It seemed that if you didn't have a civic address, the emergency people were lost. Jonny appeared to be semi-conscious and looked like he had spent the night in the bog. The workers wisely decided not to touch Jonny any further, so they waited by their truck for the ambulance.

"Must be gang stuff, you think?"

"Yeah, I don't like it, but there's not much we can do now."

An ambulance pulled up after being waved over by the workers. Medical technicians did their assessment and got Jonny onto a stretcher with an IV into his arm, making up for his less than kid-glove treatment the night before. The bleeding from his wounds had stopped, and he of course was not talking, which the technicians didn't find surprising. This type of injury was new to the ambulance techs. When the first Delta Police car of many pulled up and the officers taped the area off, the ambulance left the scene. The two city workers would be doing little work this day by the time the police were finished with them.

***

After his RCMP stop, Robert drove through the tunnel under the Fraser River and then west into the heart of Ladner. Most of Delta was flat farmland, much of it covered by massive greenhouses growing vegetables. The edges of Delta were governed by the Fraser River and marine commerce was how some locals earned a living.

He headed west alongside the south edge of the Fraser River before pulling up in front of a beaten metal industrial building sitting atop the dyke. He got out slowly and walked up the gravel path to the door, looking up before punching in the code on the pad to gain entry. He then peered past the building at the muddy river beyond, waiting for Siegfried to confirm it was Robert, and he was alone. Siegfried opened the door, sporting a crew cut that was starting to show some grey around the temples. His dark blue eyes were piercing, as if he were analyzing someone constantly.

He moved fluidly to one side after shaking hands, "Hello Robert, good to see you. I hear problems are developing. Let's get to work."

How did Siggy know this so quickly, Robert wondered. "Nice to see you too, ready to go." Robert went into a change room to get his workout clothing on.

Siegfried did his work with clients in three parts; the gym workout first, to tire his man (or woman) out, then hand to hand unarmed combat, ending with the shooting range. The target practice was done when the client was at their physical limits, hands shaking, when the gun skills might be most needed. The shooting was always in pairs, two shots in exactly the same locale, never one, or three. Most people's aim was sketchy at the best of times and when under pressure, hitting anything was problematic. Siggy led the process at a high pace, trying to go far beyond the worst situation that might be faced by the client. At the end of the two hours, and after Robert had been firing both his regular pistol, and his Beretta, he was drained.

"Thanks, Siggy, you really know how to hurt a man."

"My pleasure Robert. You should know that a Gupil chap has been found in Delta, worse for wear. You may want to restrain your team from making this an all-out war." He paused, then. "I'll be in touch."

Robert again asked himself, as he exited the building, how Siggy was so knowledgeable about something that had just happened. Immediate retribution was the last thing he wanted but it didn't seem though as if he would be getting his wish. He called Troy before leaving to fetch Farhad.

"Troy, I hear something happened?"

"Yes, a gang member was found this morning in the bog, shot up, but alive. One of the Gupils. He was taken to Delta hospital for repairs. We'll wait to see what kind of ammo was used. I'm calling all the forces to reiterate the idea of restraint. Have you talked with Thomas yet?"

"Not today, I'll call him next. Going to get Farhad now, talk later." Robert checked in with Thomas but didn't learn anything except the gangster's name—Jonny Singh. Robert then remembered that he needed to call in on the

Delta Police. Obviously, the calm the waters speech was late. It probably wouldn't be very well received anyway, and who would blame them after what had befallen one of their own. One could also plead a good case that the officers had shown some restraint. After all, Robert was under the impression that Jonny was still alive.

* * *

Robert pulled up in front of a nondescript two-storey building, headquarters for the Delta Police Force, alongside some other institutional structures. Nothing else of note was anywhere near the cluster of buildings. Apparently, the thinking was to keep the police away from the community that they were tasked to protect, if that made any sense. The real answer for its location probably had something to do with inexpensive land. Robert walked into the foyer and asked for the Chief Constable. The receptionist directed him up wide stairs to a second floor office area where he was met by an executive assistant. She ushered him into a large office with a view of the North Shore Mountains, inhabited by a smiling officer sporting large ears below a sandy crop of short hair. As soon as Robert indicated who he was, the smile disappeared, as if a cloud had passed in front of the sun.

Robert opened up with his request, "Hi, I'm here to plead for a little discretion before this whole thing gets out of hand."

"A bit late for that Robert. I heard somebody got shot up over in the bog. We are looking into it."

"Hmmm." Robert paused, then, "I'm going to get Farhad this morning to make him disappear for a while."

"Where are you taking him?"

Robert waggled his forefinger, "Nope, this is on a need to know basis. Until we solve an internal problem, no one is getting that information."

"Are you going to want more men from us?"

"Probably not, but I'll let you know. Your men may not have the most objective attitude after what happened to Gurmit. Any idea who shot up the gang member? It was Jonny Singh, by the way."

"How do you know who it was already?"

Robert smiled, but didn't say anything for a moment, then, "Whoever shot Jonny may want to be careful, lest there is some blowback. It would be good if things didn't escalate—at least until we know what or who is behind this."

"Okay, please let me know what you find out. I already told the men not to retaliate yesterday. They obviously misheard what I said." The Chief finished up by adding, "It happens sometimes."

Robert merely waved his hand as he left the office, already thinking about his trip back into Ladner, the small river town in Delta he had just passed through. His main concern was not getting shot by Farhad as he came up to his front door. His second concern was being followed. If the Gupils were actively looking for Farhad, the community was small, and it wouldn't take much for each side to bump into each other by accident. If that happened, all bets were off, gang members thinking nothing of letting loose with their hardware in public places.

* * *

That same afternoon, the Guru was sitting in his club complex in central Surrey, the large city just to the east of Delta, taking some tea with a couple of his associates. They were discussing the disappearance of a large shipment of drugs and some cash.

"We went to Gurmit's place, but the stuff wasn't there like he said it was. We looked everywhere. Maybe that torture stuff doesn't work so hot." One of the gang members said.

The Guru responded, "More likely it was there but got moved or taken by that other informer, Farhad. He is the one we need to locate. Don't worry, torture works."

The Guru wasn't concerned so much about the actual drugs or cash as the consequences that might flow from informing Edward about this matter. Edward Su ran the local Wide Bay Boys for Jacky Chow and had approached the Guru to join in on some activities. So far it had been a big break for the Gupils; they were making much more money than before and were gaining that all important status as a gang to be feared and respected. In the local solar system of crime gangs, it was something desired, hard won, and harder to keep. As he was contemplating this, one of his associates received a call on his cell. The man started cursing, then hung up.

"That was Jonny."

"How come he is not here?" The Guru had quietly noted his absence.

"Because he is in the hospital with both his legs shot up. He says cops did it. Something about payback for what we did to Gurmit. They kneecapped him."

The Guru grimaced. "So, it wasn't a shootout, or whatever?"

"No."

"Is he under arrest?"

"He didn't say. Sounded kind of drugged up."

"That was a quick response from the cops. Send flowers. No one goes to see him, is that clear? The cops will be watching the place. If we need to know something, we'll get his girlfriend to help us."

"What kind of flowers?"

"I didn't mean that literally, you fucking idiot." The Guru sat there, shaking his turbaned head. Some days, he wondered how they managed to stay in business. "We know that Farhad is a Delta undercover, so I am assuming our people are covering the area, yes? We need to find this cop."

The others at the meeting started looking at each other, which the Guru immediately noticed. "Don't tell me, you haven't started looking there yet?"

"We'll get right on it."

"Do you know what the term, time sensitive, means?" The rest of the group looked back at the Guru with puzzled expressions.

"I thought not. It means you meatheads have screwed up again. Farhad is likely gone, probably in that asshole cop, Robert Lui's hands by now." As the others in the room quickly left, the Guru thought about Jonny and what use he could make of him now that he likely wouldn't be walking again, or alternatively, what a liability he had become.

* * *

While the Gupils were discussing technicalities of how to get things done, Robert was in action, getting things done. After he left the Delta Police Station, shaking his head, he drove back north into Ladner. He kept his eyes open for any fancy vehicle that got too near to his car as he turned off to access the eastern side of Ladner. Gangsters generally, but not always, drove higher end vehicles, and black was a favoured colour. This knowledge only helped slightly, because any newcomer to Canada with some money, liked to spend it on high-end cars—Range Rovers of varying model types seeming to be the latest favourite. And in Vancouver, there were a lot of newcomers the past few years.

He pulled into the parking lot of an unremarkable group of townhouses, all stained in various shades of brown and sepia. They were depressing in the bright sun-light, so must have induced suicidal thoughts when it rained. Oddly, there was no landscaping, just buildings and pavement, something that might be standard in a more easterly city, but not in British Columbia. Robert re-checked the address again on the scrap of paper. He looked around, but no one was in sight, the place seem-ingly devoid of humanity. He walked up to the front door and pressed the doorbell, then took a step backward so Farhad could get a good look at him. The door opened after a few moments. Farhad's dark eyes glanced past Robert's shoulders to check for danger. Farhad had on newish blue jeans topped by a white and blue checked shirt. His hair was black, short, and glistening with some kind of product. He looked fit, no fat that Robert could discern. His face, with hollowed cheeks, was gaunt, similar to how a drug user might look. Robert walked into the entry hall and Farhad closed the door.

"What happened to Gurmit? I heard they found him in the river." Farhad seemed jittery.

"Hello to you too, Farhad. I'm afraid that Gurmit has worked his last case. You don't really want to know the specifics, but it wasn't good. I'm here to make sure the same doesn't happen to you. The Gupils will be looking for you, Gurmit would have given up your name." Robert answered.

* * *

What Robert didn't know was why the Gupils were so interested in Farhad and Gurmit. He just assumed it was because they had infiltrated the gang and had gained their confidence. That in itself was reason enough. Not only had they worked their way into the inner workings of the gang, but unbeknownst to Robert, they took the opportunity to liberate some drugs and money for their own use. After Gurmit's untimely death, Farhad had quickly gone to Gurmit's place and taken the stash of items to a friend in Steveston where they would be safe, in theory. Steveston was technically part of the City of Richmond but boasted a proud identity as one of the largest fishing ports in the entire country. Thus, the Guru and the other Gupils had some extra motivation in the chase that Robert was unaware of.

"Get your stuff together. You're not going to be back in Delta for a while. We have a place for you in Vancouver while I think about what to do with you." Robert wanted to get out of Delta and back to more familiar surroundings. The flatness of the river lands was bothering him. Farhad disappeared up the stairs. Robert went over to the window to surveil the parking lot and street beyond. He was tired from his session with Siegfried and getting nervous. After Farhad had retrieved a bag of clothes and some other personal items, as well as his gun, they left the townhouse and got into Robert's car. Farhad's head was on a swivel. His eyes were darting around so much it was making Robert even more antsy.

"What about my car?"

"We'll figure that out later." Then Robert asked, "I've been thinking, ever been upcountry?"

"What does that mean?"

"It means somewhere other than the Lower Mainland." Robert was starting to wonder if Farhad had been anywhere at this point.

"I was in Hawaii a couple of years ago."

Robert glanced over at Farhad. Maybe this was why they were having trouble coming out on top in their gang war, the good guys didn't appear to be much smarter than the bad guys. Robert did an interior eye roll. "I'm considering stashing you at a ranch I know of for a week or two, but I'm not sure yet."

Robert could tell by Farhad's puzzled look that this ranch idea was a foreign concept for him. They swung back onto the local highway. Robert was feeling more at ease, the dangerous part of the pick-up over. Once back in Vancouver they headed to the East Side to a safe apartment, the force not about to pony up for a pricier west side safe house. After dropping Farhad at the apartment building with a warning to keep his head down, Robert headed back to the station to check in, and pick up Camille for the ride home.

~ 4 ~

Robert and Camille arrived at the townhouse Robert rented on the East Side of Vancouver, driving up the lane and parking in the carport next to their tiny garden oasis. As it was mid-March, the garden's snowdrops and purple crocuses had faded. The tulips were springing up and the daffodils were already in full bloom, the yellows brightening against the darker greens of the newly sprouting hostas and callalilies. The garden was a mess and needed attention, but probably wouldn't be getting it any time soon. Robert looked over at Camille and smiled, the car radio almost a whisper now, unlike before her arrival into his life, when he would crank up the volume. Together, they exited the Silver Streak (his name for the older car) and headed in through the rear door of their home.

"I think we have enough fixings to make risotto." Robert said. "I'll get it going after I do some prep work. Why don't you go change and check on the kids?" Robert headed into the kitchen which he considered his domain and pulled out some chicken stock from the fridge and a large onion from the cupboard. Italian sausages, lemons, and cream completed the basic ingredients. He then yelled up to find out if the children were indeed home. A couple of short answers confirmed that the table would be full. All he needed were some vegetables to complete the dinner. He looked into the recesses of the fridge and found a half bag of green beans. It'll have to do, he thought. He was always concerned that he was making enough food for the two teenagers; they went through meals like a buzzsaw. Luckily, risotto was not a light-weight entree, so they should survive. He then pulled out a white wine—needed for the recipe, he told himself. He also poured a couple of glasses—not exactly for the recipe. After he got the mixture going, it took another half hour of slowly adding the stock while gently stirring the risotto, before finishing the dish with cream and parmesan. The children came bouncing downstairs to join Camille and Robert at the dinner table.

"How's it going at school?" Robert started as he smiled, knowing full well that he wasn't likely to find out anything about how it was going at school. He dug into his dinner.

"I think I need a new cellphone," was Sophie's response. Robert looked across the table and could have sworn he caught a glimmer on Camille's face while she appeared to be intently inspecting her risotto.

"Is there something wrong with the one you have?"

"It's too small and slow." Sophie responded. Robin was listening closely, pretending not to be, while pushing the beans on his plate around. He had a big stake in how this conversation was going to turn out, being the recipient of Sophie's phone if things went well. He knew that her phone was good, it just suffered when compared to some of the others at school. His phone, in comparison, was truly crap, and he could only hope for a replacement, as he had no money to buy a newer one.

Robert shot a glance at Robin. He knew what was probably going through Robin's mind, "But it still works, correct?"

"I guess, but not very well."

"Hmmmm." Robert paused, then, "How would you pay for it?" A bean flipped off the edge of Robin's plate as he glanced over at Sophie. Sophie offered only silence as she looked at her dad with doe eyes.

After a few seconds of this, Robert caved. "Let me think about it. I have to check the plan I signed up for first." Robert wasn't a very good negotiator. At least he had the wisdom to know this, though it didn't change the outcome. Camille smiled at him, and Robin suddenly seemed buoyant, chattering about his day at school.

* * *

Later that evening, after Sophie and Robin had retreated upstairs, Camille started relating her day as an assistant investigator in a semi-annoyed tone. "Boy, you left at the right time. The embezzlement case at the west side club that I inherited from you is a huge pain. Now, I'm the one chasing rich members around looking for clues. And these people don't seem to want to reveal much. Makes you wonder what else they are up to."

"I can imagine. Any ideas so far? Isn't it usually

someone on a committee, or one of the club staff that end up being the culprits?"

"Probably. I'll get one of them to make a mistake some-day soon, I hope." Camille smiled at the thought.

Robert started discussing the day's events from his perspective. Camille and he were sitting close to each other on a sofa in the living area next to the kitchen, pots and dishes littering the counter. The two children were up in their rooms, attending to their homework, and phones, probably not in that order. Robert's hand was on Camille's shoulder. Up until two days earlier, Robert's life had by comparison been simple and almost boring. The most important things at work for him were a couple of busts that had gone sideways for the Taskforce. Now that an undercover cop had been murdered, everything gained a new urgency, not to mention the publicity that was being generated over the matter. The television was tuned to one of the local news channels, and it seemed that Jonny's ordeal had surfaced. Rampant speculation as to whether there was a police-gang war taking place took centre stage. Very few facts were part of the discussion. Robert shook his head and clicked the television off.

"If I had to guess, I think the triads are making their presence felt here for some unknown reason. There is too much that points in this direction." Robert started.

"Why do you say that?"

"Two drug actions that went sideways for starters. By the time we had arrived at the meets, the gangs were gone. We had good intelligence, but it didn't help. They obvi-ously knew we were coming and adjusted their timetable to avoid us. Then there was the one meet that we did break up, where we managed to arrest a Gupil member, and seized a medium size drug cache. This indicates to me that they are giving up just enough to make it seem like we are making progress, which is how they work. Maybe the Gupil member was getting on their nerves or had made a mistake and he was expendable. But the real indicator is the presence of a mole. It's the only way they could have found out about Gurmit, I believe. The other gangs have never tried to do this type of thing, at least to our knowledge. On the other hand, this is how the triads operate, and they usually plant two at time, just like those *Star Wars* goofs, the Siths.

"You mean the moles are Sith Lords?" Camille smiled.

"Yeah, exactly." Robert laughed. "In fact, that's how we'll find them, flip up their capes to see if they have a light sabre."

"I haven't seen anyone with a cape at work, so far that is."

"Then I think I'm going to have to do this old school, lay a trap. In the meantime, I need to talk with my father. Want to go to that Taiwanese restaurant on Victoria Street I keep talking about?"

"Sure. I'm getting tired of hearing about it without tasting the food."

"Okay. I'll organize something tomorrow. Once we're done eating, I'll go for a short walk with my father, see what he can tell me about the triads."

* * *

Robert's father, Ethan Lui had been a young but respected chef in Hong Kong before he visited Vancouver and met his future wife. Robert had heard the rumours that Ethan had cooked for both triad members as well as members of the Hong Kong Police Force. Robert understood that one of Ethan's best friends from the old days was now a Senior Inspector for the force. Ethan was less than enthusiastic about Robert's chosen profession, probably stemming from what he had experienced in Hong Kong, so there was a distance between them that Robert continually ran up against. Robert understood this on some level, but he told himself that this wasn't Hong Kong, it was Vancouver and thus, somewhat different. He thought his father's unwillingness to see this was a failure to adapt to a new country.

What he tended to forget was that Ethan was only twenty-four years old when he had first arrived in Vancouver and met Robert's mother. After a few months of staring into each other's eyes they decided to make it formal. The fact that Ethan intended to wed Mary did not go over well with Ethan's parents in Hong Kong. Marrying outside your race was frowned upon. Mary's parent's opinions weren't much different in this respect. Ethan had to work hard on his mother and father to win them over. By moving back to Hong Kong and with much finagling, Ethan was able to wear them down. The parents were eventually charmed by Mary, but it took time. After Robert was born in Vancouver—to give him the coveted Canadian citizenship, the ice completely broke and Mary was welcomed wholeheartedly into the family. Having a son had a magical effect on things, not a big surprise in any culture. Robert had spent most of the first fifteen years of his life in Hong Kong as Ethen continued his life as a chef to the famous and infamous. Playing both ends eventually got tense enough for Ethan to finally return to Vancouver. He didn't want his young family in jeopardy because of who he cooked for and what he had learned by doing this.

***

Robert looked at his watch and realized it was later than he thought. "I'll set up the dishwasher, then I'll be up for more punishment."

Camille had a puzzled look on her face for a few seconds, then realized what he was saying, and smiled while running her fingers through his black hair, kissing him on the neck. She was unbuttoning her blouse as she left the room, "Don't be long."

The dishes had never gone into the washer so quickly, one or two gaining extra chips in the process.

~ 5 ~

Next morning, the Chief Constable of the Delta Police was alone in his office, reviewing what to do about the Jonny shooting, and when to do it. Protocol dictated that he open an investigation into the matter, but police forces investigating themselves wasn't popular with the public anymore. He knew he might have to contact the independent group set up to do this very task, he was just dragging his heels. The bar for calling them in was death or serious life-threatening injury, and since Jonny's injuries were in the grey zone, he was trying to come up with a rationale not to call in the outside body. Delta's police force was small, and he couldn't afford to lose more officers, no matter the reason. He had heard that the gangster had been kneecapped, something that qualified as a solution, or a message, a while ago in another part of the world. Raymond tried to fathom how officers on his force would resort to this kind of brutal act.

At least Jonny hadn't been killed, which would have been more serious. The aspect bothering Raymond was the rogue element. This was how bad things started, when officials on the side of law and order started taking things into their own hands. Getting away with it would just embolden them, and it would quickly worsen. There were plenty of examples all over the world. Damned if he was going to preside over this happening on his watch. Whoever was responsible would have to face the music. Raymond suspected that the officer who had done the shooting would soon be talking about it, and it wouldn't take the investigators too long before they had a suspect in hand. He was sure that his men would not cooperate with the investigation, but people eventually blabbed about their exploits. It was human nature.

*   *   *

While Raymond was pondering punishment, the Guru was thinking about retribution. There was no way a gangster could escape it; revenge was wired into the very core of their DNA. Intelligent people on the law enforcement side could use this knowledge to their advantage.

The Guru pondered using Jonny's girlfriend to make a compassion visit to Delta hospital to see if she could find out who had ventilated Jonny's legs. The hospital was situated across the street from the police detachment, which made any visit dangerous; but it wasn't like the girl was important, if she screwed up, it would just postpone the inevitable. She didn't know very much, unless of course Jonny had been talking more than he should. There was always that to consider. Around women, some of the Guru's employees acted like idiots. As long as they followed orders, everything was fine. On the other hand, any underling with a hint of smarts was an asset, but also a threat. The Guru always needed his antennae tuned for ambition; too much of it in a gang member would be a problem. This was the reason the police were able to take down a Gupil member several weeks ago, the Guru having decided the member was too focused on his own future, not the gangs'. Once convicted and in a cell, he could contemplate his own useless future to his heart's content.

The Guru was, however, very keen on getting at Farhad, and recovering what was rightfully his. The money and drugs were only part of what he was after. They were not the most important items by a long shot. The Guru had had the presence of mind to tape a conversation with Edward several months earlier, where Edward had mentioned in an offhand fashion, the identity of the man they had inside the Provincial government. The tape had inexplicably been laying with the money and drugs that Gurmit had purloined. The disappearance was what had really set the Guru off. This was leverage that the Guru needed, he felt sure, in any future dealings with the Wide Bay Boys. To have lost it to Farhad was unfortunate, even though he was unlikely to know its value. All he could think was that the police must have Farhad squirrelled away somewhere. He just needed to figure out where. He didn't think that Farhad would have blabbed to other officers about his indiscretions. Perhaps Edward would help him find the traitor, but after reflection, he ditched that idea. No sense in revealing what a leaky boat the Guru was rowing. Edward would then probably dispense with the Gupil's services, and that just wouldn't be fair.

***

Downtown, Robert was in his office, pondering his next move with Farhad. He had made up his mind to take him to Merritt, a small resource town about three hours northeast of Vancouver and stow him at a ranch house that Robert had spent time at in the past. If an attempt was made by the gangs to get at Farhad, it would be on Robert's terms. The gangsters would be off their home turf and uncomfortable, Robert hoped. What he really needed while he was figuring out who in the office to let know, was some caffeine. He walked out into the bullpen area and nodded to Gladys as he walked by. He left the building and turning south, headed up to Cafe Paulo, the favourite place to fuel his addiction. It was warm enough that thinking of summer was not out of the question. Vancouver typically had many starts and stops to this process with real heat only revealing itself in July. This was usually when real Vancouverites, who had been waiting eagerly for hot weather all year, started in on the complaining.

Robert walked into the cafe, stood in a short line, and nodded to Gilberto, the proprietor, not speaking. Gilberto pulled a double espresso and slid it over to Robert with a look of concern.

"How are you doing Gilberto?" Robert asked.

"Good Roberto, thank you. I'm thinking of taking a vacation, back to Brazil for a week or so." He waited, then. "I heard about the policeman getting killed, nasty business that."

Robert started to worry. "You're not closing, are you?"

"Carmelita will run the place while I'm gone." Robert felt an immediate sense of relief at this news. He did not want to be at the mercy of the chain coffee outlets, or the acidic dishwater served up in his office.

"We are working on it. Don't worry, we'll get our man." He thanked Gilberto and took his cup to sit by the window while he puzzled as to how to deal with the supposed mole. It was a short list of possibilities; Thomas, Gladys, and himself. Although he did not want to believe it, he had a sinking feeling that Gladys was behind the leaks—other than Thomas, no one else knew much about Gurmit's recent role. If the mole was Thomas, then everyone might as well quit the force and start another career. There was no straighter arrow in the quiver than him.

His plan was for Gladys to believe that Farhad would be driving himself to the ranch, while in reality Robert would be the one taking him upcountry and setting the trap, should the Gupils come looking to make a snatch. He would also take Tony Bortolo with him. Tony was a constable with the Vancouver Police Department and Robert had worked directly with him the previous fall. Robert also needed an alibi for being away. Having decided his plan of action, he got up and wandered slowly back to the precinct near the bottom of Cambie Street, all the while organizing the series of moves he was about to make.

* * *

Robert returned to his floor, and proceeded to Thomas's office, nodding at Gladys, who returned the gesture, indicating that Tom was in. She had a distracted air about her. Robert knocked on the door and entered, leaving the door ajar as he sat down. It was do or die days for the Vancouver Canucks as they were trying to make the NHL playoffs, so Robert started with some hockey talk.

"Heard the goalie missed one or two pucks last night." Robert started in; the Canucks having lost by seven goals the previous night. "Someone should let him know you're supposed to check the replay on the score board video after the play is over, not before."

"They'll come around," responded Thomas.

"Sure they will, once they're eliminated from play-off contention and the pressure is off." Robert laughed as he gauged his next remark. "I'm thinking of attending that short course on forensics that the Justice Institute is offering. It starts in two days. It runs for the rest of the week, and maybe I'll take a day off tomorrow before it starts. Okay with you?" Robert was looking directly into Thomas's eyes as he said this last sentence rather loudly.

"I guess that sounds good. What are you doing with Farhad?"

"I'm thinking of making him disappear up to Merritt for a while, but he'll need a car, preferably a rental."

"Gladys, can you come in here?" Thomas yelled out the door. After Gladys came through the doorway, Tom asked her to close the door. Gladys was wearing a tight olive coloured dress that dropped to midcalf with a simple gold necklace and matching earrings. She always looked like she'd be more at home in a high-end women's clothing store than a police admin pool. Today, she also didn't appear to be her usual composed self, but Robert couldn't put his finger on what was off.

"Gladys, we need a rental car. Farhad is being sent up to a ranch house west of Merritt to cool his heels. If you can get one organized by the end of today, that would be optimal. We're going to send him up tomorrow." Thomas finished, "Better rent it for a couple of weeks to be safe," then he added, almost as an afterthought, "This is the address where he'll be. Thanks." Thomas handed her the scribbled address of the ranch that Robert had given him.

"He's being sent up alone?"

"He's a big boy, he can handle himself. I can't think of anyone who'd want to spend a couple of weeks with him anyway." Thomas laughed at the thought. Gladys nodded as she left the room.

Robert stared at Thomas, then got up himself. "Think I'll go get some lunch. See you in a few days. Hopefully I'll be in one piece." As he left the office, walking slowly up Cambie he started to think about the subject of treachery, what the motivations for it were, and just as important, what the ramifications to the Taskforce would be. He thought of Gladys and doubted if money was the driver here; she made a decent living and her lawyer husband no doubt took in multiples of Robert's salary every year. If it was Gladys, was fear the motivation? Was her husband somehow involved? More importantly, how long had Gladys been with the Taskforce, and what information could she have given over, compromising what operations? This was getting to be like cold war theatrics, Robert thought, and complicated. He shook his head as he walked into his favourite lunch place on Broadway for a meeting with a plate of noodles.

***

Robert returned to his office, then called his father to see if he and Mary would like to eat Taiwanese this evening. After some preliminary conversation, his dad seemed interested in trying out the restaurant and keen to see the grandchildren, so it looked like a date. Robert called Camille, whose office was up a floor in the same building, to let her know. He then texted his two children to advise them.

He went through his list of what he would need for the trip upcountry. He realized it was a good thing that he could cook. He was pretty sure both Farhad and Tony wouldn't know a spatula from a spoon.

He called Farhad to warn him about the trip tomorrow before heading over to a local grocery store to provision up. "Pull on your cowboy boots Farhad, we're heading up to cattle country."

"What? Why are we going there?" The whining starting on the other end of the line.

"Trying to save your life, Farhad. I'm assuming that's important to you?"

"Yeah, but...." Farhad's voice trailed off, then, "How long will we be there?"

"Until the Gupil's make their move. Just get your stuff together, and don't forget your gun. I'm bringing ammo and other equipment. See you tomorrow around nine or so. We'll pick you up."

Farhad was worried about being farther from his stash of drugs and money, but he guessed it would be safe until his return. He wasn't so keen on being the 'tethered goat' however. Things had a way of going wrong in these operations. He fretted a bit about this upcoming excursion, then returned to his macaroni dinner while watching Punjabi news on the television.

* * *

Gladys Chu finished up her day around five, having procured a car for Farhad. She made a copy of the address where he was to spend some time, as well as the licence plate number and, picking up her purse, she headed home. Gladys had been feeling ill ever since finding out Gurmit's fate. This was not part of the bargain she had made a year earlier. She was feeling afraid. She had met and married her husband two years earlier, a second relationship for both of them. Gladys didn't know why his first marriage had failed, and didn't pursue the matter, although in retrospect, maybe she should have. She also didn't fully comprehend the extent of his love for gambling at first. She had been with him a few times to the local casino in Burnaby while they were dating, and it seemed like a good time, losing a few dollars for a nice night out with some free drinks. They had even been to a couple of the shows that were periodically staged in the theatre in order to bring more people to the venue. Gladys had already been working for the police for a year at that point and had passed their vetting process with no troubles.

As she stood on the train, heading east, her thoughts

were whirling. She hadn't understood that her husband would also regularly go to the casino without her, and managed to pile up a mountain of debt so large that he eventually resorted to a lender of an uncertain background in order to pay it off. That uncertainty was removed when the man learned what his new wife did for a living. In exchange for a few tidbits of seemingly harmless information from Gladys, a substantial portion of her husband's debt was magically erased. He was relieved of course, but he wasn't in the habit of thinking these things through, long term. Then, Gladys was transferred to be Thomas Harrow's assistant on the gang Taskforce. After the lender found this out, the requests for information did not stop, but started coming more often.

Edward and his assistant, Jason, could not believe their good fortune. Not only did they get an entrance to the workings of the Taskforce, but it turned out that Gladys's husband was a commercial lawyer who was now reluctantly helping the triad launder money on an epic scale. Edward seemed to have little regard for the law of averages, which the triad was pushing hard against. Successes only lasted so long in any enterprise, usually followed by failures at some point.

Once Hong Kong found out, it only made the push that much harder. In effect, they were tempting fate. All the successes and money were clouding the vision of the Wide Bay Boys, and they failed to see why their approach couldn't go on endlessly. After all, as triad members, they were not hamstrung by any of the conventions and social norms that police had to obey. Any minor mistake by the police and they would be staring down some kind of public enquiry that would make their jobs even more difficult. The triads thought this hilarious, and it was one of the main reasons they enjoyed working in North America. The authorities in China could do whatever they felt like, with no regard for society at large; as long as the upper echelons agreed, that was.

Edward and Jason were sitting together in a restaurant in Aberdeen Centre, one of the larger shopping malls that called No. 3 Road in Richmond, home. They were concerned, having just received an unsettling call from the Guru. One of his men had been shot up in what seemed to be blatant retaliation for the Gurmit episode. This was not how the police were supposed to respond. They were supposed to go on television and explain that they were trying to solve the murder of a policeman, not start shooting gangsters willy-nilly. This was a bad omen. Edward liked things to be predictable, similar to how his masters in Hong Kong liked life. Maybe using this other gang had been a mistake.

* * *

Gladys stood, hanging onto the strap below the overhead bar, trying to steady herself on the crowded SkyTrain. She was rehearsing what she would say on the phone once she got home, not noticing anyone around her, all her attention inwardly focused. She got out of the train at the Metrotown stop, one of the major centres that had sprung up around stations after the train line had been installed decades earlier. This train stop was in Burnaby, just to the east of Vancouver, and was on a high plateau of land, looking like a bad Emerald City from wherever you were in the Lower Mainland. Views from the tall residential towers however were impressive in all directions. Gladys didn't notice anything as she walked away from the station and went north a few blocks to a recently built tower. She entered her apartment on the twentieth floor, dropped her jacket on the floor and sat on the edge of her sofa, looking down at her phone. She dialled the number, which was a cut-out linking Edward to his informants, and quickly gave the information about Farhad to whoever answered. Her husband wasn't home. Being a lawyer working for a private firm, he rarely got home before half past seven. She sighed, got up and went into the kitchen to pour herself a large gin and tonic, hoping she hadn't just signed Farhad's death warrant. After she sat down and took a few large gulps, she came to the realization that she had probably done exactly that. Tears started down her cheeks.

* * *

At the end of Robert's workday, he fetched Camille, and together, they went down to their car in the underground parkade. As Robert slowly manoeuvred out of the parkade and onto 2nd Avenue Camille laid her hand on his right leg. Robert looked over and smiled.

"I have to go upcountry for a few days." Robert started. "I've laid a trap—actually two traps, and now I have to go and do my thing, and hope some people walk into them."

"By yourself?"

"No, I am borrowing Tony. We are taking Farhad up to Merritt to wait for some gang members to show up. When I was in training for the Vancouver Police Department, I met a couple of guys my age who were from Merritt and we got along really well. One of them has a ranch in the family and I have stayed there a few times over the years. The property is only a half section, but they have grazing rights all around them. It's located on one of the reserves."

"What's a half section?"

"Half a square mile, three hundred and twenty acres. Sounds like a lot, but up there, it's small potatoes."

Camille changed gears. "I'm a little nervous about tonight."

Camille had met Robert's parents only twice since she had been seeing and then moving in with Robert, so it was still a feeling out time for each of the parties. She was looking forward to this dinner with some trepidation, but with the kids present, she knew she ranked lower in the batting order.

"Don't be. Ethan can make anyone nervous, just relax. The food is going to be great." Robert drove slowly, as light rain had started to fall, rendering the streets slippery. Most of the traffic kept to its usual speed, not slowing until a near miss, or an accident happened. They pulled into the lane behind their house to pick up the kids before heading over to Victoria Drive, where all manner of restaurants and green grocers could be found. No one ethnic group had newly staked the territory, but European options were now absent in this part of the East Side, whereas decades earlier, they had ruled the roost. Robert pulled up and parked on the street. As they neared the restaurant Robert could see his father and mother in the distance heading their way, so he sent Camille and the kids in to get a table while he waited for them.

"Hi Robert, good to see you." Mary smiled as she hugged Robert tightly, not letting go for several seconds. Ethan nodded at Robert over Mary's shoulder, eyes sharp. Mary had short auburn hair cut in a bob, looking exactly like the professor she used to be. Her eyes seemed to penetrate to the very heart of your soul. Ethan was tall for a Cantonese man, and thin, belying his years of preparing great meals for a living. His salt and peppered hair was close cropped and topped a pair of equally intense eyes. Sometimes, Robert thought he had descended from eagles. As always, Mary's smile was tinged with a hint of concern. Both parents had a pretty fair idea of how dangerous police work could be on a good day, never mind chasing gangsters for a job. They followed the news and knew about what had happened to Gurmit.

"You will be careful, Robert, right?" Mary asked.

"Always, Mom."

"Let's go in. Don't get scared by the decor." Robert led his parents into what was a very basic place to eat—no frills wasted on the dining area. They could see the noodle master plying his trade in the steamy window next to the kitchen. Robert started salivating. When noodles entered the picture, Robert's whole gyroscope went haywire. He was going to need to concentrate on the actual reason for this whole meal, and it wasn't about the cuisine. The fact that he had already eaten noodles at noon meant nothing; he could easily eat them morning, noon, and night.

"Hi Gune-Gune." Robin smiled at Ethen. Sophie was grinning as well. Mary went over and hugged both of the children and then moved over to hug Camille before finding her chair. Mary had been so pleased when Robert had found someone who could tolerate a police officer's life, and that she was another officer seemed just about right. Whether it was ultimately good or bad, Mary couldn't pass judgment, she just knew that Robert was happier than he had been in a long time. She had immediately liked Camille, but Ethan, as usual, was more reserved in his judgment.

Ethan gave the interior the once over, noting the cold fluorescent lighting, the spotted linoleum flooring, the lack of any discernible art on the walls, and nodded approval to Robert. A couple of posters announcing an upcoming festival in Tai-Chung, was about it for decoration. As if some diners were about to hop over to Taiwan after dinner to take it in. The fancier the place, the better the service, the worse the food was likely to be. Robert took this as a mantra.

"Camille, you are well?" Mary asked.

"Yes, thank you, and you two? You both look great."

Ethan finally spoke in measured tones, "That is because we are. No complaints." Ethan was not big on small talk.

The waitress came to their table and the family slowly ordered all the dishes that they would need and more. Leftovers always made it home to be devoured by the kids. The feast included noodle concoctions, vegetable bowls, and ginger fried beef; the last dish being an extraordinary item invented in Calgary, of all places. For such a good dish, it was rare to find in Vancouver, and rarer still to find it done correctly. While the family waited, discussion about school filled the air. Camille and Robert listened, finding out things they wouldn't normally be a party to as the children opened up to their grandparents.

When the food started arriving, they all launched into it, dishes flying back and forth, and then silence. Ethan looked over at Robert and gave him the smallest of smiles. Yes! Robert had of course been worried about Ethan's reaction to the cuisine, but it looked as though those concerns had been unfounded. After several rounds of tea, the pace abated as everyone had their fill of the food. Robert looked over at Ethan and nodded towards the door. Ethan knew what this signalled, it not being the first time Robert had pulled the dinner conversation stunt.

"We'll be back in a few minutes. Keep eating, if you can." Robert added before walking out onto the street with Ethan.

"What's up Robert?" Ethen opened as the two walked along Victoria Street. Their breath misted up into the strangled light coming through the tree limbs from the streetlights above, new buds making their appearance on the branches.

"Sorry for this, but we have a bit of a situation at work, and I am trying to understand more about how the triads work. There are one or more gangs operating in Vancouver, and I am getting the distinct impression that they are moving out of the shadows. I'm trying to figure out why. You are going to see the results on the news. One of our people was killed the other day."

"I saw that, and you know my feelings about your chosen profession Robert. I also know that you won't let this go, so I'll tell you what I know, but it is from long ago, from another life. They consider themselves clever. The Black Societies are always hatching plans and trying to get their tentacles into everything. Intelligence is important for their operations, so like any good organization, they try to infiltrate people into places of power. I dare say you will have someone in your office who is working for them. You can also count on someone placed in government who does their bidding."

"Do they work with other gangs?"

"No. That would be highly unusual. They would use other gangs if it was to their benefit. Those gangs would probably get the impression that they were working with the triad instead of for them, but this would be a mistake."

"You used to cook for a few of them, is that not correct?"

"Everyone has to eat, and some like to eat well. Yes, I cooked for a few of them." He smiled. "I also heard things and names that eventually made it difficult for me to continue there." They had reached the end of the long city block, so they turned, and started back to the restaurant.

"If we found out who they have placed in our office, I wonder if we could use them to screw the triad up."

"Maybe. You would have to be very careful. And it would be dangerous for the person you are using."

Robert considered this while they walked. "You also had a friend in the Hong Kong Police Force, is that correct?"

"Yes, we still communicate with each other on occasion. His name is Winston Chang, and he is still working there as a Chief Inspector. I believe I saved his life near the end of my final time there."

"Really? Would he know anything about what the gangs over there are up to in Vancouver?"

"Uncertain. They have their hands full with Hong Kong issues, I'm sure." Then Ethan added, "The officer that was found dead in Richmond the other day. Is this connected?"

"Yes, I think so, unfortunately. It is why I wanted to get your view on things."

They had arrived back at the door to the restaurant. Ethan paused before entering and put his hand on Robert's shoulder. "Please be extra careful Robert, I would like my grandchildren to grow up with a dad present." He gave the shoulder a squeeze before relinquishing his grip.

"Believe me, so do I." Robert nodded, thanking his father for the insight, as they re-entered the warmth of the restaurant to see what was on offer for dessert.

$$\sim 6 \sim$$

TWENTY-FOUR YEARS EARLIER—HONG KONG

The restaurant where Ethan Lui led the chef brigade took up most of the real estate on the sixth floor of an office tower off Des Voeux Road. The window seats afforded a fine view north over Victoria Harbour, with West Kowloon providing background lighting in the evening. Lately, the Everlasting Royale had been building a well-deserved reputation for the finest of dining, mostly due to the efforts of its executive chef.

Before Ethan's arrival, the food was considered good, but expensive, the restaurant coasting on the impressive views it offered diners lucky enough to be seated near windows. After hearing less than enthusiastic rumblings from some longtime patrons, the owner decided she had better up her game. She went after Ethan, hiring him away from a formidable competitor, at no small cost. At first, she regretted her decision. Ethan took little time deciding who he could work with, and who would need to be jettisoned, but spent several weeks altering the entire menu. A few months passed, the owner starting to get panicky, when she finally noticed an uptick in customers. It wasn't only the numbers that had improved, the cliental seemed more affluent. Some diners seemed to be made of money. She asked a few questions of her friends, who provided some troubling answers. Apparently, a few members of the criminal element were frequenting her restaurant. The money was nice, but she decided some balance would be appropriate, and called up an acquaintance of her husband, a young officer with the Hong Kong Police Force.

"Winston?"

"Yes?"

"Faye here. How are you?"

"Very good, Faye. How's the old man?"

"Oh, complains, but really, he is just ducky. I have a small favour to ask if you don't mind?"

"Sure. What can I do for you?"

"We've made some improvements at Everlasting that I think you'd like. Just wondered if you and some of your colleagues wouldn't mind dropping by for a meal on occasion. There will be a discount offered of course. We've hired Ethan Lui and we couldn't be happier with the food he is presenting to our diners."

"I know Ethan. He is good. I wondered where he had disappeared to. Now I know. Of course, Faye. I'll spread the word. Hope you have enough tables, haha."

"I'm sure we will cope, Winston. Thank you, and I guarantee, you will be well fed!"

* * *

Winston and his fellow officers had been gathering more and more often at the Royale, enjoying both the food, and the police force discount. The officers discovered that some triad members also frequented the establishment, knowing them by sight. Winston quickly figured out why the owner was being so generous to the officers. Winston knew Ethan well enough to occasionally venture into the kitchen to have a word with him, but he wasn't alone in this familiarity. On one occasion he had been talking with Ethan on the edges of the kitchen action when a young triad member came in and walked up to Ethan.

"Good evening, Ethan." He glanced at Winston. "Excuse me for a second." He didn't wait for an answer after his rather rude interruption. "Jacky would like much more garlic added to his *dau mui*. Thanks." He smiled and retreated.

Ethan looked at Winston, shaking his head. "They haven't grasped the concept of what the wait staff do here, unfortunately."

"They seem familiar with you."

"Yes. I recognize some of them from my previous restaurants. They must be following me around. Everyone needs to eat, Winston, even criminals."

"Not this well. Believe me, they don't deserve it." Winston said, then changed topics, "Can you make your special dish for me tonight?"

Ethan smiled. "Of course. You realize special is a relative term, correct? Hardly anyone else orders the Singapore Fried Noodles, in fact, no one has since I got here. That's the reason it's not on the menu, it's the type of dish better served at other establishments." He didn't need to add what kind of restaurants.

"But you do it so well, Ethan." His pleading was almost pathetic, but Ethan wasn't immune to a compliment.

"Okay, okay. I'll try to jazz it up for you tonight."

"Just don't change it too much." Winston grinned before he left the kitchen to rejoin his table.

* * *

A month later, it was a Friday evening, and Winston had gathered four of his fellow officers to join him at Everlasting Royale. It was the end of a long exhausting week. The sun was setting, the windows growing dark, mirror-like, at least from the vantage point of their table. Everyone had a couple of drinks while they studied the menu they already knew almost by heart. A chicken concoction, beef hotpot, fried squid, along with a couple of vegetable dishes rounded out the selections.

"I'm getting the Singapore Noodles." Winston proclaimed.

His immediate subordinate rolled his eyes and said, "Of course you are." Like he hadn't heard this almost every time they visited Royale.

A waitress, new to the restaurant, came to take the food order. She balked at the mention of Singapore. "It's not on the menu. We don't make it here, too pedestrian."

Winston was mildly taken aback by the comments. It was very unusual for a waitress to express an opinion. He knew the dish wasn't ritzy, however, he would not be dissuaded. "Ethan Lui will make it for me." The waitress scrunched up her eyebrows, perplexed at the suggestion. Winston nodded his head slightly at her in confirmation.

He could tell that the waitress was not convinced. Looked like a visit to the kitchen would be needed, but after he finished his whisky.

Winston tilted his head to his fellow officers as a triad member they knew entered the restaurant, looked over their way, then made his way into the private dining room where obviously more gang members were meeting. The main dining area was a generous size and people didn't feel crowded, but, like most restaurants, private rooms could be booked for special, or wealthy customers. The Hong Kong officers didn't fit into either of these categories. They couldn't even rate a window side seat, but as long as the food was great, they'd keep dining at Royale.

Eventually Winston finished his second drink, and feeling relaxed, as well as developing a ravenous hunger, he got up and went into the kitchen. It looked like Hades inside, four large woks going full bore, flames leaping out of two of them, smoke being sucked away by huge roaring ventilation hoods. Sous chefs and cooks were moving back and forth in a ballet of sorts, food being ladled out onto serving platters and large bowls as new dishes were started. It was as noisy as a blacksmith's forge. Winston looked over at Ethan who was near the rear of the kitchen and signalled with his hand. Ethan nodded—he knew what was desired and went over to a cook to give his instructions. Winston smiled and retreated to the dining room.

Ten minutes later, Winston's Singapore dish was ready, steaming on the serving counter when two men entered the kitchen. Ethan immediately noted them as triad members. One of them had been a regular visitor to see Ethan, but to have two at the same time? Something was going on. He watched as they split up, the larger man heading to the cooking line where he managed to knock a large stainless steel bowl onto the floor. It made a huge clattering noise, drawing the attention of most of the people in the kitchen, but not Ethan's. He noticed the other smaller man reaching over Winston's noodle dish and doing something. It wasn't clear what he had done, but immediately, the larger man apologized loudly for his oafish behaviour, keeping all the attention on himself. Continuing his diatribe, he retreated, linking up with his mate and the two finally left the kitchen.

Ethan wasn't stupid. They were up to something. He walked over to the noodle dish and looked at it. It seemed fine. The waitress came for it, but Ethan put up his hand.

"We're re-making this. Don't touch it. I'll take it away." He took the plate and deposited its contents into large tray was used for leftovers and slapped a lid on it, snapping it tightly. He went out to have a word with Winston.

Three days later, Winston made a morning visit to Everlasting Royale, requesting to meet Ethan. They sat in Ethan's small office.

"To what do I owe the pleasure, Winston? Hope we haven't done anything wrong."

"On the contrary, Ethan. I came to thank you. I believe you saved me from a very unpleasant death. We had our scientists examine that noodle dish you didn't serve to us. Strychnine had been added. Enough to kill. I assume it's not a regular ingredient that you use to spice up the meals?"

"No. Not so far, anyway. Those fucking triad people. I watched as it happened. They used a diversion in the kitchen. Maybe we need to ban these people. This all getting to be too much. I overhear things when they invite me into their room here. I don't think I can take this anymore."

To Winston, Ethan looked worried. He hadn't seen this in his friend before. Three months later, Winston heard that Ethan had resigned his position and would be emigrating to Canada.

~ 7 ~

*TWENTY-THREE AND A HALF YEARS
LATER—HONG KONG*

Jacky Chow now led the Wide Bay Boys in Hong Kong. His nemesis, Inspector Winston Chang, with the Hong Kong Police Force, was responsible for many of Jacky's present headaches. In addition, Winston blocked the progress of a man planted years ago by Jacky as a way of getting better intelligence. If Winston could somehow be made to disappear, Jacky's man would rise to an even higher level in the force hierarchy, all the better to help business. Winston was not young anymore, but he seemed to be a forever man. He had also dodged a couple of attempts at shortening his life. Jacky was tired of the wait for Winston to retire on his own accord and had been discussing this with his Vancouver lieutenant, Edward for some time. They were hatching a plan that would finally answer their problems, or so he hoped. In the meanwhile, other business needed his attention.

Jacky sat in a private dining room in his club in Kowloon, just off Nathan Road, contemplating arrangements for a kidnapping on the Kowloon side of Hong Kong;

nothing fancy, just a play for a big pile of money from someone who could afford to part with it. Jacky had to be continually on top of his game, as he wasn't the only head of a triad trying to make his way in China. One of the things he was presently involved with was tracking a family called the Chins.

* * *

The Chin family were recent arrivals in Hong Kong from Singapore, and not entirely up to speed with local dangers Hong Kong society could pose. Spotting the Chins early and marking the son as a target was something all of the criminal gangs would be trying to do. Most of the wealthier Hong Kong set knew kidnapping to be a popular sport amongst gangs in order to re-distribute money to where the gangsters thought it properly belonged, so they took appropriate precautions. George Chin had other things on his mind.

Singapore was more orderly compared to Hong Kong, something George would soon learn about. He ran a hugely successful telecommunications business that had operations in several countries, including China. He spent so much business time in Hong Kong that after months of severe nagging from his wife, he decided to move his family out of Singapore and to the city. It would put a crimp into his lifestyle in Hong Kong, but his wife's father called the shots here. George wouldn't be running such a company without the original cash infusion from his in-laws, so he knew it was payback time. He would move his wife and son back to China.

One reason for the initial reluctance about the move was his mistress in Hong Kong. Keeping her at a distance from his wife seemed like a good strategy. However, the more he thought about it, the more he liked the idea of the move. At this point he was thinking with his balls. He would be closer to his mistress and could run over to visit her whenever the urge struck him. As long as he kept running a tight ship, there was no reason for the women to know about each other. Some seven and a half million people called Hong Kong home after all. Between his business concerns, and keeping his women from finding out about each other, the safety of his family slipped to back of his mind, way behind screwing women and making gobs of money, in that order.

Any multimillionaire with half a brain would send his son to private school in an armoured car with a chauffeur who possessed some tactical training in small arms and knowledge of what to do to avoid sticky situations. George's son, Ping, all of fourteen years old was not the beneficiary of such forethought. He would be what in popular parlance is known as a sitting duck.

* * *

Jacky had heard about George Chin's arrival in Hong Kong from a friend. After perusing the situation, Jacky asked Cedric to organize a kidnapping and the subsequent ransom note. Cedric was Jacky's righthand man in Hong Kong. Cedric took this to heart and started what any good organizer would do, surveillance and information gathering on the target. As the target was Ping, Cedric had a couple of his men follow his movements, which seemed to consist of being transported to and from school by a chauffeur from the family home. The Chins lived just south of the Kowloon reservoirs on the mountainside up Tai Po Road. The boy didn't seem to do much else that required him to be outside the family home, so Cedric knew that the main chance would be either before or after school. After confirming the pick-up and drop-off schedule, which never seemed to vary on a weekday, Cedric started planning the actual kidnapping. He wanted a van, a backup car, and asked Jacky about a place where the boy could be kept on ice. When the Chins moved from Singapore, they had picked a mansion that was conveniently located close to a major highway higher up the hillside in Kowloon. This road could quickly connect cars to several other routes affording the possibility of a quick disappearance once Ping had been taken.

* * *

The watchers that Cedric employed for surveillance work knew some of the underlings from other gangs in the city, probably far better than their bosses did. One of the Wide Bay Boys noticed a couple of their competitors on the last day of their surveillance, but put it off to a coincidence, not mentioned to his boss. They'd been spotted sitting in a car, on the side of Tai Po Road just west of where it merged onto highway seven. What Cedric didn't know was that the Chins had also been marked by another triad in Hong Kong, one of the main competitors to the Wide Bay Boys. They were in the planning stages of their own attempt at kidnapping the same boy. The situation was a manifestation of unbridled capitalism. If the gangs talked to each other to organize their malfeasance one could have theoretically charged them with being a monopoly— as if. Hong Kong gangs still enjoyed some of the autonomy that came with being a British colonial state, even if Beijing was intent on gaining more and more control over every facet of life in Hong Kong.

So, the two gangs were not aware that each was planning to kidnap the same victim. It had the makings of a tragic comedy of epic proportions; that is, if your idea of comedy included the possibility of a teenager having his life put in extreme danger by thugs. Whoever was the most efficient and acted first would get the spoils, and the gang that came in second was going to be extremely pissed off, after all, it wasn't every day that someone this rich and stupid showed up in Hong Kong. Most wealthy people spent a fair bit of effort protecting themselves, something that George Chin would undoubtably be doing after this episode concluded.

* * *

Cedric finally felt he and his team were ready and told Jacky this at his club on a Wednesday afternoon.

"Good work. Let's do it tomorrow then. Let your men know. The shop on Bute Street can be used to stow the cargo. It is not far from the boy's school, so he should feel at home. That is, if he had any clue where he was."

"Good, I will make it so. My men are eager to do this." All the waiting around and prep work grated on everyone's nerves. They all knew a big payday was in the offing if this was successful, and there was nothing like a lot of cash to get the pulses moving.

The next day dawned with a full sun rising. Early fall had arrived, so the stifling heat that usually plagued Hong Kong in the summer abated. It was a pleasure to be outside after what had been an unbearable period of higher than usual temperatures and humidity. Cedric assembled his men at a garage just off of upper Nathan Road. The team aimed for the return trip from school. There were to be three men in a Nissan van; a driver, a man who would deal with the chauffeur, and a man to snatch Ping. A second car with two men would shadow the operation to deal with any surprises if needed.

At just past three, the two vehicles drove off and proceeded up Tai Po Road to where it intersected, then passed to the north of route seven. The two vehicles waited on the side of the road for the black Mercedes to make its appearance. The car parked about one hundred metres behind the van. Farther up the route, the van occupants noticed a BMW also sitting on the verge of the road. They didn't give much thought to it, concentrating on their mirrors, looking for the Mercedes. The Wide Bay Boys were to signal with their car lights when the target car went by them as well as confirm with their cellphone. This portion of Tai Po Road saw relatively little traffic, given the few mansions scattered off it as the road made its way on up the mountainside past the reservoirs. This was the preserve of the ultra-rich who looked down upon the masses as they went about their busy lives. A private security firm roamed the area, mainly as a precaution, funded by some of the local residents. One or two foot-patrols and a car that toured around helped give the residents some peace of mind. Cedric's men had remarked on these people but had not put in the extra research necessary to determine who these layabouts were or even what their schedules were. If Jacky had known about this oversight, he would have labelled it as being sloppy and reprimands would have gone out.

* * *

The parked BMW belonged to another triad. They were doing their own due diligence, what the Wide Bay Boys had been doing the previous couple of weeks. They were not in a position yet to do what Cedric's team was about to do. However, being watchers, they couldn't help but notice the van behind them, and the car farther down the road and wondered what was going on.

A few minutes past four, the black Mercedes with Ping in the rear seat made its way along the road, not hurry-ing. The driver was in a routine now, and relaxed as he considered what club he might go to this evening after his last driving assignment was over. He was travelling about 70 km/hour as he passed by what looked like an American Buick. He slowed and checked it out as he passed by. Rare to be seeing one of those in Hong Kong. So, he wasn't paying full attention when about one hundred metres far-ther along a van pulled out in front of him from the right side of the road and angled him over to the left verge, where it stopped. He slammed on the brakes and stopped, his car almost touching the side of the van. He slipped the Mercedes into reverse and banged into the Buick that had come up behind him. Finally, his brain snapped into working mode, unfortunately too late. Two men had exited the van and came over to the starboard side of the limo with weapons drawn. The driver knew he was screwed. The Mercedes was not fortified against weapons, or much of anything. He unlocked the doors, the rear door was opened, and Ping taken, as simple as you pleased. The second man had a gun trained on the driver, who was not moving a muscle. The men were masked, so identifying the perpetrators was not going to be happening this day. The man holding the gun waved his weapon at the driver to exit his limo. Both the driver and the child were forced into the van.

At this point, things got interesting. The BMW farther up the road with two gangsters inside had done a U-turn and came flying down the road, swerving to a stop opposite where the drama had been unfolding. The gangsters could not believe that someone was poaching what they had considered their property, and they were going to do something about it, no matter how stupid the idea appeared to be. All this was happening on a very public road, one that the Wide Bay Boys wanted to disappear from as soon as possible now that they had their package. The other triad members didn't even bother to get out of their car. They lowered their windows and started firing away with their pistols at the Buick, the BMW driver hoping that his asshole partner didn't wing him from behind in all the excitement. The gangsters in the Buick were taken aback by the audacity. The passenger eventually took a bullet in his right eye, killing him immediately. The Buick's driver however, no slouch with a gun, managed to hit the driver of the other triad car in the cheek, not killing him outright, but pretty much the next best thing. Blood and some gristle shot back onto the passenger in the BMW. Meanwhile, the van had done its own U-turn, dodged the BMW and lit out of the war zone, heading back into lower Kowloon. The package was intact, but the van sustained a couple of bullet holes in the fuselage. The driver of the Buick took a couple of shots at the tires of the BMW, taking out the sidewalls, rendering the run-flat feature of BMW's tires useless. He then decided that he had had enough sport for one day and lit up the tires as he turned and squealed back the way he had come. He looked over at his dead partner in the passenger seat, brains and blood oozing onto the leather seat and shook his head. Not every day was going to be honey and roses in the Wide Bay world. The BMW sat in the middle of Tai Po Road to await its fate. Its sole remaining living occupant decided to leave the scene on foot through the trees lining the road after the Buick had driven off, his dying partner left in the BMW, to be the one to converse with the authorities, or not.

* * *

By the end of the same day, a note had been delivered to George Chin at his place of work. It asked for twenty million HK dollars for the safe return of his only son. He was not to approach the Hong Kong Police Force. His son would be released if the money was forthcoming. Failure to follow directions meant the return of Ping piece by little piece. A small finger in an accompanying plastic bag completed the gruesome message. When George opened the manila envelope in his office he almost threw up. He read the letter and looked at the finger, his brain going in a dozen different directions. He assumed he was looking at Ping's finger, and right there, decided to call the police. If this is how the gang started negotiations, then George was having none of it. So far, only George had seen the note and the finger. His regular assistant was away, and she would normally open all of his work mail.

George's call got directed through the Kowloon West Region Headquarters of the HKPF before connecting with a sergeant. He punted it up the chain of command a few levels where it landed on Chief Inspector Winston Chang's desk phone.

"Chief Inspector Chang speaking."

"My son has been kid ... kidnapped." George's voice started to crack under the strain, and he stuttered.

"Who are you again?"

"I am George Chin. I own Larkcom Industries in town here. My son Ping has been kidnapped out of our chauffeured Mercedes on Tai Po Road. I have just received a ransom note."

"What does it say?"

"I am not to contact the police under any circumstances, and they want twenty million dollars for the safe return of my son." Winston could hear a quiver in George's voice as he continued, "Included with the note was a severed finger in a plastic bag. What kind of animals would do this to a small boy?"

Winston's mind was racing. No way could the gang find out that the police were involved. He would need to instigate special procedures right away.

"Can you please not handle the note more than you have to. I will meet with you, but we must tread carefully. I will assume that someone will be watching your movements, so please leave the envelope at your place of business. An undercover officer dressed as a courier will drop by to pick it up. We will need to have some personal item of Ping's that we can use for DNA. Before we jump to conclusions, we need to check on whose finger you might have." Winston thought, then added. "Can I send a courier also to your house to pick up a toothbrush or something similar of Ping's? I would like to act as quickly as possible to forestall the gang getting any knowledge of us." George gave his address, then Winston talked with his personal assistant to get the officers in motion, being very careful not to tell anyone in his office more than needed for the task at hand.

Winston was proceeding at light speed, his actions considerably outside the normal flow of police work. Assertions and claims normally needed to be checked and verified before any action could be taken by the HKPF. However, Winston was no slouch. He knew that to take the initiative here might make all the difference between life and death for the boy. He also figured that a triad was involved, so he needed to compartmentalize this within the force so that it didn't end up on some mole's plate.

He could sense a headache coming on. How was he going to run a full-scale police operation without most of the force knowing about it? He considered his options after the phone call ended. In the end he went to his superior, explained the situation, and requested a few men from a totally different department; a traffic division or similar, some place that any semi-intelligent gangster would not bother to penetrate. What these officers lacked in experience would be made up for by enthusiasm when they found they would be working on a case that formerly they could have only dreamed about. Winston would, by necessity, need to be much more hands on, in order to guide the team, but he relished the thought of it. He doubted that the finger would turn out to be from the child, but he would let the techs figure this out.

Winston had his couriers travel in pairs, not together, but apart, one watching the back of the other. It was always useful to help identify who might be watching events unfold. This kind of extravagance was not appreciated within the department. Officers were always in short supply, but this bit of forethought prevented many problems, saving the department time. Unfortunately, it was difficult to make people in more senior positions understand this.

~ 8 ~

The day after the kidnapping, Winston had the chosen officers assemble in his large office. He was not familiar with most of them. It also seemed that only a few knew each other. A couple of them had a puzzled looks on their faces. One woman stood out among six men, reflecting the lack of progress made on the equality file within the HKPF, Winston realized. So far, Winston had not notified the bureau within the force that specialized in triad crime of what was happening. Nothing overtly suggested that a triad was involved with the kidnapping, so he felt on sure footing, but it didn't take a genius to link the two. For now, Winston kept the bureau clueless, just in case there was a leak. Carrying out surreptitious investigations within the force was frowned upon, so Winston's superior granted him authority to do it grudgingly. If there hadn't been a child involved, Winston would be doing this by the book.

* * *

Winston brought the meeting to order. "You are present today because you are going to be working on a kidnapping case. The reason that the regular detectives from the Crime Formation are not working on this is that the father of the victim was advised not to contact the police under any circumstances." He paused, then, "A finger was sent along with the ransom note. We're checking to see if it is the victim's."

There was a sharp intake of breath by one or two of the officers as they looked at each other.

"This is likely triad work, so nothing said in this room is to be repeated to anyone, understand? What we will do is monitor the developments, and when the cash drop and trade arrangements are presented to the victim, we'll arrange to be there and rescue the child. The family is the Chin family, the Chins of Larkcom Industries. Their only son was taken yesterday on Tai Po Road, not far from the family home. We found a bullet ridden car at the scene, abandoned, with a body inside. Something else went on as well as the kidnapping. The child's chauffeur was also taken."

"Why was the chauffeur taken?" This from one of the officers.

"Likely to prevent any identification of the kidnappers and news of the incident reaching the police. I am waiting for identification of the body found at the scene and any other information to be gleaned from the car. The chauffeur was not armed apparently, so what happened to the BMW is something others need to explore. For now, it is a waiting game, until the kidnappers arrange the meet to get their money. Twenty million dollars by the way."

One of the officers gave a low whistle, "A lot of cash!"

"No need to remind you that the money is not the prime

target of our efforts, the child is. He goes by the name of Chin Ping and is fourteen years old. I've arranged for a room on this floor where you can park yourselves while this case is ongoing. Anything of consequence arises? Please come to me. Do not contact any of your regular coworkers about this. I will be active in this investigation. Thank you."

With that, the officers wandered out of Winston's office wondering exactly what they were to do. They went to their new office and decided to have their own meeting. The senior officer present took charge, but after a few minutes it became apparent that the only real instruction they had received was to keep quiet about what they were doing. Since they weren't doing anything, they concluded that this order should be easy to follow. It seemed that even in a kidnapping, bureaucracy was king. Tea and coffee was their next order of business while they sat around, waiting for more information and getting to know one another.

Winston returned a half hour later and tasked three of the team to get rid of their uniforms and go canvass the area where Ping had been kidnapped for any surveillance footage. Meanwhile, in the Wide Bay world, Cedric's gang members had to dispose of a body of one of their members and clean up the Buick that had sustained considerable damage from bullets, not to mention brains and blood. The owner was in love with the car, so getting rid of it, which would have been the smart thing to do, was not an option. Cedric and Jacky soon realized that because the other gang's car was left at the scene, the police would be on the scent of what had transpired. Cedric knew they would have to move fast to get their money before the police figured out what was going on.

A second note would be sent to George at his office the next day. A courier would be used to disguise the source of the letter. Cedric also had a watcher monitoring George's office to make sure the police weren't hanging around against the triad's wishes.

****

The next day dawned with smog filtering the sun. At his office, George wondered when the next instructions would arrive. He definitely wasn't working. His wife had spent a good part of the previous evening in a hysterical fit. The police had been in contact midmorning and relayed that the finger in question came from someone else, so he breathed a sigh of relief. Temporarily buoyed by this information, he decided to visit his mistress over on Hong Kong Island. With a triad watcher tailing him, he crossed Victoria Harbour and took a taxi up to Happy Valley where he proceeded to sample some afternoon delight. The watcher wasn't totally sure what George was up to, but he had a good idea. In his mind, George was either extremely horny, or extremely stupid. Probably both, on further reflection. No matter, Cedric would be pleased to find out about this further development. He took note of the address, leaving Cedric to find out the rest as to the woman's particulars.

By the time George returned to his offices in the early afternoon, the second ransom note had arrived. It detailed instructions on the exchange of the hostage for money. The trade was to take place at 2:00 pm the next day on a waterfront promenade in West Kowloon across from Stonecutters Island. As soon as George had telephoned Winston about the details, Winston knew a boat would be involved. George, and George alone was to bring a bag with the money to the Hoi Fai Promenade just south of a group of residential towers called the One SilverSea and drop it on the seawall walk. He could then go over to a Nissan van in a parking area to find his son and chauffeur. Failure to follow these instructions would result in Ping losing some part of his body. George grimaced at this suggestion.

"You won't interfere in any way, will you?" George asked Winston.

"We will be invisible. Have you arranged for the money?"

"Yes."

"Listen to me—this is critical. After you have dropped the cash and gone to the car, you need to raise your head up and look straight up like you have spotted a hawk in the air, if your son and the chauffeur appear to be ok. We will be watching you from a distance. Don't wave or anything like that, the gang will be watching you also. If we get this confirmation, then we will try to intercept the money before it disappears."

"Okay. I will do this. But will this all work?"

"Nothing is guaranteed, but it should work." Winston had his doubts about George. It'd be a miracle if he followed any of these instructions. In pressure situations, normal people rarely did what they were supposed to.

After he hung up, he immediately called his superior and requested a police boat, but not just any police boat. This one was an undercover boat, dressed up as a junk. It had large engines and enough armaments aboard to cover any situation, short of running into a real naval ship. Winston wanted it in place this evening, so that there would be no suspicious movements the day of the event. After some moaning, his superior officer reluctantly agreed and made the call to move the asset into place. All that remained was for Winston to meet his team and hand out assignments for the exchange. The junior officers were both excited and slightly depressed, as they realized that this interlude from their normal duties was likely coming to a quick end, no matter how it turned out.

* * *

Early Friday morning, Winston and two officers from his team were driven over to the adjacent wall of towers. The easternmost building was a hotel. None of the officers were wearing uniforms, and while there were more police officers than normal in the general area, no one would notice anything unusual. Several more of the team were close by with orders to ensure that after the trade, no further harm would come to Ping. Winston did not trust the gang to just leave the area once the action was over.

Cedric had indeed stolen a speedboat for the operation, his plan being pretty much as Winston guessed. No imagination was at play here, the Wide Bay Boys pretty sure of themselves. Winston and the female officer proceeded up to the rooftop after a discussion with the hotel manager.

From this vantage point, Winston hoped to control the situation by being in contact with the various officers on the ground. Cedric had a man hanging around the hotel keeping an eye on things and looking out for police uniforms, which would be in short supply until after the exchange had happened. Winston's other officer was left to sit in the lobby, to monitor things and be inconspicuous.

* * *

At half past one, a beaten-up Nissan van pulled onto the road immediately southeast of the roundabout in front of the hotel and slid to a stop beside some trees. Winston saw this and notified the other officers on his radio. Fifteen minutes elapsed before a black BMW driven by George, made its way slowly around the roundabout and stopped at the south end. George could see the van parked about seventy feet away. Today, everyone was early to the party. George opened his car door, got out, and retrieved a black leather duffle bag from the trunk. He walked over to the promenade and dropped the bag, then returned to his car, waiting. Three men got out of the van and two came over to the bag, opening it to inspect the contents. They appeared happy and waved to the third man at the van. He joined the other two and went to the edge of the seawall where they promptly climbed down a short ladder with their loot onto the deck of a speedboat. George stood there, wondering why they didn't say anything to him, then he snapped out of his fear induced lethargy and ran the distance over to the van. He was breathing hard but looked inside and saw his son and the driver. He started to beat on the windows, then remembered to look up, which he did briefly. It was enough for Winston to issue the order to move in.

The escape boat had already slipped its lines and was ramping up speed rapidly, heading west over to Stonecutters, when a mangy looking scow came for them from the west. It pulled alongside, making way more speed than its looks suggested, and with several large guns trained on the boat, ordered it to stop. After a few seconds, and a couple of warning shots, the speedboat's operator reluctantly realized his day was over.

Winston and his assistant came down from the roof. It sounded as though everything had gone according to plan for a change. He was happy, chatting to his colleague as he stopped in the lobby to collect his other man. There was laughter and handshakes, which the gang watcher outside the lobby noticed. He decided this seemed unusual and guessed that maybe they were cops. He took a picture of the trio using his cellphone, before leaving himself. He had not heard yet how badly things had gone for his side. As Winston walked out onto the traffic circle, it was rapidly filling up with police vehicles, and an ambulance. George was hugging his son, but not before checking each one of his hands to make sure all the digits were attached. The chauffeur was sitting by the side of the road, being ignored. His facial expression indicated that he had had enough of this bullshit to last him a long time.

Winston looked around, then went over to the quay and tried to look west out onto the water. He toggled his radio and found that the speed boat had been intercepted.

It couldn't have turned out any better for the HKPF, not to mention Ping. There were smiles all around, and the traffic cops turned gang busters would be talking about this for months.

* * *

When Cedric reported back to Jacky on the total screw-up of the operation, he was officially in Jacky's bad books, an unpleasant place to be. The saving grace for Cedric was the discovery of George's mistress. He didn't tell Jacky at first, while he pondered how to make use of the information, after all, having a mistress in Hong Kong was not exactly groundbreaking news. Cedric started to research Larkcom and eventually discovered that a sizable chunk of money had appeared on the books after George had married his wife. He put two and two together. Bingo, here was George's weakness! The father-in-law had financed George, so the last thing George needed was for his cheating ways to be discovered by his wife's father. A couple of days later that he brought his case to Jacky. Jacky reluctantly realized that Cedric hadn't totally screwed up. Cedric got ready to start the extortion of George that over the next couple of years would net the Wide Bay Boys a fair bit of the capital that had gone missing on the speedboat. Cedric had redeemed himself in Jacky's eyes, and the bonus was that there were no police interfering.

* * *

Jacky and Cedric were back to discussing the Vancouver plans.

"So, Cedric, you think this will work?"

"It all depends on getting the information over to Vancouver and in the police's hands in a way that will not seem like a trap is being laid. I am thinking that we may need to send Ivy over there in person."

"I don't trust those Vancouver boys, so make it so." Jacky laid it out.

Ivy's claim to fame, apart from her beauty, was as a courier for the Wide Bay Boys. Ivy also happened to be Cedric's mistress. Jacky knew this but was unbothered by the knowledge. What Cedric did with his money was his own business, as long as the triad was properly serviced, he could have twenty mistresses for all Jacky cared. What Ivy usually transported was information, not always, but for important operations she was deemed to be more reliable than using digital communications. Jacky could be sure that any message presented by Ivy would be listened to, and only by the intended recipient. Jacky was paranoid about communications. He had seen enough movies to believe that people could do just about anything as far as electronic eavesdropping was concerned.

* * *

Cedric had done his research after Jacky told him about Ethan's cooking for some gang members years before as well as Winston and a few other fellow policemen. He had been able to piece together that Winston and Ethan had become friends, maintaining a client and professional relationship, as well as a continuing cross Pacific bond kept alive mostly by email, even after Ethan had migrated to

Vancouver. Cedric found this out from the man Jacky had planted under Winston. He had done some surreptitious monitoring of his boss's emails, nothing that Winston would ever find out about. It was only a matter of looking at emails when Winston stepped away from his office temporarily and had sloppily left his email program open.

Part of this plot would somehow involve getting Ethan to persuade Winston to travel to Vancouver where he could be dealt with at a safe distance. The Hong Kong Police Force would just think it was bad luck when they found out that Winston had been killed in Vancouver. This was the extent of the plan to date. Cedric would be communicating further with Edward to iron out some details, and timing. Jacky seemed satisfied with Cedric's progress to date, but Cedric knew that screwing this operation up would be unwise.

~ 9 ~

Back in Vancouver, after driving into the police garage at work the next morning, Robert transferred his bags, equipment, and provisions into the rental car for the journey to Merritt. As he did this, he realized the car was wrong. They needed something with more clearance for the roads they would be on. His first stop was going to be across the bridge to Yaletown where he would pick up Tony Bortolo, who was being loaned to Robert for this adventure, but this would turn out to be the second stop. Robert cursed as he made his way to the rental agency to change cars. After reflection, he calmed down as he realized this was actually a bonus. Gladys plainly had no idea what the environment was like upcountry. With luck, neither would the Gupils.

Tony was a trusted officer who had worked a previous case with Robert prior to Robert moving back to the Taskforce, so he was thankful to have Tony for the trip. They were well prepared. Along with the supplies, the rear of the SUV held two hunting rifles, two shotguns, and tons of ammo, in addition to the handguns that were part of their everyday ensemble. Robert also remembered that cell coverage was next to useless in the area where they were going to be, so he added some two-way radios, which he hoped would give them an additional advantage. Kevlar vests and a couple of pairs of binoculars rounded out the equipment. Robert was trusting in the power of surprise and knowledge of the local terrain for the threesome to overcome whatever the Gupils might send their way. Whatever happened, it would be nice to get out of the city for a few days, and the land around Merritt was stunningly beautiful.

Robert pulled up in front of the main entry to Tony's apartment tower after being forced to manoeuvre around several road closures and construction sites. Tony was waiting and came bouncing down the front steps. He got into the car after dumping his bag in the trunk, and Robert could immediately sense excitement. Tony was grinning ear to ear.

"Hey Tony. Good to see you. Let's go get Farhad." After a short pause, Robert added, "You know this is going to be dangerous right?"

"I guess, but I haven't been up to Merritt before. I'm really looking forward to this."

"No kidding, I can tell you're jacked up, but listen carefully. I am expecting trouble, and we have to be ready for anything; know what I mean? These guys play for keeps." Tony thought about this and calmed down a bit, but he was still smiling. Thank God for Tony's enthusiasm Robert thought. His had unexpectedly gone missing a few years earlier, and he wasn't counting on finding it anytime soon.

***

Meanwhile, across the river in Surrey, by midmorning, the Guru was pondering his next move. Jason had told him that his source had revealed that Farhad was moving up to Merritt, ostensibly to hide out for a while, and that he would be alone. Jason had even supplied an address. The Guru didn't waste time thinking about this; he was going to send up the troops to get this guy, sweat him to retrieve the cash, drugs, along with the cassette, then kill him. As his trust in his soldiers had never been high, he decided to send up a couple of cars—six gang members in total. Hopefully they wouldn't screw this up. Six against one sounded like reasonable odds. He was slightly worried that none of these guys had been up to that part of the province before, but it was probably Hicksville, they would be fine. He added one of his newest soldiers who hailed from a part of the Punjab just northeast of Chandigarh, where the country was similar to ranch land.

The Guru didn't think about what two cars full of East Indian men would look like to the locals in Merritt. They wouldn't be out of place in Surrey, but Merritt was a different situation, something the Guru didn't entirely grasp. He also didn't consider the fact that they'd be in the countryside, not the city, where they were comfortable going about their daily business.

He asked Manny to come into the room, and together, they started to gather a list of things they'd need for the journey and the killing.

***

Robert drove the SUV rental over to Farhad's apartment, then sat, waiting out front for him to appear. Farhad eventually came out and dumped his gear into the rear of the vehicle. He went to the passenger side to get in, but Tony was sitting in the navigator's spot. Farhad gave him what looked like the stink eye, then got into the rear seat.

"Who are you?" Farhad asked as he settled in.

"Tony, with the VPD. I'm along to help you guys out."

Farhad didn't say anything further, but Robert could discern some attitude from the back seat. After threading through the city streets, making for the highway, the trio settled in for the three hour ride. Robert picked up Highway No. 1 at the eastern edge of the City of Vancouver and prepared for the usual traffic mess that was Greater Vancouver's cross to bear, until they got past the City of Abbotsford midway up the valley. While they drove, Farhad filled the other two in on what he knew about the Gupil gang to date.

"How many people do you think they have?" Robert asked, wanting to gauge who might be coming after them. They were rolling now, whizzing past the farm fields of the valley, the Fraser River out of site for now. It was early in the year so green was not the dominant colour. Farmers were preparing their fields, and the odour of manure was prevalent. The other two in the car started complaining, but Robert shut them up, "It's the smell of money helping out some of the best farmland in the world, so suck it up."

Farhad responded, "I think around twenty or so. They

have a hierarchy like any organization, probably based on how bright or stupid they are. It is basically a South Asian gang, but they do have a few white guys as well. I'm not sure why, or how that works."

"My guess is that they will send both types to Merritt, smart ones and stupid ones. That is, if they send anyone at all. I'm still not certain any of this will pan out. But if they do come, we'll be ready for them. Do you think any of them know about long guns, or have them?" Robert asked.

"I'm unsure. I never saw any with the gangsters I met. They seem to be mostly a pistol crowd."

"If they do have rifles, they'll probably be assault types, lethal in close, but hopeless at a distance." Robert concluded. As the car approached Hope, which was the town at the eastern terminus of the Fraser Valley, mountains closed in and trees marched down to edges of the road, all heralding the start of the interior mountain ranges. Once they slid past Hope, the car engine worked harder as the road rose towards Merritt. There were other routes to Merritt, but they were circuitous in the extreme. The one they were racing up was the Coquihalla Highway, otherwise known as the Coq, a rather infamous stretch of road connecting Vancouver to the interior. Snow could hit at almost any time of the year, making life miserable and dangerous for truckers and everyone else journeying along it.

Long valleys separating mountain peaks drifted away from the road. The occasional abandoned concrete turret foundation stood guard just to the side of the pavement, remains of bases for avalanche canons used in the past to control how the snow thundered down the slopes, hopefully not onto the highway. The temperature dropped steadily as they approached the summit, rifts of blackened snow sat beside the pavement, testament to the belching exhaust from trucks running endlessly along the Coq.

Robert decided it was time to start getting his two passengers into a different head space, so he popped one of the CDs he had remembered to bring into the stereo system. Someone started singing about eighteen inches of rain, and Robert immediately heard a moan from the back seat where Farhad was lounging.

"Hey, if you wanted to listen to something else, you should have brought your own CDs, Farhad." Robert said. "We're heading to cowboy country, so saddle up and get ready." Robert grinned at Tony, who remained silent. The farther north they moved, the drier the countryside appeared to be. Tree species changed to mainly lodgepole pine and shimmering aspens, instead of the hemlock, fir, and red cedars of the coastal ranges. Views grew longer, the trees no longer hemming in the road as closely. After the car started its drop down from the summit, the air warmed a bit, but remained clean and biting. Other than the occasional rest stop or camp site, there was very little in the way of civilization apparent, certainly no places to gas up or eat until Merritt was reached. The sky cleared, becoming an impossibly azure blue. Vistas became wide and distant, with more open range than treed land.

"Once we get into Merritt, I'm going to visit the local RCMP detachment to let them know to keep their eyes open. With any luck, they'll be able to give us some warning if the thugs show up. Always good to have a bit of a backup." Robert thought a bit, the added, "Don't want to tell them too much, however. They may get over enthusiastic and complicate things."

The road dropped down to an intersection where one could either keep going, exit into Merritt, or head east to the Okanagan Valley. To the west of the highway the city looked like a map seen from above. It obviously was a small community.

* * *

"We're going to stop at an establishment in town, then head west beyond the city limits. Need to get a few more provisions." Robert added. "Farhad, you might want to keep your eyes peeled for cowboy murals. At some point in the past someone decided that Merritt should be the country music capital of Canada. Somehow, I don't think it worked out, yet. Merritt is not exactly Nashville North, but the murals are still here for all to see."

Tony and Robert heard another moan from the rear of the car. They slowed and took the exit, stopping to fill the gas tank at the only commercial enterprise at the junction. Robert believed in being prepared for anything and having a full tank couldn't hurt. They then headed west into town on a local road, heading for a bakery called the Bumblebee. There may have been more sophisticated bakeries in Vancouver, but none were better, in Robert's estimation. He purchased several breads and pastries, also grabbing something for them to eat in the car for the final stretch of road ahead. They then drove a few blocks north over to the local RCMP detachment. Robert pulled up in front of the low, fairly new industrial style building that was the standard for government offices across the hinterland of BC.

"You guys stay in the car. I don't want to give the impression that a gang war is going to erupt here, even though that's what may happen." Robert entered the detachment and asked to talk with the officer in charge, offering his ID to the officer behind the counter window. He was led through the door into an office where another officer was sitting at his desk, looking at paperwork—a very familiar scenario to Robert.

"What can I do for you?" The officer smiled.

Robert first showed the sergeant his ID, then, "You are not going to like this, but we are putting a Delta officer into hiding up here, at a ranch house northwest of here. We may be expecting company of a disreputable type following us at some point. All I'd like is for some warning if you see people coming through town that look out of place. They will likely be coming from Surrey."

The officer's smile faded like a flower quickly going past its prime. "This sounds like trouble to me."

"I am afraid it might be. Here is the number of the land line to the ranch house, and the address. It's located off an old access road called Cougar Ridge Road on one of the reserves." Robert handed the piece of paper to the officer who looked at it like it was the devil's work. He added, "Cell coverage is pretty bad up there."

"How do you know that?"

"I've been here before. I trained with a couple of guys who hailed from Merritt."

"When are you expecting company?"

"Maybe a day or two, maybe a week from now, they may not even come. I'll check in with you every couple of days."

"Just you and him?"

"I have an assistant as well, a VPD officer. We are prepared. If you need to talk to someone you could call Troy Geelham at the Richmond RCMP detachment."

"I know Troy." The officer's face suddenly relaxed.

"Okay. We'll try not to cause any commotions up here in God's country. Oh yeah, we also have two-way radios. Do you use those?"

"Yes, sometimes when we get west of here, so you can contact us that way as well."

"Great." With that, Robert waved and left the station, heading to the car for the last lap of their journey.

* * *

After driving west for another half hour, then northwest on a two-lane highway, they slowed, left the pavement, and started up a five kilometre access road only slightly more useful than a goat trail. Robert drove very slowly, dodging rocks, and potholes that could hide a large dog, when a low-slung weathered house finally came into view. They had also passed through a cattle fence, remembering to close the gate behind them. The house was perched on a wide plateau and surrounded by a large open porch providing protection to many of the main floor windows.

The wood cladding's shiny grey patina spoke of a harsh unrelenting climate. Patches of aspens were rooted in dips in the land where water could be found in what was otherwise a very arid place. One or two lumps of old snow lingered in some hollows, but most had melted off.

The house boasted a good line of sight in all directions, the result of thoughtful placing when it was built, much as Robert remembered. Tony and Farhad were both peering out the car windows at what was going to be home, for a few days at least. About forty metres behind the house stood a barn. At least it looked like a barn, sort of, if the barn was in northern Italy. Even the house was slightly different from other ranch houses, as if it had moved over from Tuscany or someplace farther northeast in Italy, like Treviso. There was stone at the base of the house, and similar stone cladding on the barn. Robert understood that the policeman whose family built the house had some Italian blood somewhere in his background. At least Tony ought to feel at home here.

The car emptied and after a preliminary reconnoitre of the house and property, they lugged the supplies and armaments into the house. Robert picked up the phone and heard a dial tone. The cellphones were practically useless, no signal evident. After picking rooms to sleep in, the three of them started to plan tactics while they ate some sandwiches which Robert put together using supplies from the Bumblebee. They sat around the dining table, looking out at the view of the surrounding land. It really was 'big sky country'. Some dark clouds were forming up in the southwest, presaging rain. It was the time of year when nature gave up some moisture to the land, and the hills greened up, until late May, when everything started to dry out. After that, cowboys moved cattle to higher ranges for the summer so they could feed on the upper grasslands, keeping hay in reserve for the winter months.

Robert started talking tactics. "They will drop their car at some point unless they are complete idiots, and come to us on foot, probably from several directions. I'm thinking that the barn may be the place to defend, not the house. I like that it has stone on the outside walls, not wood. It has a second floor that has great sight lines, in the day that is. They'll also probably cut the telephone and power lines, but that is fine, as long as we get the warning from Merritt." Robert then added, "There is a point just south of here where you can see the access road before it loops around for the final couple of kilometres to the house. We should scope that out once we get warning."

"What happens if we don't get the warning?" Farhad asked.

"Good question. We need to plan as if we get no warning. Getting warned is a bonus." Robert answered. "We'll go for a tour this afternoon. I'll show you the lay of the land. I don't believe they'll be organized enough to get up here for a day or two which will give us time to plan our tactics."

"How will they know we are up here?" Tony asked.

Robert couldn't believe what he was hearing. He looked at Tony with his head cocked at an angle, "Tony, that is an even better question than Farhads'. However, I don't think I'll answer that one, other than to say that I expect them to show up."

Tony and Farhad looked at each other with puzzled expressions, then Tony shook his head ever so gently and they continued chewing on their food. Robert expected that Tony would figure it out eventually. He wasn't so sure about Farhad.

After they finished up eating, Robert took the other two over to the barn, which was really a more sophisticated version of the house, as certainly no animals had ever been there, at least not large ones. Mice and rats always got in somehow through cracks in the walls. A workshop and a games room inhabited the ground floor while an office and some bedrooms filled the second floor. Windows allowed views in all four directions. A small kitchen and washroom rounded out the amenities of the barn.

"Nice place," Tony offered.

"Yeah, a great place to get away from all the pressures of the city. Too bad that we're bringing those pressures here, but *c'est la vie,* as they say. I just hope it doesn't get damaged." Robert turned, "Let's go for a ramble, I'll show you a few things." He led them out the rear door and headed north. Grasses and small weeds abounded in clumps. About a hundred and fifty metres farther on, the land seemed to disappear, then re-appear, farther out. They walked up to the crest of a deep ravine that was heavily vegetated. It spread over two hundred metres in either direction.

"You'd have to be really desperate or just plain crazy to approach us from this direction." Robert peered over the edge, the bottom was impossible to discern. "I wouldn't be surprised if there was a bear or two down there."

"What?" Farhad looked genuinely concerned. His eyes darted around, as if something was preparing to attack him.

"You heard me, there is wildlife out here; bears, coyotes, deer, maybe wolves, and possibly a cougar. You have to keep your eyes open as you move around." Robert then added, "If someone comes at us from this direction, they're not going to get very far, so it's really the other three directions we have to cover." Robert laughed as he continued. "But the real threat comes from marmots."

"What's a marmot?" Farhad questioned.

Tony at least knew what a marmot was and started smiling. "Something you don't want to get on the wrong side of, right Robert?"

"Exactly. Let's walk down south towards the spot where you can scope out the access road." He started loping through the bush, trying to loosen out his muscles that had tightened after sitting in the car for over three hours. Tony ran after Robert, and after the marmot conversation, Farhad wasn't far behind, having no wish to be left at the mercy of enraged wildlife. Robert pulled up at the top of a small bluff. It was early in spring but soon there would be some cornflowers and crimson poppies populating the immediate surroundings. Fresh shoots of grass were everywhere. From this vantage one could look down into a wide valley. A small lake darkened by the approaching clouds sat far beyond the trail that the three had just driven up.

"See what I mean? If you come out to the edge, you have a great view of the road, back up a bit, and they can't see you even if they knew which way to look." Robert pointed west to where the road disappeared behind a grove of fir trees.

Farhad finally asked the obvious question. "How is this going to work, exactly? We can't just pick people off as they come after us. Don't they have to shoot first, stuff like that?"

"Yeah, it's not the old west anymore, I suppose." Robert said it as if he had been contemplating just that—an old-fashioned gunfight at the OK corral. Sometimes, the modern world, with all its laws and rules became a pain in the ass. "The critical thing here is that we don't get killed. Second is that we arrest them for something, and I don't much care for what; it could be a weapons offence, it doesn't matter. If they show up, that is mission accomplished as far as I am concerned."

"What do you mean?" Tony asked, searching Robert's face.

"I mean that this is about more than just Farhad. Sorry Farhad, I know you want to be the star of the show."

"Not really, no." Farhad answered emphatically.

"Okay, don't get too excited. Let's finish the reconnoitre, then we'll plan. I want to show you west and east, then we'll head back to the house. I brought some relaxation help for us tonight." Robert didn't want the other two to know that this was really a mole hunt, but after Tony's earlier question, that might be wishful thinking on Robert's part. The group moved on, heading west to check out the terrain and cover, before reversing course and doing the same thing at the eastern end of the property. Property edges were defined by barbed wire fencing, which ran everywhere. Robert guessed that the Gupils wouldn't be bringing wire cutters with them, so they would be in a world of hurt as they tried to negotiate the landscape, particularly if they tried to attack at night, which was the move Robert thought they'd make.

***

The sun was falling, shortly to be hidden by the thunderheads moving in. Robert decided they had seen enough for one day, so headed back to the house to make dinner. Much to Tony's delight and Farhad's annoyance, it was going to be an *aglio et olio* pasta dish with a side salad. However, Farhad was happy to see Robert producing some beer that had been hiding in a bag during the trip. Garlic in olive oil was about as simple and good a dish to make as there was, as long as the garlic wasn't burned. A hunk of parmesan reggiano and some parsley rounded out the main course. The men sat and the food disappeared quickly. Even Farhad made short work of his meal.

"You guys don't have a clue what great food is," Farhad boasted, "but that was actually pretty good." Farhad had come around, at least partially. Tony stared at Farhad, knowing he couldn't cook at all, while Robert slipped away to rummage through his rucksack, eventually pulling out a brown paper bag. He sat it on the table and fetched some shot glasses. From the bag, Farhad pulled out a bottle of Irish whiskey. "Look what we have for dessert."

"This will be the only night we can do this, so enjoy." Robert said. He poured shots then sat back. "Listen to the silence. It will be this quiet until the howling starts."

Farhad's eyes darted around. "What howling?"

"The wolves and the coyotes. They like to talk at night." The discussion then became serious as they discussed tactics to deal with the expected visitors.

"I think this will be our last night here." Robert started.

"What?" Both Tony and Farhad chimed at the same time.

"The house will be what they attack, so unless either of you want to be a target, from tomorrow, we'll be sleeping in the barn with a watch all the time. We'll need to fashion a dummy or scarecrow to set up here in the dining room. They'll think it's Farhad whiling away his time at the computer. That will be one of your first tasks tomorrow. If you do a good job, we'll have a fourth and play some bridge."

Tony rolled his eyes, while Farhad looked puzzled. The gentle drumming of rain started slowly, bouncing off the metal roof and rustling the aspen leaves, then gathering force. The clouds had arrived and were shedding some moisture, rain pounding down for at least fifteen minutes before lessening. Darkness descended over the open ranges and the trio's space shrunk to the insides of the house they were in.

"I brought along some stun grenades. Not sure what we'll do with them, but they might be useful as a diversion at least." Robert continued. "I'm worried that we may not know how many they are. Nothing worse than having someone pop up behind you, just when you think you have them all." With that Robert produced a pad of paper and drew a simplified plan of the house, barn, and the surrounding land. He marked some Xs on the plan and said, "These are the points we'll move to when we know our visitors have arrived. Starting tomorrow we carry our radios at all times. We'll cache body armour, a weapon, and ammo at each spot." He poured some more shots. "The idea is to take these guys with no shooting, but you know how things go." He smiled, leaving no doubt about how he thought things would go.

"And gunfire will be heard up here. It is not as isolated as it appears." Leaving that piece of information for the other two to chew on, Robert first went to the door and opened it, feeling the coolness of the evening wash pass him. Regret was starting to eat at him for spoiling the good memories of past visits. He listened for any out of place sounds, then gently shut the door and headed to bed. He was fairly certain they wouldn't be getting much rest after tomorrow's sun rose.

~ 10 ~

The Guru worked to put a team together for the Merritt mission. As usual, weapons were top of mind, the gang believing that a gun solved all kinds of problems, which was true enough, up to a point. Also critical was the composition of the team that was to be sent. He wanted a couple of the smarter members to be part of the expedition. He also needed Manny to lead them, as Manny was adept at the information extractions that fuelled the Gupil's business. The Guru found Manny's methods distasteful, but necessary in their chosen profession. He was unsure about Manny's intelligence. Put aside the brutality, which he seemed to enjoy, not much came out of Manny's lips. In addition to the recent emigre from the Punjab, he was sending four others. He himself would not be joining this hunting trip, as he needed to be in Surrey and in control. When he wasn't around, things tended to go sideways very quickly. Somehow his thinking didn't extend to the Merritt trip, that is, how likely things would go off the rails because he had decided to stay in Surrey.

Two of the men forming the group were interlinked in a way unknown to their leader. Bobbi Atwal was a newer

112

member while Maccha Sunner had been around longer and flaunted his seniority. Bobbi had a younger sister, Safa. He had introduced her to Maccha, in a bid to curry favour several months earlier. Her first date with Maccha was a disaster. Afterwards, Maccha had said a few unkind words to Bobbi that put his teeth on edge. He belatedly realized what a moronic idea it had been.

* * *

The day after Robert's group had arrived at the ranch, the Guru gave the particulars of the target to his group. He thought that his boys were ready to go, so after a pep talk, he watched as the two cars, a BMW and an Audi, cruised out of the parking lot of his Surrey club just past three. He shook his head as the pounding sounds of Bhangra music emanated from both cars.

It wasn't long before the cars were at Hope, entering the mountains for the run up to Merritt. They were running well in excess of the speed limit in cars designed for the autobahn, so it was before five when they pulled off at the very same exit Robert had taken the day before. The gang did not bother to fill up with gas, but looked at their GPS screens, idling in the parking lot, talking amongst themselves, before deciding to head due west into Merritt. By taking the same exit that Robert had taken a day earlier, they unwittingly bypassed the RCMP detachment, which was northeast of the centre of town, thus depriving Robert's group of the possible early warning signal. The two cars growled slowly through town, the occupants unseen. What people did notice, however, were the cars.

Both sounded exactly like the high-performance cars they were. In a small town with mostly older vans, pickup trucks of varying vintages, and. some smaller imports, they stood out like they were supposed to. Gang members loved making statements, even when it was to their advantage not to. After a couple of blocks, both cars turned southwest and headed out of town, the BMW leading, onto their meeting with destiny. An older man, who had in the past been a volunteer safety officer with the RCMP, noticed the cars in the middle of town. He'd tell one of the officers later in the evening if he saw him.

* * *

After several kilometres of the narrow secondary road called Highway No. 8, the two cars slowed and pulled off onto a grassy shoulder with a drop-off. Their left wheels were barely off the pavement, giving little room to anyone passing, not that the gang members cared. The sun was dipping, yesterday's clouds having departed, so that it was directly in the eyes of each driver. The six of them gathered in front of the BMW and discussed how much further they would be travelling before the turn-off. One of the members had thought to check the location online, so they had a rough idea of how far the ranch house was off the main road. They did not however, have an idea of what kind of country they were entering. As far as they could tell so far, it looked fairly benign; in other words, they expected to be back in Surrey the next day, everything wrapped up, ready for their next adventure.

Sanji looked north and spotted some cattle grazing.

"Hey look, cows!" Sanji was excited, these being the first he had seen since emigrating.

"What a bonehead." Manny muttered, "Let's get going, I don't want to be wandering around in the dark." With that, the crews got back into their respective cars and sped off, the road slowly turning northwest as it followed the Nicola River. Just before six, the cars turned off the highway and started up the access road called Cougar Ridge. Light was starting to fade, the days being slightly longer than nights, but not by much. The BMW's driver immediately noticed that the road was sketchy in the extreme. He slowed to a crawl as they started climbing.

* * *

Robert, Farhad, and Tony had been busy preparing for the possible arrival of the gang since sun-up. Robert's warning about nighttime howling had been prophetic, and Farhad had trouble sleeping after it had started up around four. Up to that point it had been eerily silent, not something city dwellers were used to. During the morning, they had cached their weapons and other equipment at the locations sketched out by Robert the night before, then each took one hour turns at the lookout point. The day passed slowly, the men enjoying the clear sky and warming air. Farhad fashioned a crude dummy to sit at the dining table. A computer couldn't be found, so they rigged a large book to look like a laptop. They had moved the rest of their possessions into the barn, which turned out to have its own phone line. Farhad was at the lookout and scanning the road and surrounding fields when he spotted a group of deer with white tails moving through the low grasses. When Robert came to relieve him, Farhad excitedly told him about the sighting.

"Yeah, there are white-tailed and mule deer around here. See any other animals?" Robert asked.

"No, but that's pretty neat. First time I have seen deer in the wild."

"You're a real city boy, aren't you?" Robert made the basic observation.

"Yes, I guess so."

"Well, so am I Farhad, so am I. This country has its own rhythms and pace. It is a whole different way of living that most city folk don't understand or care about. I love it out here precisely because it's not the city." Robert mused. High in the sky a pair of small hawks drifted south of their position, looking for movement in the fields below them. The wind was moving softly from the southwest. Robert settled into the blanket in the shallow hollow while Farhad went off to eat.

Late in the afternoon, when the sun was low to the horizon, it was Tony who was in the perch when he first heard the low rumbling of a car engine. He was almost due for relief and was feeling drowsy. He raised his binoculars and waited. A couple of moments passed before first, a BMW, then an Audi crept across his line of sight. The binoculars were excellent, and he was able to make out three people in each car. The shot of adrenalin to his system was immediate.

He toggled the radio and spoke to Robert, "We have company. Two cars with three in each. Looks like six people total. BMW and an Audi. Look like gang banger cars to me." Tony felt a twinge of fear, dropping his pistol as he stood up. Nerves, he supposed.

"Roger that." Robert said. "Get on back here once they are out of site. They'll probably get out and walk soon I would guess." Robert then decided to be prudent and called the detachment in Merritt.

He sat back and felt decidedly ill. This meant his suspicions were correct, and Gladys was the informer in their midst. How to make use of this information was the tricky thing, but he realized that this was just more useless thinking. The outcome of this coming 'battle on the range' would likely tell the gangs all they needed to know. They would quickly conclude that they had been set up. Gladys's life would be in danger. The easy thing would be to let her meet her deserved fate, but Robert realized he did not know what had motivated Gladys to this betrayal, and to leave her to the justice of the mob might be cruel. He went over the same questions again, was it a mercenary impulse that drove her to this? Or did the gangs have some lever over her that demanded her obeisance? On the other hand, he didn't know if money was the issue here; someone had been killed, and a law enforcement officer at that. At the first opportunity, he'd need to contact Thomas back in Vancouver and warn him, but this would have to wait. Robert had more pressing things at hand.

* * *

The cars were making slow progress. The BMW driver's neck knotted up from the strain of avoiding the large potholes in the failing light, when just over a ridge, a couple of white-tailed deer stood stock still. At the exact moment the driver looked at them he missed seeing a large rock near the centre of the trail. A grinding noise was heard by all three occupants, but it ended as soon as it started, so they kept moving. They travelled another fifty metres before the oil light came on. The Audi's driver was not so enamoured with wildlife, so he dodged the rock and saved his car from the BMW's fate.

The BMW slowed to a halt, followed by some cursing.

"Why are you stopping?" Manny asked from the rear seat.

"I think I ripped out my crankcase." Getting out of the car and kneeling down, the driver looked under the engine. Sure enough, he could see dribbles of what was left of the synthetic oil in his engine falling onto the dirt. "Fuck."

Manny, who had had some doubts about this whole expedition, was now certain they were screwed. Nevertheless, as he exited the back of the BMW, he told the other two to start walking straight up the hill, and to catch up when they could. He also told them to keep an eye open for anything looking like a telephone wire, which they were to cut if they found one. The driver nodded, but he knew enough not to go around cutting unknown wires. That was the way people got electrocuted. He had a knife but no wire cutters. The men took the weapons out of the trunk of the BMW and left it by the side of the road. If they couldn't figure out how to retrieve it quietly later, they would probably have to torch it. Manny got into the other car, his bulk taking up the majority of the rear seat, and after some manoeuvring, they got the Audi around the stricken car.

The Audi was put in gear and proceeded even slower than before. They had about another kilometre or so to drive before stopping, then approaching the house on foot to take Farhad by surprise. This was the extent of the plan, which, simple as it appeared, was slowly unravelling. With the failing light, the Audi was forced to go even slower, if that were possible, so as to preserve the only car left to them and avoid the fate of the BMW. After a gully and a sharp uphill turn, they came upon a line of cattle fencing across the road with a gate in it. The car emptied as the gang members walked up closer to the gate to study the finer points of the system keeping it in place. Bobbi was finally able to get it open, giving himself a large splinter in his right hand in the process. He cursed. The cursing only grew louder after the car had motored through and Bobbi closed the gate, with him on the downhill side. Idiot, he thought to himself, why did he even close the gate? They'd only be going through it again once they had finished with Farhad.

$$\sim ~ 11 ~ \sim$$

Robert put Farhad on the upper floor of the barn with a rifle where he would have a good line of sight. The stone cladding on its walls would afford additional protection. He and Tony separated, laying in two separate gullies that were well screened by dense vegetation about forty metres from the house. Unless the gang members walked right into them, they would remain hidden, hopefully getting the drop on the gangsters as they were about to enter the house. Daylight was leaving rapidly. There were a couple of lights under the porch roof, so the general area of the house was somewhat illuminated. Farther out, dusk prevailed. Meanwhile, in Merritt, the sergeant who had received the call from Robert had called his superior to confirm what was going on, and to find out what was expected of him. He was told to dispatch three squad cars out to Cougar Ridge Road and to expect armed men. This was extremely unusual for Merritt, so pulses were racing as he organized six men to take out extra armaments. When ready, they headed west into the gathering darkness, muscles tensing up.

* * *

After a few more switchbacks, Manny decided that they were close enough to exit the car and proceed the remainder of the way on foot. The four grabbed their weapons and spread out. Manny tried to contact the other two by cellphone, but discovered there was no service. He cursed. In the half-light it was difficult to gauge footing. About ten minutes into their walk, one member managed to walk into a marmot hole and twisted his right ankle. He swore. Manny was keeping his eyes on the way ahead, so he didn't see the cow pie before he stepped into it. Curses were starting to abound.

They could see the house now, slightly above their position. It was lit up. Manny raised his arm as a signal to halt. He wanted to assess the situation and the lay-out of the property. Meanwhile the other two from the abandoned BMW had made good progress up to the point where they also came across the cattle fence. Neither of them had any wire cutters, so the only option was to go over or under. They decided that the under route was safest and each helped the other to wriggle through while the other held up the barbed wire. Swearing continued as a suede leather jacket caught on a barb and then ripped open. They split up after spotting the ranch house about one hundred metres away, slightly above them. One headed northeast, while Maccha headed due north. They walked further, then both stopped and kneeled, waiting for some sign that the others had arrived. Maccha was starting to appreciate the location of the house and the line of sight available from it. Neither man could raise the other on their cells. It was quiet, not much of a breeze was moving, enabling insects to make their presence known, adding irritation for the gang members.

* * *

The cougar was a teenage male, slightly under two years old and he was suffering, terribly hungry. At sixty-five kilograms, he was a good-sized cat. He had wandered into the territory just west of Merritt and was getting to know it slowly, having been driven out of his home turf farther west by another older cougar. So far at least, the new territory seemed to be vacant, perhaps something to do with the closeness of a human population in the surroundings of Merritt. Cougar Ridge Road didn't get its name by accident or by the whim of some marketing genius. It came by its name honestly. There had been several sightings of cougars over the years by ranchers, and it was well known, at least to the locals, that cougars occasionally hunted in the territory.

This cat came slowly from the east, pausing frequently as he sniffed the air. The light was perfect for hunting. The bit of wind that there was, moved directly at him from the west, and he smelled prey close by. He moved forward, then froze. His target was close by, mere steps from his position. He stopped, then flexed his muscles and leapt forward. In two long bounds he was on the gangster, his teeth sinking into both sides of his neck from the rear. One mangled yell escaped from the man before the cat opened his mouth, then reset his bite, sending blood flying everywhere. The main nerve stem at the back of the man's neck was severed and he quickly slipped into blackness as his life ebbed away. The cat reset his grip, hunched down, and started backing up as he dragged the body into the brush, the metallic taste of blood energizing him as he reversed.

Maccha had heard the abbreviated cry from his buddy and ran over to where he thought he was. It was then that he saw the large cat dragging his friend. He swore as he unslung his Uzi and let loose with a spray of bullets. He hit the cat several times, but he also shot his fellow gangster as well, not that it mattered anymore. Maccha watched as the bullets completed their damage, blood spurting out onto the brush where the cat settled to slowly die. Maccha couldn't believe what he was looking at. He thought that he had seen the last of big cats when he left the Punjab and its Bengal tigers.

Everyone in the vicinity heard the shots. Manny cursed up a storm, knowing that one of his soldiers had given the game away with the shooting. He immediately sent one of them over towards the commotion to find out what the cause was. Robert, Tony, and Farhad didn't know what was happening, but they knew that it wasn't one of them doing the shooting. It had sounded like a machine gun, which fit with what they knew about the gangs, but they couldn't fathom who was shooting and why.

Down in the valley below, Justine Sparrow heard the gunfire from the front porch of her house and knew immediately what it was. She knew that it didn't sound like hunting, nor did it sound like any weapons people in her band might have, but she paused anyway before deciding to call the RCMP in Merritt. The sergeant on duty was the same one Robert had talked to, so he was already on edge. When Justine told him about the gunfire, he got extremely excited. This was so much better than the usual break-ins or multi-vehicle accidents that was his lot in life to attend to. However, he only had so many cars and officers, and with three vehicles already on their way, there was only a single extra car that could attend. He sent it anyway, then got on the phone with the Kamloops detachment to explain the situation and asked for backup. Kamloops was an hour away at the north end of the Coq, but it was his best bet for help. He also notified the local paramedic facility to get an ambulance ready to go.

* * *

Robert was baffled by the shooting so he toggled his radio and asked Farhad if he could see anything.

"I saw the gunfire. Whoever it was, was shooting into the bush. And I think someone ran over to the same area from just west of your position." Farhad was trying to keep his voice low, but Robert could hear the trembling in it.

"Okay, they are almost past us now, getting closer to the house. I'm waiting until they get to the porch. Tony, you ready?"

"Yes, just give the word."

"Just be really careful—you heard the automatic fire." Robert probably didn't need to give this piece of advice, but he liked to be clear with his subordinates.

* * *

Meanwhile, Manny was waiting for a report on what had happened. In short order, two gangsters returned, having first determined that their friend was truly gone.

"He's dead!" Maccha was quivering.

"What do you mean?" Manny asked.

"A big cat ate him. Like a tiger."

"Are you shitting me?"

"I shot the cat, but it had already killed him. It grabbed his neck and bit through and was dragging him away."

Manny decided that Farhad could wait. He had to see this for himself. He told the others to stay put while he followed Maccha over to where the two bodies were. The gloom was lengthening but, in the area flattened by the attack, Manny could see that the cat looked like a cougar. A large one. He shuddered as the realization came that it could have been anyone of them chosen by the cougar. The cat had let his prey's neck loose at the end as they both lay down for the last time. They seemed peaceful, which belied the violence of the attack. Manny looked at Maccha and shook his head, nodding back toward the others. Despite the lengthening of odds, there was still business to take care of. However, Manny didn't like the way this whole adventure was unfolding. It seemed like a major hex had been placed on their team.

When the two had rejoined the rest of the gang, they looked again at the house. Now that the sun had vanished, they could see into the interior of the main floor quite clearly. Something wasn't right, Manny felt. They could see Farhad sitting in one of the rooms—it looked like the dining room, but he wasn't moving. After the gunfire, one would think he would be moving around, checking things out. Manny quietly told them to spread out, then they approached cautiously from the south. Bobbi lit a cigarette, thus screwing the night vision he had been developing.

Robert shook his head when he saw the match flare. These gangsters seemed clueless about what they were doing. He had told Farhad to draw down on the gang from the second floor of the barn, so Farhad had his scoped rifle trained on one of the group from an open window. That guy appeared to be moving slowly, with a limp, the beneficiary of a meeting with a marmot home.

Robert toggled his radio and whispered to Tony, "Okay, let's take them now." He arose and walked forward. He could see Tony approach from the southeast. They both had shotguns ready as they walked quietly forward. About twenty paces away, Robert decided enough was enough.

"Drop your weapons, this is the police. You are surrounded and outnumbered." This last item was for effect, even if it wasn't quite accurate.

Manny and three of the others froze. Crap, was all he could think. The fifth man reacted instinctively, believing he was going to shoot his way out of the situation, and started firing his AK-47 as he turned. The desperado's aim was off, both because it usually was, and his gimpy ankle wasn't helping. Bullets sprayed across the dirt, just missing Tony, but nailing a squirrel right in the head. Farhad wasted no time firing at Paal and dropped him, the bullet blowing through his shoulder, leaving him groaning on the ground. Robert watched the other gang members. It was a split hair away from getting out of hand. Manny at this point didn't know how many police were there, so he lowered, then dropped his gun, nodding at the others to do the same. As far as he was concerned, they hadn't done anything wrong, so it was better to live to fight another day.

"Get on the ground, all of you." Robert ordered.

"We haven't done anything wrong." Manny begged to differ. "We just came up here because we heard there was a place available to stay. We're on vacation." He turned and smiled, which looked creepy coming from his large, creased face.

"I beg to differ. Your pal there just tried to murder a police officer." Robert replied. "Where did he learn to shoot, the arcade at the fall fair? He's lucky we're responsible citizens, we could have opened him up like a can of tomatoes." He waited, then, "What were you shooting at back there? Chickens?"

"One of us got attacked by a cougar. It killed him, so we killed it."

"Hunting out of season as well, not to mention exceeding your bag limit. You guys are just piling up the offences. Those guns got permits? And do you usually bring guns on a vacation?" Robert was starting to enjoy this.

"Wait a minute," Manny started to reply, but was cut short.

"Shut up. Lay down and don't even think of moving." By this time Farhad had walked over from the barn and stood there surveying the damage.

Manny twisted his head to look over at Farhad, giving him the stink eye. He hadn't been in the house at all. It was all a giant trap. Shit. Added to that, it appeared that they weren't outnumbered after all. "That guy is not what you think he is." He said quietly to no one in particular. Robert heard him, however.

"Check them for weapons and cuff them. I'll look at Billy the Kid here, see if I can stop the bleeding." Robert went over to the moaning man while Farhad frisked the others on the ground. Tony watched from a short distance with his shotgun trained on the group. They could hear the engine of a car getting close. Robert prayed it was the RCMP from Merritt and not more gang members. Farhad held up an Uzi gun. This got Robert's attention.

"Who owns the Uzi?" He waited a second then, "Are you Israeli citizens? You know it is illegal for anyone who is not Jewish to be in possession of an Uzi? I'm looking at you guys but I'm not getting a Jewish buzz here. Ever been to Haifa? Tel Aviv? I thought not. You look more like scumbags to me. You'll be going away for a while on this charge alone."

What? Maccha looked at Bobbi who was lying next to him. They were royally screwed now. The gang members couldn't make sense of this. They hadn't heard of this law before, and had no idea that Robert was just baiting them for his own pleasure.

As Farad went from gangster to gangster, relieving them of their accessory weapons and cuffing them, he realized what his fate could have been had they actually caught him. The gangster he knew as Manny was huge. He must have been north of three hundred pounds. Farhad felt ill, but this was the risky life he had chosen. No one said this job wasn't without danger.

Macha twisted his face to stare at Farhad. "You rat! Know what happens to rats? They die a painful death."

"Shut your gob." Robert stepped over and prodded Mancha's back with the snout of his shotgun. Maccha stayed quiet.

A police cruiser pulled into the clearing. Robert exhaled and went over to it.

"Hi. Thanks for coming. I'm Robert. You have a first aid kit? We have a gang member with a gunshot wound. There is also a dead gangster over in the bush, but that wasn't our work."

The officer gave Robert a puzzled look but got out and went over to attend to the gangster's wound. Robert went inside and called the sergeant again, letting him know that things were under control, but there had been some gunplay, with injuries. The sergeant responded that an ambulance was already on the way. The other two vehicles pulled up, one a pickup truck; explanations were given, then the gang members were read their rights and herded into the rear seats of the cruisers. Robert beckoned to a couple of the officers and led them over to show them what had happened in the bush. They stood there, looking at the two bodies, shaking their heads.

They looked into the gloom, one of the officer's flashlights illuminating the bodies. Robert said. "Looks like a sin offering to me."

"What?" This from Tony who had followed them to the spot.

"They're not burnt, so not a burnt offering. I expect this one had a lot of sins to atone for."

"What are you talking about?" A second time.

"In the Bible."

"What?" A third time.

"You know, Old Testament, offerings to atone for sins."

Tony stared at Robert, "I wouldn't have taken you for a Bible thumper, Robert."

"Not a thumper Tony, but I've read the book, and our profession has a relation to sinners. Except usually it is man sacrificing the animals, not the other way around." He smiled.

Tony stared at Robert as he continued his head shaking. Nothing normal about his partner apparently, which was another reason he liked him.

* * *

"City folk coming to the country. Seems about right," said one of the officers from Merritt. "We are going to need more vehicles, I think. I'll radio in to get a truck to pick up the two cars. One of their cars was farther back off the side of the road, don't know why."

"You could probably wait for first light to do that." Robert offered. "Maybe the cat could go in the back of your truck."

Robert looked back at the house, relieved that it had luckily escaped the gunfire as he had not told the owner about the true purpose of their visit. Better yet, the three of them had also escaped harm. He went over to one of the officers and told him that they would stay the night at the house and come down in the morning to the Merritt detachment. Photos and statements were taken, weapons collected while they waited for the ambulance to arrive.

Robert and Tony walked back into the bush and retrieved their equipment from the nests they had occupied while waiting for the visitors, then stood on the veranda, watching the paramedics exit their truck. Robert gave a sketchy outline of what had happened to one of the officers. The officer looked at Robert with a hint of skepticism. He closed his notebook and signalled the cars that they could make their retreat to Merritt. One of the officers got into the ambulance to keep an eye on the injured gangster. After the last of the vehicles had left, Robert looked at the other two and nodded towards the door of the ranch house.

"I think we should have a celebration meal." Robert started, "We are all in one piece. Mission accomplished."

"Yeah. Any more of that beer left?" This from Tony.

"I believe there is. I'll look through the fridge to see what I can put together. You guys eat meat?"

Tony smiled, while Farhad nodded. Robert took this to mean that the steaks he had brought were going to do their duty this evening. He peered out onto the deck and saw an old grill. It looked rusted and probably not used in this century, so he decided to stick with the stove. He pulled out a bag of potatoes, some mushrooms, and proceeded to tell the other two what to do with them. What he had in mind was a smushed potato dish that was heavenly as a side to a rib-eye. Spying the bottle of whiskey from the previous evening on the counter, he poured a liberal helping to get him in the cooking mood.

While he was prepping the steaks, he started thinking about what he had accomplished with the whole wild west episode. As long as someone was here on site to judge whether the gang arrived or not; really, that was all that was needed to determine the mole issue. Gladys's life then would not be in danger (maybe). But then, the task force would eventually use Gladys to feed the gang disinformation, a prospect Robert found distasteful. And the gang would figure it out eventually, with the same result for Gladys in the end. Somehow, if it was a man who had betrayed the force, he wouldn't think twice about using him.

Then there were the stories that would come out of this episode. Robert was sure that each re-telling would embellish the events a little further. It would turn into an epic story, of that, he was sure. However, Farhad was still in danger. It would only be a matter of time before the gang members would be released and realize what had happened to them. Their offences were relatively minor, apart from the one who shot at Tony. He might be going away for a while after what he had tried. First thing tomorrow he would call Thomas and warn him that Gladys would be in trouble. Thomas would have to be the one to consider what to do with her, Robert had enough to think about. They also needed to stow Farhad back in the East Vancouver safe house for a while and hope no one found him. He knew that the Gupils wouldn't give up the hunt.

The potatoes were roasting in the oven after they had been parboiled and squashed. Tony was slowly sautéing the mushrooms, so Robert decided to give the steaks a quick sear on the stove top. The other two were feeling more relaxed than they had the last couple of days. The beer seemed to have disappeared. Robert could see them eying the whiskey bottle.

"Need some help with that?" Tony apparently always ready to come to someone's aid.

"Go ahead, I never travel without a backup." Robert replied. The other two divided up the remainder while Robert went upstairs, returning with a blended scotch, his favourite.

The table was set, dinner on the plates, the three looked at each other and raised their glasses silently, smiling at the notion of being alive, in the country, with nary a sound to be heard.

"I could get used to being out here." Robert said.

Farhad responded after a moment, "I'd go nuts pretty quickly I think."

Tony declined to speak as his mouth was filled with food, but he looked happy.

Robert looked at Farhad, something niggling at his mind, "So what did that big guy mean when he said you weren't all you were cracked up to be?"

"Don't have a clue. He seems to be the second guy in that group after the Guru, but he has never said much when I was around them." Farhad responded. "I get the feeling that he had something to do with Gurmit's death. The Guru always had Manny do his dirty work."

Robert noticed that Farhad's eyes darted around a bit as he talked. He had never conversed with Farhad much at all, and didn't know him very well, so he couldn't figure out whether Farhad was being truthful or not. Something didn't feel right, but he decided not to pursue it at the moment. Tony however, seemed to be still bothered by the biblical references earlier in the evening, "So what's the stuff about the good book, Robert?" He paused, then, "If you don't mind my asking."

"When I was smaller, and we had moved to Vancouver from Hong Kong, my mother put me into Sunday school at a local Anglican church for a year. I think she was trying to balance out the Buddhist learnings I had acquired in China, but I'm not sure. Reading the Bible made an impression."

"No kidding." Tony let the subject rest. He was a good Roman Catholic, Robert knew.

* * *

After dinner was over, Robert poured more whiskey into his glass, then flipped off the light switch that controlled the exterior lighting. He went outside onto the porch, down onto the gravel surrounding the house and looked up at the night sky. Stars were everywhere, drifts of them, so bright it was impossible to conceive of the vastness of it all. He made out one or two constellations that he knew by heart, but the rest were a jumble to him. He had spent too much time in the city and never looked up at the night skies even when they were clear. He could easily see how doing this would be a form of both entertainment and wonder for past civilizations as they looked to their gods for guidance. Like most city dwellers, it was something he missed out on entirely and didn't think about anymore. The nearby undergrowth was hushed, the silence belying the violence that had been visited on it in the previous hours. A scent of cedar drifted over from one of the few trees near the house. Robert breathed deeply and relaxed even more, enjoying the quiet, and the absence of people.

~ 12 ~

Early the following morning, before the other two had moved, Robert was on the phone to Vancouver, calling Thomas's cell. He gave a quick outline of what had happened the day before, and offered his opinion that Gladys was the informer in the group. There was silence on the other end while Thomas digested this piece of unpleasantness.

"That didn't take them long, to come after you I mean. I wonder why the Gupils are so hot to get Farhad. Something's going on here which I don't understand. Thanks for doing this. I am going to have a talk with Gladys and figure out what to do with her."

"I don't understand it either. And I am not sure how to approach Farhad on this. We'll probably see you tomorrow. We are heading into Merritt first thing today, but we may be there awhile for formalities. I'm pretty sure four of the gangsters will be freed fairly quickly, rent the first car available, and hightail it back to the city. The only thing that may stick to them are the weapons offences. Oh yeah, and hunting out of season."

"What?"

"I'll fill you in when we return. They are going to figure out that Gladys did them in. She'll be in danger." Robert paused, then, "See you soon." He hung up, then called his home. Camille answered after a few rings.

"Hey Camille, it's Robert."

"I didn't recognize the number, where are you calling from?"

"The ranch house, it's a land line. Cells don't work out here. We had visitors last evening, and things got a little frisky, but we're all okay. No injuries. The bad guys are in the lockup, for now at least. The kids okay?"

"We are all fine. They are just about to head out the door, as am I. Are you coming home today then?"

"Yes, but maybe not until the end of the day. We'll be spending some time at the local RCMP detachment." Robert knew he should be on good behaviour with the Merritt cops after all the disruption he had caused for them by his drama. Well, they could use the excitement as far as he was concerned. He'd be polite, up to a point.

"See you soon Camille." He hung up and then yelled at the other two to get their asses moving. Being spring, the songbirds were chirping and yacking it up in the alders surrounding the house. It was impossible to ignore, especially if you were slightly hung over cops trying for all their worth to not listen to the racket.

"Okay, okay. We're moving." Tony finally grunted.

* * *

An hour and a half later, the SUV, with Tony driving this time, pulled up in front of the RCMP detachment in

Merritt. The three got out and sauntered into the building, feeling like something out of a wild western movie where the sheriff and his deputies clean up the town. The receptionist already knew who to expect, so the men were ushered into the sergeant's office without delay. In the lobby, a man connected with the local paper, the *Merritt Herald,* tried to ask the group a question but Robert and his squad brushed by him.

The sergeant stood up and looked Robert's crew over from behind his desk. "You guys sure know how to cause a commotion. I'm going to be doing paperwork on this 'til the middle of summer. And now the local newspaper is pestering us."

Robert shrugged. "Our apologies."

"We have a couple of cars in storage, a shitload of firearms and ammo, a dead gangster, a dead cougar, and a wounded gangster who was sent up to the hospital in Kamloops. Not to mention four tourists in our cells."

"They still running with that tourist crap?" Robert asked.

"So far."

"I am guessing that some weapons charges could be laid on all of them, but the guy up in Kamloops needs to be charged with attempted murder. He sprayed automatic fire in Tony's general direction after they were told to stand down and drop their weapons."

"You are sure about the sequence of events?" he countered.

"Absolutely, and we identified as police officers." Robert answered quickly. "Didn't seem to matter." Robert paused then, "Where is that cat? He deserves a medal of honour."

"It was sent up to Kamloops as well for a necropsy, to see if there was any reason it attacked, other than hunger."

"Well, I still think it deserves to be on your wall of fame. Do cat attacks happen very often here?"

"Not uncommon, but cougars generally track other wildlife, not people. This one must have been desperate, or young."

"I assume those other four will be let loose soon?"

"Probably. One or two have made calls and they will all likely be released later today. Weapons charges are all we really have." After this exchange, the three Vancouver cops sat and gave their statements to other officers before being allowed to leave.

Robert looked back and smiled, "You don't have a spare cougar, do you? It'd be great to have one posted outside as those tourists are released, just to see the looks on their faces."

"Sorry. Right out of cougars at the moment."

On his way out the door, after walking by the reporter once more, Robert remembered something important, went back and asked the receptionist. "Any good coffee places in Merritt?"

"Best place is probably the Bumblebee Bakery."

"Ahh, okay, didn't know the coffee was good there." Robert had regrettably not brought his coffee gear with him and was feeling the need urgently. He wouldn't normally forget, but, as this wasn't exactly a vacation jaunt, he had other things on his mind when packing. After another visit to the local bakery, and feeling happier for a caffeine fix, they got back onto the Coq and drove south back to the Lower Mainland, Robert letting Tony drive so he could do some thinking. Robert also purchased a couple of loaves of bread. The other two looked at him with questioning eyes. He ignored them. They didn't have families to feed and wouldn't remotely think along those lines.

Robert settled into the back seat of the car, leaving the other two officers in the front to talk amongst themselves. He wondered whether any of the gang members they had just finished with were responsible for Gurmit's death, and if so, how they would ever find out. From what Farhad had said, Manny seemed to be the likely culprit. It would be difficult to prove though. Someone from the Gupil group would have to be turned, and asked or made to testify against the others, but it seemed a stretch. He needed to have a sit-down with Thomas as soon as possible. He wondered how Thomas's conversation with Gladys was going, and what he would do with her. Was it possible to use her in some way? It certainly would help the group if they could penetrate the triad in the same way that the Taskforce had been compromised. Nothing like sowing some seeds of doubt into the enemy lines to create confusion or uncertainty. This is what has happened to the Taskforce, Robert realized; we're running around, looking over our shoulders, uncertain as to who to trust or what actions to take.

* * *

That same morning, the Guru had received a phone call from Manny. After the unexpected contents of the call, the Guru slowly worked himself into a rage. Not only were his men complete idiots, but Robert Lui seemed to have outmanoeuvred him. He was trying to come up with a good way to tell the Wide Bay Boys, but he couldn't think of one yet without looking stupid. It was really none of Edward's business after all. It wasn't Edward's drugs and money that had gone AWOL. And, he was now missing two members of his menagerie, not to mention the weapons that would need replacing. Then there was the call to the lawyer in order to get the other four out of custody, never an inexpensive conversation.

At the end of Manny's call, he told the four to be at his club by ten the next morning for a *tete a tete*. He then started contemplating with distaste the task that Edward would be planning for him, and how to accomplish it with the least amount of commotion. His conclusion was that this was impossible. All hell would break loose. In this case, it would be very apt. He wondered what was behind Edward's request, and how he would calm the waters after it had been done. Perhaps Edward had other levers to accomplish this, but it seemed doubtful.

* * *

Back in Delta, the Chief Constable was not making any progress in finding out who had waylaid Jonny. A couple of officers had interviewed Jonny at the hospital, but as expected, he wasn't saying much of anything. What was surprising was the lack of information from the police side. The officers had obviously closed ranks to protect whoever had done the shooting. Either that, or the guys who did it weren't talking, a proposition Raymond found hard to believe. The ballistics report had come back from the slugs found in Jonny's knees, and they matched standard issue police ordinance. Not really surprising, but not helpful either. He had no appetite for checking every Delta Police handgun to see if there was a match to the ammunition used. There also didn't seem to be any progress on Gurmit's murder. The coroner confirmed that Gurmit died from drowning, his lungs had the combination of river and salt water in them that could be found in that part of the Fraser River as the tide turned. Other than this fact, the police were not having any luck with the investigation. The houseboat inhabitants in the Richmond slough were not talking, understanding that gangs might be involved. For their future health and well-being, they'd remain silent. Gang shootings seemed to be an almost daily occurrence in the Lower Mainland, and no one wanted those people back visiting.

* * *

The Guru had convinced Jonny's girlfriend, Mattie, to finally make a visit to the Delta hospital to see if she could get any information out of Jonny as to who had shot him. She was reluctant on several counts; she didn't like hospital and she was unimpressed with how the date night had turned out, especially with being stiffed for the dinner bill. It also seemed like Jonny's dancing future was in jeopardy. She was re-evaluating her relationship with Jonny.

She eventually decided to go, after some persuasion from the Guru in the form of cash, but the trip was a bust. The police had an officer in the room while she visited, so she learned next to nothing. Jonny was to be moved out to a rehab facility in Vancouver called GF Strong, where they would see if Jonny could be made to walk in a straight line again. Hospitals never had enough beds for their patients, so moving them as soon as possible was standard practice. She wouldn't be visiting GF Strong, no matter what the Guru wanted. Mattie liked her boyfriends to be good-looking, able to spend money on her, and, oh yes, have the ability to walk. Jonny would be coming up short on that last asset, so she'd be on the lookout for a new beau.

When Mattie called the Guru to report what she hadn't learned, he exploded. He cursed, then threatened her if she didn't toe the line and do what he wanted. She wasn't impressed or afraid, obviously unaware of how gangs dealt with people who disappointed them. She knew that Jonny and her were over as an item, so the Guru could go stuff it. Luckily for her, the Guru had larger problems to deal with at the moment, but he mentally put a black mark against her name, for future possible action.

* * *

Robert and his small band of men retraced their steps in exactly the reverse order taken a couple of days earlier after arriving back in Vancouver. Robert kept Tony with him instead of dropping him at his condo and they drove back to the Vancouver Police Headquarters on Cambie, parking in the underground garage. After transferring the remains of the supplies, weapons, ammo, and the other equipment out of the car, he left Tony to deal with the equipment and return the car, while he went up to his office. It was half past four, so the regular shift was almost done. As he walked onto the floor, a couple of people waved at him. He noticed that Gladys was missing, so he went straight to Thomas's office. The door was ajar, so he assumed correctly that Thomas was inside. He peered around the jamb. The occupant did not look happy.

"Hey Thomas."

"Robert. Welcome back. Good work, I think." Thomas elaborated, "Don't get me wrong, you guys did great. It's just that this whole situation is turning into an octopus. It is starting to get out of hand." He gestured to the spare chair on the other side of the desk, inviting Robert to sit. "Shut the door first please."

"What happened to Gladys?" Robert asked.

"I had a talk with her. You were correct. It was she who was giving information to someone on the other side. She does not know who, she only has a phone number. We are trying to trace it, but it is likely a cut-out. Turns out that her lawyer husband got her into this through his gambling debts. And before you say it, the vetting was clean. This all happened after we checked her history, so it appears that we need to do something other agencies practice, that is, ongoing reviews of our people." Thomas shifted in his chair, while he looked out the window at the lowering light, watching some crows meander over the building, heading east.

"I told her that she didn't look well, and she should

take a few days off. I am not sure what to do with her. And there is something else, her husband has been doing some money cleaning for someone." Thomas added. "Probably the same people."

"Sounds like a mess." Robert answered, "They may not necessarily conclude that she ratted them out you know, she easily could have got a detail or two wrong when she relayed the information about Farhad." He continued, "However the husband must have met someone to do what he is doing. This may be a way into the inner workings of the gang. The chief mucky mucks should reward us handsomely if we can come up with this connection. They have been pretty free with their mouths for a while now about curbing money laundering. And I mean the politicians, not our betters."

Thomas was silent while he studied the sky, then he turned to Robert, "Let's not forget that there is likely another mole planted somewhere, maybe more than one. And I am unsure how thorough our bosses want us to be in our investigations. My guess would be, not very. Someone has let this go on for years, so we're going to need to be careful."

Robert remained silent for a moment, then, "We may have to hide them both."

"What? Not arrest them?"

"It makes sense. If we can figure out that Gladys's husband may be the key to the triad in Vancouver, then they will do the same, unless they are complete idiots. Putting them in remand might not be a smart move." Robert sat thinking. "We need to protect them. They aren't going to like it. It'll be a big hit to their lifestyle, but maybe an explanation about the alternatives will get their attention. We could use that safe house in Ladner that Farhad was just in. It's pretty bright and cheerful." Then he added, "Not really. They'll probably run out into the middle of traffic after a couple of days there. Better than prison though. I don't think they'd be safe in there."

"I'll arrange it in the morning." Thomas concluded.

"Ok, I'm heading home. See you tomorrow." Robert got up slowly and walked past his office over to the stairs and headed up to check on Camille. He arrived on the floor and gave it the once over. It was his place of work only a year earlier when he had been pursuing an unusual case in Vancouver for the Vancouver Police Department. He saw Tony at his desk, and closer by, Norma, one of the civilian admin assistants, was just wrapping up her day.

"Hello Robert, how are you?" Norma seemed to have finally gotten over the issue of Camille moving in with Robert.

"Good, good. Nice to see you, Norma. Is Camille in?" Norma nodded over to the office that was formerly Robert's. He went up to the office door, stuck his head around the frame, and smiled. "Hey."

"Robert, you came back! In one piece?" She smiled back. "No wonder you left the VPD for the Taskforce, this office is so small. I am now understanding why you were always out for coffee."

"Funny. Let's get out of here and go home if you are finished up that is."

$$\sim\ 13\ \sim$$

The next morning, Thomas Harrow was in his office before eight. He had come to a decision about Gladys, and her husband. He was going to suggest that they change locales for a while in order to save their lives, per Robert's suggestion. Thomas was under no illusion what the gangs would do if they felt threatened by people they used. He had a friend a while back whose hairdresser went missing one day, never to be seen or heard from ever again. No body ever found, no nothing. There was a bit of talk about what her boyfriend had been up to, but he had suffered the same fate at the same time, both erased off the face of the earth, as though they had never existed. Talk about cold cases, that one was an icicle.

He decided to get Gladys into the office, along with her husband, to explain the facts of life. He waited a few more minutes, then dialled her number, "Gladys, Thomas here. I would like to talk with you and your husband today, if possible, in person."

Gladys sounded groggy, "I'm sorry, I just woke up. Why do you want to see us?"

"We think your lives may be in danger. It's up to you, but you may want to hear what we have to say."

"I am not sure if I can get Terrance to leave work or not. Can I call you back?"

"Yes, of course, but I would impress upon him the importance of this meeting, if he wants to keep doing what he does for his law firm." This last item was a bald-faced lie, but Gladys didn't quite understand how their lives were about to change. There was no way Terrance would be able to continue his life as he knew it. The sooner they both understood that, the better. At least that's what Thomas told himself. He also started thinking about who he was going to get to replace Gladys. He needed someone as soon as possible, as keeping everything straight with all the people comprising the Taskforce was no small task. He would ask Robert if he had any suggestions once he showed up at the office.

* * *

Robert came in later that morning, having taken his sweet time waking up with Camille, after being absent from home for a couple of days. As soon as Robert walked onto the floor of the Taskforce his first thought was coffee. He walked by Thomas's office and peered in.

"Want to go discuss hockey while we drink some coffee?"

"Sure thing. I have talked with Gladys. I told her and her husband to come in at two for a discussion." Thomas stood up, grabbed his jacket and they left the floor taking the stairs down. Together they ambled up Cambie to Café

Paulo. It was cloudy but a touch of warmth was in the air, another grey day in Lotusland. They walked into the café and Robert waved to Carmelita who was running the La Cimbali machine. She had another helper in to man the point-of-sale machine while Gilberto was away. Robert was hungry after his morning at home, so he also selected a croissant from the glass display case. Carmelita slid the Americanos across the counter with a broad smile. Robert stood, staring at his coffee, shaking his head while Thomas took his and retreated to a window table.

"This won't do Carmelita."

A deep look of concern spread across Carmelita's face. Robert had never shown anything but extreme satisfaction with the service at Café Paulo.

"What's wrong Roberto?"

"Can't drink coffee out of a glass, Carmelita. Would you mind pouring it into one of your mugs?"

"Of course, Robert. But if you don't mind, why?"

"I don't know, glass makes it taste bad, and I'm not sure why. All I know is that for me, glass does not mix with coffee." After Carmelita had made the irrational change in coffee containers, Robert retreated to the table Thomas was sitting at. He looked at Robert curiously.

"What was all that about? Did she make your coffee too strong?"

"As if." Robert responded. "Just a container mix-up was all."

Thomas looked at his glass mug and then at Robert's ceramic mug. "You are nuts, you know that don't you?"

"Maybe. You think they'll make it?" Robert changed subjects after he sat down.

Thomas was confused, "Gladys you mean?"

"No, the Canucks of course." Robert was questioning the hockey team's ability to make it into post-season play.

"You weren't kidding when you said we should talk hockey. Okay, I think they'll make it. They have a good schedule the rest of the season, even if all the teams are turning on the afterburners to get in. The majority of their games are at home. I also like the cut of that rookie's jib."

"Jib? What are you, a sailor now?"

"It's a common nautical phrase."

"Okay, I didn't know you were a nautical kind of guy. And just for the record, I'll only give them a fifty-fifty chance. You need great goaltending in this league, and after they managed to inexplicably trade both of their best goalies away, that part of their game is dubious at best. And dubious is not a nautical term."

Thomas peered back at Robert, shaking his head as he sipped his Americano. "You're too wound up about those god-damned Habs to make any sense. That Camille really did a number on you."

"Don't worry, my son is still a Canucks fan. There is that to consider."

Thomas smiled. "Thank God for the younger generation."

"I agree. Speaking of the younger generation, Tony did well on our country jaunt. He is still keen as all get out, unencumbered by our perspective on things."

"That's good, I'll let his superior know that." He then

changed gears, "When Gladys and Terrance show up, I am going to show him a few pictures of people we have been following at a distance. See if any are the ones he met when he first got involved with getting his gambling debts erased."

"Back to business." Robert sighed.

"Yes, and any ideas on a replacement for Gladys?"

"How about Norma from up a floor. She's been efficient for that group, at least when I was there. I don't know if she would be available, but she is good. They probably won't want to lose her, but you carry some weight I understand."

"I'll check on her security clearances, see how long ago they were done. Don't want to be repeating the same mistakes over and over, do we?"

"Probably a good plan." Robert paused as he swallowed the remains of his coffee, happier as a result, "Maybe we should get back." Then he had another question, something that had been niggling the back of his brain. "Do you know anything about Siegfried Damler?"

"The special forces guy? Not very much, no. Why do you ask?"

"He seems remarkably well-informed, that's all. I was curious about how that could happen given how tight we like to keep things."

Thomas remained silent as they walked back down Cambie, then, "I'll see what I can find out."

"Carefully, of course." Robert added unhelpfully.

Thomas looked sideways at Robert as they entered the police building and nodded.

* * *

Later that same morning, Manny and the other three adventurers showed up, one by one at the Guru's club in Surrey. They had been sprung from custody the previous afternoon by the Gupil's lawyer, rented the largest car they could find in Merritt, and sailed back to Surrey. Manny was in a foul mood, and his large girth did not make for a comfortable ride for Bobbi, who shared the rear seat with him. The BMW and the Audi remained in the impound area of the RCMP detachment in Merritt where they would gather dust over the next months; two less status symbols masquerading as cars roaming the streets of Surrey.

The Guru sat at the head of the table in his meeting room, stirring some sugar into his tea, watching as the team members slowly entered and took their seats.

"What do you have to say for yourselves?" He paused, "Manny?"

Manny shifted in his chair before answering in his deep voice, "We were set up it seems. There is no way we could have predicted what happened to the one killed by that cat."

The Guru looked at Manny, "There were six of you, against three as I understand it? And a cat, an unarmed cat at that. Your tactics obviously leave a lot to be desired. I don't care whether they were laying in wait for you or not. Ever heard of surveillance and assessment before you act?"

Manny did not have a comeback for this comment.

He knew their whole expedition had been too hastily mounted and executed. Their gang had walked right into it, and he knew it. The Guru didn't exactly prepare them as to what going out into the country was like. He probably didn't appreciate the difficulties any more than Manny did, but Manny wasn't going to mention this lack of information from the top. It was on him to properly mount the expedition, and he had failed.

"What is our next move, gentlemen?" The Guru asked.

The others around the table looked at each other, surprised to be asked this.

The Guru chuckled a bit, "Just kidding. I know you idiots don't have a clue what to do next. That's why I'm running this outfit." The Guru never tired of putting his members in their place, even if it was a slightly dangerous thing to do. As long as the money kept flowing, he felt he was on safe ground. Manny was not impressed, but he knew enough to keep his feelings to himself. There would be a day of reckoning, he hoped. That time had not come yet, however.

"Revenge." That one word was left hanging by the Guru. He did not elaborate on it. Everyone in the room knew what it meant. The trick was in how to accomplish it. "In the meantime, I have to promote a couple of men to take the places of the unfortunate ones you left behind in Merritt."

Manny spoke, "By the way, when you get some new guns, don't get any Uzis."

"What do you mean by that?"

"It's illegal for someone who is not an Israeli to have an Uzi."

The Guru couldn't believe what he was hearing. "Who told you this?"

"The cops up at Merritt."

"I'm finding it hard to comprehend what morons you all are. And if I told you that lamb vindaloo had rabies in it, would you stop eating that dish?"

The gang members looked at each other, none wanting to be the next one to speak, so the Guru continued, "As far as I know, there is no such law, and anyway, aren't half the weapons we have, illegal? You guys are total idiots. Someone is pulling your chain, and apparently, it's not very hard to do."

The meeting devolved into discussions of the day to day issues with running drugs, outwitting their rivals, and re-arming themselves. As the others talked about what each of them needed to do, the Guru was contemplating how to get at Farhad, and retrieve his possessions. He was sure that what the Wide Bay Boys were suggesting he do would help in this regard. The trick was how to achieve his own ends without pissing off the triad gang. He guessed that they had their own agenda that he was not privy to.

One by one, the four men left the room. The Guru hardly noticed them as he was deep in thought. The others noticed the distance that had swiftly overtaken their leader, sitting at the table, looking at his tea, as if some divination could be achieved by the reading of the leaves. Even Manny was impressed by how quickly the Guru had withdrawn from the conversation. He thought that he understood his boss only about half the time, which was way more than the others in the room. The rest of them were dumber than table legs. This was Manny's kindest assessment of his fellow gangsters right now. Although, after the Uzi fiasco, he wasn't entirely sure about his own intelligence.

* * *

Terrance and Gladys showed up at the Cambie police station after two. Gladys led Terrance slowly up the stairs and onto the floor where she had formerly worked and checked in with the receptionist. She was dreading this meeting. The two of them then sat waiting for Thomas to come get them, Gladys avoiding looking at any of her former coworkers, even though they had no idea yet what had happened. Eventually, Thomas made his way over to them and lead them back to his office. He closed the door after asking them to take a seat. On a side table were ten photographs of varying quality, all surveillance photos taken of people the Taskforce was interested in.

Thomas started in, "I take it that Gladys has told you why you are both here, correct?" He was looking directly at Terrance.

"Sort of." Said Terrance. He didn't look too sure of himself. Unusual for a lawyer, Thomas thought.

"You are here because your gambling problem has screwed up both of your lives. It has led indirectly to the death of a police officer. Not something we take lightly. Therefore, a time of reckoning has come. A second operation has just concluded where once again, because of your actions, our people were put at extreme risk. And once the gangs that you are dealing with figure out what happened and why, your lives will be in danger as well. They don't give a second thought to getting rid of people that are a liability to their business or themselves as you may have noticed from the news every week."

Terrance and Gladys looked at each other nervously. They obviously hadn't expected Thomas to be so blunt.

Thomas looked directly at Terrance. "I'd like you to take a look at some pictures on the table over there. See if you recognize anyone." Terrance rose and went over to the table, giving the ten photos the once over. It didn't take long for him to pick one out.

"This one is the guy who I went to about my loans. His name is Jason, at least that's what he told me. He was introduced to me as someone who could help me out with money problems. It was through another gambler acquaintance at the casino. I don't recognize any of the others."

"Where was this?"

"The casino in Burnaby, the one close to the highway."

Thomas was silent, thinking. "I would not recommend spending much more time at your home, or place of work. We would arrest you, but don't think it is safe for you to be in remand. We have a safe house you can stay for a while until we figure out what to do with you. If I were you, I'd be working from this home for the next couple of weeks. The townhouse is located in Ladner. And I wouldn't be advertising this fact to your friends and family. They have a way of blabbing about things that would make it easy to find you by people you really don't want finding you. We think a couple of gangs are involved here; one may be a triad."

Gladys remained silent, but her eyes widened at this last revelation, knowing that she was the source of the police problems, probably contributing to an officer's death. She wondered what charges Thomas would bring against them but did not want to be the one to raise this issue.

Thomas gave Gladys a slip of paper with an address on it as well as a set of keys. "This is the address of the place down south. An officer will drive you home to get your clothes and then take you down there." He stared at Terrance, "We will want to talk to you about your money laundering activities for the gang. I'll call you when we are ready to have that conversation." With that, he let them go, watching as they stood, waiting for the officer. He shook his head, not liking their chances.

* * *

After the couple had left, Thomas went over to Robert's small office and entered, leaning against the doorframe. "Terrance identified one of the photos as a Jason, who had arranged for his loans to disappear. He apparently hangs out at the Burnaby Casino on occasion. I'm going to have surveillance put on this Jason and see where he leads us."

"Sounds like a plan." Robert said. "You should use our best assets for this job. We don't really want them to know we are onto them until it serves our purpose."

"No, we don't, I agree." Thomas concluded their conversation. He went back to his office to call someone he trusted in the Attorney General's office to ask questions about Siegfried Damler.

With that, Robert had had enough for the day. He looked at the paperwork on his desk and shook his head—it could wait for another day. Dialling Camille's number on his cellphone, he found that she was out on the west side of the city following up some leads in her case. He told her she could have the car to get home, he would take the hard route home before getting some groceries to make dinner. He then left and walked up to Broadway to catch one of the jam-packed double-long buses that trundled back and forth along the transit corridor, spreading radiance and joy wherever it went.

A week later, Safa Atwall was at home in North Surrey, when she got a ring on her cellphone. She was taking information technology courses at one of the local technical universities but did not have classes today. Her older brother, Bobbi, lived on his own. Even though he was essentially a full-time gangster, family was important, so he always kept an eye out for his only sister. They communicated with each other daily on their small devices. Safa had only a vague understanding of what Bobbi did for a living, but she liked the extras that seemed to come with the lifestyle.

The first time Safa met Maccha, the Gupil gang member, she admitted to herself that she was attracted to him. Bobbi had let her tag along to a dinner that had been organized with a couple of the other gang members. One of them also brought a girlfriend along, so Safa was not the only female at the restaurant gathering. Bobbi had been unsure about the idea of Safa joining the dinner, but it was early days for Bobbi. He was still excited about the whole gang thing, not to mention the prestige that he thought came with it. He wanted his sister to see how others respected him now that he was part of a brotherhood. The fact that it was a criminal group didn't really seem to register on Bobbi; that is, as long as the money kept rolling in and no one got killed. For his part, Maccha was also interested in Safa. He had thanked Bobbi in an offhand way for bringing her to the dinner and for the introductions. As a more senior member of the Gupils, Maccha felt he carried substantial weight, and that other gang members should show him proper deference. As with all gangsters, it was about perceived respect, who owed respect to whom, and who deserved it in return.

It wasn't long after that first meeting that Maccha had called Safa up and offered to take her out to dinner. Safa had demurred at first, talking with her brother to see what he thought. Unfortunately for Safa, the first thing that Bobbi considered was himself; how this dating thing might reflect positively on him and his chances to move up the rungs. Bobbi didn't know Maccha that well, but he wasn't thinking straight, so he told Safa that it sounded like a good idea. Family all of a sudden came second, instead of where it should have been, top of mind. Bobbi also neglected to ask any of the other gang members what Maccha was really like, another oversight.

In the end, Bobbi had pulled Maccha aside and told him that he had had a word with his sister and that she would now be willing to date him. Maccha looked at Bobbi without saying anything. He considered Bobbi to be a pussy, and here was proof. He decided right there to wait, not call Safa, but let her stew a bit. He had other girls that he could date in the meantime.

After a couple of weeks had gone by, Maccha called Safa and offered to take her out to dinner. There was a flashy Indian restaurant that a local celebrity chef had opened in south Surrey. It was located at the end of a newish ersatz commercial village that had all the character of a big box store. Someone was trying desperately to manufacture history so that the village would look charming, not successfully. This was the setting for their first date, which did not go smoothly. The food was outstanding but there were mixed signals on both sides of the table; not fully understood, but hardly uncommon, especially on a first date. In any event, Safa ignored some of what had transpired, still interested in Maccha.

* * *

The caller was going to try again, "Hello, is this Safa?"

"Yes." She had not recognized the phone number displayed.

"It's Maccha here. I wondered if you would like to start over. We didn't seem to get off on a good footing at our last dinner together."

Safa was silent for a few seconds, thinking. "Okay, what did you have in mind?"

"There is a new restaurant on Scott Road that I have heard about, very good food. Then, maybe a movie?" Maccha had inadvertently chosen the same restaurant that Jonny had dined at, eating his last decent cuisine for a long time.

"Which movie?" Safa was smart enough to know what most men wanted to see—action films like the interminable

Terminator movies. She really wasn't interested in seeing any of that stuff.

"There is an Indian movie playing close by. It's about two grandmothers, but it is in Hindi with sub-titles. It's supposed to be good."

Safa was surprised. This didn't sound like something a gangster would be going to see. Maybe the movie was really good, or just maybe, something else was going on. She decided not to think too much more about it before accepting, "That sounds good. When did you have in mind?"

"Are you free tonight?" Excitement was building at the anticipation of what he thought was to come.

This was awfully fast. Safa hesitated, gauging whether she needed to study this evening, then agreed, "What time?"

"Pick you up around 6:30?"

"Ok, see you then." She told him her address before ending the call.

* * *

Edward Su decided that it was past time to check on his favourite go-fer gang. It wasn't just his favourite; it actually was his only go-fer gang. The bosses in Hong Kong forbade using more than one gang at a time to do the dirty work that sometimes needed doing. Edward wasn't sure why this was, but he guessed that in the past someone had used two gangs or more in a local situation, and it hadn't turned out well. He could understand that. The Gupils seemed to be one step up from a cow as far as smarts were concerned. But he also thought it would be fun to have two gangs doing his bidding, each trying to outwit the other in order to curry favour and move up the food chain. He called the Guru, to get him out of Surrey and onto more favourable ground. After several rings on the cellphone, the Guru finally answered.

"Hey buddy, time to meet. Why don't you come to Richmond. You know the restaurant, the one at Aberdeen. How about 6:30 tonight?" Edward knew that the Guru hated being called 'buddy', which is why he did it. "And don't bring anyone with you." He added this for good measure, knowing that the Guru didn't like being at a disadvantage where meetings were concerned.

The Guru grunted his assent to the meeting, "See you this evening." He was okay with attending the meeting by himself. He didn't need his associates seeing how he was really treated by the triad gang. The Gupil's perceptions of his control and strength over his followers might be called into question, and that would be annoying.

*　*　*

At half past six in Surrey's north end, Maccha pulled his low-slung Mercedes slowly into the driveway of Safa's home. He let it rumble for a few seconds before shutting it down. The street was devoid of pedestrians, but one or two neighbours noted the appearance of the car from their living rooms. There had been rumours about Safa's brother. This seemed to be one more confirmation of those stories. The tinted windows, flat black paint job, chopped appearance of the ride, and flashy chrome rims all added up to someone wanting to be noticed. Maccha had been oh so lucky that he hadn't been asked to drive up to Merritt. His ride would likely be behind enemy lines if that had happened. Now he was free to continue raping and pillaging in style, as he liked to think of his activities.

He swung his legs out of the driver's seat and walked slowly up the stairs to the front door. He was wearing black gabardine slacks, a white dress shirt, and a mustard yellow blazer. He was about to knock on the door when it opened. Safa appeared, sporting an indigo dress that was hugging her body tightly under a light jacket. Her hair was gathered into a ponytail, and her makeup was layered on heavily. If she was feeling iffy about the date, she was not sending out the correct signals. Maccha smiled and led her down the front steps, stumbled a bit and almost fell down the rest of the way. Safa looked at him from behind with a tilt of her head. Was this guy a goof? He did not even bother to see if her parents were around, let alone greet them and introduce himself.

* * *

At around the same time, the Guru pulled his Range Rover into the giant parkade next to the Aberdeen Shopping Mall in Richmond. The shopping centre's name was pulled from Hong Kong, which in turn had taken it from a city in Scotland. Cantonese developers from Hong Kong had been responsible for a fair bit of building in Vancouver and its surrounding cities over the previous thirty years, hence the British names that kept cropping up on their developments. A gentleman standing by the car entry talking on a cellphone warned Edward that his dinner date had arrived, apparently alone. Edward was all about keeping one step up on everyone he dealt with.

After the Guru had entered the restaurant and explained to the greeter who he was looking for, he was led to a private room off the main dining area. Edward was sitting with Jason at the circular table which could accommodate twelve. The chairs were mahogany with a cream brocade seat and back. The carpet was deep maroon, and typical Chinese art depicting mountains and water within intricate frames covered the walls. The Guru guessed that the table was also mahogany, but it was covered by a large ivory tablecloth. The whole room had the ostentatious and syrupy feeling not unlike what the Guru was used to when he went out for dinner in a higher end Indian restaurant. Edward motioned with his hand for the Guru to sit across from him. A selection of dumplings and wontons were on offer with hot sauce, mustard, and other condiments sitting alongside the dishes.

"Welcome. Please help yourself if you are hungry." Edward paused, "There are a few more dishes coming." He was feigning politeness before he pulled the knives out and started twisting them into the Guru. He waved at the server waiting by the wall to leave the room. The help at the restaurant didn't know who the customers were, only that they carried clout, and were to be obeyed, no questions asked.

Outside the restaurant, at a coffee bar farther down the mall, Benton sat, cooling his heels. He was one of the Taskforce watchers picked to see where Jason would lead them. He was not alone. His partner was doing some window shopping farther down the mall. They would not contact each other, but one would pick up the trail if the other felt compromised. Both were Cantonese by heritage, blending into the population of the mall, where any white person stood out like a ghost. Benton had not known who Edward was but was familiar with the Guru. A few surreptitious pictures were taken, the Taskforce shortly to have any doubts removed about who was behind the problems of Terrance and Gladys. Benton and his backup were so far unaware of the watchers on the triad side, and equally, the triad was unaware that they were being tailed. If it wasn't so potentially deadly, it had the makings of a comedy.

Benton had taken a quick stroll into the restaurant after the Guru had shown up, perused the menu and then left. He couldn't see his subjects in the main dining area but knew the fancier restaurants had side rooms for special clientele. He had spotted what looked like one when a server came out, quickly closing the door. A good place to set up a listening device, as long as the room wasn't swept regularly, which was a distinct possibility. The restaurant might be a regular meeting spot. Benton made a note to return to the restaurant soon to do this, on the premise of inspecting the room for a special party rental. One thing was certain, they would be able to spot the Guru's turban from miles away, he was wearing a bright yellow one today.

* * *

Edward was dressed in a dark grey suit, black Ferragamo

Oxfords, and a light blue shirt, tieless. Jason was more informal, wearing the currently popular jeans with a sport coat look, that says, 'I don't know how to dress—I'll just copy other people'.

Edward looked intently at the Guru and fired his opening salvo, "Word has it that you're running short on people these days." There, he had said it. The Guru now understood that Edward knew exactly what was going on with the Gupils, as if there was any doubt. "Heard you had a few problems out in the hinterland. You know the countryside can be hazardous, or maybe you didn't allow for this, I don't know."

The Guru's saffron turban waved a bit as he looked from Jason back to Edward, "We ran into some unexpected problems during our trip to Merritt, I'll agree. Nothing we can't handle."

"I heard one of your men also got himself shot up in Delta. Makes one wonder if you people know what you are doing at all."

The Guru quietly started to seethe. Who was this guy to talk to him like this? "Good thing I am not the only one with problems."

Edward paused. What was the meaning of this comment? He knew he had hit a nerve, but where did the Guru get the effrontery to say something like that?

The Guru noted the reticence of Edward to say something, so he launched into it, "You have a problem which impacted us. I assume you know about it?" He was pretty sure that Edward didn't know about this particular problem, he just wanted to twist his own knife here.

Now Edward was concerned. He always had the upper hand in these conversations, and it was troubling that he now didn't. "What are you talking about?"

"To put it bluntly, your information source sucks. We were set up and paid a heavy price for it in Merritt."

Edward stared at Jason. The triads didn't make mistakes. At least that was the party line. But it sure sounded as though something wasn't right in Lotusland. He looked back at the Guru, "What happened exactly?"

"We were chasing an undercover cop who had penetrated our gang and were going to deal with him exactly the way we dealt with the other one in the river a couple of weeks back. However, it turns out that they were waiting for us. They knew we were coming. That asshole Robert Lui was there. We were told by you guys that Farhad would be up there by himself. It should have been simple. It was anything but."

"Were you there?"

"No. I needed to be down here."

Edward glanced at Jason again before asking his next question, "Can you snatch someone for us, and keep them for a while?"

The Guru had been waiting for this request after earlier hints, but needed more information, "I suppose. Who is it?"

"In good time. We just need to know if you can do this. If not, we'll look elsewhere."

"No, no. We can do it." The Guru didn't want Edward going anywhere else—that would be the end of the Gupil's sudden rise in the world, and quite possibly, the end of the Guru.

"Excellent. We will be in touch. Meanwhile we have an issue to take care of thanks to what you have told us." Edward smiled thinly at the Guru, no mirth in it at all. "You can go if you wish."

The Guru hadn't eaten a morsel of food but was happy to get out of the room. He'd eat when he got back to Surrey. He pushed his chair away from the table and rose, nodding at Jason and Edward as he exited the meeting.

* * *

Edward picked at the dumplings as he thought. The more he considered, the worse the story seemed. They would use their own people to deal with this. The Gupils definitely lacked the sophistication needed for this task.

He was looking at Jason. "You are going to talk with this Gladys person, and bring her in. We must deal with her quickly." Jason nodded as he considered how Gladys's husband could be a problem as well. The husband knew Jason, having met him a couple of times when his money problems had turned into trouble. Jason didn't mention this to Edward, not wanting the aggravation it would bring. Then there was the money laundering that Terrance was doing for the triad. Things were getting complicated.

Outside the restaurant, Benton noted the Guru leaving, impossible to miss, but stayed put, reading a copy of one of the local Chinese newspapers, more interested in who else might come out the door. Unfortunately for the watchers, Edward and Jason ate some more food before leaving, but the half hour wait was worth it. When Jason exited, talking to Edward, Benton tilted his head at them so his partner would get some photos of the pair. Benton and his partner stayed put a while longer and were relieved that they did. As Edward and Jason walked down the mall two more young gentlemen joined them. These two had been loitering separately by a couple of the other stores and were obviously watchers themselves. Prudence dictated the two cops wait slightly longer, in case there were more stragglers, before each of them left in separate directions.

Over on Scott Road, at the new Indian restaurant, Maccha and Safa had settled into a booth and were perusing the menu choices. Fortunately for Maccha, the two undercover cops, Dal and Michael were off this evening, so were not in the restaurant where they had turned out to be regulars. There was no doubt that having got away with it once, and still troubled by the death of their colleague, they would have taken more revenge without a second thought. They knew most of the Gupil members by sight and Maccha wouldn't have stood a chance. The two had stayed away from the restaurant for a while after the Jonny event, but the food was so good that they eventually caved, at some considerable risk to themselves if their Head Constable was still intent on finding who had shot Jonny.

After the food arrived, Maccha asked a few questions of Safa about her school and courses, things he had not the slightest interest in. When he was not staring at her, which made Safa uncomfortable, he was looking around the restaurant to see who was looking at them. He was basically a peacock who had only one thing on his mind and that was getting Safa out of her tight dress. He planned to drive to the movie theatre after the dinner, but that was about it. He really had no interest in the movie. Everything he was after would be in his car.

The couple each had some *Gulab Jamun* with ice cream as dessert to round out a feast of specialties that kept them busy for almost an hour. Safa was sated, and feeling at peace, while Maccha who normally would be feeling slightly sleepy, was getting excited in anticipation of what he thought was to come. He waved for the bill.

"What time does the movie start?" Safa asked.

Maccha had no idea. "Pretty soon, we should get going." The server came over and Maccha settled up, leaving a rather large tip, befitting a big man around town. She smiled at him, ignoring the fact that Safa was sitting there. He liked the look of their server, and she had rather large breasts. He made a mental note to come back to the restaurant another day, to see if he could hook up with her.

They made their way out to the Mercedes. Night had fallen, and the cloudy sky did not afford any moonlight. They got in, and Maccha started, then gunned the engine, pulling out onto Scott Road, heading south. The strip mall where the cinemas were located was only a few blocks away. In a couple of minutes, Maccha was turning left at 72nd Avenue then left again into the mall parking lot. He drove slowly past the entry to the cinemas, trying not to run over any of the people making their way across the road and into the box office. He kept going, turning again into a smaller parking area, hived off from the larger ones by a row of hedges. The Mercedes was the only car in this area. He drove over to a stall against a row of trees and killed the engine.

"Why are you parking all the way over here?" Safa asked, concern in her voice.

"So no one scrapes my ride. People don't know how to drive around here."

This was a good explanation as far as Safa was concerned. She relaxed for a moment, before noting that Maccha had loosened his trousers. Was that what she thought it was? A second later Maccha's right hand grabbed the back of her head and pulled it towards his crotch. Her face jammed into his erect penis. Her immediate reaction was horror. However, she was no shrinking flower. She acted as she had been taught in her self-defence classes, improvising on the spot, and what was immediately available were two balls, which she grabbed with her right hand and squeezed for all she was worth. The breath went sharply out of his lungs, and he felt immediately nauseous. He was shocked that Safa had gotten temporary advantage of him. His next move would have repercussions, but he wasn't in the habit of thinking very hard about anything. He pulled Safa's head upright and swung his left fist at her head, landing in the vicinity of her left eye. She screamed, which caused Maccha to loosen his grip on her hair. She grabbed the car door handle and bolted from the car, bleeding from the force of the blow. Maccha also went for his door handle and started to get out of the car, then realized that Safa had already run through the landscaping screen onto the sidewalk of a very busy street, screaming as she went. He thought better of chasing her, moaning as he got back into the car, and was about to drive away when he noticed Safa's purse on the floor. He grabbed it and chucked it out the car window, before driving back the way he had come, groaning and cursing.

Meanwhile, Safa had nothing to staunch the flow of blood from her face. She was trying to wave down a car to get some help, but the streetlights illuminated her face and when people slowed, they saw the mess and thought better of stopping. She looked back through the undergrowth that lined the parking area and saw the Mercedes leave but wasn't thinking about her purse. She was thinking how stupid she had been not to have seen the signs of what Maccha was planning. She was crying now, her mascara running down her cheeks as the shock started to wear off. She was also starting to think. At that moment, a car finally did stop and a woman in the passenger seat opened her car door, asking if they could help.

"I tripped and fell. Could I borrow a cellphone, so I can call my brother? He will come and get me." Safa decided not to send up the alarm, at least not until she had talked with her brother. The woman gave Safa some tissues to help clean up her face, and a cellphone. She dialled her brother, told him she desperately needed a ride, and gave him her location, that was it, nothing else. She knew he would go nuts when he saw her, but better to have a calm Bobbi driving to get her, rather than an enraged Bobbi. There was no thought given to calling either her mother or father. They would lambaste her for going out with Maccha in the first place.

"Thank you for the help. I appreciate it." With that she waved off the couple in the car, preferring to stand alone on the street to wait. She had stopped crying. She was angry now, furious at being blindsided by Maccha. That guy was a piece of work. She needed to convince Bobbi to leave the gang, but how?

* * *

Fifteen minutes later, Bobbi drove up and slowed in the curb lane as he saw Safa. Stopping in front of her, he saw her face as she opened the door to get in and was alarmed.

"What happened?" He saw the bruising start around her left eye, and the dried blood down her cheek, mixed in with mascara. "Are you ok? Should we go to the hospital?" Bobbi was unsure how serious the injuries were.

"I fell, can we just go to your place? I don't think I need to go to the hospital." Safa was tough, no doubt about it in Bobbi's mind.

"Okay, but what happened?"

"I tripped. Let's get to your place first, then I'll tell you." Safa was also smart. She knew exactly how Bobbi would react. Better not to be driving when she told him.

"Let's go, then." Bobbi was skeptical as he looked over at Safa and rested a hand on her shoulder, trying to comfort her as he put his car into gear and headed east, deeper into Surrey. As a gang member, Bobbi had an income that most young people would envy. He was able to afford a two-bedroom condo high in one of the new towers springing up around Surrey Central, the supposed new city centre for the growing metropolis. They headed there. He had an extra bed, so as far as he was concerned, Safa could stay as long as she liked. He knew how controlling their parents were, but if he explained that she was just hanging out with him a couple of days, things would be fine, he hoped.

After they got up to the apartment and some tea was made, Safa finally explained what happened to her. Bobbi predictably blew a gasket and started swearing, making various threats about what he was going to do to Maccha while walking around his living room. Safa remained silent, relieved that he could let off steam in his home, not while driving.

"You should think carefully before doing anything Bobbi. Let it sit awhile, let him wonder." She wasn't sure if this was correct advice or not.

Bobbi paused, looked at her, still fuming, but stopped his ranting. "Revenge served cold?"

"Exactly."

"Also gives me time to figure out how to deal with him." He paused, "I'm really sorry that I allowed this to happen. I wasn't thinking straight."

"Well, I was interested in him at first. I just didn't know what an asshole he was."

After another round of tea, they both decided that they had had enough for one day and turned in. First, Bobbi sent a text to his mom before his parents got more worried. This done, he climbed into bed and started to think about options for dealing with Maccha. It was a long time before he fell asleep.

The next morning, at the cinemas, one of the mall cleaners tasked to do a round of the exteriors and parking lots happened across Safa's purse and brought it into the mall's management offices. Safa's phone was in the purse along with her wallet. The only address noted was her home address, so that is where the call went to. Bobbi had texted his mom the night before to let them know that Safa would be staying with him for a day or two, no reason given. The call from the mall about discovering Safa's purse puzzled her mom. She tried calling Bobbi's phone, but he wasn't answering, too focused on what he would do about Maccha.

~ 15 ~

After his dinner meeting with Edward and the Guru, Jason made a call to the person he used as a cut-out in order to contact Gladys. His man eventually called back and said that Gladys was not answering her texts or phone calls. Concern grew. He tasked the man with contacting Terrance, and to also check the couple's apartment in Burnaby. He then sent one of his watchers into Vancouver to the police headquarters on Cambie Street for any sign of Gladys. He also sent another watcher to Terrance's law firm in Burnaby. It'd be dangerous to surveil the police building as this was not a fifteen minute tour of duty, but probably an all-day assignment. Jason knew that it wouldn't be too long before Edward came calling, demanding to meet the wayward couple, then deal with them. He was starting to sweat.

* * *

At Cambie Street, Thomas Harrow received a call from Deputy Chief McKnight, something that rarely occurred. "Thomas?"

"Yes, Chief." Slight concern noted.

"Word is that some questions have been asked about Siegfried Damler over in Victoria. Are you the one instigating this?"

Thomas felt rattled, trying to gather his wits before answering, "Maybe."

"Siegfried is off limits, got that?" He waited, then, "Making myself clear here?"

"Sir, yes."

"Good." The line went dead. Thomas sat, looking at the receiver before slowly depositing it back on the phone base. It seemed fairly certain that his contact at the Attorney General's office was now off limits as well. He didn't like where this left him.

* * *

Robert Lui spent his day on Cambie Street going through paperwork on his desk while musing about recent events. He wasn't getting anywhere as far as what the triads were really up to. His thoughts then started drifting to food, and what he would make for dinner that evening. The weather was cool, so his best thought was a *penne aux gratin.* He knew Sophie and Robin would love it, and Robin had a hockey practise later that evening, so it could be considered carbo-loading. That is, as long as Robin didn't have five helpings of the pasta dish. He was musing about this when Benton came by his office and peeked in.

"One of those watchers is outside our building."

"What?"

"When we were tailing Jason yesterday at Aberdeen Mall, there were a couple of men doing lookout duty when the Guru arrived for the meeting. One of them is outside, hanging around."

Robert stood up and followed by Benton, went to Thomas's office.

"We've got company, Thomas."

"What do you mean?"

"Benton thinks one of the triad watchers is outside, keeping an eye on our building."

"Thanks Benton, do you mind stepping out for a second, need to discuss something with Robert."

"Sure, no problem. Did you get the pictures we took yesterday at Aberdeen? The guy with Jason?"

"Yes, thanks for that."

Benton left and searched for a coffee station.

"Looking for Gladys is my bet." Thomas said once the door had closed.

"How much did you tell Gladys and her husband anyway?" Robert asked. "Did you explain that they had to be cut off completely from their life for a while?"

"I did that, but who knows if they were paying complete attention. I get the feeling they'll screw up somehow, probably by contacting their family members, and it won't take long, I'm guessing."

"Well, if someone does try for them, we should be watching. Catch them in the act. What do you think?"

"Not sure I have the manpower for that, but it's probably wise. If I was the triad, I would make a move to grab them or kill them." Thomas waited, gauging whether he should broach the Siggy topic, then, "I have been warned off Siggy by the higher-ups. And believe me, I was cautious about who I talked to in Victoria."

"Interesting." Robert sighed, nodded, then left Thomas's office, walking slowly back to his own office. He went over to Benton on his way to thank him for his sharp eyes. But then, this is what they were paying Benton for. Nevertheless, he was on task and Robert liked to acknowledge good work when he could. When he got back to his office, he looked at his desk, but couldn't think of anything further he wanted to accomplish, so he called Camille and headed for the exit, thinking of dinner.

* * *

Once they arrived back at the townhouse, Robert got to work on the pasta dinner, after pouring out some Sauvignon Blanc for himself and Camille. He had Camille fix a salad to leaven the heaviness of the *penne*. Robin and Sophie were happy to hear what was on offer at the table, and for a change, the conversation was animated amongst the four of them.

"I checked your cell plan, and it looks like we could do something. It expired several months ago." Robert directed this at Sophie. He looked over at Robin, whose grin indicated he would be getting Sophie's phone, a small triumph. "Do you know what kind of phone you want?"

Sophie was startled to be asked this. "I have a few ideas."

Robert surmised that these ideas were based on what her friends used. He had a limit on what he was going to spend but didn't let her know this. Instead, he switched gears. "Got all your gear ready, Robin? And I don't know if you should be having that third helping of pasta. I really don't want to see it all over the ice later this evening."

Robin smiled and kept eating. "Our practices aren't that tough. Besides, this is really good, Dad." Robin was playing Peewee level house hockey. It was the age when the players stopped listening to their coaches and did whatever was considered fun, or trouble. This included getting into on-ice fights whenever possible. Robert knew that whatever those poor referees got paid, it wasn't enough.

"Okay Robin, finish up and let's get going."

* * *

Camille tried connecting with Sophie again after Robert and Robin left for hockey. Sophie was studying her phone on the sofa. Camille was dealing with the dishes. "Hey Sophie, do you want to go to a mall this weekend to see about that new cellphone?" She knew this was top of mind for Sophie, but the offer didn't solicit much of a response.

"Maybe." Sophie grunted. "Will Dad come?"

"I thought it would be just the two of us, maybe go for lunch as well. What do you think?" Camille was really trying.

"I think I'll wait for Dad to do it, thanks." Sophie smiled, then rose, turned, and walked upstairs to her room, closing the door.

There was nothing overtly rude about the reply, but there was no way in that Camille could see. She went over and dropped onto the couch, mildly depressed. She had come into this situation expecting that it wasn't likely to be easy, but she hadn't guessed how hard it was turning out to be. Nothing in her life so far prepared her for this. The two children were also teenagers, a time in life when everything went bizarro anyway. She thought back to her time in Montreal, and whether any of her friends had gone through something similar, but nothing. She was the stupid trailblazer here. She decided to call her sister in Montreal to unload some of the anguish on her and see if she had any ideas.

* * *

On the way to the ice rink, Robin and Robert talked about the Vancouver Canuck's chances of getting the playoffs. Robin watched the Canucks whenever he could as all their home games were televised.

"Maybe we should try and take a game in before the season is over, what do you think?"

Robin smiled. "That would be awesome, Dad." There was nothing like attending an NHL game to see just how large many of the players were, and how hard they hit each other.

"I'll try for a Saturday game if I can." Robert wasn't looking forward to the next hour. The novelty of watching the kids do drills and practise plays had worn off, but it was part of being a hockey parent. Some rinks had second-storey restaurants that also served beer and wine, but Robin's home rink wasn't one of those. Robert didn't need the distraction provided by alcohol in public settings anyway, and all the other parents knew what he did for a living, so being a role model was part of the deal. After they pulled into the parking lot, Robert smiled to himself as Robin lugged his huge hockey bag into the rink. He had hauled that bag around and was surprised at how much additional weight the players donned in order to protect themselves. Robert himself, could barely skate, so he was impressed by how quickly Robin had taken to the game, and the fluidity of his skating given all the equipment that he wore.

Two days later, it had become obvious to Jason that Terrance and Gladys had gone to ground somewhere. Neither had shown up at their places of work. Jason's men had confirmed this. Jason had ascertained who the couple's immediate relatives were, so he put a couple of his watchers onto those people as well. His resources were getting strained. The Wide Bay Boys had kept their crew on the small side, keeping potential problems to a minimum. But in situations like this, Jason wished he had more people. Using the Gupils for this task was not allowed by Edward, so Jason had to make do. When Edward had learned of the disappearance of Gladys and Terrance, he had not been amused. It was obvious that the police were involved here in some way. Gladys and Terrance wouldn't have figured out on their own that they were likely in danger.

"Do whatever you need to do but find these people. We need to know what they told the police. And you had better not fail me." These were Edward's words to his lieutenant. Jason was pretty sure his life would be in peril if he failed, so he had impressed upon his watchers the importance of their task. Jason had seen a movie where it appeared as though government agents could track and find anyone through their cellphone use. He bitterly wished he had this capability, but his triad was not that powerful, at least he assumed they weren't. There was no knowing for sure how high up their influence went in China. He knew that very few people would stop using their cellphones, even if they were told to. However, they were in Vancouver, not China, so Jason was doing his search 'old school', tailing people.

A day later, Thomas asked Benton to do some field work. He was told about the safe house in Ladner and who he was to keep an eye out for. To Benton, this sounded like a very boring task, but he decided that complaining about it wasn't going to get him anywhere, so he went to get a fleet car and made the journey down south. He also found out that someone would spell him off, so it could have been worse. Before he left the fleet lot, he gave the car a once over, finding a Kevlar vest in the trunk. He considered this on the sloppy side. Usually, all equipment and armaments checked out had to be returned. He put his service weapon in the glove box, then decided to stock up on a few snacks and refreshments for his assignment.

* * *

After a week of hibernation in Ladner, Gladys was going stir-crazy. She and Terrance were trying to keep a low profile, but the effort was getting old. They had hardly ventured outside their door. The neighbours probably thought that the place was operating as a short term rental suite, what with different people going in and out, so they didn't approach anyone who showed up to stay. Apart from getting groceries and some liquor, the Chus had not gone anywhere.

Terrance had been trying do his work in a remote fashion, which satisfied his partners up to a point. He still needed to meet some clients face to face and was pondering how to accomplish this on the sly. The Burnaby based law firm he worked for had been accommodating so far, but the longer he stayed away, the more of a problem it was turning into. One particular client had been pestering the firm to meet with Terrance, so they called and impressed upon Terrance the need for this to happen. He called the client and arranged to pick him up in front of the office, then head over to a local cafe. This seemed safe enough to Terrance. Shortly before eleven he headed off to Burnaby, picking up the client a half hour later. The cafe was only a block west from the firm. Terrance parked on the street, and they went inside to conduct their business, ordering some coffee and pastries.

A grey Camry had been parked up the street, the occupant noticing Terrance arrive. A half hour later, Terrance came out, got into his car, then pulled out into traffic heading west over to Knight Street, which connected south to one of the few bridges making a crossing of the Fraser River. The grey Camry followed at a distance; the driver satisfied that he had not been noticed. Rain clouds had gathered and were about to let loose with their heavy load. It was commonly understood in Vancouver that the farther south one got from the North Shore Mountains, the less rain there was. Today, however, would be an exception to the rule. It was going to rain everywhere, and hard. The Camry driver would be happy about this as it made his job easier, being able to tail his prey closer than normal.

* * *

Benton saw Terrance leave the townhouse complex at eleven, but remained where he was. His mandate was not to follow everyone all over, but to watch the safe house, so he stayed put. He assumed that Terrance was just stepping out for some groceries. At least it was some action, in what was proving to be the worst duty of his short career.

He was about to leave for some coffee, when Terrance returned, parking in his usual stall. Just as he was about to turn on his ignition, Benton noticed a Camry slowing and stopping on the street. The driver didn't get out, his engine idling. Benton pulled out his binoculars and, bingo! He had no trouble identifying the occupant as one of the watchers from Aberdeen Mall. He swore to himself, wondering how the man had latched onto Terrance. He could see the man talking on his cellphone, so he knew the secret was now out. He dropped lower in his seat, so he wouldn't be discovered himself, and called Robert.

"The Chus are blown. One of the Aberdeen watchers is here as I speak. And I can see him talking on his phone, so...." He trailed off, uncertain what to do next.

"Craps, that didn't take very long. They probably won't waste any time doing something about it. Stay put and I'll get you some backup. Don't reveal yourself. We'll leave that to others." Robert had to think quickly. He made a call to get some cars moving, then ran over to Thomas's office where he told him what was happening.

Then he asked for advice on what they should do. "And I really don't want Benton to reveal himself, unless there is no alternative."

"These people are under our protection. Instruct the backup to intervene on site. No wild chases through the streets of suburbia please." Thomas answered.

Robert left the office and got on the radio to the cars proceeding to the townhouse, to give them their instructions. He also called the Delta Police and asked for a couple of squad cars to attend, but at a distance, no sirens. He then got hold of Benton to advise him what was likely to happen.

Benton stayed put and hunkered down, waiting for the backup. He occasionally lifted his head to observe the Camry, which didn't seem to be doing anything. He pulled his service weapon out of the glove compartment, checked the clip, and flipped the safety off. The Camry's occupant was probably waiting for his own backup before proceeding. Benton was apprehensive about what was going to happen. He was somewhat used to dealing with the regular gangs in the Lower Mainland, but not with triad members. He wasn't sure how they would act, or react, if the police intervened.

***

A dark grey BMW pulled into the parking lot. It had tinted windows. Benton wrote down the licence number and waited. Three men got out and proceeded to the front door of the townhouse where Gladys and Terrance were. Benton couldn't believe that this was happening in broad daylight. These gangsters were either stupid, or desperate. He radioed Robert to tell him what was happening, and Robert relayed the information to the other cars. The ghost cars were almost there, while the Delta cars were waiting just down the street. The three men opened the door by kicking it in. Apparently safehouse doors weren't that safe. Lewis made a mental note to tell Robert about the hardware problem.

After a couple of minutes, about the same time that the front door re-opened and five people came out, the two ghost cars pulled into the lot, doors opening with officers piling out. Meanwhile the two squad cars up the road came alive and careened into the lot. One officer went over to the Camry with a drawn weapon, while the others surrounded the group with Gladys and Terrance. One of the gang members had a gun aimed at Gladys's head. The other two seemed unsure what to do. This uncertainty saved the day as far as Gladys and Terrance were concerned. Five officers stood with drawn pistols aimed at the gang members, and they weren't moving despite the threats from the man with the gun aimed at Gladys's head. His English wasn't on point, so the officers just stood there pretending they had no idea what the man was saying. The officer's behaviour was unorthodox. Usually, it was all about negotiation at a distance, but in this case, all ten people were within a few feet of each other. After twenty seconds of this, the gangster lowered, then dropped his gun as he realized that the officers didn't seem to care whether he blew a hole through Gladys's head or not. He knew that Edward wanted to find out what Gladys knew, so killing her was really not going to happen. Gladys's eyes were as large as they could get without exploding. When the officers rushed in to arrest the three gangsters, she collapsed onto the pavement where she lay, sobbing, while Terrance knelt beside her, offering comfort.

*　*　*

Jason tried to contact his watcher, the one who was tailing Terrance from Burnaby, first by a cellphone call, then via a text message. Neither method worked, so he tried the cell of the man who was in charge of the snatch team sent to reclaim Gladys and Terrance. Nothing. It was as if they had left the country. They always responded. As a result, Jason was concerned that something had gone wrong with the pick-up. That couldn't be. They had just discovered Terrance's location themselves. Unless it was all a set-up, exactly like what the Gupils had walked into in Merritt. Reluctantly, he called Edward, and gave a quick synopsis of what he thought had happened. Edward swore of course, then gave Jason his marching orders.

"Okay, I've had enough. Contact the Guru and tell him to make the grab that I talked to him about. I am tired of playing these games. If they want to play tough, then we will respond in kind. Meanwhile, find out what happened." Edward knew that if this went on, they would shortly be out of gang members and out of business. This wouldn't go down well in Hong Kong. It was fortunate that they had the Gupils to call on to do this type of work.

He congratulated himself on his foresight, forgetting the trouble the Gupils had gotten themselves into recently.

* * *

Back in Ladner, the officers cuffed the four triad members, and took them back to the police station for processing. One of them, the Camry driver, was protesting that he had nothing to do with whatever had happened. The police didn't care. They had found a handgun in the Camry, so accountability would get sorted at the station. The Camry and the BMW were being cordoned off, waiting for forensics to attend, before they would be shipped back to the impound lot.

After they had departed, there was one Delta Police car left and the couple of ghost cars from Vancouver. Benton got out of his car and went over to the group.

He explained who he was. "I'll take the Chus back to Vancouver. They're going to need a new place to live for a while."

The Delta officer responded, "They need to make a statement as to what happened before they return to Vancouver."

"I'll drive them over there and wait." Benton looked at Terrance. "Go get all your stuff. This address is no longer usable." Word was going to get back to whoever was running the gang that they had screwed up. Tempers would be frayed, and Benton wanted out of Delta.

~ 16 ~

In Surrey, it was early afternoon, and the Guru was preparing for the most important and riskiest move of his career as a criminal. He had received his marching orders from Jason. His mission was to kidnap two children, and not just any children, but children of a policeman. All he had to do was to take them and hold them for a while. He didn't even have to deal with the police or deliver ransom notes. Those complicated issues would be handled by Edward. It sounded straightforward, that is, if kidnapping was a normal thing to do. Edward had his own reasons for doing things that went beyond the Guru's understanding. All he knew was that unholy hell would break loose once this was done. He had even considered turning Jason down. The problem was the connections that were generating much of the Gupil's income now came from the triad. Stepping away from that would likely put his own life in danger once the rest of his gang realized the money had essentially stopped flowing. He shook his turbaned head, realizing there was no easy answer to his dilemma. His life before becoming head of the Gupils was starting to look a lot more attractive.

191

He made a call to Manny, then started on his team selection. He decided that on this item, not every gang member would be included. He knew that the police had marked quite a few of his members, they just hadn't caught them red-handed as the Gupils went about their business. So, his solution was to compartmentalize this action. The fewer gang members who knew what was going on, the better for keeping the kids securely. The gang had been monitoring the children's movements, and the Guru needed two teams to do the kidnapping, as they never walked home from school together. Grabbing them on the way to school was out as some days they were driven by Robert or his girlfriend. There was no rationale to when this happened, so after school it was. He assembled his teams accordingly and got hold of two bland panel vans free of windows in the rear cargo area. He had organized the vans a few days earlier in anticipation of what was to come. Satisfied that his teams knew what to do, he sent them off.

* * *

Across the strait in Victoria, the capital of British Columbia, where the government tried to run a province larger than some countries, the Ministry of the Attorney General was making a big deal about mounting a war on money laundering. This only became their latest craze after some intrepid reporting by journalists had brought the problem to light and people started to ask uncomfortable questions. The money washing had been making all kinds of people extremely wealthy for a long time, and was not something to be interrupted, that is, if you wished to live a long and successful life. The government appointed a commission to root out the causes and explain some remedies that could be taken. The commission's real purpose was to lay blame on a few people, preferably politicians from the previous government. This was bound to take a long time and accomplish nothing. It would be a show for the public, like most commissions, while the criminals would make some adjustments and continue with their god-given right to make as much money as humanly possible. The rest of society could go screw themselves. The Wide Bay Boys had managed to plant someone into the Gaming and Enforcement Ministry at a high level, but this was only part of the government's problem. Naked self-interest amongst the bureaucrats and politicians counted for many of the problems rearing their head.

***

Chip Diamond, who worked for Gaming and Enforcement within the Ministry of Attorney General, sat in his office looking out over the inner harbour of downtown Victoria. Immediately below his view, just west of Wharf Street, lay the local float plane fleet. These planes were a handy connection for businesspeople as they transited from downtown Vancouver to downtown Victoria with minimum effort. Victoria and Vancouver were not very far from each other, the problem was that the separation included the expanse of the Salish Sea. Other coastal communities were connected to this transit miracle, but the Vancouver to Victoria run was the busy and profitable link. It was no longer an inexpensive flight. Businesses, as well as the government it seemed, were only too willing to shell out any price the airlines asked for the easy access. Chip immensely enjoyed the view afforded by his office, watching the planes come and go in the harbour when he wasn't busy.

He was feeling self-satisfied as he perused the car brochures on his desk. Audi made so many nice models, he was having some trouble selecting one that he felt complemented his super-engaging personality. He had done a search online, but after visiting the dealership he also had the hardcopy brochures of the cars that interested him. As one of the Assistant Deputy Ministers to the Gaming Branch of government, he was well compensated. However, what he was contemplating purchasing was precious even for that salary.

Chip had a second income stream that almost no one else knew about, and the bonus was that it was entirely tax free. This money enabled him to treat not only his family, but some of his work associates, and more importantly, a few politicians extremely well. He had connections as well in the Ministry of the Attorney General. But, no one was more important than number one. He deserved this car. All he had to do was rein it in a bit, not to get too ostentatious. Chip didn't want people to start asking awkward questions. The model that he really desired, if he had to be honest with himself, was quite expensive, north of a quarter million dollars. He could afford it; this was the galling thing. It would just complicate his life, however. People would start whispering, and he hated whisperers. He and his wife had separate bank accounts, so technically the money shouldn't be a problem, but his wife was another person he didn't want asking unnecessary questions. She hadn't questioned anything so far, including the recent fabulous vacation in St. Tropez. When nice things are happening, there is a propensity not to ask any questions, lest the good times suddenly stop. A couple of the other car models would start tongues to wagging, so he had to dial it back, settling on one of the high-end sedans. Elegant and quick, nearly perfect. Perhaps when he had made some more money, a younger woman might be on order, and maybe a change in venue to a more luxurious and warmer location. Victoria was nice but tended to be chilly in the winter. He'd do some forward thinking about the possibilities soon.

This decided, he focused back onto Jason's latest request. Jason wanted to know where the cash limits were being put in place at casinos across British Columbia. Gangs were known to arrive at casinos with bags of cash that they would exchange for chips. After some gambling, they would suddenly decide it was time to leave, trade in their chips and receive a cashier's cheque for the amount. Suddenly, the money was cleansed of any link to the drug trade. Magic, and it worked every time. If a cashier became uncomfortable with the transaction and took it up with their superiors, they were told to follow orders. Casinos funnelled tons of cash into local municipal governments, keeping tax hikes lower than what they normally would be. This caused a lot of looking the other way when questions started being asked. Chip's other job was to help Jason out with some insider information from time to time, as well as some friendly persuasion to his fellow bureaucrats. For this, he was handsomely compensated.

Life was grand for Chip, no icebergs that he could see. He forgot that icebergs were mostly invisible, a minor detail, at least until he bumped into something unanticipated, and it became a major detail. Chip made a few phone calls, and it wasn't long before he had a short list of casinos out in the hinterland that still seemed to be accepting larger cash amounts when gamblers came a-calling. Jason's associates would just need to do some extra travelling. It would do them good to see the rest of British Columbia, Chip thought. It was a beautiful province, and more people needed to get out and explore it, even if they were criminals.

* * *

In downtown Vancouver, the producer for the radio morning show on the people's network mused about doing a segment on gangs. She was always looking for ideas to help fill the agenda, preferably topics that were current and controversial. The gang issue was one of those never-ending stories and she felt it was time to milk it again. Nothing like getting the listening public riled up about something to boost the ratings. She normally wouldn't consider the gang wars that seemed to be a permanent part of Vancouver's background, but the recent killing of an officer, and the apparent retribution on a gang member had forced the issue onto the front pages. Usually, the sporadic violence was between gang members with the public generally left out of it. But like winter, it always came, regardless of what everybody tried to do about it.

The more she thought about it, the more she liked the idea, maybe get the host out into the community, into the heart of Surrey, where much of the action seemed to take place. The CBC loved going on location, but she could already hear the whining from the citizens of Surrey, saying their city was unfairly represented as being a haven for gangs. Unfortunately, or fortunately, depending on how one viewed these things, Vancouver Asian gang action had died down, so Surrey was the closest municipality where one could reliably say that gangs were active and making news. The show host didn't like going on the road, in fact, he could be a real pill about the whole thing. Luckily, she had some heft in the organization, so her word generally carried the day. She liked the whole idea enough that she put a couple of her minions onto the task of organizing something. With any luck, they might get creative and come up with a new angle on the problem.

* * *

A couple of days later, her team thought they had struck gold. Through a community worker in Surrey, they had been able to contact a former gang member by the name of Dev. He had recently extracted himself from the Gupil gang and was willing to talk about it on morning radio. This was the kind of coup that the other radio stations could only dream about. The gang member had been near the bottom of the totem pole a far as smarts was concerned, so the Guru wasn't overly worked up about him leaving. He had also been on the outside of many of the operations and he didn't know all that much. If he got uppity, the Guru could always have him taken care of.

However, Dev's departure had been noted by a couple of other members; one being Bobbi, the other was Sanji, a newer gang member. The breakout by Dev had given Bobbi some hope about being able to leave himself. Sanji, however had a different view. He thought it treasonous to leave like that. He had spoken to a couple of the other members about it. They agreed, but also knew enough to let it be. The Guru would know what to do about it, and when. What Sanji saw was an opportunity to work his way up the ladder. Being relatively new to Canada, he figured that showing some initiative would be a good way to prove himself. Besides trying to gain respect of his gang mates, he was also working on improving his English. He did this by listening to the radio, in particular, CBC AM, where they talked all day long. It wasn't a bad way to pick up some English. This was how he found out that the traitor would be appearing on the early morning show to discuss gangs. The CBC was promoting the show to amplify ratings. Excellent. Sanji would be there to make his mark, and in doing so, would lift the radio station's ratings off the chart.

* * *

Robin and Sophie usually walked to high school together, if they weren't driven, but came home separately. Today was different in that they were walking home together. They weren't alone either. Sophie walked with her friend, Rose. Robin liked Rose, a lot in fact, but in no way would he let anyone know this. This was why he was tagging along, a little behind the girls. Rose was a couple of years older than Robin, therefore she barely acknowledged his existence. Rose and Sophie were close, like sisters to each other. Rose Esmeraldo grew up in a conservative Filipina family. She had only brothers to contend with. Being protective, her parents had made sure that Rose attended a few self-defence courses, just in case. Ironically, neither Sophie nor Robin had the benefit of such instruction, their father being too caught up in his pursuit of criminals to think about such matters. Even after his two children had been approached to join gangs at school a year earlier, this piece of insurance had not crossed Robert's mind. If it had occurred to Robert, he probably would have cast the thought aside, knowing that chances of a teenager coming out on top against a gangster would be very low.

Today Sophie had dressed up and was wearing a pair of black ankle boots that boasted very solid heels instead of the footwear she usually favoured, sneakers. Sophie and Rose were walking slowly on a side street a couple of blocks from the high school they attended, Robin trailing behind by a good several metres. It was after four and as they ambled along, all three were looking down at their phones, per the custom of half the world.

Robin was vaguely aware of a truck as it went past him, then swerved to a stop with a squeal of the tires. This caught his attention. He looked up ahead at a dark van with no windows as the side door opened and two men jumped out, one after the other. They were wearing what looked like bandannas over the lower half of their faces. In seconds they were on the two girls. Then his attention was diverted by the sound of a second van skidding to a stop right beside him. It looked to be brown. Why he was focusing on the colour was beyond his comprehension because what was happening was alarming in the extreme. He started moving off the sidewalk onto the front lawn of the house he was walking by. Two men jumped out of the second van and grabbed him almost instantly. One wrapped something foul and sweet over his mouth. In seconds, everything went black. One of the men dragged Robin back to the open door of the van, and the second man picked up his feet and they swung him into the back. The two men jumped in, and the van gunned it out into the street, narrowly missing the first van. The men's directions had been very specific; concentrate on their target and don't worry about anything else. However, as he drove by, the driver of the brown van could see that things were not going smoothly for the men from the other van.

The first pair of men were having difficulties. One man pushed Rose away, while the other one grabbed Sophie. They had not been prepared for dealing with two girls. It took about three seconds for Rose to reach into her bag and grab a small can of bear spray. She ran back at the man who had pushed her and started firing the spray at the back of his head. He made the mistake of turning his head to see what was being done to him and caught a face full of the spray. He was blinded by the red hot liquid and doubled over, starting to scream. This startled the second man who had a grip on Sophie. Sophie saw her chance and stomped down hard with her heel on the instep of the man holding her. She heard something crack as he released his hold of her. It appeared that sneakers were not a match for proper shoes. He bent over double while cursing up a storm; the pain hitting the roof of his skull for an instant. The girls saw their chance and ran for their lives, screaming as they ran. It took only a few seconds for the first van's gangsters to realize that they had botched the whole operation. They hobbled into the back of the van, and the driver gunned it out onto the street as its door was being closed. It clipped the corner of a parked car before chasing after the brown van.

The girls ran for a bit then looked back. The vans were gone, so they slowed down and went up to the front door of the next house they came to. While Rose rang the doorbell and hammered on the door, Sophie realized that her phone was back down on the sidewalk where she had dropped it. She hesitated, then ran back to retrieve it.

"What are you doing, Sophie?" Rose yelled. She started to shake as the realization of what had just occurred sank in.

"Getting my phone. I dropped it. I have to call my dad!" She yelled back.

The front door opened slowly to an older Filipina woman dressed in a printed dress of indeterminate age. Rose's Tagalog was sketchy at best, so she spoke English.

"Can you call the police please? My friend's brother has been taken."

The older woman wasn't quite sure what was happening, but she could see Rose trembling in apparent distress.

"Come in please."

Rose realized that she also was without her phone. She must have dropped it when she was pushed aside, "I need to borrow your phone, quickly."

"Yes. Wait here and I'll get it."

Rose got through to 911 as Sophie was walking back up the entry walk. She was starting to cry as she realized what had just happened to her brother, and what had almost happened to her and Rose. After a frustrating minute of the responder establishing the bona fides of Rose, he dispatched a cruiser to the address. The three heard a siren within twenty seconds, rising louder as it approached, but it could have been three days later for all the difference it would make now. Robin was gone. Sophie's call to her dad went to voicemail. After leaving a very hysterical message, the only other idea she had was to try to call Camille at the police station.

"Camille speaking."

"They took Robin!" Sophie was almost screaming at this point.

"What? What are you saying?" Camille could see the name of the caller, it was Sophie.

"Men took him. They kidnapped him. And they almost got me too."

"Where are you? Have you called 911?"

"There is a car coming, we can hear the siren. We were on our way home. We're in someone's house." The sentences tumbled out.

"Who is we, Sophie?"

"Rose is with me. She saved my life I think."

"What address are you at? I'm going to go get your dad and we'll be right there. Don't leave where you are." Camille was already moving, heading down the stairs to Robert's office. When she got to his office, his door was closed, so she swung it open. Robert was on the phone and didn't look pleased to be interrupted. Then he noticed the grim look on Camille's face as she made a slashing motion across her throat.

"I have to go. I'll call you back." Robert concluded.

"They've taken Robin, let's go." Before Robert could even process what Camille had said, she was grabbing him by the arm and they were running to the stairs.

"What did you say?"

"Robin has been kidnapped. We're going to where Sophie is right now. Apparently, they tried for her as well but failed somehow. Cruisers are responding as well."

Robert couldn't believe what Camille was telling him. When they got to the garage, Camille told him that she would drive, afraid of what Robert might do once the news sank in. For a change, she drove very quickly along Broadway.

In the neighbourhood east of Knight Street where Sophie and Rose were, several more squad cars responded, and the street was fast becoming a no-go area.

One of the cars turning up at the scene belonged to a local television station. The reporter tried but failed to get anyone to make a comment on what was happening.

* * *

Camille looked over at Robert as she drove. She was going as fast as she could reasonably go given the traffic, but it felt like ages before they arrived at the street. Robert was grim and didn't say anything until they arrived.

The woman who had let Rose into her home could not believe what was happening. Several policemen were in her living room talking with the two distressed girls. She did the only thing she could think of, and that was to start making some coffee and tea for the group. The next thing she knew, two more people came in and rushed over to hug one of the girls. Must be the parents, she thought. It was at this point that the officer in charge thought it would a good idea to vacate the home they were in, lest details of the obvious upcoming investigation get out. They thanked the woman and walked out her door without sampling any of her refreshments. She looked disappointed to the last officer leaving, but he thought he heard praying as the door closed.

* * *

The officer in charge of the scene knew he had a problem right away with Robert being there. Logic dictated that Robert would be too close to be a part of the investigation. He wasn't even with the VPD at the moment, and this mess was definitely under their jurisdiction, at least for now. But he wouldn't exclude Robert from the questioning for now.

Sophie and Rose explained what had happened from

their viewpoint and gave descriptions of the men they had dealt with, at least as much as they could. The police put out bulletins about the two vans to VPD cars, as well as to adjacent municipalities in the hopes someone might get lucky. Then the police started a canvass of the neighbours to see if anyone had cameras on their porches, or if anybody else had witnessed the events. Several of the houses had cameras. It was just a matter of getting in touch with the owners, many of whom didn't seem to be home. The officer in charge was hopeful that because the men were only covering part of their face; identities could be found out, that is, if any of the cameras had recorded the action.

Robert addressed the commanding officer, "If you are done, we'd like to take Sophie home. We'll also take Rose and drop her at her home as well. I think they have had enough for one day."

He nodded, "Can she come down to the office tomorrow for follow-up?"

"I'll bring her in when she's ready, and Rose as well."

"That would be best."

"I'll call you in the morning and confirm a time." Robert gathered his family, what was left of them, and with Rose, headed to the Silver Streak. They ignored a reporter who tried to pester them for some information. Camille drove over to Rose's family's home. Robert walked Rose up to her front door and waited as Rose opened it and yelled for her mother.

Maria came to the door, worry evident in her eyes. "What's wrong?"

Robert explained what had happened. Maria's eyes

widened in horror as she digested the news, tears starting as she hugged her daughter.

"Rose saved my daughter, Maria. You should be proud of her."

This did little to stop the tears, but Maria searched Robert's face. "Robin?"

"They got him." He looked down, starting to feel shaky himself. "Rose will need to come down to the station tomorrow morning for statements. I'll pick her up, okay?" Did he imagine the hint of reproach in her face? Deserved, he supposed. A talk about the hazards of hanging around with an officer's daughter would be in the offing for Rose.

Maria nodded, then backed into her house, slowly closing the door.

With that, he turned and left, returning to his car. A thousand thoughts were racing through his head, most of them not of the good variety. His stomach felt terrible, as though a knot was twisting it into a crumpled bag.

* * *

Robert said that he would drive home. Camille was starting to worry; Robert had not said a thing to her since leaving the scene. She had never seen him like this. As they neared their townhouse, Robert finally spoke, "You okay Sophie? They didn't hurt you, did they?"

"I'm worried about Robin. No, we didn't get hurt." She started to cry again. Camille put her arms around Sophie. They were both in the rear seats of the car. Sophie surrendered to Camille and buried her head in Camille's shoulder.

"I never should have gone back to the Taskforce." Robert said quietly as he pulled into their carport. Camille didn't know how to respond, so kept silent. Once inside their home, Camille made some tea, and then foraged inside the freezer before pulling out some frozen soup for a dinner of sorts in case anyone was hungry. Robert went into the front den and got on his cell to talk with Thomas.

Thomas answered immediately, "Hello Robert. Is Sophie okay?"

"I think so. She is kind of tough, actually both those girls are. It's probably why they were able to escape. I'm worried sick about Robin though. I don't know why they would do this. It doesn't make any sense to me." He was feeling seriously ill.

"Yeah, if it's about getting at Terrance and Gladys, this is way over the line. If it's something else, I am at a loss. The VPD is hopefully getting some security footage from a couple of nearby homes. We'll see what this tells us, but it seems to be the Gupils from the girl's descriptions." Thomas paused, "We are going to make the Gupil's lives very hard. The word is going out. I expect they will duck for cover for a while."

"You'll find those vans burning somewhere soon." Robert said.

"Yeah. That's my guess as well."

"See you tomorrow, Thomas. I need to call my parents now." As he said this, he contemplated what his dear father would say to him. It didn't help his stomach.

"Right. There are a few things we need to discuss tomorrow." Thomas concluded, but the line had cut out halfway through what he said. He now knew beyond a doubt that having Robert come back to the Taskforce had been a mistake.

The late news on the local television stations led with the story of the kidnapping of a policeman's child. It was a sensation, not that the news people had any clues about the story at all, but they guessed correctly that this was an item that was going to be of extreme ongoing interest for some time. Robert missed the news this night, not needing anything to further stoke his fires. Dreading the expected response, he finally called his father.

"Dad."

Ethan and Mary had already seen the television news story about the kidnapping. "Hello Robert. I don't know what to say, so I'll keep quiet." The unsaid words were already echoing through Robert's mind. "Is Sophie okay?"

"Yes, she's doing as well as you could expect. I'll be taking her down to the station tomorrow for another interview. We'll be doing all we can, but it really is a waiting game. See what they want when they contact us. I hope Robin is okay."

"Call us when you hear something. Is there anything we can do?" Left unsaid was what would happen if nobody called from the other side. Ethan didn't want to broach that with Robert just yet.

"We'll let you know tomorrow, okay Dad?"

"Yes, our prayers are with you and Robin." With that Ethan hung up. Robert sat, looking at the phone, feeling like he should be doing something, but unsure as to what that might be. He looked over at the rear door. Robin's street hockey stick was resting beside the door frame. He prayed that wherever Robin was being kept, that he was being treated well. He concentrated on that stick and willed thoughts to flow through it to his son as though it was a one-way radio transmitter. "I'll come for you Robin."

Robert got up and went into the kitchen to the cupboard where he kept his whiskys. He chose one and poured a generous shot, slid some ice from the freezer into the glass, then slowly went upstairs. As he moved, thoughts were piling through his mind, most of them, not good. There was no way he was going to be bound by whatever police code there was about how to conduct himself in such a situation. Whatever it took to get his son back, he was going to do it. A take-no-prisoner mentality was slowly growing in his mind. And the whisky wasn't proving to be a deterrence to this. As he entered their bedroom, Camille noted the fierce look in his eyes. She guessed correctly that whatever the Vancouver Police Department had in mind for Robert, he would be doing his own thing. She knew that Robert would not be let onto the case, as he was not remotely able to be objective. Well, she knew Robert, and it would be at everyone's peril to dismiss him.

In Surrey's northwest, against the Fraser River, industrial buildings ruled the landscape. Fields of damaged cars sat, the battered remains of every accident that had happened on the roads of the Lower Mainland for years. Warehouses, body shops, some companies that actually made things, and trucking outfits ruled the area. Wharves and concrete plants functioned here. Anything that could use the water as a highway was located at the river's edge. It was desolate, cold, and not a place for humans. As one of the ways to launder drug money, the Guru purchased property from time to time; condos, industrial sites, it didn't matter. One of these places was where the Gupils were keeping Robin for the time being.

The day after the kidnapping, the Guru drove his pickup truck into the parking area beside a small metal building, utterly like every other building in the area. It was the same building where Gurmit had answered questions in several weeks earlier. The difference this time was that the hostage was to be kept alive, on ice, as a bargaining chip to be used by the Wide Bay Boys. To what end, the Guru couldn't guess. He did know however that a lot of pressure was going to be applied to his gang in the next few weeks by law enforcement. He let the word out to all his members to keep their miserable heads down. It was a given that the police would make the Gupil's lives as difficult as possible until Robin was returned to his family.

He walked into the building and surveyed his crew. He had heard about what happened on the East Side of Vancouver. Today, his turban was aubergine.

He tilted his head a bit and chuckled, "Which team was the successful team?" He already knew the answer to his question by Maccha's limp and the decidedly red face of another of his men. He was just being his usual asshole self.

"It wasn't us." Maccha said. He was not having a good week where women were concerned. His balls were still sore from his date gone wrong. Now he had a slight fracture on the top of his foot where Sophie had made a definite impression.

"Refresh my memory, you had the girl to get, correct?"

"Yes." He responded quietly.

"A real tigress apparently."

"She had help." The reply, defiant.

"Another girl if I'm not mistaken." He could discern hints of smiles on some of the other's faces. "They'll be talking about this for ages I think." The Guru neatly summed it up. "It's a good thing Paneet didn't screw up his task. We would officially be out of business if he had." This wasn't strictly true, but the Guru liked to rub it in when he could. "Who has the boy seen?"

"Just me." Paneet responded. "He is shackled in the other room."

"Keep it that way." The Guru considered, then, "You'll be getting a bonus this month. I am thinking of taking it out of the pay for the non-performers."

Paneet thought about this, didn't like it, but kept quiet. Now the other two would be angry at him. As well, gang members sometimes considered what they could get charged with in the unlikely event that they were caught. It was another cause to worry, as all the blame would attach to himself. The extra money was always nice, but he wasn't keen about the babysitting duty. This was bound to cut into his night life.

The Guru's next discussion with the triad was going to be difficult. After some consideration, what he wanted was more money. He was sure that his gang was going to be ravaged by the fallout from the kidnapping, so compensation was due. He fortunately had the bargaining chip in his possession. In his view the triad had made a mistake in using the Gupils to do their dirty work. He assumed Edward would be furious to learn that they only managed to get Robert's son, and not the daughter. But he guessed that getting both the children would have been a bonus and one of them should be sufficient for whatever Edward had in mind. The more he thought about it the less he liked what he had done, and it had nothing to do with morals. Having the police department after you with extra incentive was bad enough, but having the kid's father on the hunt was not going to be pretty. He wished now that he had said no to Edward and suffered the consequences.

Before the Guru left the building, he took Paneet aside. "Make sure you take care of the boy. And do not let him escape or be rescued by anyone. Understand?"

Paneet didn't understand but nodded his assent anyway. Was he supposed to kill the boy to prevent him being rescued? The directions were a little hazy to put it mildly.

* * *

Robin was feeling better, after an awful night. He vomited a couple of times when he came to, the first time on the floor, the second time in the pail when he saw it. Paneet had not been amused and forced Robin to clean up the mess with his hands. Robin didn't know what time it was or where he was. The room he was being kept in seemed to be about three metres square, with a dark green paint job and a stained concrete floor. A single light bulb provided illumination from the ceiling. A cot, a bucket on the floor and a table with a chair were the extent of its furnishings. A bottle of water was on the table. It didn't take a genius to figure out that his being in this room had something to do with his father's work, but he didn't know what the specific reason was. It was cold, not freezing, but not Hawaii either. He shivered.

The Guru left the building, got into his truck, and went back south to his club to make the call to Edward. He had acquired a certain amount of paranoia over the years and tried to avoid using his cellphone for important calls when he could. He had forgotten about old-fashioned phone taps, which used to be the preferred way by law enforcement to find out what other people were up to.

The club's phones were not presently tapped, as far as he knew.

He went into his private office and sat down in his leather chair, like some senior executive of bad things. He studied the phone for a few moments, then summoned his courage and made the call to Edward.

"It's about time you called me." Edward started in.

"I was checking on the boy, and I don't like using a cell for important calls."

"How come you didn't get the girl as well? I saw the news. You guys are incompetent."

"That may be, but we have the boy. I assume one child will be enough for you."

"Don't assume anything with us."

"Fair enough, however I have been thinking. I will need some more compensation for this. My gang is going to be savaged by the police, so I think it only fair."

Edward could not believe his ears. The effrontery of this man to renege on an agreement with a triad spoke to an ignorance of consequences. Then it got worse.

"As you will note, we have the boy." This was followed by silence while Edward considered his options. He decided to project an aura of businesslike calm despite the obvious threat. He knew that he could always deal with the Guru later after the triad had what it wanted. And right now, the Gupils had the bargaining chip, not the Wide Bay Boys.

"What do you want?" Edward posed the million-dollar question.

The Guru had been thinking about a number, and

eventually he realized he should have asked for twice as much as what he had originally agreed to, so he took this number and doubled it, being no stranger to negotiations, "I'd like an extra half million."

"You must have rather large balls to make a request like this."

The Guru didn't answer, but waited, expectantly.

Edward sensed that this man wasn't going to be the patsy that he first appeared to be, "I'll give you an extra one hundred thousand. That is way more than some other groups would have done this for, I remind you. In fact, I could get someone killed for less." This last item was the obvious threat it was meant to be. However, the Guru was not to be dissuaded this day.

"A quarter of a million more, and we will deliver the boy to you."

Edward knew he was being played here, but he needed that boy for his masters overseas, "Okay, you will get your money. I will be in touch." With that, the connection was severed. Edward was angry, but he put his feelings aside and thought about Hong Kong.

After the call was finished, Edward telephoned Jacky in China, "We have one of the Lui kids. We can send the message if you wish." It was 6:30 in the morning the next day in Hong Kong.

"I thought you were going to get both of them."

"It didn't work out. We got the boy."

"The boy is good, but I am not very impressed with your work. I have decided to send Ivy over to deliver the request in person. She is leaving shortly and will be there in about fifteen hours. Do not harass her. She will make her own arrangements when she arrives in Vancouver. Afterwards she will meet with you to get an update on your business there."

Edward thought this over. Not sending any message to the police would drive them crazy. It might even cause them to do something unexpected; maybe not the police, but quite possibly Robert Lui. Then there was the 'update'. Hong Kong obviously had little trust in Edward, so he'd handle Ivy with care, once she appeared.

***

After a night of not sleeping, Robert got out of bed, feeling drained. Moving slowly, he called out to Sophie to get her awake, then went to take a shower. They, along with Rose, were expected down at police headquarters. After both Camille and Robert were dressed, they sat at their dining table across from one another, sipping coffee quietly, waiting for Sophie to get ready. Robert made a couple of calls, first to the high school to confirm what the administration already knew, Robin and Sophie would not be attending for a while. Then he called Rose's mother to arrange to gather Rose. Maria wished to attend with her daughter, so the car was full. On the drive, Robert was quiet, but Camille knew he was seething inside, probably revisiting every decision he had made over the last several months.

***

After they arrived at the Cambie station, the girls were

led into a conference room by another female officer where they were given some drinks before the interviewing started. Robert and Camille were asked to go to Thomas's office. Maria was shown the waiting area and given some tea.

After they sat across from Thomas, he started. "How are the girls, Robert?"

"They seem okay, considering." Robert responded.

"And how are you two holding up?"

"Okay, I guess."

"I know that can't be right." Thomas searched Robert's eyes, "I have a full team working on this with the main VPD investigation, you should know that, Robert."

Robert just nodded, waiting for what he knew was coming.

"You understand that you can't be part of this investigation, correct?"

"Not a surprise."

"Neither can Camille. She is too close."

Robert and Camille looked at each other. Nothing said so far was unexpected, but it hurt all the same.

"Have you heard anything yet?" Camille asked.

"Nothing. The vans were found early this morning. They weren't burnt and are being transported to the forensic garage."

"Where?"

"North Surrey, by the water. A trucking firm called it in to the RCMP. They noticed the vehicles in their compound. The caller hadn't heard about the kidnapping but said there is always something unusual going on in that area of the city, so they check their lands daily as a matter of course."

"What do we do now?" Robert did not in the least want to be asking this, but he knew it was expected of him. And he knew the answer before Thomas opened his mouth. He just wanted to force Thomas to say it to his face.

"Take some time off Robert. You're not going to be much good to the Taskforce the way you are. We'll keep you informed."

Robert knew this last item was a lie, and there; he had heard the expected, 'Get out and leave us alone to do our work'.

"Any idea why they did this?" Robert asked.

"No. If you have any, let us know."

Robert signalled to Camille, they got up and left the room without saying anything to Thomas. Thomas sat at his desk, feeling like the cad that the force's bureaucracy demanded he be.

After Robert and Camille left the office, Robert ignored the questioning looks from some of officers and administration people that he worked with. He walked up a floor with Camille, who still had a job to do.

"I'll wait here for Sophie and Rose to finish up, then take them home." Robert said.

Camille looked at him, knowing how hurt he was by the talk with Thomas, "Yes, a good idea. I'll make my own way home. Try not to worry too much." She knew how lame that sounded.

Robert then made his way over to the admin person outside the interview room and raised his eyebrows.

"I think they will be a little while longer, Robert."

"Ok, I'm going to step out for some coffee, be back in a few moments." He left the building and made his way up to the comfort of Cafe Paulo. When Robert entered the cafe, Gilberto noticed him right away and beckoned him over to the counter. He reached across and put his hand on Robert's shoulder, "Roberto, I heard about your son." He said quietly.

"I appreciate the concern, thanks Gilberto."

"You'll get the bastards, right Roberto?"

Robert smiled thinly, "I hope to." He was suddenly unsure about coming to the cafe. What he wanted was to be anonymous, not to be pitied.

Gilberto pulled a double shot espresso and slid it across the marble top. He held up his hand when Robert made to pay. "No Roberto, please. If there is anything we can do...." his voice trailed off.

Robert nodded and went over to his favourite seat. As he looked out the window, he started to do what he should have done a day earlier, that is, to think. Enough feeling sorry for himself and his family. If he was going to get Robin back, he was going to need some leverage with this gang. And so far, he didn't even know which gang had done the deed, or even why Robin had been taken. His guess was that the Gupils were behind it. The lack of any communications was also worrying. Usually when someone wanted something, they let you know what it was, especially with police scouring every bit of the Lower Mainland, putting pressure on known associates of any gang member. He shook his head, finished his coffee, and stood up, tipping his head slightly to Gilberto as he left the cafe.

After Robert returned to the police station, he collected the two girls and headed home. Sophie wanted to spend the rest of the day with Rose, so he dropped them off at Rose's house, and asked Sophie to let him know when she needed a ride home. Back at the townhouse, he made a short list of who he could trust at headquarters. He was going to need some surreptitious help, and going through Thomas would be a waste of effort. The one officer with the VPD he knew who could help would be Tony. Camille could be the cut out, as they still worked together on Vancouver cases, and the investigation was the property of the Vancouver Police proper, not the Taskforce. The other person he felt he could trust was Troy Geelham out in Richmond. He put some water on the stove to make coffee, then went to sit in the living area where he stared at the ragged garden beyond the glass.

* * *

Over at the CBC offices in downtown Vancouver, excitement was building for the morning show producer. The latest developments only heightened interest in the gang topic, even if there was no actual evidence that a gang was behind the kidnapping. Facts never got in the way of a good story, so she was putting the final touches on the plan to do a remote broadcast the next week, on Thursday. This would give the minions time to make their final site preparations and for some advertising to hype the show.

The production was going to be held in the grand entry lobby of the Simon Fraser University campus in central Surrey. This campus for SFU was actually a second choice for the building owners. Originally, an exciting new university, designed to be one of the largest in Canada for arts and applied arts was to be the tenant, that is, until the government of the day decided not just to cancel the project, but the whole university. It took time but eventually SFU was lured into making a Surrey presence, one they would not regret, given the rate at which Surrey was growing.

The producer was mulling over sending the weather person along with the morning host. She could talk about gangs and weather, as if that made any sense. It would be nice to get them both out of the CBC building for a day. Arrangements were made with Dev to make his appearance. Sanji, being the attentive English student as he listened daily to the broadcasts, began smiling as he understood when and where Dev the traitor would be appearing. He could hardly wait. Sanji had received instructions to keep his head down, but he also knew that initiative was usually rewarded in the gang.

After finishing his coffee, Robert got fidgety and decided a road trip was needed. He couldn't sit around in his home doing nothing, so he got into his car and after threading through his neighbourhood, headed south, eventually heading to Richmond to visit Troy in the RCMP detachment there. Troy sat with Robert in his office and calmed him as much as he could.

"There is always a reason behind their moves, even if it

is a stupid or hard to fathom reason." Troy started, "They will be letting you know soon enough."

"I know, I know. I just don't know why they picked my family."

"I agree. It's not like you know any of those people personally, do you?"

"No." He looked down at Troy's desktop.

"If I hear something I'll let you know Robert, you know that right?"

"Thanks Troy. I'll stay in contact. Think I'll go out to the dyke for a while."

Troy's promise to keep Robert in the loop wouldn't be countenanced by Thomas, but Troy liked Robert and the friendship would win out. Thomas could go to hell if he thought Troy would keep Robert out in the cold.

* * *

That decided, Robert left the RCMP detachment and headed west on Steveston Highway, until he came to one of the roads connecting south out to the dyke edging the Fraser River.

Eventually, Robert pulled into a parking lot along the edge of the river but stayed in his car, facing south, watching the wind ripple across the foreshore grasses in silvery jade waves. Rows of metal-capped black pilings with a couple of seagulls atop each of them marched well out into the Fraser River, broken and splintered by decades of weather; grouped in two pairs, like long-legged lovers tied to each other, but decapitated at the waist. They were the remains of long abandoned wharves.

Tide was at an ebb, the wet sand stretching in dips and banks up to the edge of the moving channel hundreds of feet away. Robert looked up and saw two eagles cutting large arcs on the thermals, wings not working at all, looking for easy pickings on the shore, or in the river itself. Today they were not being harassed by gulls or crows, who typically wouldn't shy away from making the much larger bird's life hell. The gulls seemed content to sit on the pilings, ignoring the larger birds above them. To the southeast a sleeping, snow-covered Mount Baker stood on guard over Washington State and the Fraser Valley. Robert's car was stopped just east of Steveston atop the dyke. He looked west at an island just across from the shoreline. It was originally a sandbar that had been enlarged around the turn of the 20th century by dredging and ship after ship from countries all over the world dropping ballast before picking up full loads of canned salmon. A line of rocks appeared to connect the island to the mainland at its eastern tip. The rocks had a darkened patina that spoke of being underwater half the time from the tides. The island itself had become forested over the years but was inaccessible most of the time due to the tidal movement of the river. Beyond the line of rocks, Robert could discern some masts belonging to fishing vessels, all part of Steveston's fleet.

* * *

Robert wasn't the only driver sitting on the bank of the dyke in the long parking area gazing south, but he suspected he was the only one with a kidnapped son to worry about. Watching a river roll by seemed to be good for sorting one's life out, and the larger the river, the larger the problems it could handle. This last item was a theory, but it made sense to Robert. He rolled his window down and could smell the foreshore grasses. The sun warmed the interior of the car. He came to the obvious conclusion; whatever it took to get Robin back, he was going to do, career be damned. Shaking his head, he knew he should head back into Vancouver to go pick up his daughter and see if they had any food in the house worth eating for dinner.

~ 18 ~

The next morning, Ivy Sun was sitting in the business class cabin aboard a Cathay Pacific flight, bound for Vancouver from Hong Kong. She reviewed her instructions from Jacky before crashing out for some midflight sleep. The stewardess in charge of the cabin was pretty sure that Ivy was a movie star that no one knew the name of. Subsequently, sleeping Ivy became the topic of heated debate in the galley amongst the other flight attendants.

Edward was in his home, a penthouse condominium in central Richmond, counting his troops. The problem was that he only needed one hand to do this. Things weren't going well. He had lost three helpers in that screw-up of a snatch attempt on Gladys and Terrance in Ladner. They had preliminarily been charged with attempted kidnapping and had not yet been released on bail. The fourth man on site, who had tailed Gladys to her hideout, had been released, as his only sin was having a weapon in his glove compartment, for which he had a permit. He had one other young man who he had not yet decided on whether to admit to the inner workings of the triad. If he needed more men in a hurry, he was going to need to talk to Jacky in Hong Kong. The problem was that Jacky didn't like sending men over to Vancouver; they had a propensity to want to stay once they found out how nice Vancouver was. The only thing that Jacky had going for him was that Vancouver's night life was dead boring by comparison to Hong Kong's; not a small thing for a gangster who liked to show off and spend money.

* * *

Edward made a call to the triad's lawyer to find out when the three men in remand might be released. After all, this was their first detected offence. The three had no convictions that Edward was aware of, but that didn't mean they were unknown to police. The lawyer told him that their position was that the three were merely asking Gladys and Terrance out to lunch. They didn't seem to have any comment on the bashed in entry door, or the waving of guns in the couple's general direction when the police arrived, so until the police sorted through the various stories, the three were going to remain in remand. However, someone was going to need to come up with a convincing argument to the judge for them to remain in custody. A Vancouver prosecutor assigned to the case was working with Thomas to present the best story they could to hold them without letting out too much of the Taskforce's investigation into the open. The judges made the law enforcement side of things work really hard to prove their case each and every time—everybody innocent until proven otherwise. Edward thought he would have his three men back soon, but until then, he might have to lean on the Gupils a while longer. He found this prospect distasteful after the number of times they had screwed up, but he saw few other options.

Edward's next move was to get Robin out of the Gupil's hands so that he had control of the situation, not the Guru. To that end, he was arranging the agreed payment to the Gupils after the blatant extortion call from the Guru. Ivy was due to land in Vancouver any time, and he had to be prepared to do whatever she requested of him. She was like some consular official or ambassador from Jacky and had to be treated as such. Edward didn't really feel like explaining to Ivy why Robin Lui was not in his hands.

To finalize things, he needed a place to stash Robin, and a minder so that Robin didn't wander off. The place was not a problem; he had a leased maintenance shed in a harbour area of Steveston that could be used. The baby-sitter was trickier with his limited manpower. In the end, he decided to leave the problem to Jason after staring out his living room window for half an hour. His view was west, over the Oval, another leftover building from the 2010 Winter Olympics that had hosted the long track speed skating. He liked the view but had to admit it was getting eroded bit by bit with all the additional residen-tial buildings going up along this arm of the Fraser. Pretty soon he was going to need to move his home, to get the better view that he used to have and deserved again.

* * *

Over in North Surrey, Robin was feeling somewhat better. He had shaken off the sick feeling left over from the ether that had been used to kidnap him. He wasn't close to one hundred percent, but being a bit of an athlete helped him recover quicker than some would have. Two things consumed his mind at the moment: how bored he was, and how he was going to escape. Luckily, the escape dilemma won out. He was sitting on a metal chair, his right wrist tethered with a lengthy chain to a metal table that seemed to be securely bolted to the concrete floor. An empty takeout container that had contained a basmati rice concoction was sitting on the table beside a half full bottle of water. At least they weren't starving him, Robin thought. The old cot sat by the wall. He had lain on it, but it was extremely gross, probably filled with bugs.

His minder was not in the small room. He was next door; at least that is what Robin assumed. The times he needed to go to the bathroom, he yelled at the door, and it opened to reveal Paneet. The toilet room was adjacent, but he had to leave the prison cell to get to it. Paneet released the tether from the table and brought him to the toilet room. The first time he had requested to go, he glanced at the immediate area. Paneet was living in style compared to Robin; he had a couch, a low table with some magazines and what looked like a small computer on it. A table and a couple of chairs were a little farther off with the evident remains of a much different class of meal than what had been served to Robin. There was also a small space heater adjacent to the couch. It looked to be a kerosene type model, which got Robin to thinking. He also needed to scope out the rest of the room to see where a possible exit was, and whether Paneet was alone, or had unseen help.

One thing on his side was that Paneet wasn't very large. He didn't look like some of those pictures Robin had seen on the television of thugs from Mexico, Columbia, or even some of the infamous gangsters from up the Fraser Valley that were in the news. Those people were truly scary looking. Paneet was thin, wiry, and not much taller than Robin. The best thing Robin would have going for him would be the surprise factor. He assumed that the kidnapper knew far more about fighting than he did. The only fighting Robin had done was on the ice, and that was only twice, with no clear result.

Nothing in Robin's short life had prepared him for this, so he needed to think things through before he tried anything. At least he had the intelligence to come to this conclusion. He was sure that he would have one shot at this. If he failed, things would likely get harder for him. One other thing he assumed—he'd been taken because he was to be traded for something. What that was, was a mystery. It couldn't be about money because his family was strictly middle class and didn't have much money. If they did, he was pretty sure his family would be living in their own house instead of renting it from someone. It was likely something else, probably related to what his father did with the Taskforce.

* * *

Ivy Sun's flight landed at YVR, Vancouver's airport in Richmond, just after six in the evening. She had slept on the flight but was tired none the less. She found travel fatiguing, no matter how easy the airlines tried to make it. After clearing customs without trouble, she exited the terminal and arranged for a town car to take her to the Fairmont hotel on Vancouver's waterfront, a trip that took about forty minutes going against rush hour traffic. She had considered staying at the hotel attached to the airport, but knew she would be dealing with Ethan Lui, who resided in Vancouver, so Coal Harbour it was. She enjoyed visiting Vancouver, having been to the city several times. Ivy found it a relaxing break from the frenetic pace of Hong Kong. She checked in, towing her small carry-on suitcase, and went up to her room. She looked out the window at the view of the North Shore Mountains and Burrard inlet. Relaxation immediately started to set in. She was using her own name this trip, after all, she was merely conveying a message, and checking up on the locals. She expected to be in town for a couple of days at most.

After opening her suitcase, she undressed and donned the luxurious bathrobe provided by the hotel. She then perused the menu for room service before choosing a selection of sushi and some miso soup. She liked to eat lightly when she travelled, it helped the body adjust to being somewhere else entirely. After she ordered her food, she sat in the guest chair in front of the large picture window and pulled a manila folder out of her briefcase. It contained a two-page history and description of Ethan Lui along with an old picture that must have been taken twenty years earlier. She studied the picture. He was a handsome man, no doubt about it, with steel grey eyes. He was standing in his whites at the side of a banquet table where some men and women were drinking, with the remains of a meal strewn across the table. It was obviously a high-end restaurant in Hong Kong somewhere. She didn't recognize anyone else in the photo, but it was taken a long time ago. She had been a teenager when this had happened, her life not mapped out yet. She re-read the bio in the file and noted Ethan's contact information. She planned to sleep tonight and deliver the message the next day in the morning. If everything went as planned, she expected to be on a Cathay flight the following afternoon, flying west back home.

A knock sounded on her door. She answered and her dinner was placed on the table by a smiling young man. He was smiling because he hadn't realized he would be delivering food to what was obviously a movie star, he just couldn't place her was all. Movie people often stayed at the hotel and were always the topic of discussion amongst staff. After he departed, Ivy sat down at her table, contemplated the food, and the task that awaited her the next morning. After finishing the delicious sushi, she decided a bath would help her to relax. She filled the tub, slipped out of her bathrobe and underwear, stared at herself critically in front of the mirror. Not bad, she thought, before she went to the tub and slid into the hot water.

* * *

Robert Lui had spent that morning at home thinking and waiting for any news of Robin. There had been nothing. It had been decided that the two girls would have one more day off school, so they spent the day with Robert in the townhouse. Camille was at work in the police station, but as far as she knew, no news had come in. The camera footage from a couple of the adjacent homes near the action had revealed nothing of value. Robin's cellphone and knapsack had been recovered from the scene by the sidewalk where he had been taken. Tracking his cellphone to possibly find his location was not an option. The police had taken and examined the two vans, and little was found inside that would link to any known criminals. The gangsters had used gloves, and apart from fibres, there were no fingerprints or blood for that matter. The men doing the abduction were going to be hard to identify because their faces were half covered, but a couple of detectives were working on this. As far as she was aware, there had been no contact made by whoever had kidnapped Robin. She was working on her embezzlement case but was finding it extremely hard to concentrate. In the end she gave up and left the office at about half past three, heading home to be with Robert.

* * *

At about this time, a meeting started in the Vancouver Police Chief's office. Present were Caleb Woo, the Chief Constable for Vancouver and his Deputy, David McKnight. Also in attendance were the two heads of the Major Crime and Organized Crime divisions. The last person in the room was Steve Christie, the intrepid leader of the detectives working in the trenches. The meeting would have taken place eventually, but after a 'helpful' question from the Mayor to the Chief as to what was being done about the kidnapping, Caleb decided to find out exactly what was going on. The four senior administrators were staring at Steve, waiting to be illuminated by his handling of the situation. Steve was uncomfortable in the extreme, not being prepared for the inquisition. He usually counted on having more lead time. The police board, which represented civilian oversight, and which the mayor chaired, had been asking Caleb pointed questions which he felt only his duty to kick down the chain of command until they landed at the feet of Steve.

"What is happening Steve? I don't think we need to remind you how embarrassing it is to have a policeman's child kidnapped off the streets of Vancouver. It makes us look a little on the weak side, don't you agree?" This opener came from the Chief, "Was this Robert Lui fellow part of your department?"

Steve was relieved to have an easy question to answer while he was frantically searching the depths of his mind for some way out of this mess, "He used to be under me last year, but he transferred back to the gang unit a few months ago. You may remember the Eden Gardens case? He was the lead detective on it."

Caleb remembered all too well the social ruckus the case had caused on the west side of Vancouver, but was cagey in his reply, "I seem to recall something."

Steve's brain at last kicked into life, of a sort, "We have a full team on this case and are exploring all leads."

Caleb smiled unpleasantly, "We're not the press here. I don't want to listen to crap. I want the real story."

Steve swallowed. His mouth was unaccountably dry,

and there were no refreshments in sight, "We don't really have any leads so far, and the kidnappers have not contacted us or Robert." He paused, then added, "As far as we know."

"What the fuck does that mean?" Caleb leaned forward. All the people in the room had children, so the concern was not academic.

Steve was starting to sweat, "We took Robert off the case, as well as his partner, Camille, who works in my department. Robert is on paid leave, and we have not heard anything from him. We think gangs are behind this."

"Do you now? Did you come up with this explanation on your own, or did your group suggest it?" The sarcasm was getting pretty heavy, Steve having dug himself about a metre down into the ground. He remained silent while he tried to marshal what few remaining thoughts he possessed.

Caleb continued, "You want to hear what I think you should do?" He was glaring at Steve, who wisely waited some more, not wanting to finish off his own grave.

"You had better get your best people on this. We really don't want open season on police children, do we?" Caleb's face was on the dark side at this point, as he tried to restrain his anger, "Get out. I want some progress on this case the next time we meet." Steve nodded and almost ran from the room.

Caleb looked at the two heads of divisions while he shook his head, "Is this the best you have gentlemen? I am not filled with confidence at this point. I'll spin some bullshit to the mayor for now, but we are going to need some results soon. Can one of you get me a summary of this detective, Robert Lui please? I want more details about this man." With that directive, the meeting was ended.

* * *

The next morning at about nine Ethan Lui received a phone call at home. Mary picked up the phone, then called Ethan who was drinking tea while reading the morning paper in the dining area.

"A woman on the line for you, Ethan."

"Who is it, Mary?" Not many people called Ethan anymore.

"No idea, she wouldn't give a name."

Ethan went into the kitchen, "Hello?"

"Is this Ethan Lui?" In Cantonese.

"Yes, who is this?"

"It doesn't matter. I am calling because I would like to meet you about a matter of mutual concern."

Ethan sat down. Mary saw his face darken. She suspected maybe this was about Robin but was uncertain.

"Is this about Robin?"

Now she was certain.

"Victoria Restaurant, downtown, one hour. Come alone." She hung up.

Ethan sat, dumbfounded. How was he mixed up in this? After a couple of seconds reflection, he knew exactly how he was involved; his past was surfacing. His first thought was to get in contact with Robert, but no way was he going to call him. He thought the VPD might be listening.

The caller had said come alone. He was going to comply. He would call Robert after the meeting.

"Who was that, Ethan?" Mary asked.

"The kidnappers, I think. But I am not certain. She spoke Cantonese. I am to go to the Victoria Restaurant downtown. It is in the base of one of those large hotels if I am not mistaken. She did not mention anything else, not Robin's name, nothing."

"Are you sure you shouldn't call Robert?"

"He will do something crazy, I think. I'll go and meet her to see what this is about. It is a very public place. I need to get going, the meeting is in one hour." He went to the front closet and retrieved his coat. He looked at Mary as he got ready. "I'll call from a public phone when I am done. Don't call anyone please. I am worried about our phones."

Mary looked at him after he said this, wondering if he was going to be as paranoid as their son. Ethen left the building and walked hurriedly north to Hastings Street to catch a bus heading downtown.

About a half hour later he exited the bus, then walked a couple of more blocks to the designated restaurant. He stood in the lobby, looking out across the large Chinese restaurant. A woman sitting against the far wall stood up and beckoned him. Two thoughts crossed his mind as he moved towards her, the first was that she was bloody beautiful, and the second was that she knew what he looked like. He didn't like what that implied. As he walked over, she sat down, waiting.

"Please sit. Would you like some tea?" Ivy started in Cantonese.

Ethan sat but remained silent, staring at her with his intense gaze. She felt some pressure at this lack of response.

"We are meeting like this because I don't trust phones. As you may have guessed, this is about your grandson. We are requesting Winston Chang be at the exchange." She stood up.

"That's it? Is Robin ok? What exchange? Why Winston?"

"Call this number tomorrow morning if you have arranged it. One word will suffice—yes. You will receive instructions after that. And don't involve the local police." With that, she turned and walked out of the restaurant.

Ethan thought about following her but was unsure. What if she had minders? She was gone in seconds anyway. The opportunity was missed. He got up and asked for a public phone. The waitress looked at him oddly, who used public phones anymore? She directed him to the hostess who let him use her phone at the hostess station if he was quick about it.

He called Mary, "It is about Robin, and Winston. I am going to text Robert to come over. I'll be home in about forty-five minutes." He hung up quickly. The entry was filling up with hungry customers, and he wanted to get out of there. He left the restaurant and stood in the mall against a wall while he sent a message to Robert.

Winston from Hong Kong? Mary didn't know any other Winston. Her mind was whirling as she started hitting the dining room table with the flat of her hand. She could not believe what was happening to her family.

* * *

Robert was perplexed at the text he had just received.

"Camille, I am going over to Dad's place for a visit. He was going to come by here, then backed out. Something is not quite right." He swallowed the remainder of his coffee and stood up.

"Shouldn't you call him and ask?"

"No, if he didn't call, there must be a reason. He rarely texts anyone." He went up to his room and picked up his guns, both of them along with their holsters, then looked at himself in the mirror. He looked like crap. He fastened both guns to his body, then returned back downstairs. Camille saw the SIG Sauer and immediately became concerned.

"What do you think is going on?"

"Don't know. That is why I am going prepared. I'll text if things are ok. I'll say something like, 'will stop for milk on the way home' something along those lines."

Camille stood there, knowing why Robert was scared, but wondering if he was going over the edge with his fears.

"Just take it easy driving over there, okay? I am going to head off with Sophie to school and then take the bus into work."

Robert smiled, the first time he had done this in several days, even if it was a bit forced.

"Rodger dodger." With that he walked out the door.

Robert sped east to where his parents lived in a condominium on Renfrew Street. He parked on the street and sat there, watching for anything unusual. After five minutes he got out and went up to the lobby door and got buzzed in.

As he entered the suite his eyes met his mother's.

"You have heard something."

"Yes, a lady called your dad to meet downtown, but didn't tell him what it was about."

"Why didn't he call me?"

"I don't think he was sure what it was about and wanted that before telling you."

Robert was silent. Mary came over and hugged him.

"Let's see what he says, he should be home any minute now."

Ten tense minutes went by before Ethan walked in the door.

"What happened?" Robert asked.

"I met this Chinese lady at the Victoria Restaurant downtown, and she didn't say very much, but it concerned Robin. She said she wanted Winston Chang at the exchange, and that if I arranged it, I was to call a number tomorrow morning and say yes. That was it, she up and walked out." After a pause he added, "And don't involve the police."

"What? Exchange of what for Robin?"

"That wasn't clear. Since you are on leave, I guess I am following her instructions about the police. She spoke Cantonese the whole time."

Robert sat down at the dining table. "Sounds like a triad."

Ethan nodded. Robert looked at Mary and gave her a wrinkled smile while he wiggled his hand with his thumb and little finger sticking out. She knew exactly what he was signing for, some coffee. She went into the kitchen to put more water on.

"Not a lot to go on." Robert said. "Can you contact this Winston Chang, ask him if he would come over?"

"I will, but you realize that once I ask him, word will get out—at least I think it will. People are going to notice if a Chief Inspector ups and leaves for Canada suddenly."

"This whole thing sounds funny, doesn't it?"

"Yes, but for Robin's sake, I am going to make the call to Winston. I believe he will come. He thinks he owes me a life debt."

"How?"

"I suppose I saved his life. It was just before we decided to emigrate permanently."

This was news to Robert. "I should try to meet this woman. Do you think she is local, or from Hong Kong?"

"I believe she is from Kowloon from the way she spoke."

"Hmmm." Robert stared into nothing, motionless, then started a bit when his mother brought the coffee to him. "We should assume that the VPD will be watching us somehow. If they aren't yet, they soon will be."

"That is what I thought Robert. It is why I texted you instead of calling."

Robert smiled at his father, grateful that his parents were no one's fools.

"I wonder what they want, other than Winston?" Robert said slowly. "I am going to attend this meeting tomorrow if you can set it up. When you call her tomorrow; just say Victoria Restaurant, 11:00 am., nothing else, then hang up. Call her around ten so she doesn't have time to think. I will go there early and arrange to rent a side room. You will need to be there because you know what she looks like."

Ethan looked at Robert but knew his son would not be dissuaded from whatever he thought would save his child. He could not blame him, rather, he was proud that Robert was swinging into action.

Robert finished his coffee, then excused himself, wanting to get back to Camille with the news, "Let me know somehow if you are successful with Winston." With that, after kissing his mother, he departed, eyes darting every which way as he made his way back to his car. In the car, he texted Camille to say he would pick up milk, then drove home.

After Ivy had walked out on Ethan, she decided to do some shopping to kill the day off. She'd contact the local Wide Bay Boys after she finished with Ethan but would call Cedric to report once she returned to her hotel room. She walked over to Howe Street and visited the Holt Renfrew store, a high-end Canadian retailer. Ivy was basically window shopping, not finding anything very special, at least to her standards. After an hour of this she wandered over to Alberni Street where the smaller, more exclusive shops such as Hermes and De Beers were located. She treated herself to a scarf from Hermes before heading back to the waterfront for a stroll along the seawall just north of her hotel.

After walking for a while along the edge of Coal Harbour, watching the float planes come and go, she decided she had had enough fresh air, and thought she'd better report to Cedric. It would be early morning in Hong Kong, but too bad. At least Cedric hadn't had to come halfway around the world to perform this stupid task. She often wondered what those Wide Bay Boys used for brains. In her view the message could have been delivered in so many easier ways.

Back in her room, she briefly considered using her cell to call Cedric, but instead used the hotel phone. It rang several times before a groggy Cedric answered it.

"Wake up sleepy head."

"What time is it."

"Time you should be up." Ivy knew enough not to use names when on the phone.

"What do you have to report?"

"Message delivered to the elder, face to face this morning. I should have an answer tomorrow morning, and then I will check with the locals and return to Hong Kong."

"Good. Please call our people in Vancouver and confirm the package is okay and in their hands."

"Do I have to?"

"Please do this, and don't use your cellphone."

"And what is the name of this person again?" She was a trifle ticked off at this extra work, as little as it was.

"Edward, or his assistant, Jason." Apparently, Cedric forgot about the injunction against names over the phone.

"Fine, I'll do it. Have a pleasant day." This last comment came out petulantly as she hung up.

On the other end, Cedric sat looking at his phone. It was one of those days when he wondered if Ivy was worth the trouble, but he already knew the answer. He would have her in his bed as soon as she returned from Vancouver.

Over on Renfrew Street, Ethan called Winston Chang on his direct line at the Hong Kong Police Force offices. It was early in the morning, but Winston arrived at his office by 7:00 am every working day.

"Winston speaking."

"Hello Winston, it's Ethan calling, from Vancouver."

"Ethan, great to hear your voice. What has it been, a year or more since we last talked?"

"Probably Winston. It is good to hear your voice as well, but you may not like what I have to tell you."

"What, is Mary okay?"

"Mary is fine, it is my grandson." Here he paused a moment, "He has been taken, apparently by a triad gang."

"Oh, Ethan. I had heard something about a kidnapping of a policeman's child in Vancouver. News does not stay in one country in today's world. This was your grandson?"

"Yes, his name is Robin. They finally made contact today in a very unusual way. I received a phone call this morning to meet a woman in downtown Vancouver. I met her. I'm pretty sure she is from Kowloon by the way she talked. She said and I quote here, 'We are requesting Winston Chang be at the exchange.' That was it. She got up and walked out without saying anything else."

There was silence on the other end of the call for a

moment, "I wonder why they would want me there, and why would they send someone from Hong Kong to deliver the message?"

"Unknown. I am going to try to meet again tomorrow morning. My son wants to be at the meeting. I don't know if that is wise, but he will not be dissuaded. They also seem to want an answer tomorrow about your participation as well."

"Have you told the Vancouver Police about this?"

"Not yet, other than Robert, but he is actually off the case. Too close it seems. His partner, who is also a VPD officer, has also been restricted from the case. They are not a happy couple right now. The woman told me not to involve the local police, but that seems to be a pretty standard line these days."

"Yes, it is." Winston paused. "I think I can come over to help you, but I need to check first to see why they would want me out of Hong Kong. Let me get back to you. It might be late your time." Winston's first thought was that a gang was up to some shenanigans in Hong Kong and wanted him out of the country while they did whatever it was they were planning. His own safety did not cross his mind.

"That's fine. Don't worry about the time. No one is sleeping much here anyway."

"I understand." Winston ended the call. Ethan and Mary sat, looking at each other across their dining room table. After several minutes, Ethan decided to let Robert know that he had made contact with Winston, so he sent a cryptic text to him.

'Made contact with HK, will receive reply tonight. Talk soon.'

Robert smiled a bit to himself after his phone pinged. His dad was coming through. He realized, not for the first time, how lucky he was to have parents like Ethan and Mary. It was late in the day and Camille had not arrived home from work. She was commuting the hard way, by bus. Robert had kept the car so that he could pick up Sophie from school. He had also been to the grocery store and after a moment's thought, started a simple spaghetti sauce for dinner.

Down at the Cambie VPD offices, a detective by the name of Rodney Fister had been put in charge of the kidnapping. Rodney had two children himself, so Steve assumed his motivation in this investigation would not be lacking. Robert Lui was the best detective on the force by a mile, but unavailable after being told to stay away.

Rodney had convened seven officers in a meeting room, reviewing what they knew and didn't know. Tony Bortolo was not in the room, as the higher-ups had decided that he was too close to Robert, having worked with him several times. However, a close friend of Tony, Vito Cotoni, attended, thus providing an inadvertent conduit for information on the case to get back to Robert.

"Let's get this meeting going. Where are we on the identification of the kidnappers?" Rodney started in after the last officer had sat down at the table. Two officers had been reviewing all the available video from house cameras on the street in question. After winnowing out all the extraneous video, they were left with one camera that had half decent shots of the two guys who had tried to get Sophie. They had then tried to use a version of facial recognition software to match what was only the top half of the two faces to some photos the police had on record of Gupil gang members. The VPD's copy of the software frankly sucked, as it was a beta version of what more senior bureaucracies had. Another camera had caught the action surrounding Robin, and this footage was being reviewed.

One of the officers started, "We have some photos that we think are a match to the two suspects." He added, "We also have some shots of the men who took Robin, which he might corroborate, once we spring him."

Vito spoke up, "I think we'll need to get those girls back in here to see if they can identify some pictures. It'll be like a line-up, but with photos. Because the faces were half covered, it's going to be a stretch for a match to be made, but it is our only lead. There was very little of use gained from the forensic examination of the vans. Some material that matched to the pants that Robin was wearing, and some other fibres probably from the perpetrators, but nothing else. It'd only be useful once we had these guys."

"I agree. Someone get over to Camille and see if it can be arranged. The sooner, the better." Rodney then brought up the obvious sticking point, "Have we heard at all from the kidnappers? And if we haven't, has Robert?"

"No one has heard a peep from Robert, and nothing has been received here. It's not natural." This from one of the sergeants in the room, "What has it been, three days now? Something is not right about this whole thing."

"Since Robert is off the case, he may have received

something and not told us. It would be just like him."
Rodney considered Robert to be a peacock. What Rodney
thought should be done was to put a tap on Robert's
phones, and keep an eye on him, but he wasn't about to
reveal this in front of his team. Once the team realizes that
they are tapping the phones of their own people, everything would go to hell. He decided to go see Steve Christie
after the meeting and ask. Steve was his immediate superior, and Robert's old boss.

"Keep on the lookout for any Gupil members. Someone
is bound to surface eventually and make a mistake. They
are not the brightest of people." Rodney then ended the
short meeting and went looking for Steve.

Rodney went over to Steve's office and looked in. Steve
was present, although it was uncertain as to what he was
doing. His work at the moment seemed to consist of staring out his window at the view. Rodney knocked on the
door frame.

"Can I come in?"

Steve twitched a bit as he came back to reality from
wherever he had been, "Sure, have a seat. What's up?"
After the inquisition at the hands of the Chief a couple of
days earlier, he had made sure the team was beefed up.
But he plainly had only a vague idea about the quality of
people in his department.

"We haven't heard anything from the Lui kidnappers
so far. We are thinking that maybe they contacted Robert,
but he has not told us about it."

"What makes you think that?"

"He never plays by the rules if he can get away with it."

Steve thought about this piece of news for a few seconds, and reluctantly had to agree. "So, what do you propose to do about it? He has been sent home on temporary leave."

"We'd like to tap his phones and keep a watch on him."

"How would you like it if we tapped your phones, Rodney? I don't think so. If you want to keep an eye on what he does, feel free, but keep me in the loop on what you find out. Just remember, it's his kid who went missing."

Rodney felt chastened after the exchange but got the message. Now he had the authority to tail Robert. As far as he was concerned, this was a big win, and he intended to exploit it to the fullest. He went back to his office and thought about who he would task to cover Robert. No one who knew him that was for sure, otherwise they might not do a tip-top job. Unfortunately for Rodney, he didn't know about Vito and Tony's friendship, so the constables he chose to do the work were pretty much blown from the beginning of their task.

* * *

Meanwhile, downtown at the Fairmont, it was late afternoon when Ivy decided to finally give Edward a call, again using the hotel phone.

"Edward speaking."

"I am calling on behalf of Jacky. Is the package secure? I have made contact and should know tomorrow morning what their response will be."

"Yes, the package is good. We are ready for the

exchange." This was a white lie, but then she hadn't exactly asked if Edward had the boy, had she? "How are you doing, is there anything you need, like some company while you are in town?" Edward wasn't above rooting around in another man's effects. After all, he had heard the stories about Ivy's beauty.

"Fuck off. Concentrate on your job." She paused, "I think I will let Cedric know about your impertinence."

Not likely, Edward thought, "Okay, if you change your mind, you know where to find me."

Ivy was actually pleased at Edward's unexpected suggestion, but she was still tired from her flight. She would think about it over dinner. She decided to head down to the restaurant in the hotel where, after giving the menu a once over, she ordered a seared sablefish dish. While she waited, she decided to have a cocktail called a 'Pretty Bird' whatever that was. As she sipped the drink she felt suddenly revived and came to a decision. She would call Edward back and get him down to her room for some fun and games, so that her trip wouldn't be a total waste of time. She had seen pictures of Edward and Jason in Kowloon, so she knew that he was a good-looking gangster. As she contemplated what was to come, she got excited enough to call him from her table, thus breaking the no cellphone rule. She was horny enough that she didn't care.

When Edward answered, she simply said, "Room 2732, Fairmont Pacific Rim Hotel."

He smiled, then left his condo to head downtown. The Guru could wait for his money, there were more important things to be done, such as being a gracious host for a particular visitor to this fair city.

***

Camille eventually arrived home from work after almost an hour of walking, waiting, bus riding, and more walking. What was usually a twenty minute car ride, took twice as long on a bus, on a good day. This was not a good commuting day. The waiting around was the worst part, and Camille's humour was tested. She stepped through the door to the aroma of a sauce simmering on the stove top and immediately felt her spirits lift.

"Hi Robert, home." She called out. Robert wasn't in the kitchen but in the front room, on his laptop. She went in to talk with him.

"They want Sophie and Rose back downtown tomorrow to look at some pictures. Rodney is the lead detective."

Robert rolled his eyes. "That is the best they can do?"

"Apparently. As you know, neither I nor Tony are to have anything to do with the case, but the good news is that Tony's friend, Vito is part of the team. I'd say we will be kept up to date."

Robert nodded.

"And they are getting suspicious about us. They haven't heard anything from the kidnappers. Rodney came and questioned me. Asked if we had heard anything. I said no one from the gang had contacted us. Which is true enough. What happened with Ethan?"

Robert's face darkened, "Not surprising given who the triad is after. I doubt anyone down at headquarters knows the connection that my dad has with the Hong Kong Police Force."

"What do you mean?"

"They want Winston Chang at the exchange. He is a senior officer on the Hong Kong Police Force."

"Why? And what exchange?"

"Don't know the answer to either of those questions yet."

"My guess is that our friends down at headquarters will try to watch us going forward, maybe even try for our phones."

"Yeah, don't know if they'll be successful with getting our phones tapped, but I wouldn't put it past them to try to keep an eye on us. I wish we had a different car."

"I need to use your car tomorrow to get the girls down to the station. Why don't you ask your father. He still has his car, doesn't he?"

"Great idea. He has to come with me tomorrow anyway, if we get a meeting set. You could drop me tomorrow at the Commercial SkyTrain station and I'll pull a dipsy-doodle to lose anyone that might tail me before I meet up with him." Robert seemed to relish the thought of playing with the VPD. "I bet Thomas will call me tomorrow to see what I am up to."

"Let's eat Robert, I'm sure Sophie is hungry.

"Good idea. I'll put the linguini on." As he went into the kitchen, he couldn't help thinking about what Robin was eating, or not eating. Camille briefly wondered why Robert wanted a car, when he just as easily could go downtown on a bus, but the thought flitted away.

***

During dinner, Robert brought up the kidnapping with Sophie. "I heard Rose had bear spray."

"Yeah. She nailed the guy good when he turned to see what she was doing. I think she picked up the idea at a self-defence course she took."

"I'm going to find a course for you and get you in. Something I should have done long ago."

Sophie smiled back at her father as she slurped up the pasta from her fork. "I'd like that."

After dinner was done and some reassurance given to Sophie, Robert retreated alone to the den where he started thinking about all the pieces that needed to fall into place during the next twelve hours. He was going to need a few prepaid phones, so that he and Ethan could continue to communicate without worry. While he didn't think the higher-ups would countenance tapping his phones, it wasn't hard to do, and if some eager beaver down at headquarters got it into his mind to do it, he would be screwed.

He wasn't totally sure what would happen tomorrow, but decided to call Farhad to see how he was doing, as he might be needed. It turned out that Farhad had not been behaving himself; he had gone back into Delta to retrieve his car, but none of the Gupils had seen him. They were keeping their heads down as much as Farhad was, for different reasons. Other than this escapade, he was bored out of his skull. Robert let him know that his assistance might be needed soon. Farhad had heard about the kidnapping on the news and smiled at the thought of actually doing something. He was starting to like Robert.

Robert called out to Camille and told her he was going out for a few moments. He needed to get those cellphones tonight. There would be too much going on tomorrow. He left and walked several blocks to a strip mall on Fraser Street that had a mobile shop, which was getting ready to close up for the night. He purchased four prepaid phones using cash, which made the owner smile. This accomplished, he headed back home, his head on a swivel all the way. As far as he could tell, no one was following him. He knew the signs.

Once home, he put some coffee on. He was determined to wait up to see if his dad heard back from Winston. Camille's cellphone lay on the dining room table. Robert had suggested that Ethan use her number to call him in the interim until they had more secure phones. Camille headed up to bed after calling Rose's mother to explain the need for Rose and Sophie to appear again down at the police station. Robert called the Victoria Restaurant and reserved a side room he knew was available to rent.

* * *

At half past midnight, Camille's cell rang. Robert picked it up after the second ring.

"Dad?"

"Hi Robert. Winston called back and has agreed to come over to Vancouver. He is not coming alone, either. One of his most trusted assistants will be joining him. He should be here in about a day or so. I am unsure of the time differences."

"That's great, Dad. Good news." Robert paused a bit before asking, "Dad, can we use your car tomorrow? I am going to get Camille to drop me at the Commercial train station just to make sure I am not being followed, then I'll link up with you to drive downtown. Camille has to use our car to get Sophie and Rose down to the station tomorrow to look at more photos." This explanation came out longer than he intended, but his father didn't seem to notice.

"Okay Robert. What time will you get to my place?"

"I am going to leave here early, so about nine or so."

"Fine. See you then." Ethan hung up the phone.

Robert sat at the table for a while longer, contemplating what was to come tomorrow. Outside, at the north end of the lane running behind their home, a dark blue Crown Victoria pulled up to the curb of the cross street and cut its engine. The watch mounted by the VPD had officially started. The two officers inside the car had some coffee and a couple of sandwiches to get them through the night. They were slated to be relieved at nine the next morning after what was sure to be a very boring night.

Before he went up to bed, Robert checked the actions on his pistols and their clips once more before putting them up in a cupboard out of sight, ready for tomorrow.

$$\sim \; 20 \; \sim$$

Dawn broke with sunshine for a change. Camille hadn't slept much, mostly because Robert hadn't either, moving around relentlessly most of the night, until finally finding sleep around 4:30. Robert woke, not feeling at all refreshed, but it was of little consequence. He was keyed up and ready for action, whatever form it took this day.

"Can you drive me over to the Commercial station before you take the girls downtown? I can make my own way from there." Robert asked.

"Sure. I'm going to shower first."

Robert grunted his assent. He wished he could have joined Camille in the shower, but today wasn't the day for this type of monkey business. He went down to the kitchen after yelling at Sophie to wake up, heading for the coffee implements. He made his coffee the old-fashioned way—water dripped through a paper filter. Not for him, the fancy home machines, he liked things simple and unadorned after experimenting with every method known to man. After getting the coffee made and confirming that Camille was out of the shower, he went upstairs to prepare himself for the day.

Robert and Camille sat drinking their coffee across from each other, not saying anything. After finishing, Robert went over to the front window, then the rear one to see if there were any watchers. He couldn't see any, but that didn't mean anything.

He yelled up at Sophie. "We're leaving, Sophie. Camille will be back shortly to get you. See you later." Sophie yelled back something, but it was unintelligible.

"Ok, action time." Robert said with a small grin at Camille. They went out the rear door and got in the Silver Streak, Camille driving. They drove slowly down the lane to the north end turning right, where Robert promptly spotted the police car. It might as well have had a big sign on it saying stakeout car.

"It's always depressing to know you're right." he said as they passed by the car, Robert waving to the two startled officers in the car. Camille had a smile on her face as she headed east to Commercial Street. The driver managed to spill some coffee on himself as he quickly turned the key to start the engine.

"Wake up!" He yelled at his partner, "They're moving, and they've seen us." Their car was facing the exact opposite direction from Camille's move, so the first thing the driver had to do was pull a U-turn on East 27th. He executed this smoothly enough and started heading east, but Camille wasn't exactly waiting for them to catch up, so The Streak had a good block lead on the police car. At Victoria Street, Camille turned north.

"Keep it at the speed limit, Camille. I don't really care if they close the gap, I'll lose them when I get on the

SkyTrain. Slow down when you hit Broadway and I'll jump out." Robert had a light jacket on and some equipment; both of his weapons, his badge, and cuffs, just in case.

The Streak followed Victoria north as it curved, then became Commercial Street. Robert had his eye on the rear mirror. He could see the chase car getting closer. Camille slowed to almost a stop as they approached the station where two train lines crossed. It happened to be the busiest station on the whole system, and at the most crowded time of day—the morning rush. Robert figured that whoever jumped out of the car to follow him better be in the shape of his life if he wanted to keep up with Robert. Fat chance he thought. He knew most cops were not the fittest people after being on the force awhile.

"Okay, Camille, thanks, wish me luck," as he first squeezed her shoulder, then opened the door and leapt from the car onto the sidewalk. He ran up the station stairs after paying the fare. The station accommodated two platforms for two different lines, so after he got up to the main platform, he headed for the lower one, which was the Millennium line, the newer of the two lines.

Back on Commercial, the tailing car backed off a bit as they saw Camille slow. The cops swore as Robert had leapt out and ran into the station about a half block ahead of them. They weren't prepared for this.

"Shit. I'm going to try to follow him." The cop in the passenger seat said. "Drop me as close as you can to the station." This cop was at an immediate disadvantage, having only used the system once or twice in his life. Not only didn't he know how stations were laid out, but he also had no idea how complicated the Commercial station was. He ran up to the fare gates, and with no money ready he decided to vault over the gate. This didn't faze most of the regular transit users in the least, however he was lucky that a transit officer didn't see him do this. They took their job seriously and would have jumped on him, putting his chase to an end by nabbing another scofflaw.

He ran up the long flight of stairs to the main platform and immediately started looking for Robert. It was packed on the waiting area with the outbound and inbound rail lines on either side of the crowded central platform. He had no idea which direction Robert would be headed. He moved through the crowds, not seeing him. As far as he knew, no trains had stopped as yet, but one was fast approaching from the east, heading into Vancouver. He had almost reached the end of the platform—no Robert. The train stopped, and people jammed onto already full cars. He turned and watched. No Robert. It was then he saw the sign directing people to the other commuter line that he had missed. Craps, maybe he was in the wrong place. He started running, dodging commuters as he went. He hit some stairs, the longest flight down he had ever seen. He ignored the escalator and took the stairs three at a time, hoping he wouldn't break an ankle. He hit the bottom and turned right, running onto the platform as an outbound train stopped. He was already winded. He stopped and looking ahead, spotted Robert at the far end getting on the outbound train. He slid through the door of the same train just as it closed, and started to move up the car, hoping to get close enough to watch Robert without him noticing. Pretty good, he thought to himself. No way was that detective going to outwit him. He started to calm down, moving confidently along the car.

Robert had been keeping a watch, and noticed an officer arrive on the platform just as the train arrived. He walked onto the front of the train and sighed. The next stop was Renfrew, which was where he wanted to get off, however he stayed on, waiting for the opportunity that he knew would present itself. The next station, Rupert, did not offer what he was looking for. At the Gilmore stop, what he was waiting for, happened. A train going the opposite direction was stopping as Robert's train pulled into the station. The doors opened, Robert waited, counting down. Just as the doors started to close, he slid between them and crossed the platform, getting on the inbound train. As the two trains started in their different directions, Robert looked across the platform and, smiling, waved to the helpless cop on the outbound train.

Robert relaxed slightly and started to focus on the next stage. He got off at the Renfrew stop and exiting the station, starting an easy run north. He had several blocks to cover before he arrived at Ethan's condo and no time to lose.

The cop on the train to nowhere pulled out his cellphone and called his partner.

"I lost him. He's heading back into Vancouver somewhere."

"Shit. I'm already halfway back to the station."

"What about me?" He whined.

"I'm sure you can find your way back downtown, can't you?"

"Asshole." So much for that partnership.

* * *

Robert arrived at his parent's suite after getting buzzed into the building.

"Hey Mom, Dad, are you ready?"

"Waiting for you, son." his dad answered, "Should I make the call?"

"Let's do it—short and sweet, remember." It was just after 9:40 am when Ethan dialled the number he had been given, which was Ivy's cell number. In her haste the previous day, she had given out her cell number instead of the hotel number. Ethan could tell it was international.

"Hello?"

"Victoria Restaurant, eleven." He clicked off the call and looked at Robert with a questioning expression, "Correct?"

"Great, let's get going."

Ivy sat looking at her cell. This wasn't supposed to happen. And why had she given Ethan her cell number? She had given him explicit instructions, and really wasn't prepared for something going off-script. For the first time since arriving in Vancouver, she was unsure of herself. She debated calling Cedric, but decided not to until after she met Ethan. She would meet this elderly man and finish her duty. She took her time but finished a light breakfast in her room, then got dressed. Edward had stayed several hours, but she eventually kicked him out after getting the satisfaction she had been craving as well as the information she was tasked to get. She packed her small case and after taking a quick look around, left the room. At the front desk, she checked out, confirming her bill was correct, then asked the host to check her case. She said she would return later to pick it up before heading to the airport. The host booked a limo for noon on her behalf.

* * *

Farther south, at the Cambie police offices, the watcher had returned without his partner. He parked the undercover car and reported to Rodney, rapping on the doorframe of Rodney's office.

"He gave us the slip. And he knew we were watching him."

"Crap." After a bit of thought he offered, "He's up to something."

"You think?"

Rodney looked back at Jimmy, his eyes narrowing. He didn't like being sassed but wasn't quite sure if this was what was going on, or if Jimmy was just stupid.

"What happened?"

"Camille drove him by the Commercial SkyTrain station, and he jumped out. My partner followed him but lost him in the transit system."

"Where is he?"

"Don't know. I didn't wait around. No telling where they would end up."

"I guess." He paused, waiting for his brain to engage a

bit more, "Maybe I'll go have a talk with Camille. You can fuck off."

At least now Jimmy knew that his piece of impertinence had been noted by his superior. Rodney walked quickly over to Camille's small office. He didn't waste time knocking on the half open door but walked in.

"Where is Robert? What is he up to?" No pleasantries offered.

"Hello Rodney. Would you like a seat?"

"Screw off. I want to know what you two are up to."

"What business is it of yours?"

"We were watching you to see if you had heard anything from the kidnappers."

"Nice. Always good to know you are trusted by your coworkers."

"So where did he go? My man lost him on the transit system."

"You should get better men then." Camille then changed tack. "He told me he was going to Brentwood to buy some extra cellphones. He is scared that you guys might decide to tap his phone. But I told him that the VPD wouldn't do that, would they?" She smiled, knowing it might drive Rodney over the edge, watching as his eyes seemed to grow and his face redden. Would his head explode? Then he calmed slightly.

"This isn't the last of this." Then he added, "It's not even your kid that went missing." Camille stared back at him, stone-faced, not believing he could say what he did. Rodney quickly twirled and left her office without so much as a parting 'good day'. Camille shook her head and started pondering what other local police forces she might find employment with. Things were not looking rosy at Cambie Street.

* * *

When Robert and Ethan arrived in the centre of Vancouver, Robert parked in an underground lot adjacent to the Victoria Restaurant. Robert and Ethan walked into the shopping mall that opened into the restaurant. It was sparsely populated due to the time of day. Robert went up to the hostess at the entry and identified himself, asking to be led to the room he had rented. The hostess smiled and led him inside. There were some menus on the table as well as some tea, so Robert took a seat and poured himself a cup. The hostess asked him to let her know when his entire group was ready to order. Robert smiled without saying anything.

Ethan stood in the entry foyer, looking for Ivy. He didn't have long to wait. Ivy had arrived early to figure out if a trap was being laid for her. She saw Ethan just before he saw her. He appeared to be alone, so she walked up to him. Just as she was about to demand an explanation for disobeying her orders, he told her in Cantonese to follow him to a private room where they would not be disturbed. The hostess nodded approvingly; she knew good-looking people when she saw them. There must be some kind of big deal movie lunch going on. He opened the door and ushered Ivy in, with him following so she could not back out.

"Who are you?" She asked in Cantonese to Robert. He

sat there without saying a word, arms on the table in front of him, fingers interlaced. He understood what she said but felt it better that she didn't know, waiting for his father to offer an explanation.

"This is the father of the child that you kidnapped. He speaks English." Ethan answered after he had shut the door.

"You were given explicit instructions, which you disobeyed. You have put your grandson in grave danger. You may never see him again now." Again, in Cantonese.

Robert twitched slightly, which Ivy noticed.

"Winston has agreed to come over to Vancouver per your request." Ethan said this slowly.

Ivy looked puzzled, "Then why are you jerking me around? This is not going to turn out well for you because of your impertinence." She wasn't sure what the meaning of this meeting was, but she was tiring of it quickly. "I am going to leave now. You had better hope you haven't screwed up all your lives."

"Sit down and shut up." The words came from Robert's lips as if they had been scratched on a chalkboard. In stark English. He reached into his jacket. The SIG Sauer came out, resting in his hand. "You aren't going anywhere just yet."

It was slowly dawning on Ivy that this was a police officer she was dealing with, not some civilian who hadn't a clue what was happening. She started to feel uncomfortable, and unsure where this was heading.

"Where is my son?"

"I don't know." She assumed that Edward had him but wasn't certain.

"Why do you want Winston here?"

"I don't know."

Robert sipped some tea while looking at Ivy. He waited, watching her discomfort grow.

"It is unfortunate that you don't seem to know much. I think I am going to arrest you and keep you until the fog in your brain drains away." Robert stood up, took out his handcuffs, and before Ivy could do anything, had her hands cuffed behind her back. Ethan was surprised, not knowing Robert's intentions.

Robert got his badge out and with his right hand, opened the door and frog-marched Ivy out through the general dining room and past the hostess, whose jaw dropped six inches from the floor. The three quickly re-entered the parking lot after a short walk through the mall and went over to Ethan's car. Ethan got into the driver's seat while Robert manoeuvred Ivy into the back seat where he sat beside her, the gun trained on her again.

"We're going to East Vancouver, Dad, south of 41st. I'll direct you when we get close."

"Okay, Robert." Ethan hoped his son knew what he was doing, but whatever it was, it didn't sound like they were going to a police station. Forty minutes later and after a slap to Ivy's head when she thought she might voice her opinion as to what was happening, they drove up to the rear of a four-storey apartment building, where Farhad was cooling his heels. The three of them managed to make it up to Farhad's floor without running into anyone else.

Robert knocked and waited. After they got into the apartment, Robert explained to Farhad that he was to take care of Ivy for a few days. Farhad looked at Ivy and told Robert that he thought he could accomplish this task. He was grinning. Suddenly his life was a lot more interesting. Robert gave him the keys to the cuffs and left, letting him know that he'd be in touch.

As Ethan and Robert got back into the car Ethan finally spoke, "So that wasn't really an arrest, correct?"

"Maybe not."

"More like a kidnapping?"

"Words, Dad. We need some leverage."

Ethan couldn't argue with that.

Back at the Fairmont hotel, a limo was waiting in the auto court for a certain Ivy Sun. The concierge looked around, then asked the front desk if she had picked up her case from left luggage; but no, after checking, she confirmed that it was still there. He shrugged and went out to ask the driver to remain another ten minutes if he could. Inside the Victoria Restaurant, the hostess was becoming busy but was still perplexed by the apparent arrest of a movie star. Maybe it was part of a movie being shot, but then there would have been cameras and a lot of other people around, no? She would watch the news when she got home, confident that the local television station would have all the answers.

* * *

In Hong Kong, Cedric was waiting for an expected call from Ivy. He was looking forward to seeing her tomorrow.

He knew what time her flight was supposed to leave and decided to call her himself after waiting almost two hours. Ivy's cell rang. On Vancouver's East Side, Farhad looked at it and decided to answer. The caller rattled off a string of phrases in Cantonese that totally eluded Farhad, so he answered in Punjabi, telling the caller to screw off, then ended the call. Cedric looked at his cellphone, puzzled as to what the hell was going on. He re-checked the number he had called. It was correct. He tried again. This time, answering in English, Farhad was more succinct, "Fuck off." Then he broke the connection again.

Cedric understood this with no problem. What it meant however, was a big question. He decided to call Edward in Richmond.

"This is Cedric. Is Ivy with you?"

"No."

"Have you seen her?"

"We met briefly last evening, but I haven't heard from her since." Edward was wondering how much Cedric knew.

"She is not answering her phone. Someone else answers when I call."

"Maybe she lost it. Did you try the hotel?" Edward thought this was a good answer.

Cedric didn't even bother replying. He hung up, then called the Fairmont.

"Hello, I am trying to contact an Ivy Sun. Has she checked out yet?"

"Just a second." After a pause, the reply came. "Yes, she checked out and left her suitcase with us until she returned to go to the airport. The limo waited fifteen minutes, but she didn't come back. That was an hour ago. Her suitcase is still with us."

"Okay." He severed the call and sat thinking. He decided to go talk to Jacky. He'd know what to do. A short walk later, he entered Jacky's club and went up to his office. After telling Jacky what was happening over in Vancouver, Jacky stared back at Cedric.

"She's been kidnapped, you moron. Check Cathay and see if she got on the flight. My guess is that Robert Lui has taken her as a bargaining chip."

"Shit."

"Exactly."

"So, what do we do now?"

"Get in contact with Edward and tell him to send a finger to the cops to show them we are serious. And check with our man at the HKPF to see if Winston is leaving town or not. Do you know if Ivy delivered the message?"

"Yes, she called me and confirmed." He waited, then, "A finger from the kid?"

Jacky looked at Cedric while he rolled his eyes, "What kind of man do you take me for? Tell them to use one of the fingers they have in their freezer."

Cedric knew exactly what kind of man Jacky was, and knew it wouldn't bother him to harm anyone, including a child if it furthered his aims. Which is why he had asked the question.

After Edward heard from Cedric, he thought it was about time to get control of the Lui kid. For that, he was going to need a quarter of a million dollars to grease the trade. He called Jason and told him to get the cash to-gether, unlaundered was fine. The Guru could do his own cleaning, not that he would tell the Guru the money was possibly tainted and marked. After all, wasn't that what made life exciting, surprises? He was fast tiring of the Guru anyway.

He called to arrange the trade. "Hello? It is Edward. I need the Lui son now. Where do you want to do the exchange? We'll have the money."

The Guru was off kilter. He wasn't prepared for this to happen so quickly, but after a pause he responded. "We can do it in North Surrey. When?"

"Later today?"

"Ok. Here is the address. It is in an industrial area by the river. Five?"

After Edward had written the address down, he called Jason back to tell him the time of the exchange and to bring a few men with him to the meeting, just in case. Jason thought about this for a moment but could only come up with two names of men not in custody at the moment. He hoped it would be enough.

Edward then relayed the message about the finger. "Send it over to the Vancouver Police today. Include a note with it. I'll tell you what to say. Use a courier service with the usual cut-out. The Ivy Sun girl is missing. I think that either the police arrested her, or, more likely, Robert Lui swiped her, probably as a bargaining point. I don't believe our Hong Kong brethren are very impressed with us." Edward had to admit that he was starting to have some respect for Robert. He was definitely no pushover and would likely cause more problems for his group.

~ 21 ~

In North Surrey, Robin was tiring of being the captive. After getting over his initial fears, he was still plotting an escape attempt. Paneet had been on solo guard duty ever since the kidnapping. He had been spelled off once for a night, but that was it. He was in a foul mood. To this point in his ordeal, Robin had purposefully been a model prisoner; doing what he was told, with a minimum of talking. The whole time, he gauged his captor and assessed his possible tools. Surely the police would be looking for him. The one asset he had was the tether with the chain on the end. The only time he was loose was when he went to the toilet in the next room and had to carry the chain with him. Robin was pretty sure there was only one person watching him, so all he had to do was overpower him and then run. This, unfortunately, was the extent of the plan. Surprise would be his only advantage. He had done his best to look scared the whole time, even though he wasn't.

Paneet was dissatisfied, but he had to admit that kidnapping a youngster was pretty easy. It wasn't like the kid was going try anything. He seemed to be scared out

272

of his wits and didn't look very strong. If Paneet thought about anything, it was what he would do with all the extra money that was due to come his way. He was hoping that his duty would soon come to an end so he could get paid and get out to the clubs.

Robin had been following a pattern when he went to the toilet. When he had finished and came out, he walked only a few feet past Paneet, who inevitably, was sitting at his table looking at his cellphone or computer. After walking by Paneet, he would wait as Paneet arose, then he'd enter his cell with Paneet following to re-attach the tether to the table with a lock. Paneet sat in a manner that was perpendicular to Robin's path; not with his back to Robin, but not facing him either. In Robin's mind, this would be the closest he was going to be able get in order to spring an attack.

Today was the day, Robin decided. He wasn't sure what day it was anymore, and he had no clear method of telling what time of day it was, let alone how many days had passed since his abduction. He had had enough of this crap. He wanted to see his family again, and as odd as it sounded, he wanted to be back at school.

* * *

Down at Cambie Street, a manila envelope arrived just after two in the afternoon, courtesy of a courier on a bicycle. Like any large organization, the envelope was passed onto the secure mail room where it was scanned, then opened carefully. One always had to be careful about the potential for powders, or explosives in a police station. The contents made the opener draw a sharp breath,

"Shit," was her first comment. She looked around and called out for her colleague. She was starting to hyperventilate. The coworker came over to her station.

"Look at this!"

The colleague was staring at a small finger in a plastic baggie. She felt ill. She had seen a lot of things come through the mail system, but this topped them all. There was a folded piece of paper in the envelope as well, but both of them knew enough not to touch it. They called upstairs to get a detective down to pick up the grisly message. The two waited until an officer came down from higher up in the police kingdom to remove the offending message, then decided to go for a long coffee break. And when they finished that, they'd be leaving for the day, citing mental trauma.

The officer retreated up to the fourth floor heading straight for Rodney Fister's office.

"Hey Rod, got something for you." He smiled, dropped the envelope onto Rodney's desk and didn't hang around for the show. Rodney stared at the departing back of the officer. He was getting annoyed with the disrespect he appeared to be garnering. It wasn't just some on his team, but also people who he really had very little contact with, who didn't give him the proper respect usually afforded a senior detective. Maybe they needed traffic duty to help with their attitude adjustment.

After this train of thought petered out, he looked at the manila envelope sitting beside his keyboard. It looked slightly fat, having a bulge in its centre. He assumed it was okay, after all, it had come through the mail room. He picked it up and looked in, and immediately dropped it on his desk. After some loud cursing, he grabbed it and emptied the contents onto his side table, not believing his eyes. Obviously, someone knew what was in the envelope but didn't communicate it to Rodney. His conflicting emotions soon resolved themselves as he picked up the note that accompanied the finger. He would worry about the respect thing later. He guessed this was going to be about Robin Lui. He unfolded the note carefully with a pair of tweezers.

'WE WANT WHAT IS OURS. MAKE SURE OUR DIRECTIONS ARE BEING FOLLOWED AND WINSTON IS THERE OR MORE PIECES OF THE SON WILL BE SENT TO YOU.'

That was the sum of the note. He picked up his phone and called Vito Cotoni.

"Vito, get the team together in the room. I just received a message from the kidnappers. Get in here after you have organized the meeting. I have something that needs analyzing."

A couple of minutes later, Vito entered Rodney's office. When he saw what was on the table he blanched. "*Porco Nero*" was all he could manage. "Is it Robin's finger?"

"Not certain about that. Can you take it over to forensics and see who it belongs to?"

"Sure." What Vito thought he would do is ask them to check on other matches first, before scaring the daylights out of Camille by asking her for some DNA linked to Robin. Such forethought was rare in the force, and even rarer for it to be acknowledged by anyone. Vito was proud of his mind, which had received some molding by the Jesuits in Montreal at Loyola College. It was unusual for someone trained by the Blackrobes to become a police officer. He went down a couple of floors in the building to the Forensic Identification Unit offices and had a quiet word with the officer on duty. The officer got the hint that the Lui kidnapping was involved here, so he moved the work to the top of the list. His mission accomplished, Vito headed back up to the team meeting that was starting. As he walked towards the team room, Rodney appeared from his office doorway and beat him into the meeting. There were nine officers in total attending.

"We have finally heard from the kidnappers." Rodney started off, as he waved the note that had arrived. Fortunately, today he was wearing latex gloves, as usually, he wasn't above mucking up a piece of evidence due to carelessness. He read out the short note, then, "And a finger was sent along with this message." Rodney liked the shock value that this added to the proceedings. There was a sharp intake of breath from a couple of the officers.

"We're checking out the finger, but in the meantime, the rest of the note needs some deciphering." He paused, then when no one said a word. "Any ideas? Any of you?"

"Who sent the note? And who is Winston?" A bright spark asked.

Rodney's eyes did a mega-roll as he considered how he was going to solve anything with this group helping him. "It appears that there is an exchange to take place, but we seem to be short on details. Vito is working on whether the finger belongs to the kid or not."

Then a second officer asked. "How do we know what is ours, when we don't even know who it is who wants it?"

"Good point. We'll leave it to you to figure this part out then, shall we?" Rodney stared at the officer. Vito watched the proceedings, holding his tongue. Several of the group shifted uncomfortably in their seats, but no one offered anything further.

"Fine, meeting's over. I'll figure this out myself." With that, Rodney, who hadn't even sat down, turned and left the room, slamming the door behind him. Vito sat, watching the reaction on the faces of the officers around the table. They ranged from puzzlement to disgust. He was starting to fear for Robin if this was the best the department could muster. He knew that Rodney was short on leadership skills, but this was a breathtakingly inept example of it.

Rodney decided to confront Camille with the note. Jarring her might be his only way to find out what she and Robert had been up to. He looked over to her office and noticed the door partially ajar. He immediately strode over and knocked on the door frame as he entered the room, not waiting for a reply.

Camille was startled. She had been concentrating on some paperwork regarding her ongoing case. She looked up, "What do you want?"

Rodney had a smirk on his face, "We received a note from the kidnappers."

"Why are you smiling? Is something funny here? What did it say?" Camille started to tense up.

Rodney repeated what the note said, and as Camille's eyes widened, he stuck the dagger in, "And there was a finger attached to the note."

Camille screamed, "What?" Then, louder, "You bastard!"

Norma, who had not departed for the floor below just yet, ran over to Camille's open door, "Is everything okay?" She surveyed the two occupants, sensing the animosity that the curse had illuminated.

Rodney was brief, "Get lost Norma. Everything's fine." He then closed the door. He was intent on finding out what Camille and Robert knew, and politeness was not on the menu. He was going to be lucky if anyone he worked with ever did anything for him again. "I want to know what you know about the message, right now."

Thanks to Norma however, Camille had gathered her thoughts, and just sat there, staring at Rodney. There was no way in hell that she was going to share anything with this poor excuse for a detective. "If we have anything to say, you'll be the last one we talk to, Rod." She knew he hated the abbreviation to his name.

"How would you like to be suspended?" When Camille declined to respond, he turned and as he left. "Fine, I'll make that happen then."

* * *

Camille wrote down what Rodney had said, then called Vito on his office local phone line to find out what he knew about the finger. There was no answer, so Camille left a message. Her thoughts were spiralling. Could the triad really have cut off one of Robin's fingers? She desperately needed to talk with Robert but was not going to do it at the station. Norma came back to her office, "Are you okay Camille?"

"I don't know Norma." Tears were starting now, "That guy is such an asshole."

Norma was unsure about what had transpired, but she tried to comfort Camille as best she could, rubbing her shoulder gently. Camille took a moment; composed herself, rose, and told Norma that she was fine, just needed some coffee. Norma watched her receding back, shook her head, and returned to her desk. Meanwhile, Vito had left the aborted kidnapping meeting, making it back to his desk to play his pending phone calls. The message from Camille worried him. However, he was wise enough not to return the call, but instead, dialled up Tony and relayed what he knew, and that forensics were looking at other matches for the finger. He would tell Tony promptly as soon as the results were in.

Camille left the building, turned left, and made for Cafe Paulo. As she entered the cafe Gilberto waved to her. It was a slow time of day, mid-afternoon, when most people had had their caffeine fix or three already. She had Gilberto pull an Americano, so she could linger over it.

"How are you, Camille?"

"Okay, Gilberto, thanks for asking."

"How about Roberto? I haven't seen him for a couple of days. Any news on the child?"

She really didn't want to explain. "He's doing okay. We are working on things." She tried to smile as she took her cup and went to sit by a window.

Taking out her cell, she called Robert, the coffee momentarily forgotten, "It's me. The department got a message today." She read out what she had scribbled, then, after Robert had gasped, she told him about the finger, and how the whole thing had been presented by Rodney.

Robert swore, which Camille had been expecting, then, "Why don't you come home, we need to put our heads together."

"Ok Robert, I'll be home soon, love you." Camille didn't bolt, but finished her coffee in a measured fashion, thinking about how her life was changing, not in a good way. Robert's children added a layer of responsibility that she had not anticipated.

* * *

In North Surrey, Robin was sitting at his table, screwing up whatever courage he could find. Suddenly, he was less sure of himself. He was about to try something he had no experience with, that is, attempting to kill or incapacitate someone. He hit the table with his hand, then yelled out to Paneet, "I need to go to the toilet, please." Then he waited, Paneet usually taking his sweet time about opening the door. Robin knew he had to follow his routine, lest Paneet twig to his nervousness. The door finally opened, and Robin stood up while the shackle was unlocked. He then slung the tether and chain over his shoulder and walked out to the toilet room. He didn't look behind him but assumed that Paneet went back to usual position at his table, studying his cellphone.

He stood in the small room, getting more nervous by the moment. Finally, he flushed the toilet and opened the door. Paneet didn't glance his way, so it was game time. Robin strode resolutely to where Paneet was sitting and before Paneet could look up, Robin had the chain wrapped around his neck and he was pulling back, twisting as he yanked. The chair toppled over but Robin hung on for all he was worth as Paneet's arms flailed uselessly, trying to make contact with Robin's head. It didn't take long for Paneet's efforts to falter, then his body went limp. Robin hung on for a few more seconds as they both lay on the floor. He pushed Paneet over onto the concrete floor and looked for the exit, which wasn't far away.

Robin exited the building and looked around, breathless from his exertions. He wrapped the tether and chain around his forearm. A soulless landscape of weeds, ruptured concrete, and chain link fencing commanded his view. At least it was daytime. Unfortunately, at the same moment, a vehicle was rolling into the parking area about fifty metres away, a Range Rover, followed by another car, a BMW by its looks. He turned around and ran for his life in the opposite direction.

The Guru was in the Range Rover. He swore as he realized that Robin was trying to make an escape. However, he didn't get too excited. There was nowhere for Robin to run to, unless he was a swimmer, that was. The only way out was the gate that the Guru had just opened. The entire perimeter of this compound, as ramshackle as it looked, was actually very secure, razor wire topping chain link being the fencing of choice. He got out of his vehicle and stood there. He nodded to Maccha, who was accompanying him for this handover to Edward. Maccha strode off towards Robin, while the Guru contemplated yet another embarrassment in front of Edward, who was getting out of his BMW.

"Troubles?" Edward's insult was brief. Jason exited the passenger seat, while two other associates got out of the rear seats, watching Maccha trying to catch the escaping chicken.

The Guru tried to keep what cool he had left, "Where is the money?"

Edward signalled to one of Jason's men, who went behind the BMW and opened the trunk. He pulled out a bag with handles that looked as though it should have laundry inside it. What it had was the opposite of anything laundered. The man dumped it at the Guru's feet.

"It's all there?"

Edward spread his hands out either side of his body in the classic stance of an aggrieved soccer player from the southern hemisphere, "Come on."

It was at this point that two things happened almost simultaneously, Maccha caught up to Robin and grabbed him, then the door to the building slammed open and Paneet strode out looking worse for wear. He spied Maccha coming toward him with Robin tightly in his grip. As Paneet started to run towards the two, the Guru yelled at him to stop. This only slowed Paneet somewhat, enough for Maccha to put Robin behind him and stick out a straight arm into Paneet's face, adding further insult to Paneet's lousy day. Maccha hit him hard enough with his flattened palm to knock him back onto his rear, where he sat, blood dribbling down his face from his nose.

"Didn't you hear the boss?" Maccha asked Paneet.

The Wide Bay Boys were enjoying the antics of the Gupils, chuckling amongst themselves. The Guru was tiring of the farce and signalled to Maccha to release Robin. He could care less if Robin ran for it or not, he was no longer the Gupil's concern. Maccha hauled Paneet up off the gravel and handed him a handkerchief for his nose, then the three Gupils strode over to the Range Rover with their money. Edward had his men grab Robin before he tried to make another run. Two of them then stowed Robin in the trunk of their car. Edward was still smiling as they departed the wasteland. For his part, Robin was exhilarated that he had attempted something, but was unsure about what had just transpired. It seemed like he was being traded, but why? And how did that Paneet character spring back to life?

***

A secretary who worked for an adjacent trucking firm drove by the tableau after she had ended her day. Her attention was captured by the two shiny cars sitting close to the road. They seemed wildly out of place. She also thought she saw someone chasing what looked like a kid farther off close by the river's edge. She slowed down a tad, staring at the scene but kept driving, not bothering to look again. She knew enough to keep her nose out of other's business, particularly in this part of town. The gangster's attentions were captured by the Maccha/Robin escapade, so they didn't notice the car driving by. Something didn't seem right about the scene to the woman, but nothing clicked until later that night when the segment about the kidnapped policeman's son was repeated on the late local news. She decided right away to call 911 to tell her short story. After conversing with the emergency tech to verify her bona fides, she was transferred to the Vancouver Police station where the night shift was working the drunk watch.

"I think I might have seen that kid who got kidnapped this afternoon." She started in on what was going to be a very brief story. The desk sergeant took the notes, and while there was little to indicate that Robin was involved, the location of the sighting and the cars involved made him take notice. After taking all the particulars the lady had on offer, which weren't many, he decided to bump it up a notch and called Vito Cotoni at home, who was just about to head to bed.

"It's probably nothing, but I just received a call from a lady who thinks she may have seen Robin late this afternoon. It was at an industrial yard near where she works in North Surrey, by the river."

"What else? Is there an address?" Vito's heart was starting to race. After taking down the information, including the time of the sighting, he decided to call Rodney at home. Rodney was not pleased to be getting a work call this late, but reluctantly agreed they better spring into action. He called the tactical squad and requested a unit be sent to the North Surrey address. He then called the RCMP, whose turf it was, and explained what was happening. They dispatched several cars to the scene with orders to cut off the area, but not approach as yet. Rodney then decided to share the news by calling Steve at home. If Rodney's evening could be disturbed, then fair was fair.

In the end, and after much manpower dispatched, it was mostly for naught. The site was completely vacant, but evidence of someone's incarceration was abundant. The forensic people would be busy for a while.

Next morning, the lady from the trucking firm noted the extensive display of yellow tape along the roadside on her way to work. So, she had been right! After she had set up her station for the day, work took a back seat to tales of kidnappers for her fellow employees.

~ 22 ~

What had started out as a nerve-wracking time for the Guru had turned out far better than he could have imagined. He had an extra quarter of a million dollars in his possession on top of the original one hundred thousand he had negotiated, and he was freed of taking care of the policeman's son. One of his men had driven back to the industrial site the morning after the handover to clean up, but he kept going, the police tape telling him all he needed to know. The negative side of the ledger noted the loss of this North Surrey hideout, some embarrassment in front of the Chinese lads, and hurt feelings harboured by a couple of his associates. The extra money more than made up for those difficulties. It was Thursday, and he decided to have a meeting to assess the state of the union. The Guru didn't listen to or watch the news very often, preferring to remain in his own world, thus depriving him of some basic facts before he started his meeting.

* * *

Earlier that same morning, the CBC had aired their morning radio show in the grand lobby of the Simon Fraser

University campus in Surrey Central. Needed equipment had been installed and checked the previous evening, all in readiness for the 5:00 am start time. Because of the remote location, some of the talent didn't show up until half past four, put out by the extra travel involved, not to mention the disruption to their routine. It was enough to give the producer a mild headache.

The host arrived grumpy, and after getting briefed, perused the script for the morning. He knew that an interview was set for around 6:45 with someone called Dev— apparently an ex-gang member. His brief was to interrogate Dev about gang life, how he got out, and what he was doing now with his life. The airtime before the interview was to be taken up with background to the gang story and recent developments. In addition to Dev, another former gang member would be in attendance, expounding on the benefits of the school visit program he led. There were no uniformed RCMP officers attending, despite the CBC's request to the City of Surrey, however one plainclothes officer was tasked to keep a watch on the show. He appeared and immediately made for the coffee on offer to help pry his eyes open. His personal schedule was never what one would consider normal, but to think these people willingly got up this early every day for work boggled his mind.

The show started live at five on the tail end of the local news. The first ninety minutes went smoothly, the lobby slowly starting to come alive with a few students and office workers who worked in the adjacent tower. Dev had appeared just after six and was prepped for his part of the show. At 6:35 he was led over to the table where he would be sitting alongside the host. He settled into his chair with the proffered headphones, nervous, not having done anything like this before. A few more people gathered around, anticipating what was to come after all the shilling that the CBC had done for this show.

* * *

Hovering in the background, around nine metres away, Sanji was standing beside a small group. He was nervously walking back and forth wearing an oversized windbreaker. His right hand was nestled inside the front of his jacket, cradling a pistol complete with silencer. The undercover officer had noticed Sanji's agitation and was watching. Sanji waited until the host introduced Dev, then took out the gun, aimed, and fired a few shots. Sanji was not a great marksman, and nine metres in an unfamiliar environment is a stretch for even very good gunmen. Dev had leaned back a tad, and the first bullet went by his face, through the front of the radio host's throat, grazing his windpipe. It was a serious wound but not critical. The second and third shots didn't hit anybody. Sanji wisely decided that his best chances were gone, so he turned and started running, right past the surprised plainclothes officer. He turned, dropped to a knee, carefully aimed his SIG Sauer, and took Sanji down with one shot to the back. He was definitely a better man with a pistol than Sanji. He walked over to where Sanji lay, got on his cell, and called for an ambulance for the shooting victims. He bent down to check Sanji's pulse, which, after a moment, he found to be absent. He then looked back at the broadcast table, which had reddened significantly.

One of the CBC crew was trying to staunch the blood flow from the host's throat, first aid being part of his training. People were running around, some were screaming, all in all, quite the start to the day. It was not clear at the moment, but the host's future on-air career would be over, even after the ministrations of the medical profession.

The officer looked out over the lobby, checking that there weren't any more people aiming to cause mayhem. Well, this was way more interesting than he had been led to believe. He decided to go over and pour another cup of coffee while he waited for the calvary to arrive. He knew his professional life was basically screwed for a while. Using a firearm in public was bad enough, but killing a perpetrator was going to end up in a long internal investigation, with him as the centrepiece. However, to the upside, was suspension with pay, something he had always dreamed about.

The star of the show, Dev, was disconcerted, feeling lucky to have escaped injury. Maybe a lower profile in the future might be on order. He felt radio didn't really seem to suit him.

* * *

Back at the Guru's club, his soldiers were slowly meandering in. It was after lunch and the Guru had called in all but the lowliest of his men, the ones who had yet to prove their worth and bone fides. Twelve gangsters filled the seats, the Guru at the head of the table. He did a mental head count, remembering that three of them had sadly left his employ.

Someone was missing. "Where is Sanji?"

Bobbi sat still, looking around the table at the other faces. A full two thirds of them were looking down, studying their phones. Maccha stared back at him, his phone in front of him, on the table. No one seemed to have a clue that Sanji had died that morning. So, whatever they were looking at, it wasn't any of the local news networks. He found it hard to believe how out of touch they were with everyday events. His leader didn't appear to be any better informed. "Sanji may be a while—he's dead."

Maccha, who was sitting opposite Bobbi, spoke first, trying hard to put a stick in Bobbi's spokes. "How do you know this? Did you kill him?"

"I heard it on the news, you idiot."

Maccha rose and lunged at Bobbi from across the table, but Bobbi was alert and backed away just enough to escape Maccha's grasping fingers. He smiled at the loss of control. This infuriated Maccha further.

The others were not aware of the issues between the two, but the Guru had had enough. "Sit down!" Then he continued. "What do you mean, he's dead?"

"There was some kind of shootout at the SFU lobby in Surrey this morning and he got killed by a cop. The news feed didn't say much else, but they ID'd him. Must have been stupid enough to have his wallet with him." Bobbi looked around the table and decided to take the risk, "Am I the only person here who knows what's going on?" This provoked some murmurs and a couple of curses directed at him. Manny looked at him thoughtfully.

"It seems so Bobbi." The Guru responded. He was impressed. It took balls to say that amongst this group. The loss of Sanji, however, was not welcome news. His group was now down four gangsters and counting. He wondered if the killing was further retribution for things his gang had done recently.

However, he still had a meeting to run. "Despite several screw-ups by some of you, we have come out two hundred thousand dollars ahead from this kidnapping episode." He was not going to tell the group how much he had really freed from those triad boys, but the news perked up the meeting.

"Unfortunately, we seem to have lost the use of our property at the river, so there is that on the minus side. You each will get eight thousand dollars, with some extra for the crew that did the job and looked after the package." This money would be in addition to their regular pay, so the local restaurants and clubs were going to be doing well for several days. Smiles broke out around the table. The good times for a few would only last until some of the cash made its way to a local bank and got flagged as marked drug money.

There was a bar at one end of the room, which the Guru decided to break open for once. "Help yourselves to a drink if you wish."

Excited conversation broke out. This was unprecedented. Most of the group quickly got up, crowding around the table. Near the far end of the table, Bobbi sat watching, considering how little attention was paid to Sanji's demise, as if he were a disposable item, no longer needed or even to be thought about. Bobbi stayed in his seat, staring at the table. Several cellphones were sitting there, forgotten for a few minutes, including Maccha's. A germ of an idea that had been rolling around in his brain for a day exploded. Revenge was going to be sweet, and the best part was that he would be out of the fray, that is, if his plan worked out. All he needed was to get his hands on Maccha's phone for a minute to put his plan into action, not a minor problem. He decided to act right away; screw the risk, while the drink fest was happening. Maccha's back was to him as he nattered away at Manny at the far end of the room. Manny was not a fan of Maccha and was doing his best not to listen to whatever ramblings came from his lips.

After a few moments of frivolity, the Guru wanted to get back to business, so he continued loudly while the throng was pouring drinks, "We need to find the Farhad traitor. I want enquires put out, and I want him found. Is this clear?"

The Guru was getting mixed up. As recently as a few days ago, the gang had been warned to keep their heads down, on the watch for a cop reprisal for the kidnapping. Now they were being told to get out there and find some-one. It was as if magically, the police would now be chasing the triad boys and leaving the Gupils in peace. The Guru was not great at looking at things from different points of view. As the gang members started talking amongst them-selves, drinks in hand, the meeting devolved again into the finer points of running drugs in the Lower Mainland. The Guru was left wondering how much smaller his gang would be by the end of this episode.

* * *

In Vancouver that morning, Robert and Camille started their day with same depression hanging over them that had accompanied the previous days. Camille was readying herself to go into work, dreading another run-in with Rodney, knowing that Steve was useless at protecting her, as he seemed to be with most things. The guilt in Robert's mind was unceasing.

The landline rang, "Camille here."

"Camille, it's Tony. Results came back on the finger. Turns out that it used to belong to Gurmit."

"Oh. Thank God, but that is still gruesome. Thanks for calling, Tony. I'll see you soon."

"Wait, there's more. Last night we think there was a sighting of Robin. A lady saw some men chasing a kid in an industrial yard in North Surrey on her way home from work. She didn't twig to what she had seen until she saw the late news. She called it in, but by then the place was cleared out. But it looks as though Robin was being held there according to traces in the building. Good news of a sort, I think. The lady didn't say much else, but she did notice the vehicles, one being a Range Rover, and the other one looked like a BMW." He paused, then before breaking the connection, "They would have to be pretty stupid to not realize we'd find out who the finger really belonged to. See you at the office Camille."

"What?" Robert was jittery, any good news welcome.

"It wasn't Robin's finger. It was Gurmit's. And someone saw Robin last evening at an industrial yard in Surrey. It was empty by the time officers showed up though but there was evidence that he was there. Maybe he was being moved." She told him about the vehicles.

Robert smiled thinly as he started thinking things through. "So, if the Gupils dealt with Gurmit, how did the triad get the finger? It looks to me like I was correct. The Gupils are working for the triad, doing their dirty work. A Range Rover sounds like the Guru to me." He got up to refill his coffee cup. "Doesn't leave us any farther ahead though. Maybe I need to have a discussion with the triad girl we have."

"Well, I sense that you are already light years ahead of Rodney in this investigation." She changed gears. "I've got to get going. You'll get Sophie to school?"

"Yup. Take care Camille and watch your back." He kissed her before returning to his coffee and his meditations on gangs. After a while at this and getting nowhere, he downed the last of his third cup of coffee and called his father. If the police were watching his home, he had to assume they were monitoring his calls. He used the pre-paid cellphone he had purchased a couple of days earlier. He had left one with his father, leaving him with two spares for future problems.

"Hello Dad. How are you?"

"I'm good Robert. I believe that Winston lands sometime later today. I will wait for his call, but I don't know where he will be staying, might be the airport hotel."

Robert relayed the news he had about Robin, and his belief that there were two gangs involved, then, "I think I'm going to visit Farhad to talk to that woman, but I may have to sneak around. I'm sure I am still under surveillance by the VPD. Contact you later."

Two officers, replacements for the previous pair who were no longer getting along, were indeed sitting in another Crown Victoria at the end of the block, and they had noted Camille leaving. She waved at them as she drove by. They then realized the problem they had; a target with no vehicle (they assumed) and they could only monitor either the front or the rear of the residence, but not both. The driver radioed in that they needed help. The detective on the other end helpfully told them to stuff it and do their job. They sat, thinking up a strategy to cover Robert, but by the time one of them worked up the initiative to actually get out of the car and do a walk-by, Robert had left the townhouse with his daughter. He knew exactly how lazy the men were. Once they were in their car, it was as though the doors were welded shut, and nothing short of a bomb, or the end of a shift, could get them out of it.

The high school was in the opposite direction from where the ghost car was sitting, so the officers had no chance of seeing the couple. As Robert walked, he started thinking about Farhad and how much longer it would be before some bright light at the station decided maybe they should keep an eye on him as well. He'd have to be careful as he approached the safe house, checking for people out of place.

"We think Robin was spotted last night, over in Surrey."

"What? Did we get him back?"

"He was gone by the time the police showed up, but...." The news was a positive, of a sort.

"I can't stop thinking about him." Sophie said, staring at the pavement.

"We're going to get him back." Robert affected an air of bravado he in no way felt. At the school he said good-bye to Sophie, kissing her lightly, then kept walking over to Knight Street to hop a bus south towards Farhad's hideout.

* * *

In Kowloon, at the same time, it was early morning the next day and Cedric was jumpy. He had decided that he needed to travel to Vancouver to rescue his mistress. All he needed was Jacky's blessing. Which to be frank, was a bonus, if granted. He didn't give a damn whether Jacky gave it or not, but he thought it courteous to ask. He texted Jacky, then headed over to the club, where Jacky spent the majority of his time ensconced in luxurious living.

He walked up to Jacky's office and knocked before entering. "Hey Jacky."

"Cedric? To what do I owe this visit?"

"Think I am going over to Vancouver to get Ivy."

Jacky looked back at Cedric with a totally neutral expression. It was as if Cedric hadn't said a word. Then, "Good. I was going to send you anyway. I heard from my man at the HKPF. Winston Chang is on his way over there. I need you to be there to make sure Edward doesn't totally screw this up. Take a man with you. I want to make sure about this. I want Winston dead. Got it?"

Cedric smiled, "Ok, see you in a couple of days." He turned and left. He hadn't even sat down. He got what he wanted, but as he walked out of the club it dawned on him that now, essentially the whole damn operation was resting squarely on his shoulders. Not exactly what he had in mind when he started the day. When would he learn to keep his trap shut? He had strolled into that meeting like a sheep ready for the axe. Plus, he still had to rescue Ivy.

He returned to the cubbyhole he called his office and had his sometime assistant book some flights, as well as hotel rooms. His next concern was who to select for this adventure; someone who could keep his mouth shut, and good with weapons. Many were either/or but not both, so in the end he ended up taking his most trusted man along. He hadn't been to Vancouver previously and spoke only Cantonese, badly.

* * *

Back at the office on Cambie Street, a detective received a phone call, put through by the admin assistant. The message was extremely short, and the caller wasn't speaking very loudly, "Manny Dhillon killed Gurmit." Four words and the connection was severed, but the detective had a record of the caller's number. He sat in his chair mulling over what he had heard, wondering why someone would tell him this.

He stuck his head around the partition and beckoned Vito over. He could have gone to someone more senior, but thought he'd speak to someone he trusted first. "Vito, let's go talk." Rick led Vito down the corridor to a small meeting room, entered, and shut the door.

"What's up Rick?"

"I just received a call telling me who killed Gurmit."

"Hmmmm." Vito had sat down, but Rick paced around the small room.

"Exactly. Is it real? Is it revenge? Or someone trying to cause trouble? Apparently, the killer is someone named Manny Dhillon. Do you know the name?"

"Nope. The Taskforce?"

"Yeah, they'll know. Think I'll get the number traced, then go see Thomas."

"Wonder if it's anything to do with the kidnapping." Vito testing waters. Rick offered up silence, but he was thinking. The killing and the kidnapping were by far the most important crimes that had the attention of the VPD. And he knew that Vito was working the kidnapping. Opportunities like this were not to be squandered.

"We think it was the Gupils who did the deed. Wonder if this Manny chap is a Gupil?" Again, nothing from Rick. "Can you let me know what Thomas says?"

"No worries, Vito. I'll see what I can find out."

Vito nodded his appreciation as they both exited the room. Rick returned to his desk and asked for a trace on the number that had registered on his phone. He then twiddled his fingers while he waited, sensing this was somehow important. Vito knew that what he had learned should probably get to Tony but waited—there might be more. He decided to go up the street to Cafe Paulo for coffee, Robert not being the only addict on the police force. As he entered, he noticed Camille sitting by the window in what was Robert's former territory. He waved but didn't come any closer, not wanting to queer the pipeline before it had a chance. Other officers showed up at the cafe from time to time, and people talked.

Camille was gathering her wits after another tongue-lashing from Rodney. He was feeling the pressure from above due to the lack of progress. Naturally he shunted it down the line like the good bastard he was. His suggestion to get Camille put on permanent leave had not been well received by his superiors, only adding to his anger level. Over coffee, Camille pondered her situation. She decided to check back in, then head home. She had seen Vito and knew not to approach, but his nod suggested something.

* * *

Rick finally got the name off the phone trace, so he took a trip downstairs to see Thomas Harrow. Gladys seemed to be missing, so he went up to Thomas's door and rapped on the frame.

"Come in."

"Hi. My name is Rick Santos, from upstairs." He decided to close the door and take a seat, so Thomas knew something was up. "I received a call a little while ago, very short and to the point, and I quote, 'Manny Dhillon killed Gurmit'. That was it. So, I traced the call. It came from a phone registered to a Maccha Sunner." He tried for nonchalant as he asked the golden question, "They both Gupils?"

Thomas didn't answer quickly, so Rick knew he had hit the target, "We'll bring them both in. Thanks Rick. You are with?"

"Investigations, upstairs. Under Rodney Fister."

"My condolences."

Rick smiled as he left the office. Thomas got on his phone and gave the order to grab both men. He was careful not to say why he wanted them apprehended, lest they arrive at headquarters in less than pristine condition. He didn't care if he had no evidence, he'd get them into the station and make their lives difficult for a while. And after some thought, he was sure that interviewing both at the same time would make for some interesting interaction—maybe a fight, who knows. At the very least, he hoped one of them would make a mistake.

* * *

Robert had made his way to Farhad's apartment after getting off the bus several blocks away. He took his time, approaching slowly, watching all the way. The sky was lead grey, matching what his brain felt like. As he approached the entry to the building an older couple strolled along toward him. He kept walking as they passed beside him, nodding his way. He exhaled, knowing they weren't watchers. More talented surveillance people might have boldly acknowledged him as they had, but he knew people in the VPD didn't rise to this level. He walked further, then pivoted and strode up to the entry phone at the front door.

Farhad answered his door carefully, allowing Robert

into his apartment. Robert noticed an angry mark on the side of Farhad's forehead, which he pointed to.

"She tried to get sporty with me. I had to sort her out."

Robert's questioning eyes prompted more, "She's fine. Not so bossy anymore."

"How are you doing?" Robert asked.

"Good. I had to improvise a few things to keep her at bay, but on the whole ready to do something else I think."

"I don't think this is going to last much longer. Things are coming to a head. I need to ask her a few questions. I'm sure I won't get anything out of her, but thought I'd try. Can you bring her into the living room?"

Farhad went into one of the bedrooms, unleashed Ivy and led her into the room where Robert sat, waiting. Robert immediately noticed a small bluish bruise next to her left eye, the result of Farhad's ministrations. If Robert was going to find out anything, he knew he'd need to be subtle. He started out with a simple observation in Cantonese, "You look like a mess."

Ivy was startled by Robert's Cantonese, then tried to recover. "This ape hit me."

"Sure about that? Looks like you walked into a door." Robert then sat silent for a few moments, waiting for her discomfort to grow.

"You will regret keeping me here." Ivy tried some bluster.

"Yes, it is most unfortunate that you have to be here, but it is hard to see any future for you until my son is safely returned to me."

"Jacky will have your head for this." It came out before Ivy could help herself.

It was more than he could have hoped for, but he tried to go a little further anyway. "Does Jacky have my son?"

"Fuck off."

He had gotten one piece of information from her, so it was time for insults, "I'd ask who you work for, but you don't work for a living do you?" This was met with sullen silence. "You probably make your way in the world by screwing your way around Kowloon." Ivy's eyes were flashing at this accusation, but she held her tongue. How did this cop know she was from Kowloon?

Robert nodded to Farhad, who rose, grabbed Ivy, and marched her back into the bedroom. When he had made sure she was confined, he returned. Robert gave him one of the burner phones he had, "My number is programmed in. I'll be in touch soon. I think this is all going to play out in the next day or two. How? I wish I knew, but I have a feeling it's going to be messy. You sure you can handle her? You'll probably have to move her at some point."

"That's what trunks are for Robert, moving things. I'll be fine."

"Keep your eyes open Farhad, the VPD may put a watch on this place. I'm not exactly the flavour of the week these days. And thanks for this Farhad, I owe you."

Farhad was feeling more confident these days. In addition to getting his car back, he had also visited his friend in Steveston, who had agreed to hide Farhad's goods in exchange for some cash, of course. Everything seemed under control, and he was even starting to appreciate Ivy.

But he wasn't letting Robert know. Farhad smiled and patted Robert on the arm. "We'll get him back Robert."

Robert wished he had the confidence to agree, but he didn't feel in control of anything as he walked out the apartment door. Robert exited the building, not spotting anything suspicious. To Robert, this seemed about right with Rodney leading the investigation. He was always two steps behind the action.

~ 23 ~

In Vancouver, Thomas's men put in the request to the Surrey RCMP to bring both Manny and Maccha in for questioning. Officers had been dispatched, two cars to each of the known locations where the men were thought to live. It was late afternoon, after the Gupil meeting ended, and Manny had returned to his condo to chill before heading out to spend some of his new-found money. Maccha however headed straight to a bar after the meeting, so avoiding the unpleasantness of a trip downtown, at least for another day.

The cars pulled up to Manny's condo tower. Two men were sent to cover the parkade exit, and the remaining main floor exit. The remaining two waited until someone was leaving through the front lobby. They flashed their badges and gained entry. The actual arrest went smoothly enough. Manny answered his door calmly and surrendered to the officers. In his mind, he hadn't done anything wrong. For their part, the two officers were relieved that Manny didn't make a fuss, as there was considerable doubt as to whether they could have handled him on their own if he had resisted. Manny took up a full two/thirds of the rear seat in the squad car as it departed for King George Highway. It didn't take long for Manny to discern that they weren't headed to the Surrey RCMP premises, but instead, into Vancouver.

"Where are you taking me?"

It was the first thing Manny had uttered since his arrest.

"Downtown, Cambie Street." Came the terse reply. Manny thought about this but decided not to answer. Fifty minutes later, travelling opposite the rush hour mess, the car arrived in the underground sally port at Cambie Street. The VPD took custody of Manny with the necessary paperwork completed. An officer led Manny directly to an interview room and manacled him to a table to wait. Manny tested the cuff and decided that he could rip it off the table if he really wanted to, but tried to remain calm. At three hundred and thirty pounds, many people thought he resembled a huge pile of jelly. The opposite was true. Sure, some lard featured in the collection, but there was also significant muscle. The RCMP officers had been correct in their assessment that Manny could be physically very dangerous. Manny sat at the table, drumming his fingers, wondering why he had been taken in. He had been responsible for several bad things over the years, but nothing had stuck to him to date.

The door swung open, and Thomas entered the room, alone. He wasn't worried about his personal safety, until he saw Manny. He could have several officers in the room in a few seconds at any sign of trouble, if necessary, but in this case, it might not make a difference.

Thomas sat down across from Manny, placing a manila file folder on the table. "Do you know why you are here?"

"No."

"We received an interesting phone call today. It said, and I quote, 'Manny Dhillon killed Gurmit.' And you are Manny Dhillon, correct?"

Manny sat, thinking. "Anyone can call you and say whatever they like."

"This was a Maccha Sunner, apparently. He is being picked up as well for questioning." Thomas watched as Manny's eyes widened ever so slightly, a look of menace creeping onto his face. "I believe he is an associate of yours."

"So what?" He was affecting nonchalance, but Thomas suspected Manny was contemplating seriously altering Maccha's physical makeup once he got his hands on him.

"So, if we get him in here and he confirms what we heard, you will be charged with murder of a policeman. How does that sound?"

"Sounds like you guys are fishing. Do you have a licence?"

Thomas smiled at the impertinence. "What do you know about the Lui kidnapping?"

"Nothing."

Knowing the interview was over, he rose, walked out of the room, and motioned for the officer waiting to take Manny to a cell. Manny remained calm. He knew they would have to charge him with something in order to keep him more than day in custody, and until that happened, he wouldn't be calling a lawyer, the Guru, or anyone.

* * *

As Thomas walked onto his floor heading to his office, a forensic technician strode over to him, nodding at the open door. Thomas gestured for him to enter ahead of him. Thomas closed the door. The tech remained standing.

"You're in charge of the Gurmit killing, correct?"

"Yes."

"Our analysis of the scene where Robin Lui was being held out in Surrey indicates that Gurmit spilled some blood there."

Thomas's eyes darkened, "Makes sense, I guess. They'd have a place where they do their interrogations. Not any-more, for now at least. I want those bastards so badly."

The tech nodded, sensing the fire building in Thomas, "I'd better get back."

"Thanks for this. Keep it quiet please."

* * *

Robin was again sitting in a room that wasn't much different from his previous place of imprisonment. Maybe there was a book on this stuff, how to decorate a room to keep a prisoner depressed. He wasn't totally sure about what had happened a day earlier after his aborted escape attempt, but it felt like he was being traded or sold to a different set of thugs. His present guard was Chinese, and again, not much larger than himself. But if he had to guess, the new guard wasn't going to be the patsy that the previ-ous guy had been. He had no idea where he was, but he had heard a low-pitched distant sounding whistle go off earlier in the day that could have been announcing noon, or the end of a shift maybe. Robin's new guard was one of the men on probation that Jason resorted to. His men that had screwed up the Gladys snatch had only been released from custody on significant bail this day so he decided to put a new guy on babysitting duty, but only after making sure he knew what kind of trouble Robin could get up to.

For his part, the only thing Robin could possibly be optimistic about, was that maybe he'd get some Chinese food out of the deal, given who his minder was. The food in his last cell was pretty horrible. He wondered how Sophie was doing, and how Rose was doing. Ah, Rose, beautiful Rose. He knew what she probably thought about him, which was nothing much, but maybe his stock with her would rise, if he got out of this alive that is. He wondered how his hockey team was doing without him.

* * *

Robert returned to his neighbourhood mid-afternoon after his conversation with Ivy and had a thought. He walked along Fraser, stopping at a pastry shop. He purchased four eclairs and a couple of coffees to go. He then walked north on Fraser to East 27th Avenue and made his way slowly along the sidewalk until he came up behind the Crown Victoria belonging to his watchers. He rapped on the passenger side window, startling the drowsy officer. He looked at Robert and after quickly realizing who it was, displayed a distinctly guilty mien. The window lowered.

"Figured you guys might need a sugar fix. How's it going?" Robert being merciless.

"Funny." After a pause, "But thanks." Then after some more thought, "You didn't drop a mickey in the coffee, did you?"

Robert smiled before rubbing it in a little further, "It doesn't appear that I need to do that, does it?" He then turned and walked up the lane waving at the officers with the back of his hand, heading home.

"Asshole. But a nice asshole I guess." The officer divided up the sweets and gave a coffee to the driver. "Somehow reminds me of a movie I saw a long time ago." The driver's reply was garbled by one of the eclairs meeting its demise.

* * *

Robert slowed as he came to the rear of his townhouse, remembering easier times, when all he had to worry about was a crazy murdering psycho on the loose in Vancouver. Now, he was worried about whether his daughter would make it home safely from school, not to mention whether his son would be returned to him. He walked into the home and called out. Sophie answered, and a second teen's voice joined in from upstairs, probably Rose. He relaxed slightly, then his thoughts turned to dinner, and his father.

Farther south, at Vancouver's airport, an EVA flight originating in Hong Kong was landing. On board was Winston Chang and his assistant, Lee Pin. The Cathay Pacific travel experience was denied the two, the HKPF budget not allowing for such extravagance. EVA's definition of business class didn't exactly match what other airlines offered, and Winston was trying hard to see what was different from the tourist class section farther back in the plane. After the long wait to exit the plane and clearing customs, they walked up a couple of levels in the terminal to the lobby of the Fairmont YVR hotel and checked in.

* * *

Earlier that afternoon, a call had been received at the VPD station on Cambie. The call ended up being accepted by Thomas Harrow. He was informed that Chief Inspector Winston Chang would be landing in town today, per the request from Vancouver. He should be afforded the usual courtesies.

After the call ended, Thomas sat, wondering. He hadn't called Hong Kong and couldn't come up with a reason why someone would come all the way over the Pacific. While he dialled the number of Deputy Chief McKnight, a thought blossomed. Could it be Robert? After the call ended, Chief McKnight confirming that he had made no such request, Thomas was pretty sure who was behind this. Two questions surfaced, where was this Inspector Chang, and why was he here? And if the HKPF people thought the inspector was coming to see the VPD, what exactly was going on? He decided to boot it along the chain of command to get a few answers by calling Steve Christie.

"Steve, it's Thomas. I want you to find a Chief Inspector Winston Chang who apparently arrived from Hong Kong today. Find out what he is doing here. Thanks."

The line clicked dead, and Steve sat, staring at his phone. It was unusual to be asked to do something this specific, so he was flummoxed. Steve was used to filling out reports on manpower, training, and attending meetings. He did what any good bureaucrat would do and called Rodney, repeated what he had been asked to find out and hung up. Rodney swore. How was he supposed to solve a kidnapping if he was asked to run around looking for police officers from foreign countries. Didn't those higher-ups know where their brethren were? Why was it up to him to do this shit work? He decided to bump it down a level and called in Vito, "Can you find a Winnie Chan for me? He was supposed to have arrived today from Hong Kong. He is a cop apparently."

Vito nodded, left Rodney's workspace, and headed back to his own seat to think for a second. It didn't take more than that to put the pieces together. He dialled Tony and told him who he was supposed to find.

"That name sounds kind of odd, but I'll relay the info. Thanks." Tony responded.

With that done, Vito proceeded to try to find a person who didn't really exist. It also wasn't on the top of his priority list, so he didn't get going on it for another hour. Meanwhile, Tony walked over to Camille's office, which was empty. He decided to call her using his cell to relay the information. She had just arrived home, and after answering the call, considered the information for a moment, realizing who they were trying to find.

"Tony, could you do something for me?"

"Of course."

"Could you get back to Vito and ask him to only look for that specific name? No variants if possible."

"So, he'll be searching using the wrong name?"

"Pretty sure that's what's going on."

"No problem." Tony was smiling.

* * *

It was only after more than fifteen minutes had elapsed that Rodney was able to put two and two together. He belatedly remembered the note from the kidnappers about a Winston. Must be the same guy! Brilliant. This was why he was in charge of the kidnapping file. He started a tuneless humming to himself, sure that he would be solving this case before the end of the week.

* * *

After Tony's call, Camille dropped her phone on the dining room table and grabbed Robert, who had just come down the stairs after confirming that Rose could stay for dinner. Wrapping her arms around Robert, she squeezed as tight as she could. Robert hugged Camille back, resting his head in her hair, breathing in her scent, trying to put his worries aside for a moment.

"Winston is in town."

He lifted his head, "How do you know this?"

"Because someone at the station found out and they are now looking for him, under the name of Winnie Chan." She laughed. "Sounds to me like something got scrambled, but that's who they're looking for, nobody else, I made sure of that." Camille then relayed the rest of the story as she knew it.

Robert was satisfied that, for now, Winston would be firmly on their team, not the VPD's, for whatever was to come. He briefly thought about dinner, and decided it was time to raid the freezer. He had no intention of cooking anything good until Robin was returned. He rooted around and found some frozen soup and a bag of scones. The soup was split pea and bacon, so the teenagers shouldn't be complaining, too much.

Robert's prepaid phone rang. He grabbed it immediately.

"Robert?"

"Yes, Dad. Nobody else would be answering this, correct?" Robert wondered if the general concept of burner phones eluded Ethan.

"Okay. Winston has landed and contacted me. I'm planning to meet him tomorrow morning here at my place. Is that good?"

Robert considered it briefly, "Should be fine, but the VPD know he is in town and are looking for him. Can't figure why they don't know where he is staying, but that's the VPD for you. Camille has put them off the scent, but I don't know how long that will last. I'd like to come and meet Winston, but I'm a little unsure if I can make it out of here un-followed. I'll call you tomorrow morning when I figure it out." A simple thought came to him.

"Camille. Can you go out back and re-park the car, so the nose is facing out of the carport?"

"Sure, although let me do it after I drive Rose home." She looked at him. What was he up to? She tossed a questioning look at Robert. He smiled, "I'm going to hop in the trunk tomorrow while you take Sophie to school.

Then I'll get out and go visit my dad. That is, if you'll open the trunk."

Camille didn't smile. "I'll think about it."

Dinner talk was kept light for the girls' sake, the real conversation held back until Rose was taken home. Sophie had retreated upstairs to her room and cellphone, the dishes left to their own devices. Robert and Camille sat across from each other at the dinner table after she returned from her taxi duty. Robert started, "I'm going to need some backup for what's coming."

"You know I'm here for you, Robert. You don't need to ask a question like that."

"Yes, but you realize it will probably get you booted off the force, don't you?"

"I think I'm already halfway gone thanks to that Rod jackass."

"I wouldn't put too much stock in that character. He has limited influence, and skills for that matter. But when they realize you have been actively helping me, your employment options may be severely limited. I'm pretty sure I am out after the fools I've made them look like. It's not difficult to do, that's the concerning thing."

"How do we let the kidnappers know that Winston is here?"

"I bet they already know somehow. My concern is that they will be picking the time and place to do whatever they are planning. Puts us at a great disadvantage. Plus, there is only you and me. I'm guessing Winston and his assistant aren't armed." Robert paused, "I better get that extra gun out and clean it up."

"Tony will help us if we ask him."

"No, I don't want to screw up his career as well. This whole thing is on me. Farhad will be on our side. He doesn't work for the City of Vancouver, and he has their courier after all. She is pretty good-looking. I'm assuming they want her back."

"How good-looking?"

Robert backpedalled, "Not that good-looking."

"But enough for someone to want her back."

Robert could only smile lamely. "I'm going to go get that gun."

* * *

Later that night, in Surrey, an RCMP car was waiting in front of Maccha's apartment tower. Just after one, the officers spotted what looked like Maccha walking toward the lobby entrance after leaving a taxi. He had a young girl on his arm. His right hand was on her ass and the walking was not exactly on the straight and narrow. The officers exited their car, went up to Maccha, showing him a badge. The younger officer had his hand on the grip of his pistol, safety off. When the subject of an arrest was a drunk gangster, life was unpredictable. The older officer carried a billy club low down, next to his leg. In no way was this countenanced by the force, but Reg was old school. Tasers were for sissies. As expected, once the officers told Maccha who they were and what they wanted, he flew into a show-off rage, cursing and spitting. This behaviour didn't last longer than it took Reg to administer a gentle tap to side of Maccha's head, knocking him down. As stars whirled around his head, he was cuffed, then thrown into the rear of the cruiser while the girl stood there, slowly realizing her night was over, but not sure what had just happened.

The younger officer knew it was just a matter of time before modern times caught up with Reg and he'd be put out to pasture. Video available from security cameras was everywhere. Then there were members of the public, who thought they were Francis Ford fucking Coppola, filming anything they thought remotely similar to police harassment or brutality. As if all the perpetrators were angels. It was only a matter of time and circumstance. But in the meantime, Reg quietly went about his business, cleaning up messes.

The cruiser then followed the same pattern established earlier in the day by Manny's capture, heading into Vancouver and depositing Maccha into the care of the attending officer at Cambie Street. He ended up in a lovely holding cell until he could be interviewed the next morning. The officers then headed back to Surrey, a satisfactory end to a long day. On the other side of the world, Cedric and his helper boarded an EVA flight bound for Vancouver. They would arrive exactly a day after Winston and Lee landed.

* * *

The next morning, in Richmond, Edward was sitting in his condo puzzling out how he was going to accomplish what needed doing while getting richer, and without losing his life. He had just been informed that Jacky was sending Cedric and another man over from Hong Kong to assist him. This was both bad and good news. He intensely disliked having his actions monitored by other people, but he could really use the extra men for what was to come. He supposed Cedric was coming to rescue Ivy. He didn't care what happened to Ivy. His short evening with her confirmed a quickly formed opinion that she was rather too full of herself; an attribute that was likely to result in a short life given who she hung around with, despite her beauty. The call from Jacky also confirmed that Winston was on his way to Vancouver as well. So, the pieces were falling into place.

Rain battered his living room window as he made a call to Jason and told him to come over for a war council. He normally didn't like conducting business from his home, but he knew he would be moving soon, so it mattered less. His motto was, the fewer people who knew where he lived, the better. All they had to do was to get their hands on Winston, then give him to Cedric. It sounded simple, but Edward knew it would be anything but.

His entry phone finally rang, and he let Jason enter the lobby, but not before carefully ensuring that no one else was in his company. Once Jason was inside his suite, he offered him some tea, then they sat in the living room watching the wet greyness cling to the outside of the windows.

"I think we'll do the exchange at the Columbia Fish Yards where we have the kid stashed." Edward started. "We can leave by boat if the roads are blocked."

"Really? You think the cops will be there?"

"I don't know Jason. They might be."

"Then we should take a crappy car, I don't want to lose my Mercedes."

Edward sat, thinking. "We can't let them have any preparation time. Who is the contact again?"

"It's the cook, Robert's dad. It is the only number we have. He is the one who knows Winston."

"I guess we have to wait until Cedric arrives from Hong Kong. Is he getting here today?"

"Late this afternoon."

"How many men do we have?"

"Six, plus the young guy taking care of Robin. But two of them are watchers, maybe not so good in a fight, if it comes to that."

Edward didn't respond, thinking. "Might need a couple of Gupils, to round out the team. Cedric supposedly is bringing someone with him. So, eight or ten on our side." What he was thinking was that the numbers sounded okay but having men from several different groups signified trouble. "I think tomorrow is the day. I want to be rid of the kid, and all this nonsense." Patience wearing thin, Edward was trying to imagine what could go wrong.

"Can you get someone to bring our boat across from Ladner today? I want it in position. And one other thing, tell our contact in Victoria to activate the man he has. I want him for two reasons, I want backup in case something goes wrong, and I want him to take out Robert Lui at the meeting."

"You mean kill him?"

"Brilliant Jason, you really are catching on quickly." The sarcasm, thick.

Jason nodded, trying to think how this was going to turn out well for their gang. His guess was that it wouldn't, but there was no arguing with Edward. Then he attempted to remember who knew how to drive a boat in their crew. Edward certainly didn't, not that it stopped him from trying. A single day trip on the water a year ago was all it took for Edward to be captivated. He bought a power boat shortly after, and kept it moored in Ladner across the Fraser, south of Steveston. Jason was certain that Edward had only been out in it a couple of times maximum. It was another toy, a perk, for a group that loved its symbols of power. Edward also had a couple of 150 hp Mercury engines installed after the purchase. These replaced the engines that came with the craft—against the advice of the seller. The boat had not been designed for such powerful engines; but his protestations were a waste of breath, Edward wanted speed and power. The boat could fit nine or ten in a pinch. Jason knew that the Gupils would be left behind whatever happened at the meeting, so it would suffice if events turned against the Wide Bay Boys and they needed a quick exit, provided everything worked out.

* * *

Down at Cambie Street, Maccha was put in a large interview room, solo for now. Thomas thought he would start the interview, and then bring Manny in to see if some fireworks would break out. The larger room would give his officers space to work if some calming tactics were needed. He was under no illusion what damage Manny could cause if he felt so inclined.

Thomas entered the room, noting Mr. Sunner's dishevelled look. Hung over, at a guess, and none too happy after spending a night in a cell. Maccha's greased hair stuck out at stylish angles, except it wasn't on purpose for a change.

Maccha, not one for waiting around, "I want a lawyer."

"What for?"

Maccha looked confused. "Why am I here?"

"For a conversation, nothing more." Thomas answered smoothly. The man on the other side of the table didn't appear to be overly bright. Thomas had a nose for smarts and this one seemed deficient.

He continued, "Do you know a Manny Dhillon?" Thomas could almost see the cogs slowly turning behind Maccha's eyes. Should he answer? Should he lie?

The coin finally landed, on its edge. "Maybe. Why do you want to know?"

"Well, he seems to know you, and he doesn't appear to be super happy with you right now."

As bad as Maccha physically felt at that moment, all of a sudden, he felt worse. He tried to swallow but couldn't, his mouth dry. "Could I have some water?" Stalling for time to think. Thomas was mildly impressed, maybe this guy wasn't so slow. Something bad wriggled into Maccha's brain, "Is he here?"

Thomas didn't respond, watching Maccha's distress grow. He stood up, grabbed a plastic bottle of water from a side table, put it on its side and rolled it across to Maccha.

After a couple of moments Thomas decided to start in. "We received a phone call yesterday from your cellphone saying that Manny Dhillon killed Gurmit. Would you care to comment on that?"

Maccha was in mid-swallow and managed to spew a mouthful of water onto the table, just missing Thomas. His eyes were getting larger by the second. "No way I made that call. You must have screwed up."

Thomas looked at his notes and rolled off Maccha's phone number, "That correct?"

"Yeah, but." His voice dying away.

"Maybe we'll get Manny in here. See what he has to say. What do you think?" This last being purely rhetorical. He was already rising and signalling for Manny to be brought from his cell. This time, however, he was going to have two of his larger constables in the room with him, just in case. Thomas returned to his chair and stared at Maccha, watching his discomfiture worsen.

"I'd like to leave if you aren't going to charge me."

"And miss your buddy? Wouldn't dream of it. Let's wait till he shows up. Then you both can leave together."

Manny was uncertain as to why he was being led back to an interview room after he had successfully rebuffed the policeman's challenges the day before. This lack of clarity was removed when he entered the room. He made a lunge at Maccha from several feet away, but it was a mock attack. The two officers who had a grip on him tightened their holds as the trio lurched forward a couple of feet. They were not much smaller than Manny, so the situation was under some kind of loose control. Maccha was close to relieving himself under the table, but managed to hold it in. Manny stared at Maccha while he was led to a chair across the table from Maccha.

Manny started in, despite himself, "You are dog meat." His inner voice told him to be quiet, but he had to air something.

"I didn't call these guys."

"Shut up." Manny responded.

Thomas was mildly disappointed, but he supposed this was the extent of interaction for now. He didn't want to reveal anything further to these two, such as the DNA evidence gleaned from the room where Gurmit had been tortured. He realized Manny was far brighter than he appeared. "Okay then, time for both of you to leave. We'll remain in touch; how would that be?" Again, silence. Thomas was disappointed in himself. He was starting to miss Robert. "The officers will escort you to the front desk where you can retrieve your possessions."

Once outside on the street, the pair of them stood in the rain. Manny called a driving service to take him back to Surrey. He ignored Maccha, for now that is. He already had a plan to deal with him and would not be waiting very long before he implemented it. The car drove up and Manny got in, the protestations of Maccha taken away by the wind and rain. Maccha was by now getting very worried.

Upstairs, on the fourth floor, after checking all the likely hotels, Vito had come up empty in his search for a Winnie Chan. He strode over to Rodney's office to report his lack of findings. Rodney was confused, Winnie Chan?

Something didn't sound quite right. After a couple of choice curses, Rodney called Steve using the office phone to relay the lack of progress.

After the connection was severed, Steve sat, looking at his phone, then he dutifully called Thomas, "Hi, Steve here. We couldn't find anyone called Winnie Chan in town. Is there anything else you need?"

"Winston Chang, you moron! Should I spell it for you? Chief Inspector Winston fucking Chang. From Hong Kong." He was yelling, the loss of control uncharacteristic.

~ 24 ~

Robert shuddered as he woke. His tee-shirt was damp. Dreaming, he was wandering around inside a police station. He looked out the window and seemed to be in Merritt. A call came from inside Rodney Fister's office. Rodney was sitting at his desk, on which nine fingers were displayed - Robin's fingers. "I'm waiting for the tenth, then we can spring into action." Rodney grinned at Robert. "We'll get him back, no problem." The dreams were becoming more and more vivid as the days passed, manifesting the incompetence that Robert felt permeated the investigation of his son's kidnapping. He shook his head, looking over at Camille, who was still dozing. The dreams were just more confirmation that Robert was going to be the one to bring Robin home, no one else.

After a quick breakfast of toast and a shot of coffee, Robert was ready for another day of playing hide and seek with the VPD. He checked his firearms, including the extra gun he was planning on giving to Winston or his assistant. He stowed it along with its holster and some extra clips of ammunition in a small knapsack. Camille sat waiting patiently by the back door as Sophie collected her things for school. The weather was drizzly and cool, another perfect 'made in Vancouver' day. Robert needed to be at his parent's place, no different from a couple of days earlier. Alternate tactics were called for today, hence the trunk idea. The VPD officers on watch were slow, but not that slow.

This time, they were almost caught. As Camille was closing the trunk lid over Robert, one of the officers was walking up the lane, apparently using some old-fashioned initiative after prying open the door of his cruiser. Camille smiled at him and waved before getting into the Silver Streak, Sophie in the passenger seat. The officer came up to her window, which she opened after a brief hesitation.

"Ma'am. Hope you are fine today." The small talk brief. "Where is your husband?"

Not one to lie to the authorities, she said. "I am not married, but if you are referring to Robert, he is laying down right now."

"Sorry about that. Have a good day." He didn't smile, just touched the brim of his cap with a finger in a lazy salute.

Camille just shook her head at the idiocy of it all as she headed off up the lane towards Sophie's high school. Sophie smiled at Camille, liking the charade. "Fooled them again, Dad!" She yelled loudly, so Robert could hear. Camille glanced in the rear-view mirror. The officer was still standing in the lane, not certain, but suspicious that somehow, he had been duped, again.

***

After she dropped Sophie at her school, Camille circled back north to link up with the SkyTrain line at the Commercial station. Before getting to Broadway, she took a right and then drove a short way up a lane, parking behind a garage. She got out and opened the rear door, releasing the seat back so Robert could get out of the trunk without a big display. He crawled out, blinked twice, and pulled himself out of the car. "Thanks Camille, great work back there."

He smiled grimly, kissed her, then wheeled around, heading north up the lane toting his knapsack. Camille stood watching, wondering if he would hold it together until Robin could be liberated. She reluctantly returned to the driver's seat to make the journey west to Cambie Street where her own work-hell awaited.

Robert took the same route to his parents' place as before, but without all the hijinks of a couple of days earlier. His senses were extremely attuned to the people around him, knowing that making an ass of some watchers would only make them re-double their efforts to find out what he was up to. He also needed to keep an eye out for regular car patrols. If the officers didn't know him personally, they would certainly have his picture on their dashboard screen to refer to as they did their rounds. His neck was knotting up from all the swivelling his head was doing.

Robert gained entry to his parents' apartment and was welcomed with a bear hug from his mother before he could take another step. He kissed her, then asked if the guests had arrived.

"They're here, in the living room, with your father."

He followed his mother into the room. Winston stood up, along with another Chinese gentleman. Ethan introduced Winston as well as Lee Pin.

"I'd forgotten that two of you were coming." Robert opened.

Ethan asked, "Is this a problem?"

"Far from it, Dad. I'm very pleased to meet you both. Dad has told me a few stories." Left unsaid was what these were about. Winston smiled and shook Robert's hand. Lee Pin didn't smile, waiting. His English wasn't totally on point.

"Lee Pin is my assistant. He is along to keep me out of trouble."

"The more people, the better. Thing is, I have only one extra gun with me. I thought you wouldn't be bringing weapons on the flight." Then he realized that he could part with his Tomcat. "However, I have a Beretta that one of you could use."

"I can take that. Give the real gun to Lee. Other than qualifying each year, which I barely manage, I am a little rusty."

"Okay, it comes with an ankle holster." He bent down and undid it, giving it to Winston who looked it over. The group then sat down. For the next half hour, Robert slowly told the story of his child's kidnapping, as he understood it.

"I went to question the courier yesterday. She didn't say much but did let out that she works for a man named Jacky."

Winston looked at Lee. "Jacky Chow is the leader of the Wide Bay Boys in Hong Kong."

"That adds up. They have a chapter in Vancouver that seems to be behind this whole mess."

"Directed by Jacky." Winston added.

"Directed by Jacky." Robert repeated. "We don't know why."

"Well, if they requested me to be exchanged for your son, then it must be for them to kill me. I can't think of any other reason for all the trouble expended on this charade." He thought a bit, then, "I have been a thorn in their side for a long time. They are probably tired of me." Winston smiled wanly. "I checked with my office back home to see if anything important was happening, but it is quiet, so I believe my analysis is correct."

Mary, who had been listening quietly, looked distressed at this conclusion. She correctly assumed that if this was the reason behind the whole mess, then serious injury or death for someone was going to be a likely outcome of the exchange.

"I am going to ask Camille to get us some extra equipment for the meeting." Robert excused himself and went into the kitchen to call her using his prepaid phone. After he returned, talk resumed about what would likely happen. "I'm guessing that we won't get much time to react when they contact us again, it would shift the balance if we could prepare more."

Robert was thinking tactics, "Responding in layers might be the only way to tip the balance. Show up as only two or three people with more behind, make them become uncertain. Winston, myself, and Farhad, with that girl in tow. Camille and Lee Pin could come in behind us. It'd put them off kilter."

Winston pondered this, "In Hong Kong, they like to use the water to get around when they can, if they need to escape."

"Even if they do that here, it doesn't help us locate where they might meet, there are too many arms of the river running through too many communities." Robert responded. "The important thing for you two is to get some rest. You've come a long way, and you can't be at your best when you don't know where you are, or what time it is. Where are you staying?"

"The hotel at the airport."

"My comrades are looking for you, wonder if maybe you should check out, move to a place with a lower profile."

"Comrades?"

"The Vancouver Police Department were alerted to your presence in town, but they don't exactly know why you are here or where you are staying. Not sure who alerted them. Since I have been cut off the case, I am doing my own thing, and the comrades are not happy. They have a twenty-four-hour watch on my townhouse."

"Did they follow you here?"

"No. I've been able to elude them several times. It is depressing how easy it is. But if we get a call to come to get Robin, I may not have the luxury of avoiding them again. It is kind of hard to tell whether it would be an advantage given the situation, or a total cluster fuck, excuse my language."

"I think I understand. I would guess that my comrades were the ones who called the VPD." Winston said. "Do you have an idea of where we could stay if we move?"

Ethan spoke up, "There is a suite here I believe, that is operating as one of those rogue hotel things. No one in this building is happy about it."

"You mean an Air BnB?" Robert asked.

"Yes, I think so."

"Let's check it out and get you moved if it is available." Robert paused, then, "And Lee, maybe you could go out there to collect both your things. They'll be looking for Winston. I think I'll drive you. We should leave right away."

* * *

Down on Cambie Street, after the tongue-lashing from Thomas the evening before, Steve Christie had decided that delegating wasn't working, so he was using his personal aide to make some calls to find this famous Winston Chang. It took her exactly one phone call to locate him at the Fairmont YVR. She shook her head. Who put these guys in charge? It seemed to be a miracle that Steve could get to work fully dressed some days.

Steve looked at his roster of available men and picked Rick Santos to be the one to head out to the airport to pin this Winston down and find out what he was doing in town, Steve not being in receipt of what the kidnappers note had said. Steve was feeling good about himself, not considering if Winston would be in his hotel room in the middle of the day. For Steve, this would be a step too far.

Before Rick departed, he beckoned to Vito, his new-found buddy, "Hey Vito, I have to go out to the airport to interview a Winston Chang. He's staying at the Fairmont."

"Sounds good. Let me know what you find out." He watched Rick leave, then called Tony to start the underground information relay.

For the second time that day, Robert was barely one step ahead of the VPD. He was sitting in his dad's car in a lay-by in front of the Fairmont Hotel at the airport. Lee Pin came bouncing out the door and over to his car with a couple of small carry-on suitcases, having checked out. A VPD squad car passed his and pulled into the area used by police to park their cars. Robert recognized Rick Santos getting out. Robert slid a little lower in his seat and pulled a magazine up in front of his face. Lee looked puzzled as he got into the car after stowing the bags in the rear seat.

"Looks like they are on to you. Let's scram."

Lee understood the danger, but not the idiom. Robert put the car in gear and swung out into the busy traffic lane and hit speed bump after speed bump. This was where their airport tax money was going, he realized, to prop up the speed bump industry. By the time he had rounded to the exit road, he had lost track of how many bumps they had driven over, but his head felt rattled. Just one more reason to hate airports he supposed.

After a discussion with the front desk, Rick was not unduly surprised to find that Winston Chang had checked out. But to realize that he had just missed the check-out was disappointing. However, Rick was no slouch as a detective, and after finding out that Winston had been accompanied by a second man whose name was Lee Pin, he realized that the Chinese man he had noticed on the sidewalk as he entered the terminal was probably one of the two. He asked for and received some cooperation by the YVR RCMP security officers. He wanted camera footage of the lay-by area. It didn't take long for him to focus in on the man getting into the car. The hotel clerk, who had obligingly joined Rick, confirmed that this indeed looked like the Lee Pin who had just checked out. Rick wrote down the licence number of the car and left. Before firing up his car however, not being a cold-hearted bastard, he made a call to Vito and let him know that soon, maybe in about a day, the VPD would be looking for the car attached to that licence, thus giving Robert's team a temporary and short-lived reprieve. Tony relayed this to Camille, who was getting ready to leave for the day, heading to pick up Sophie from school. Before leaving, she went over to Tony's desk to ask him for the equipment that he had volunteered to get. They went down to the locker room where she grabbed a bag, along with a few extra clips of ammunition.

"I think something may happen tomorrow." The concern in her voice was palpable.

"Let me know if you hear anything, okay?"

"Yes, I will." Robert's admonishment not to include Tony fell by the wayside. She knew that numbers might well turn the tide in whatever happened. "Thanks Tony."

* * *

After Robert had made his way back to his parent's

home, they found that the suite in Ethan's building was available, so the Hong Kong guests moved in. Robert thanked his parents, leaving Ethan to play host for a dinner out for the guests, and headed home the hard way, by transit. It was after he had arrived home that Camille called him, warning him that his dad's car was going to be the subject of police eyes at some point tomorrow.

"I think I'll go and trade cars with your dad's if that would be okay with him."

"I'll call him and tell him, good thinking Camille. See you soon." Robert ended the call. After Camille had done the car transfer with Ethan, who was just about to go out with his guests for dinner, she arrived home in Ethan's car. Robert came out to tell her she had one more task, to pick up Sophie who had spent the afternoon with Rose. The watchers at the end of the street had not noticed Camille in her alternate ride, so they were a non-issue.

Robert sat at the dining room table, staring out the window at the neglected garden, thinking about Robin, dinner, and what the kidnapping had done to their lives. If tomorrow was the day, then he was going to have to be at his finest. The rain had stopped, sunlight glinting through the water drops on the wild looking flowers and weeds. His father's car pulled into the carport with Sophie and Camille aboard. After they entered the kitchen, question-ing looks sent Robert's way, he announced his dinner idea. "Eggs. We're having breakfast for dinner." Sophie smiled and went upstairs to her room while Camille flopped onto the couch.

"I don't think I can take much more of that place I work for." Camille led off.

"After tomorrow, I think we'll both be casting about, looking for other options, no matter what happens." As he said this, he brought a couple of glasses of wine over to Camille.

"Thanks. I agree." She raised her glass, "Here's to Robin, one more night, then home, I hope."

Robert didn't say anything, looking at his wine. "Is the equipment in our car?"

"Yes. I'll take your dad's car to work tomorrow. If they are looking for it, it'll be right under their noses, so it should be safe."

"Okay then, we are as ready as we can be. I'm going to pray tonight." With that he got up, went into the kitchen, and started the prep work for omelettes. After dinner, Robert checked his Bible, searching for something appropriate. He read the short Psalm 23 that most Christians knew by heart, then Psalm 140—about deliverance from the evil man. He closed the book and put it aside, calmed. Then he started imagining what could go wrong in the next couple of days.

* * *

Exactly twenty-four hours after Winston's plane had landed, the same flight brought Cedric and his cohort, Ho Li-Fan to town. Li-Fan's head was looking every which way. He could not believe the mountains, the water and all the trees as the 747 slowly descended over the Salish Sea. As a first-time visitor, it looked like a natural paradise.

He had heard that Cantonese had been the main language for the local BC Chinese for a long time, so he anticipated being able to get along fairly easily. After the two had checked in to their hotel, Cedric dialled Edward to tell him that they had arrived.

Edward's response was simple, "We are doing the exchange tomorrow around noon. You better get some rest. We'll be meeting at the Columbia Shipyards in Steveston, near the old Britannia site. I trust you can get there on your own."

Cedric was replying, "We need some guns..." as Edward was in the process of hanging up. Did he hear right? These visitors from far away wanted him to supply weapons? Why couldn't they use some of those Jackie Chan movie kung-fu moves that Hong Kong was famous for? Hell if he was going to help them.

Cedric sat, looking at the phone. Asshole, he thought. The police would be better hosts than this man. He beckoned to Li-Fan, "Let's go get some food." He was hungry after eating almost nothing on the flight.

Edward now knew that tomorrow would be the day of days. He could be rid of the kid, and hopefully rid of Cedric and all his useless aides. Then he could get back to making money, maybe finding that wayward lawyer and his wife to deal with. He called up the Guru, "Hey buddy, need you to help us out tomorrow. We're doing the exchange with the kid you took and need a little extra muscle just to be on the safe side. I'd like you to appear, and maybe one other, I don't care who."

The Guru gave this some quick thought, and the first

thing he thought of was money, not his safety. "I'd like some consideration for our presence."

Edward had been expecting something rude like this, "Fine, I'll give you five thousand."

The Guru didn't hesitate, "Okay. Where and when will this happen?"

Edward gave him the details and cut the call. All he had left to do was to call the cook the next morning to get their side to attend. He wasn't about to give them more than an hour's warning before the exchange.

Manny waited until mid-afternoon before gaining access to Maccha's building. Dressed roughly as an overly large delivery man with a wide-brimmed hat and holding onto a small box, he followed an un-wary resident into the lobby. He knew where Maccha's suite was and walked quickly up the five flights of stairs to his floor. His concern wasn't whether Maccha had actually ratted him out, that was between him and his God. He was just going to do what needed doing. He walked up to the door, stepped back and basically walked right through it. Splinters of the jamb showered onto the floor, the door banging against the wall behind it. A neighbour heard the bang of the door, then several muffled thuds through the adjoining wall, followed by silence. She didn't know what to make of it, but wisely stayed in her home for a while before eventually venturing into the hallway. She looked left and right. Seeing no one, she decided to slowly walk down to the next entry door. It was wide open, the frame damaged, wood fragments all over the carpet.

"Is anyone home?" She had seen Maccha a few times

and knew him by sight only. He had never bothered to answer her attempts at being a sociable neighbour. Her first query wasn't very loud, so she tried again. No answer. She tentatively entered the apartment but didn't have to take more than a few steps to see Maccha laying face down, a growing maroon stain on the carpet around his head. A sharp intake of breath, then she screamed as she backed up. She collapsed onto the hall floor.

Another neighbour ventured into the hall, "What happened?" After she was directed to the shattered opening, she felt ill, but just as quickly, gathered her wits and called 911. She tried to comfort her prostrate neighbour until the floor turned into a busy no-go zone. Maccha was strapped to a gurney and trundled away, balanced between life and death. The neighbour was subjected to twenty questions by a couple of officers, none of which she could answer very well. In the end, all the officers would have was some security video from the lobby and the elevator, which they could only hope would give up some answers.

~ 25 ~

Edward sat in his living room, fidgeting, wanting this day to be done with. The day had started sunny, but clouds had moved in from the southeast, the usual source of swirling storms. Just before 10:30 am he made his call to Ethan.

"Hello?" Winston and Pin were in the room with him.

"Is this the cook?"

Ethan barely controlled his anger at the insult, "Yes."

"We meet at noon at the Columbia Shipyards. Bring Winston, and that girl I assume you have, Ivy Sun. Then you can get your grandson back. No police other than Winston, do you understand?"

"I understand." Ethan wanted so dearly to say more, his restraint almost more than he could manage. The call ended. Winston and Pin could overhear the conversation, so Ethan went immediately to the planned call to Robert.

"They want to meet at noon at the Columbia Shipyards, wherever that is."

"It's in Steveston. Drive your guests over here and I'll take over."

"They said no police."

"I'm freelance now, dad. I'm going."

"Winston says to tell you that they'll probably leave by boat. It follows the pattern of how they do things in Hong Kong."

"Ok, good to know. Get over here quickly please." He broke the connection and immediately called Camille on her cellphone.

"The meet is on for noon at the Columbia Shipyards in east Steveston. They'll likely leave by boat after it's over, Winston thinks. Go down right to the end of Number Two Road in Richmond and turn left. There is a tiny village of sorts where we can organize ourselves. Park on the street." He then called Farhad to relay the same information.

At last, thought Farhad, action time, and in Steveston. If he was lucky, he could pick up his loot after it was over, or at least check on it. He called his fisher friend to warn him.

At the same time, on Cambie Street, Camille walked slowly over to Tony's cubicle. She beckoned with her eyes when Tony looked up, nodding her head to a small meeting room. She wasn't about to say a thing with Rodney's moles listening. After Tony shut the door, Camille spoke quietly, "The meeting is on for noon at the Columbia Shipyard in Steveston. I'm going down there. You shouldn't come, Tony. It'll reflect badly on you if you're not following orders."

"Maybe, maybe not. I'm not too concerned, but good luck Camille." They both left the room, more than a couple of pairs of eyes on them as they walked by. Tony didn't follow Camille but veered over to Vito's desk. He signalled Vito to join him.

"Feel like going down to Steveston for some fish and chips?"

Vito looked at Tony like he had lost his mind. Nobody travelled that far for lunch. Then it dawned on him.

Tony spoke in a low voice, "I'm going to provide backup for Camille. The exchange is happening at noon. Let's draw some equipment on the way to the car." Then he added, "By the way, she doesn't know we are coming, but we better let her know when we get down there. Don't want confusion, do we?"

"Can we go for the fish'n'chips when we're done?"

"Suppose so, if it turns out we're still hungry. The whole thing might go sideways."

Ethan was driving Robert's car with his two guests as passengers. He came west along East 27th then slowed and turned into the lane. He passed directly by the surveillance car, whose occupants immediately sat upright. The occupants all looked oriental. Winston and Pin noticed the VPD car as they passed by, but it didn't register on Ethan. He drove up to Robert's townhouse and stopped in the carport.

Inside, Robert and the two guests donned bulletproof vests under their shirts, procured by Camille the day before, and made sure their armaments were in working order. Ethan watched them, trepidation growing from witnessing something he wouldn't normally be a party to. Robert's stomach was in knots again, his fear growing as well. As confident as he appeared, his nerves were on edge. There was too much he didn't know about his opponents, so many things that could go wrong. His advantage was the knowledge that the gang's motivations were pretty clear and simple, directing their actions every time. Money and self-interest drove these people, what happened to others was of little concern. If Robert got hold of Robin, and he couldn't even be sure the gangsters would keep their side of the bargain, he would need to be shielded from whatever erupted afterwards.

* * *

At the end of the lane, the watcher's car started idling, one of the officers walking slowly up the lane, wanting to know what was happening. He was within two houses of the Lui residence when Robert's car backed out of the carport, then lit out up the lane heading south. The officer had seen Robert at the wheel, so he wheeled around and ran back up the lane, signalling his partner to get moving. Robert looked in his rear-view mirror and had seen the watcher, so he knew they would be tailed to the meet. It wasn't something he would worry about anymore. All his energy was focused on the upcoming exchange. He felt that Winston's analysis was probably correct, that the end goal to all this was Winston's demise. So, he had more than his son to consider. As he drove over to Knight Street to get on the bridge south, he occasionally looked in his rear-view. The Crown Victoria was doing its job. There was no chance of losing them, so he didn't waste energy trying.

At Cambie Street, a call was put through to Rodney Fister, "Robert Lui is on the move, and he has a couple of oriental guys in his car." The watchers were reporting in. "Looks as though they are heading south, and it doesn't seem as if they care that we are following."

"Which bridge?"

"Knight Street."

"They are probably heading to Surrey. Stay close and don't lose him, or don't bother coming back." Rodney hung up. He wasn't impressed with his team of tails to date. He sat, thinking. An unusual thing for Rodney to be doing. A moment later, Rick Santos peaked his head into Rodney's office. After sitting on some information for half a day, he thought it time to share.

"I got a match for the plate that I picked up at the airport when I just missed Winston Chang. The car belongs to an Ethan Lui." He dropped the paper with the car make and associated address on Rodney's desk and promptly left. This interrupted Rodney's thought process, leaving him confused for a moment. Winston Chang? Weren't his superiors looking for this guy? Matching this information with the report of oriental gentlemen in Robert's car he had just received was a step too far—like a monkey constructing an atom bomb. His first thought was to report to Steve, to get him off his back. His second thought was about the message the police had received with the finger. Winston is to be at the meeting. Confusion reigned as he walked over to Steve's office.

Edward sat in the front passenger seat of the Chevrolet, with Jason driving, and two other gang members sitting in the rear. Edward had decided not to bring everyone along. Having Cedric attend with his goon would be problem enough. The asset that Edward requested of Victoria would be doing his own thing. No one exerted control over him, but he was reputed to be reliable. Give him a task, and he would accomplish it with a minimum of fuss. Not inexpensive by any means, but dependable.

Frankie, who was one of the men sitting in the rear spoke up, "I got the boat over last evening. It's tied up not far from the shed. I also cut a boom across the east end of the channel, in case we want to leave that way. Less traffic for sure."

Edward grunted in reply. He had decided that however this turned out, they would be leaving by water. The car they were in was of no value. It would be his gift to the police. He didn't know what a boom was but trusted that Frankie had things covered. Two fast cars waited in Ladner for the final leg of their getaway. Frankie didn't have a boating licence and wasn't even aware that you needed one to operate any pleasure craft in the province. He had obtained a pleasure craft licence when they bought the boat, but this was just a piece of paper to register the craft. He knew where the throttle was, and he knew where Ladner was, that was about it.

Edward hoped Cedric could find his way to the meet so he could take control of Ivy but wasn't overly concerned one way or the other. On the eastern edge of Steveston, Jason drove down to the end of Trites Road, entering the large shipyard. It was just after 10:50 in the morning, rain threatening. Jason headed towards the water's edge then turned right, passing a row of bedraggled looking fishing boats perched on stilts. He parked next to the battered metal building he had rented a year earlier. Piles of tarped off fishing gear sat to the land side, but in front of the building, a clear view of Shady Island was available. To the west, sat several fingers of boat slips, most of which were filled with fishing boats of all ages and sizes, none from this century. Amongst them was Farhad's friend's trawler. A smaller new power boat sat moored, Edward's toy. Everything seemed to be riding at almost the same level as the work yard, testament to the coming high tide.

* * *

The Guru drove his Range Rover to the meeting, Bobbi his tag-a-long for this adventure. The Guru hadn't received the memo about not taking good vehicles to a place where they were likely to be lost in action. He had brought Bobbi, as his second, because he liked the moxie on display at the latest gang meeting. Bobbi just needed some seasoning was all and actions like these were excellent ways to get it.

Bobbi wondered what this was all about. He hadn't received much in the way of explanation from the Guru; just that it would be lucrative, and oh yes, bring his gun. The Guru had used an online map to find out where he was to show up, but it really didn't tell the whole story. There seemed to be a couple of entries to the place. It was also in a part of town that he had not visited before, so the disadvantage was multiplied.

Bobbi was disconcerted, having discovered that the Guru now seemed to trust him more than the others, the opposite of what he wanted. How was he going to escape the gang if he kept being drawn deeper into its dramas?

The Guru was following his app to lead him to Columbia's main entry. He drove slowly south past some buildings and boats. One of Edward's men was waiting at the end of the alley and signalled him to turn right. After driving about fifty more metres, he stopped and got out with Bobbi. Edward and the Guru stood looking at each other, mutual disdain on offer. The door to the closest shed opened and out walked Jason with the minder, and Robin, squinting, even with cloudy skies, drizzle starting to mist down.

Back at the entry to Columbia, a taxi dropped off Cedric and Ho Li-Fan. They were not impressed that no one was on hand to greet them, but after a moment they started walking down the main street. Eventually, after a couple of wrong turns and dead ends, they happened upon the tableau preparing itself for the exchange. Cedric looked over at the Guru and asked, "Who are these two?"

"Extra help, in case."

* * *

An hour before noon, Siegfried Damler grabbed his rifle bag, a small rucksack and headed down to the private dock on the Fraser behind his industrial shed. This was where he kept a small but speedy boat. It had a shallow draft, enabling Siegfried to beach it, allowing him access to a wide variety of shorelines. Today, he wasn't travelling very far, just across the wide mouth of the Fraser's south arm, on a course northwest to Shady Island, off Steveston.

He noticed that the tide was high, likely very near its peak. There wasn't much small boat traffic on this stretch of the Fraser, but one had to keep on the lookout for the occasional ocean-going freighter, tugs towing barges of every description, and large commercial ferries. He had donned his camouflage hunting outfit. His goal, to kill his one-time client at the behest of people in Victoria who lavished much more money on him for his services than the local police forces ever could. Siegfried was troubled by this, pretty sure that this was some kind of sin on a couple of levels. He shook his head—all that training for naught. Crazy world. Still, business was business. Today, he wouldn't be giving Robert the opportunity to get close to him to possibly demonstrate whether he could best Siggy. Not that this was even a remote possibility, but better to keep things clean. Although he had motored by Shady Island once or twice, this would be his first landing. Another reason to dislike the whole set-up. If he had had more time, he would have mounted an expedition to check things out.

* * *

Shady Island lay just south of the Columbia boat yards, and was uninhabited, other than by the occasional teenaged beer party. He planned to take Robert out from there with his favourite sniper rifle, a Blaser R93. The German gun had been designed to be flexible, its barrel and bolt heads could be switched out in order to change the calibre of ammunition he could select. The target would not be far away, and it wasn't like he was going after a moose or an elephant. He didn't want a shot to travel through Robert and kill or maim other people. He was very precise in this way, keeping his transgression to a single action. He went for a smaller calibre shot; it would still be lethal, properly placed. The only intelligence lacking was exactly where his target was likely to be.

After beaching his boat, he walked across the narrow island and came to the north side, a journey all of sixty-five metres. He then realized that the shipyard waterfront went on for over three hundred metres and was dotted with buildings, sheds, along with tarped gear, and boats, both on land and in the water. This new information bothered Siggy greatly. He disliked impreciseness. He also didn't want to be moving around once he found his nest, as he would be easily noticed. Usually, he had time to reconnoitre before doing a job, but no warning had been given to him, just an urgent instruction to attend and kill someone. Something desperate was going on, of this, he was sure. He should have told them no. He slowly moved around amongst the trees on the island, finally choosing a firing position that covered the widest number of possibilities. If the target was somewhere else, or hidden by all the onshore gear, he would just abandon the whole thing. He settled into the undergrowth behind some sparse branches with a couple of snacks, some water, and his binoculars. He could see a few people walking around the shipyard. They did not look like fishers.

* * *

At the south end of Number Two Road, where you

could not go farther without ending up in the Fraser River, Robert swung his car left and parked on the street. Farhad's car was up ahead; Farhad lounging against the rear passenger door, seeming to be in conversation with someone. It had started spitting a light drizzle, but nothing a Vancouverite would take seriously. Robert got out and went up to Farhad, who was talking with Ivy, sitting in the passenger seat.

Robert wrinkled his eyebrows at Farhad. "What gives?"

"We've reconciled. She's not so bad."

Ivy looked up at Robert, a slight tug to the corner of her lips, then she winked at him.

Robert had no time to fathom what was going on with these two. He shrugged.

* * *

As Winston and Pin came over to join them, Ethan's car pulled up behind them with Camille at the wheel. At the same moment, the VPD car tailing them rounded the corner and drove slowly by the group. Robert ignored it.

"Winston, Pin, and I will drive Farhad's car over to the boatyard, with Ivy, I guess. Farhad and Camille should follow a bit behind us in my car. I don't want them to know there are more of us coming." Robert said.

Camille's phone rang. "Camille, it's Tony. I have Vito with me. We're coming down to Steveston for some fish and chips. Are you interested? And if so, where can we meet?"

Camille smiled, "I'll be at the Columbia shipyard. It is at the south end of Trites Road. We'll be there just before noon." She looked over at Robert, "We're going to have a little extra help. I told them not to, but I guess they didn't understand what I said."

"Maybe stay back at the entrance to link up with them. I think we can ignore the guys who tailed us down here. They're trying to figure out what's going on. This whole thing will be over before they understand what's happening, I hope."

In the Crown Victoria, the officer riding shotgun was conversing with Rodney again. "We're down at the south end of Steveston, not Surrey after all. Robert is here, along with a couple of Chinese guys, and a Punjabi looking fellow. Your favourite detective also just pulled up, Camille."

"Shit. Something is going to happen. Where are you again? I thought they were going to Surrey."

"At the south end of Number Two Road in Richmond.... craps, they're moving." He cut the call.

Robert had pulled out and with a quick U-turn, zigzagged west a half kilometre to the Columbia entry. The officers watching were momentarily baffled that Camille didn't follow. That Robert had changed cars didn't help things either. This gave Robert a head start, which they wouldn't make up before he entered the boatyard. They drove right past the entry, heading west, ending up amongst some heritage cannery buildings and low-rise condominiums. They puzzled as to where Robert was heading and how they could have lost him so quickly. As a result of them leaving to pursue Robert, Camille and the three other officers could now proceed west to the

Columbia entry with no one watching them. Camille was keeping her phone on, directly connected to Robert's, so she could listen in on what was happening to get a better understanding of what awaited them. Four extra officers weren't very many. Police always liked to outnumber their foes by a large factor, so this action felt bad from the beginning.

Robert drove slowly towards the water, head swivelling back and forth, his hands gripping the steering wheel so tightly, it hurt. The street was wet, puddles surrounding garbage and weeds. Building fronts, boats, and cars received the once over, nobody in sight. The windshield wipers were moving on Vancouver time, every three seconds. The buildings were grey and dun coloured; rust and dents from years of abuse, doors, windows, every detail seared itself into Robert's brain. At the end of the alley, he looked left, a newish looking large ice plant blocked the way. He checked right and past a pile of crab traps saw the group of people looking back at him.

* * *

Siegfried was sitting up straighter as more and more people joined the party. His count was up to ten, but as far he could tell, Robert was not among them yet. He had been told to wait until after Edward had left the scene if possible, so he settled back. The target would be farther than he had planned, as they were not directly across the water from him, but nothing he couldn't handle.

* * *

Robert drove no further. The three of them got out as he muttered for Camille's benefit, "Looks to be nine or ten of them. Better call Troy for more help."

"Okay." Camille asked Tony to call the RCMP detachment for backup. "And make sure no sirens." Farhad got on his cell and called his fisher friend, who was on his boat, the Ocean Disputer, per Farhad's request a day earlier.

"Can you move into the channel slowly?" Farhad was relaying the request that Robert had made, to try to force any escape boat back to the east end of the channel.

* * *

Four people got out of Robert's car. Oddly, Ivy stayed with their group as they slowly approached the gang and made no attempt to run over to them. Robert could see Robin now. He smiled to himself, even knowing that nothing had been yet resolved. They slowed, until no more than ten metres separated the two groups.

Robin yelled, "Dad!"

"Send over Winston and the girl, then you'll get your son." Edward started. Several of the gangsters had their guns out, easy smiles on their faces, sure of their control.

"The girl stays with me until Robin is at my side, then you can have her, with my condolences." Robert noticed a smile on Edward's face as he accepted the insult. Cedric was not so forgiving however and started in on Edward in Cantonese. Robert grabbed for Ivy's arm, but she swung it away. "I'm not going anywhere." Ivy said in a low voice to Robert in Cantonese. Robert remembered what

Farhad had said. Maybe she was switching sides? He was confused.

Winston looked grimly at Robert, then slowly walked over to Edward. As soon as he was amongst the gang members, a couple of them frisked Winston, quickly finding the body armour he was wearing, but nothing further. Bending down to find the Beretta strapped to Winston's ankle apparently was too much effort, so he remained armed. At this point, Edward signalled to the minder who had hold of Robin to release him. Robin sprang forward to Robert with a yell as his shackle was removed. They hugged each other fiercely.

"Thank God you are finally with me Robin." This was the agreed signal for Camille to move in.

"Send Ivy over." Cedric demanded in Cantonese.

"Think she wants to stay in Vancouver." Robert answered in English.

Edward couldn't help smiling again. Edward and Jason started to back up with their new hostage, heading to the gangway behind them, the other triad members following. Cedric was puzzled by Ivy's apparent change of allegiance. The Guru and Bobbi looked equally confused, uncertain what was going on as Camille rounded the corner with the other three officers. RCMP vehicles were piling up at the entry to Columbia, officers spilling out with weapons drawn. Robert sent Robin toward Camille just as he got hit by what felt like a sledgehammer in his side. He pirouetted as he fell. The sound of a rifle shot arrived at the same instant. Farhad immediately raised his gun and fired at the two Gupil members remaining. The Guru was wearing his aubergine coloured turban this day, but he should have opted for a bulletproof version. Farhad's first shot went through the turban, then his upper forehead, blowing a wide hole out the top rear of his skull. He was dead before he reached the ground. Bobbi immediately dropped his gun to the ground and raised his hands, hoping he wouldn't be taken as well. Robert realized that someone had taken a long shot at him, so he stayed down, pretty certain that a rib or two had been broken despite the protective vest. Robin returned and knelt beside him trying to see if his father was still alive. Robert winked up at Robin, trying to reassure him, and pulled him to the ground.

"Stay down, Robin."

Now that Robin was safe, the focus split between retrieving Winston somehow, and not getting shot by whoever had tried for Robert. Edward's gang headed for their boat, a couple training their guns on the wharf where more and more officers were arriving.

Siegfried, watching with his binoculars, noticed that a few officers were looking back at Shady Island. He couldn't see Robert moving, so concluded that his shot had hit the mark. He started to back up, crawling so as not to reveal himself, deciding it best if he left the party. He felt some regret about what he had done, certain that he would have to atone for this somehow.

* * *

In the boatyard, no one fired a shot after Farhad had dealt with the Guru, but tension was heavy. The officers didn't want to lose Winston after what he had done for Robin, but a straight-out gun fight on the wharf could turn out badly. The gang started to squish onto their boat, Frankie having started the engines. Edward directed one of his helpers to rope Winston's hands together before getting onto the boat. Winston knew it was now or never, so he bent down, which puzzled the helper, and came up firing with the Beretta. He winged Cedric, who was unarmed and about to get on the boat. Someone fired back from the boat, hitting Winston once in the stomach, knocking him off the dock and into the water. Tony decided that firing his gun was now okay, so he let loose, hitting the boat a few times, which was moving into the channel. Nobody aboard was hit by Tony's bullets, but one gangster returned fire, causing the group of officers to hit the ground.

Farhad was on his phone, alerting his friend. The boat was a fishing trawler, large and slow. Its size would encourage Edward's boat to turn around. It started heading west after clearing the arms of the dock and moved slowly across the narrow channel, spooking Frankie. He spun the speedboat's wheel violently, turning the boat one hundred and eighty degrees. He opened the throttle up, heading east. After an initial hesitation the boat quickly hit forty-five knots. The large wake started to jostle the tied up boats in the harbour.

Robert struggled to sit up, watching the boat head east, picking up even more speed. "Watch this." He said to no one in particular. Then he asked Lee Pin, "Can Winston swim?" Meanwhile Vito dropped his equipment belt and dove into the channel to try rescuing Winston.

Just as Pin was answering, the boat's keel hit the now invisible rock breakwater connecting the east tip of Shady Island to the shore, completely cleaving the bottom of the boat from the superstructure. The barrier was the same wall of rock that Robert had seen a couple of weeks earlier when he was parked along the dyke at low tide. Bodies flew through the air as the boat blew apart after striking the hidden barrier. Camille got on her phone to call the emergency rescue force that operated a hovercraft in the area.

"I don't really know, but I doubt if he swims." Pin said eventually.

* * *

Robin stooped down to hug his father again, tears starting to flow, "Thanks Pops, I knew you'd come." Robert winced from the hug but tried to hug Robin back. He opened his jacket and shirt, exposing a gash where the bullet had hit his vest. "Might need some medics here Camille. Has someone pulled Winston out?" His chest pain was pretty severe, but there didn't seem to be any blood from his body.

"Already in motion Robert."

"Are you okay Robin? Did they hurt you?"

"No, not really. Just bad food, Pops."

"You have all your fingers?"

Robin looked at his dad, cockeyed. "Yeah, why?"

"They sent a finger or two to the station, that's why."

An ambulance had arrived, and some techs came inside the tape that was being set up to keep the boatyard workers back. Most of them knew what gunfire sounded like and had come over to see what the commotion was.

Farhad wandered over to where his friend was docking his boat, checking in to see that his cache was still aboard where he had left it. It was, so he relaxed. He'd be back eventually to reclaim it after all the drama was finished.

* * *

The VPD officers in the surveillance car had finally solved the mystery of where Robert had gone by following the converging RCMP vehicles back to the scene inside the boatyard. They parked in behind and called Rodney.

"Looks like the action is over here, boss. I can see Robert and I think his son is with him. A couple of bodies are on the pavement. Can't tell too much else yet. There are a ton of Mounties here."

"Get closer and report back." Rodney responded decisively. He was not happy. If Camille was on site, then credit for solving the kidnapping might not fall into his lap. He had to come up with operation 'Screw Camille' fast.

The first ambulance took Winston, who had been fished out of the channel in rough shape from both the gunshot and his lack of swimming ability. After initial statements, Robin and Robert followed in a second car to the Richmond General Hospital; Robin for a check over and Robert for his chest problems. Camille, Tony, and Vito were left at Columbia to answer questions. Farhad received special attention for his straight shooting of the Guru. The police on site were satisfied with the explanation of events but a special investigation into the shooting would be started no matter what. Officers killing civilians was frowned upon, even if they were gangsters.

At the hospital, Robert used his cellphone to call Ethan, "Hi Dad, we got Robin, but Winston has been shot I am afraid."

"What?"

"There was some gunplay at the exchange, but Robin is safe now. Winston attempted to shoot his way out when the gang tried to get away and crashed their boat."

"That's horrible news." Robert could hear the tension growing in his father's voice.

"I know. We are at the hospital now getting checked over, and Winston is here as well, in surgery, I think. We'll get you and Mary over tomorrow to tell you the whole story, okay? Lee Pin is fine and here with me. I'll wait until Winston is out. We'll get Lee back to you somehow later today."

"Good news about Robin, we are relieved to hear that." Ethan didn't really want to ask anymore.

"Yes, see you tomorrow. I'll call when I know more about Winston." Robert ended the call. Just breathing hurt.

A minute after he had finished with his dad, his cell rang. The nurse attending him was frowning. If he hadn't been a detective, he was pretty sure the nurse would have taken the phone and chucked it in the garbage. Signs prohibiting cellphone use in the emergency ward were everywhere.

"Hello? Robert here."

"Robert, it's Thomas, are you and Robin okay?"

"A little worse for wear, but we're good."

"Good, good. It sounded like quite the commotion from what I've heard."

"Definitely. A real mess, but I think the gangs are busted up because of this."

"No doubt. Would it be possible for you and Camille to come by tomorrow?"

At last, to the crux of the call, "Sure, I think so. Morning?"

"That would be fine Robert, get some rest. See you tomorrow."

It was not until the next day that the stories about the gangsters' meeting with the Fraser River were pieced together. Frankie, the pilot, met his demise at the windshield, breaking his neck with the sudden stop to his forward progress after leaving the driver's seat. Jason and Cedric drowned, their swimming capabilities nonexistent. The remaining occupants made it to Shady Island, some with broken bones, where they sat, wet and depressed before being picked up by a police boat. Attempted murder and kidnapping charges were on offer for these four, even Cedric's accomplice from Hong Kong couldn't escape the mess. Bobbi Atwal was going to be charged with being an accessory to kidnapping, but he was already talking about deals to be made without even waiting for legal advice. At least Edward had access to his lawyer. Without the Guru, Bobbi would be left at the mercy of a publicly appointed defence lawyer.

Questions were being asked about how a senior member of the Hong Kong Police Force was present at the meeting. Robert's guilt at this was mitigated by the return of his son. The story behind Ivy's detainment by Robert hadn't seen the light of day so far. Farhad seemed to have some-how charmed Ivy into remaining in the Lower Mainland and she had remained mum about being held by Farhad. Robert didn't know what the story was, but perhaps, with Cedric now history, Ivy fancied her chances in Vancouver. She hadn't been taken into custody after answering some questions. It remained to be seen what Edward would say, but so far, he was concentrating on his own predicament.

* * *

Robert and Camille rose from their best sleep in weeks. After a quiet breakfast they checked in with Richmond General Hospital to see how Winston was doing. He was on the mend, but it would be a couple of weeks before he would be approved to fly home. They then headed downtown to Cambie Street for the dreaded meeting with Thomas Harrow. Robert guessed that his career with the Vancouver Police Department was over. Camille's future seemed less certain. As they both walked onto the floor for the meeting, Norma saw them and smiled, waving. It seemed that Thomas had secured her transfer to be his assistant. A few people came over to shake Robert's hand and hug Camille. Thomas was watching this from his office door. He had read the preliminary site report, four dead and five in custody, all this with Robert at its centre. He waved the two into his office and shut the door.

"How is Robin doing?"

"Fine. He is going to spend the rest of the week at home, but the whole thing seems to be sliding off his shoulders.

I suspect there will be some mental anguish when he has had a while to process things." Robert answered smoothly.

"Yes, yes. I hear someone took a shot at you?"

"A vest saved my life, fortunately. Not a large calibre bullet it seems. Cracked a couple of ribs though. Hurts like hell."

"But it wasn't from the people on site?"

"Seemed to come from Shady Island, across a channel. Someone was waiting for me."

"Camille, Steve would like to have a word with you upstairs if that's okay?" Thomas asked.

"Now?"

"Yes."

Robert had been expecting this. Camille reported to Steve, not Thomas.

As soon as Camille left, Thomas got down to it, "It looks like the local triad boys are out of business for a while. And I don't know where the Gupils will end up now that they are leaderless. All thanks to you."

Robert started to sense some hope.

"But I am afraid you are somewhat of a loose cannon, and that is putting it kindly, Robert. Four dead people in a very public fashion is not how we do things here. I also now have to explain to Hong Kong why one of their senior officers won't be coming home anytime soon, if he even survives his injuries."

"I checked again with the hospital, and he will survive, but you are correct, he will be a guest for a while."

Thomas continued, or rather finished, "Unfortunately, I must put you on paid leave while we determine your fate, but I have to be honest, it isn't looking good for you around here."

"I wouldn't have it any other way." He responded, "But I also wouldn't have done anything differently either, to get my son back."

Thomas nodded. Thinking about his own family, he couldn't blame Robert one bit. "We'll be in touch Robert. You should leave your badge and gun with Norma."

With that, they were done. Robert went over to his office and picked up a couple of items before leaving. He went upstairs a floor to find Camille, nodding to Tony. Camille was already done and waiting.

"Let's go to Café Paulo. I need a fix." Robert said. As they left the building, Robert looked questioningly at Camille.

"I've been put on desk duties for a month, no change in pay. I think I might just survive this."

"Good news Camille." He paused, then, "I've been put on ice. They are going to terminate me, I know it." The sun was shining for a change. "Guess I can keep a closer eye on the kids while I figure out my future. They entered the café. Gilberto yelled when he saw them, very excited to welcome back his now most famous customers. After the usual banter with Gilberto, they took their coffees and sat by the window, trying hard not to think for a change. Robert savoured the rich flavour, hints of cocoa making it even more satisfying.

He shook his head, what was he now, a sommelier of coffee? This was probably going to be his last for a while at Gilberto's place, hence the stupid tasting notes to himself.

"I haven't the courage to tell Gilberto that I might not be around. I'll let him know, eventually. That is, if I am still here myself."

After they had finished up, Robert touched Camille's arm, "Let's go get some food for tonight. Have to up my game with Dad coming over." They waved to the proprietor as they left.

As they shopped, Robert's brain fired up again, trying to guess who would have taken a shot at him. He was sure the bullet came from Shady Island. It was only accessible by boat most of the time. Why he was targeted from there was less clear, especially when they were standing toe to toe with the two armed gangs that were the source of his family's problems. The only person he knew who had sniper abilities was his trainer, one Siegfried Damler, but that didn't make any sense. If indeed it was Siegfried, then someone must be telling him what to do. Robert could come up with no reason Siegfried would want him dead.

* * *

Despite what happened to Winston, Robert was determined to have a good dinner to celebrate Robin's homecoming. His parents had agreed to come, bringing Lee Pin with them who was going to fly out the next day. Sophie had been encouraged to invite Rose as well, to Robin's hidden delight. Robert sent Camille out to the local barbeque shop on Fraser Street to pick up some *char siu* along with roasted pork and a duck. He was going to unleash his wok to make a chicken and peanut stir fry. A noodle pillow, steamed *bok choi*, and pea tips with garlic would round out the feast. After Camille returned with the meat, sampling was done to ensure quality control. It was difficult to stop the sampling once started.

Around the time Sophie arrived with Rose after school, Robert started in on the prep work. His parents and Lee Pin showed up just after five, so Robert made sure everyone had drinks. He continued his prep work, now under the eye of his dad, who was doing his best not to appear interested. Robert wasn't fooled.

Although the events of yesterday were so fresh in the participants minds, they didn't want to ruin the dinner by discussing them amongst the rest of the family. However, with the teens upstairs, Ethan couldn't help himself. "Unfortunately, Winston is not my first friend to have suffered gang violence, so I have a certain view of these things that will probably not change until I pass on. I had hoped that this part of my life was over, but...."

Robert gripped his dad's arm. "I know. After today, it looks like I will be leaving the VPD soon, so please don't fret about me."

Lee Pin looked pensive. "Winston doesn't have his own family. I have talked with my superior back in Hong Kong, and they want me back. Otherwise, I would stay until Winston is better. I talked with the hospital today. It looks like recovery will take a while."

Robert raised his whisky glass, "Here is to Winston Chang, who did this for a child he didn't even know. He is a saint in my book." He looked at Pin, "Please tell your comrades in Hong Kong what a hero he is. We will be praying for him, and visiting." They all raised their glasses silently. The doorbell rang. Robert went to open the front door and was face to face with a reporter from one of the local television stations standing on the welcome mat, a cameraman just a few steps back focusing on Robert.

"Could I get a comment about the events of yesterday down in Richmond? Were you responsible for some of the deaths—."

Robert shut the door firmly, cutting him off in midsentence without saying a thing. He returned to the kitchen where Camille raised an eyebrow.

"Just the media, looking for someone to help them do their job. Looks like we'll be harassed for a little while, until they get the message."

Camille looked at Robert, "Which is?"

"No comment. In fact, don't say a word to any of them. They'll soon go elsewhere." With that, he yelled to the teenagers upstairs to get down to set the table. Pretty soon, the table was covered in small bowls, dishes, ladle spoons, chopsticks with their holders, and trivets for the serving platters. Water glasses, teacups, and more wine glasses filled the remainder of the available space. Linen napkins underscored the type of meal it was to be. Once Robert had finished with the wok and directing his sou chefs, the food was transferred to serving large platters and taken over to the dining table. The aromas and steam coming off the plates drew smiles from everyone.

"Here is to Robin, who displayed character and resolve throughout his ordeal, even attempting a prison break. Cheers!"

Robin had a huge grin on his face as he took a small sip

of tea, then launched into whatever dish happened to be closest to his bowl, the others following suit.

Robert wasn't done however, "I would be remiss if we didn't also cheer Rose and Sophie for their admirable actions to avoid getting taken in the first place."

Robin's smile turned sheepish when he parsed what this could mean, but then shrugged and went back to eating. He had some catching up to do after his less than desirable diet of the last week. Silence reigned while the food disappeared. Ethan nodded at Robert. Yes! He was always concerned that his skills wouldn't meet Ethan's high bar.

After more tea was poured, the teenagers were excused, and discussion turned to Lee Pin and his impending return to Hong Kong. He talked instead about the triad they had been duelling with for decades.

"That man who died on the boat was a top man for the Wide Bay Boys, I'm sure of that. And if you say their head man here was the one arrested, then they will be in trouble. Upheaval will follow. Others will try to crowd them out."

"The other gang lost their leader as well, so you are correct. There may be more violence coming." In deference to Mary, the group stopped their talk of gangs and instead mused about the older days in Hong Kong when Ethan and Mary had lived together there. Pin's flight was not until noon the next day, so they stayed up late, drinking too much whisky before the guests left.

* * *

A day later in Ladner, Siegfried checked his bank account online expecting to see another fat addition to his balance, but nothing. He had already received fifty percent of the fee as an advance, so was not unduly worried about the delay. A short time later a text message arrived, **Return the deposit. Mission incomplete.** That was it, short and definitely not sweet. What had gone wrong? He flipped on the television and watched the local news program. Of all the dead people at the scene, there was no mention of a VPD officer. Shit. He was sure he had hit Robert. It didn't take him long to figure it out. Bulletproof vest. He should have stuck with the higher calibre ammunition, then the vest wouldn't have mattered. This was not good in several ways, not least of which was possibly having Robert Lui coming after him if he concluded who had taken the shot. Siegfried was pretty sure it wouldn't take him long to do this. He was not afraid, but definitely concerned.

* * *

In Kowloon, Jacky Chow had not heard any news from Cedric. After Jacky checked with a news feed, he realized what a monumental screw-up had occurred. Jacky had lost his lieutenant and it sounded as though the Wide Bay Boys had been decimated in Vancouver. Although not mentioned, it seemed that Cedric's man was in custody also. And there was more bad news. It seemed that Winston Chang had survived being shot and was recovering in Richmond General. But a disaster was looming; his man at the Hong Kong Police Force said that a promotion to take

Winston's position temporarily would likely be going to Lee Pin, not his man. Outrageous! All his scheming was for nothing. It was enough to drive a man to drink. He went to his whisky cabinet and poured three fingers, though it was just shy of eleven in the morning.

A few days after Robert's celebratory dinner, he was at home pondering his future when the doorbell rang. He went, checked, and let in Farhad Gil.

"Hey Farhad, how are you? Out of purgatory?"

He smiled, "In one way, I am. Back in my own place for now but thinking of moving. The shooting thing with the Guru will take a while, I think. I am on paid leave from the Delta force. My dream actually."

"Ivy?"

"Yeah, looks like we are an item, for now anyway. Who would have thought? I just wanted to drop something off for you." He paused several seconds, then, "You were correct. Gurmit and I took some of the Guru's stuff. That's why he was keen on getting us. This is part of it. I think you will know better than me what to do with it." He dropped a small cassette into Robert's hand.

Robert looked at the tape, then at Farhad. "Do you know what's on it?"

"I think you should be careful with it." With that, Farhad nodded and let himself out.

* * *

In deepest Surrey one Manny Dhillon sat in what was formerly the Guru's chair at the club. He was now the de-facto leader in charge of what little was left of the Gupils.

A creepy grin spread over his face as he contemplated life and how he was going to re-make the gang after his own image. It was not going to be pretty.

* * *

Robin eventually returned to high school, and to no one's surprise, he became the chosen one. He couldn't tell his story enough times, and of course, embellishment started to add even more lustre to the tale. His dad had told him to rein it in, but that was next to impossible. And best of all, Rose was now talking to him. He also became the star of his hockey team, ability or playmaking having nothing to do with it. It was only at home when it was quiet that the realization came to him of how lucky he had been to escape with his ten fingers still in place, let alone being alive. His dad had quietly filled him in on what the gangs had done to previous hostages, and their disregard for the mores of civilized society.

Camille smiled at Robert after returning from her day at the office sorting through paperwork, "Guess where Sophie and I are going Saturday?"

Robert shrugged.

"The mall, to get her a new cellphone."

"She doesn't want me along?"

"Apparently not needed." Camille's smile had turned Cheshire-like.

About the Author

Glenn Burwell was a registered architect who practiced in Vancouver, British Columbia, for almost forty years. He's seen all sides of the local development industry and how it affects the lives of people living in the region. This is his second novel. Robert Lui was introduced in The Chapel of Retribution. Now retired, Burwell is working on more stories of detective Robert Lui, manages a small tomato and herb garden, and continues to keep an eye on the never-ending saga of housing problems in Vancouver.

You can contact Glenn through the Somewhat Grumpy Press web site, SomewhatGrumpyPress.com

Help independent authors and small presses by leaving a review at your favourite online retailer.